Buddhahead
Trilogy

U.S. Copyright Office
Registration No. TXu 1-998-491

AUTHOR'S NOTE

The tale you are about to embark upon will cover a Japanese family's migration to America up to the present day. It is a fictional story endeavoring to convey their hardships, racist encounters, struggles, hopes and ambitions from a humanistic perspective. Much akin to the experiences of other people of color who arrived here from distant shores, it is a story about striving for equality, acceptance, and finding a sense of inner peace within an Anglo European-dominated culture that often misreads differences in skin hues, cultures and identities as threatening.

As the story of this fictional family unfolds, a different writing style appears in the later chapters. This shift occurs as the passage of time becomes contemporary; the writer interjects sequences of his life experiences into the story as opposed to relating it through a narrative style.

This isn't to say that the fictitious character becomes the writer; rather, the character(s) are a conglomeration of the writer, friends, family, comrades, associates, neighbors, his imagination and even enemies—most here today and some with us in spirit. He thanks all with whom he has had the honor to share insightful moments— without you, there is no story.

Nick Nagatani

CONTENTS

CONTENTS

BUDDHAHEAD TRILOGY

Part I

Issei

THE BEGINNING

Hiroshima, Japan
July 1897

KICHIGARO NAGATA'S ability to mask his inner thoughts and feelings, was a self-taught survival tool that kept outsiders at a safe distance by maintaining an outwardly calm, stoic presence. Today, in the center of his *hara* (gut), an excruciating, cramping sensation made it exceedingly difficult for Kichigaro to maintain a calm exterior. This nauseating ache was different from the everyday hunger pangs to which his body was conditioned. The ache sprouted from seeds of doubt concerning a stressful family matter that Kichigaro had internalized and silently endured through the changing of seasons.

Sitting in an erect posture on a hard wooden western chair, intensified Kichigaro's discomfort. He knew that by relaxing his shoulders and slightly bending his stiff upper body forward, the tightness in his stomach would ease. However, Kichigaro was determined to endure its pain and not show any visible signs of distress to the agent sitting across from him.

The agent, a fellow countryman, was dressed in western clothing, a sight becoming common in the city. Beneath his weathered black topcoat, he wore a neatly pressed white shirt with cuffs slightly frayed, a black bow tie, black pants, black socks, and scuffed leather black shoes. A black derby hat hanging on a coat rack in the corner of his small office room, completed his costume. He had not always dressed western-style, it was only after he impressed his *hakujin* (white) bosses by steering countless men and boys into their offices to sign labor contracts, that his bosses recognized his value as a recruiter. Eventually, they retained his services and rewarded him with a small stipend along with a few articles of handed-down western-style clothing. The agent diligently studied his *hakujin* masters and did his best to emulate their foreign mannerisms, mimicking their speech patterns and voice inflections. The *hakujin* found him to be both amusing and often comical. Through his persistence and endurance, he was eventually elevated to the position of a Nippon recruiting agent. They set up him up with an office: a tiny room with a sign hanging outside which, when translated to English read, "Pacific Northwest Railroad Company."

The agent sized Kichigaro up to be just another desperate rice farmer fallen on hard times—a poor rice farmer dressed in field clothing, loose-fitting cloth pants, a matching color *happi* coat fastened at the waist by a strong cord, and straw sandals secured by twine lacing to protect his tanned feet. The agent had enlisted so many of these types of rice farmer and jobless city folks that he had lost count. Unbeknownst to Kichigaro, the agent had his own concerns. His *hakujin* masters had implied that soon Japanese workers would no longer be needed nor welcomed in America. If this rumor turned out to be true, then his own future was uncertain. Not wanting to dwell on this thought, he nonchalantly reached across the table that separated himself from the rice farmer and placed a paper contract in front of Kichigaro for his signature.

He spoke, "Nagata-*san*, as I have already explained, by signing this contract you are obligating your son, Kenji Nagata, to work for the Pacific Northwest Railroad Company for three years. Our company will send him to America, provide work, pay monthly wages, feed, clothe and house him for three years. After he fulfills his three-year duty to Northwestern Pacific, he will be free to leave. Of course, his travel, food, clothing and housing expenses will be deducted from his monthly pay."

As the agent spoke, Kichigaro remained stoic. He was well aware of the terms and conditions of the contract that would obligate his second son, Kenji, to leave his village for a life of uncertainty and hardship in a foreign land. Although he knew the terms of the contract were one-sided, he masked his disdain from the agent. His few interactions with fast-talking merchants and western agents had taught him that it was advantageous to remain quiet and let them think that he was slow of mind because by acting this part, their arrogant nature would eventually lead them to reveal their true intent.

When Kichigaro did not demonstrate any change in demeanor to his prearranged speech nor reach out to mark his name to the contract, the agent became concerned. Perhaps he was changing his mind. "Nagata-*san*, this may be your last chance for your son to have this opportunity. There are growing complaints from the American government that too many *Nihonjin* (Japanese people) have entered their country and soon no more will be allowed to enter America." Kichigaro detected the nervousness in the agent's voice, but he was still in no rush to sign the paper. Generations of planting and harvesting rice on the family plot of land had taught him the virtue of patience. A person can never allow himself to feel totally content. When the harvest is plentiful, a family will be fed and protected through the winter season; then suddenly, without warning or reason, Nature can become angry and cast hunger, hardship and famine on a family—even an entire village. Nature's laws aren't to be questioned and cannot be controlled. One learns the virtues of patience and understands that the only item of permanence for a rice farmer is the family land, passed from generation to generation through the family's *chonan* (eldest son). Unfortunately, during the current difficult times in Nippon, the Nagata plot of land was no longer able to sustain and feed Kichigaro's expanding family.

Contrary to the agent's concern, Kichigaro possessed no doubts about signing the contract. What he may have lacked in spontaneity was balanced by a focused deliberate thought process. He had agonized for months, going back and forth over this pending decision. He kept his final decision from his family, because as the Nagata family *chonan*, he felt that the burden and weight of this decision rested solely on him. His last and perhaps greatest concern was telling his *okusan* (wife) and family that their second-born son, Kenji, was leaving the family to go to America.

"Nagata-*san*, I don't mean to rush but there are others waiting to meet with me." The agent's whimpering plea brought Kichigaro back to the moment. For the first time since he entered the small office room, he focused his attention on the agent sitting directly across from him. Casting aside the agent's western-style clothing and mannerism, all that remained was a weary, nervous, scared person holding a writing quill and offering it to him. Kichigaro took the quill and marked his name at the bottom of the contract. With the contract settled, the agent handed Kichigaro a paper with the date, time, and name of the steamboat, where his son, Kenji Nagata, was to report. Kichigaro took the paper, stood, bowed, and left the room before the agent could engage in any idle chatter. Once outside, Kichigaro was not surprised to find that his stomach cramps had yet to dissipate. Now came the most difficult part—traveling home to the village in Matsuyama to tell the family of his decision.

ISSEI

Issei, pronounced (ee-say) is a combination of two words, ichi, *meaning one, and* sei, *meaning generation. Issei is the name given to the first generation of Japanese people that immigrated to North America.*

Hiroshima harbor
August 1897

A LOUD CONTINUOUS monotone drone blaring from the horn of the Dollar Line Steamship, did not deter its Japanese passengers from rushing to the port side railing as it left Hiroshima harbor. The railing was densely packed, three rows deep. Within this mass, Kenji Nagata managed to squeeze into a slight opening along the rail. This youthful group of Japanese immigrant passengers stretched over one another, each trying to position themselves closer to the rail, frantically waving arms, shouting "*Sayonara!*" while desperately trying to capture one last glimpse of their family members amongst the crowd left ashore.

It was not necessary for Kenji Nagata to gaze into the crowd—his *sayonara* with his *otoosan* (father) had taken place hours earlier, immediately before he boarded the anchored steamship. The farewell between father and son was a simple ritualistic bowing of their heads, followed by a heartfelt meeting of their eyes. With his second son now safely aboard the steamship, Kichigaro Nagata began his journey back to his rice patch in Matsuyama.

As the Dollar Line headed out to open sea, the image of Japan's coastline slowly began to fade. Finally, all that remained was the blue horizon across the expanse of water. When Japan's coastline vanished, the passengers' frantic nervous energy also disappeared, replaced by a disquieting silence.

As the group of immigrants slowly disbursed, Kenji Nagata remained at the rail, blankly staring out at the vastness of the sea, his thoughts fixed upon his family. Four days ago he and his *otoosan* left the village of Matsuyama to travel to Hiroshima. Kenji vividly recalled the scene of his final *sayonara* with his grieving *okaasan* (mother), *niisan* (older brother) Ichiro, Fumiko, his brother's pregnant wife, *obaasan* (grandmother), and his two *imooto* (younger sisters), Yoshii and Hana. Although his send-off occurred only four days ago, it now felt like a distant memory.

He and *Ootosan* spent the past four days and three nights together—they walked, walked, and walked some more. When they stopped it was either to eat the rice balls, pickled radishes, and dried fish, that his *okaasan* had packed for their

14

trip, or to sleep under the dark sky filled with hundreds of twinkling stars. Little conversation took place between them, but Kenji understood that his *otoosan* was a quiet and private man. During their travel, Kenji hoped that his *otoosan* would tell him the reason why he signed the paper, sending him to a place called America. This conversation never took place.

Although last year's rice crop was smaller than anticipated, the family had experienced leaner harvests and still managed to feed themselves. He surmised that perhaps *Otoosan* made his decision after his older brother, Ichiro, moved his new wife Fumiko into their already-crowded home, adding another mouth to feed in addition to his two *imooto* and aging *obaasan*. His fate in being sent to America was probably sealed when the family noticed Fumiko getting sick every morning followed by the growing expanse of her abdomen.

Otoosan's decision for Kenji to leave home, work and send money back to the family, did not catch Kenji totally by surprise. He heard of other young men from Matsuyama and surrounding villages leaving their homes to find work in the city in order to benefit their families. For Kenji, leaving his family and village to find work in the city would have been difficult enough, but to be sent to a foreign land was beyond his comprehension.

As he gazed at the ocean focusing on nothing, Kenji was so absorbed in his thoughts that he lost track of time; he now stood alone at the railing. However long, it must have been a while—the sun was no longer directly overhead, as the beginning stages of dusk settled in. Before leaving the railing, his last thought was to envision a triumphant return to Matsuyama, bringing back riches from America, as his proud *otoosan* and *okaasan* hosted a welcome home feast in his honor. Clinging to this vision, he left the railing.

A typical profile of the ninety-plus Issei immigrants aboard the Dollar Line was that of a young, second-born son from a poor family. Only a few had willingly volunteered to migrate to America to seek opportunities not available to them had they remained in Japan. The majority were aboard because of duty and obligation to their families. This was their first experience of being on their own. Their separation and emotional trauma had the additional physiological hardship of being out at sea. From the moment the Dollar Line hoisted anchor, leaving safe harbor for the open sea, one had to reorient ones balance and equilibrium. The perpetual motion of the ocean waves rocking the boat and the constant humming of the ships engine caused tightness in ones head, fluttering pupils, and nausea. The terrible-tasting rations they were fed made one feel even worse. Kenji, who had worked in the fields all of his life, had tanned yellow-brownish skin. He wondered if the color of his complexion had turned the same yellowish-green color he now noticed on many of the seasick farers.

Nighttime was intolerable—all ninety were cramped in an overcrowded compartment below deck. If one was fortunate, he could find a bit of comfort on a thin mattress on one of the twenty double-bunkbeds alongside the ship's hull. The remaining Issei slept on thin mattresses placed on the hard wooden floor. The compartment lacked ventilation; personal space and privacy were non-existent. The steamship's bathing facilities were off limits to the Issei immigrants; they washed themselves daily, by scrubbing their bodies with damp cloth rags. Every night, trapped below in this cramped sweltering dungeon of sweat, body odor, and passed gas, Kenji barely slept.

The group of youthful Issei immigrants boarded the Dollar Line as strangers, each possessing his own anxieties, fears, hopes and dreams. Like Kenji Nagata, they were taught not to share their personal life with anyone outside the family.

Often, when a group of strangers share a traumatic experience so harrowing that it takes one outside of ones inner self, that event can become the catalyst in forging a bond within the group.

Such a unifying event occurred on the sixth night aboard the Dollar Line. What started as distant roars of thunder soon amplified into a chilling, piercing howl that penetrated the ship's depth. Humungous waves arrived with overpowering strength which towered over the ship and its passengers, exposing their weakness and helplessness. In the depths of the ship, each violent thrust of the ship sent bodies shifting from location to location. Lacking secured structures to grasp, all one could do was curl up into a fetal position and hug the ships floor. No one dared to stand and be thrown about like a *judoka* (judo-practitioner) novice, fighting a seasoned black belt. Just as it seemed like it could not get any worse, it did. The thunder roared and pounded like a titanic taiko drum, the angry ocean swells bounced the ship sideways, up and down, and in every imaginable direction, as if the deities were playing a game of catch with it. With every jolt, the trapped Issei were helplessly tossed about the ship's hold. As they rocked and rolled in the depths of the ship, Kenji closed his eyes, waiting for the inevitable.

When Kenji awoke, it took but an instant to reorient himself, but the boat was still afloat and he was alive. His emotions were mixed: he felt like crying and laughing at the same time. Surveying his surroundings, he saw that many Issei had staggered topside, some vomiting over the railing. Most were in sitting positions adjusting their clothing and tending their aches and pains. Kenji sat up and examined his body; his knees and elbows were raw and scraped, but other than an overall body soreness, he was fine. Kenji gathered himself and went topside to greet a new day.

For this Issei group, the turbulent Pacific thunderstorm was their "icebreaker." Following this white-knuckle experience and for the remainder of their trek across the Pacific, the young Issei slowly began to intermingle and interact. Friendships were forged; past lives, dreams and ambitions were shared. Listening to the others converse, Kenji learned that they shared common backgrounds. They were the second or third sons of families and contracted to exchange their labor for promises of riches in a country that required more workers than were available. After fulfilling their labor agreements, they envisioned returning to Japan, rich and prosperous. Kenji even met a few Issei whose labor contracts were with the Pacific Northwest Railroad Company, the same company to which he was contracted.

However, this Issei group did not evolve into a cohesive family. Groups and cliques formed, based on personality, compatibility, and backgrounds. The most prevalent distinction among the Issei was whether one came from the country as opposed to the city. Those from the city were fewer in number, but generally louder in voice, walked with a swagger, and more opinionated. Most of them viewed themselves as more sophisticated and superior to their country counterparts.

The majority were country-bred Issei.They were more apt to listen than to talk, and were less likely to talk about themselves and their past lives. By in large, the city slickers' pompous attitudes did not bother them because it was evident from their soft hands and bodies that they had never experienced real work and in due time they would learn humbling lessons of toil, labor and how to conduct oneself.

At the ripe age of twenty-four, Masao Iwata was the oldest Issei of the group. Having been raised in the country, his family sent him to find work in the city when he was sixteen. After enduring the hardships in both city and countryside, he believed that economic opportunities in Japan were limited. Unlike the other immigrants, Masao had signed a work contract by his own choice. Masao was probably the only one aboard the Dollar Line that possessed a strong suspicion that the majority of his Issei traveling companions would never return back to Japan. He did did not want to dampen their youthful enthusiasm and spirits, so Masao kept his opinions to himself.

Among a gathering of males, a few mean-spirited bullies will often try to impose their will over those they perceive as weak. Aboard the Dollar Line, a handful of city boys from Hiroshima entertained themselves by bullying Issei from the country. They generally engaged in sharp tongue lashings, mocking and taunting less sophisticated country Issei. The harassment never elevated to the level of beatings because the rest of the Issei would not have tolerated it. However, it didn't deter them from pushing, shoving, and roughing up a country boy when they knew that they could get away with it.

The mean-spirited Hiroshima crew perceived Kenji Nagata's quiet nature and slight build as confirmation that he was just another country bumpkin needing to be taught a lesson. The adage that one's inner resolve and strength cannot be measured by outside appearance was certainly true when applied to Kenji Nagata. Although quiet by nature, he was not socially backward or ladened with self-doubt. He had been raised to believe in himself; his quiet confidence was often misinterpreted as backwardness. Despite Kenji's slim build, he was wiry quick and his body was hardened through years of working the fields. He had inherited his slim build and inner resolve from his *otoosan*. As a child, Kenji saw his *otoosan* test his judo skills against competitors from surrounding villages at the annual harvest judo competitions.

Kichigaro was the reigning champion who defended his title year after year against competitors of all shapes and sizes, until bad knees from the wear and tear of stoop labor forced him to stop competing. From watching his *otoosan* compete, Kenji learned that the biggest and strongest do not always prevail; if this were not so, his *otoosan* would have never defeated most of his opponents. Kenji learned that by outthinking and anticipating an opponent's next move, an adversary's strength could be countered and used against him. For years he saw his *otoosan* utilize his quickness, balance, anticipation and tactical planning to either throw or outpoint opponents of greater size and strength. His *otoosan* was taught judo by Kenji's *ojiichan* (grandfather). In turn, he trained both his sons, Ichiro and Kenji, keeping judo a Nagata family tradition. His *otoosan*'s "dojo" (training place) was any place where grass and terrain was firm but soft enough to absorb flips and throws onto the ground. Although Kenji's body always ached after *Otoosan*'s judo sessions, he always looked forward to the next training session. As he grew older and became stronger, he began to give as much as he received during training sessions. He had been looking forward to the upcoming harvest festival because it was to be his first entry in the judo competition. He rationalized his disappointment in not being able to compete by reminding himself that even in America, he would find time to train. He would return home stronger and with greater skills to win and defend the *judoka* title, just as his *otoosan* did.

Early one morning, after over three weeks at sea, three Hiroshima city boys gathered by the ship railing. A line for morning food rations was beginning to form but the trio were not in any rush to join the line. Once the rations were ready to be served, their usual practice was to cut to the front to be served first. While idly killing time, waiting for breakfast to be served, they spotted Kenji Nagata heading toward them. They had seen Kenji before but this was their first opportunity to harass him. As Kenji approached, the three spread out side-by-side blocking his path. Kenji sensed trouble and unable to pass by, he stopped in front of them and softly said "*sumimasen*" (pardon me). They snickered and got mouthy but Kenji neither moved, nor listened to what they were saying. Instead, he tensed his body, spread out his feet to balance his weight, and intently watched his opponents' movements. When the trio saw that this country bumpkin did not cower like the others they became enraged and shouted, "*Baka!*" (fool). Kenji remained still, continuing to focus on their movements and not their mouths. The biggest of the trio then made the mistake of underestimating Kenji's slight build and misinterpreting his silence for weakness. Suddenly with outstretched arms, he lunged at Kenji, trying to overpower and push him onto the ship's deck. Instinctively, Kenji countered his movements by quickly crossing his right foot over his left foot, and in the same motion grabbing hold of the upper left collar of his attacker with his right hand, and gripping the right belt area with his left hand. He then pivoted sideways, leaned forward, and used his attacker's momentum to toss him over his right hip onto the hard wooden deck. The sound of the body cleanly-thrown onto the deck was loud and crisp. Suddenly there was absolute silence, followed by groaning from the body laid out on the deck. His opponent's two cohorts meekly stepped aside allowing Kenji to pass.

Kenji didn't know it yet but his early morning encounter was going to turn into a life-altering moment. During this time, Masao Iwata was squatting on the ship's deck, waiting for the food line to shorten, when he observed someone walk past him on his way to the food line. Next, when he saw three troublemaker-types block that person's path, Masao sensed a scuffle was about to happen. Masao considered the harrassment child's play for other than hurt feelings, there were no real injuries and these occurrences generally took place when virile young men were thrown together in tight quarters with too much idle time. Feeling bored, Masao watched this early morning encounter unfold, but when he witnessed Kenji standing up to his harrasser, then skillfully throwing his bigger opponent to the deck, he was impressed by the young man's skill. What impressed Masao even more was the focused and calm manner with which he handled the situation. Masao thought to himself that he would make it a point to find out more about this young Issei.

Getting acquainted with Kenji Nagata was not a difficult task. The more Masao became acquainted with him, the more he took a liking to him. He found this quiet young Issei to be focused, centered and respectful. Kenji was equally receptive to befriend a person with Masao's worldly experience. Soon, the two would eat their meals together and spend idle time in each other's company, These two activities were the basis of the majority of their daily routine. Without verbalizing it, they forged a bond—Masao took on the role of an older brother and Kenji that of a loyal younger brother. By the time the Dollar Line entered San Francisco Port, Kenji and Masao had formed a friendship that would last their lifetimes. By fate or fortune, Masao's labor contract was also with the Pacific Northwest Railroad Company; however, since Masao negotiated his own contract he only had a two-year rather than a three-year obligation.

After six weeks crossing the Pacific Ocean, the Dollar Line dropped anchor in San Francisco Harbor in late September, 1910. During this time, Kenji Nagata had turned 18 years old. It was three days before Kenji and the other Issei were taken to the Angel Island immigration processing center, the West Coast equivalent to Ellis Island. When the time finally arrived to register their immigration status, Kenji and his fellow Issei stood in a long line waiting their turn to be processed. Masao had prepared Kenji for this moment by telling him that when they asked him questions in English, he was to recite his name aloud, "Nagata, Kenji."

When Kenji's turn for processing came up and the white man sitting behind his desk spoke an alien language to him, Kenji responded, "Nagata, Kenji." The man looked confused and asked him the same question in English and again Kenji responded, "Nagata, Kenji." This was repeated two more times. Finally, in frustration, the man wrote something on the paperwork in front of him and dismissed Kenji with an abrupt wave of his hand, shouting out "Next!" As Kenji stepped away from the immigration station, the immigration clerk, tired and irritated from having to figure out all the names of these slant-eyed aliens, placed Kenji's immigration paper in his finished bin. Kenji's immigration papers read:

Last Name: Kingi

First Name: John Doe

According to the archives of United States immigration records, Kenji Nagata never immigrated to America in 1897. However, a young man named John Doe Kingi did.

COOLIE LABOR

West of the Rocky Mountains

AFTER CLEARING IMMIGRATION, the Pacific Northwest Railroad Company wasted no time in picking up and transporting their Issei laborers. By the end of their first week in this foreign land, they found themselves leveling rugged terrain in preparation of laying down railroad track. They were issued western work clothing, boots, mallets, shovels and picks. Their base camp was somewhere in the middle of Montana. It was the railroad baron's grandiose plan to build a transcontinental railway system, connecting the Atlantic Ocean to the Pacific. To accomplish this herculean task they exploited the cheapest labor available. While Kenji and the western work crew laid track in an easterly direction, eastern work crews simultaneously duplicated the effort in a westerly direction, with the goal of merging the two tracks in the Midwest, at a place called Kansas City.

The weather in Montana fluctuated to the extremes. Temperatures ranged from below zero freezing cold in the winter to sweltering summer heat, often over one hundred degrees. The Issei laborers had difficulty adjusting to the harsh weather fluctuations and to the life as "coolie laborers." Even Kenji, who had worked ever since he could walk, found the elements and working conditions nearly intolerable.

The labor camp was comprised of several rows of tents; each tent housed twelve workers, with six cots on each side of the tent. Oriental workers were the driving labor force for the railroad company: the Chinese immigrants were the majority, followed by Japanese Issei, and a small sprinkling of Filipino immigrants; all of the railroad overseers were white. The work day began at the crack of dawn and ended after the sun set. The sounds of clanging steel mallets, picks and shovels, breaking rock, leveling land and pounding steel ties to mount track, was the language they spoke. They lifted, carried, pulled, pounded, and leveled the earth on every type of terrain imaginable—hills, valleys, slopes, wet soil, dry soil, up mountains, down mountains, and if necessary, straight through mountains. Mother Nature's obstacles were overcome by erecting bridges to go over them or by going straight through them with picks, shovels, and explosives. The harsh weather conditions made no difference to their overseers. Laborers were injured but as long as he could stand and walk, he was expected to work; there was no such thing as a minor injury. A high fever, a common cold, the flu, or intestinal problems were considered minor. The few "legitimate" reasons that excused one from working were injuries resulting in breaks, fractures, loss of limbs, and the permanent excuse of death.

The coolies were expendable. During Kenji's three-year obligation, he witnessed permanent injuries and deaths caused by boulders dislodged from mountain tops crushing workers, the mishandling of explosives, and faulty trestle supports toppling workers to their deaths. A worker's worst fear was to sustain a crippling injury that would take away or limit his capacity to work—this would be an insurmountable tragedy. A disabled worker was no longer useful to the railroad company and would immediately be terminated from his contract, without a return ticket home. In such a devastating predicament, one could only hope that a person had the foresight to save enough wages to purchase a ticket home, or at least to buy himself some time, even if only for a short while, to consider his options while stranded in a foreign land with limited work opportunities.

Every tenth day, the workers were given a day to rest. The base camp was so far away from cities or towns that the workers were confined to the camp quarters. Even if there were nearby towns or cities, Orientals were not welcomed, and entering such a hostile environment was dangerous. Towns west of the Rocky Mountains posted signs in shops, eateries and bars, which read, "No Dogs or Chinamen Allowed!" If a town with honky-tonks existed that welcomed Orientals, Kenji Nagata would have opted to stay behind to rest his aching body—besides, he was not interested in blowing his tiny savings.

Months passed before Kenji adjusted to the daily demands of railroad camp life. The workdays were long and physically taxing. At first, after a strenuous day's work, there were instances when Kenji would be so physically drained, he would eat supper then fall asleep on his cot fully clothed, only to wake up a few hours later to repeat the routine. As he slowly adapted to his new life, his body hardened, and instead of allowing his mind to constantly wander, thinking about his family and village back home, he disciplined himself to focus on his immediate surroundings. Kenji realized that such an adjustment was necessary for both his mental and physical survival. In his short time there, he had witness laborers get injured due to a lack of focus and concentration.

A daily routine Kenji practiced in Japan was an early morning deep-breathing technique which he found beneficial to continue in his new surroundings. It was not a Zen-type of meditation practice which required years to perfect; his was simple, practical, and self-taught. Even as a young boy, Kenji was an early-riser and was always the first in his family to awaken every morning. In the peaceful quiet of the early morning, he would inhale through his nose, allowing his breath to enter his lungs and flow to the center of his core. In the same breathing rhythm, he would evenly exhale his breath through his mouth. While breathing deeply he would empty his mind by concentrating on nothing. Kenji saw how clearing his mind every morning, helped him start the day in a positive frame of mind. Upon arrival in America, he continued his early morning breathing routine.

The major stabilizing factor in Kenji's new life was his *tomodachi* (friend), Masao Iwata. From the moment they arrived at the Montana base camp, they were inseparable; they were placed on the same work crew and assigned to the same tent lodge. They did not engage in idle gossip, respected each other's privacy, were cautious when selecting friends, and were fiercely loyal to those befriended. Placed in surroundings without family support, Kenji and Masao respected one another as brothers.

Early one morning, around six months after his arrival in America, Kenji still lay in his cot, ready to begin his deep breathing. But on this morning, he was unable to empty his mind: a troubling thought lingered and bothered him enough to disrupt his morning meditation. When he awoke his first thought was that it was payday; he always looked forward to sending a portion of his scant wages back his family in Japan. This would be his sixth payday since arriving in America. Instead of clearing his mind, Kenji began to mentally add and subtract his monthly wages from his expenses. He knew the pay from the Pacific Northwest Railroad Company was more than he could have earned had he stayed in Japan, but, each month after settling his monthly expenses with the railroad for lodging, food and items purchased at the company store, the bulk of his wages went back to the company. After sending most of what was left of his earnings back to Japan, it left him with only *skoshi* (little bit) for himself. He further calculated that by the end of his three-year contract, he would only have enough saved for a few good meals, some new clothes and a one-way ticket back to Japan, but not much more.

This was the first time since he arrived at base camp that Kenji felt uncertain and insecure. He realized that despite his strong back, he was nothing more than a cheap laborer—an unwelcome stranger exiled in a faraway foreign land.

Kenji remained troubled and one evening, a week after his epiphany, he finally asked Masao, "Why didn't you tell me, after all this time, that I would barely have enough saved to return back to Japan?" Masao sat quietly and after careful contemplation, his eyes met Kenji's troubled but inquisitive gaze. "Kenji, it is not my place to tell you something that was always right in front of you. I can tell a boy how to think, but a man has to think independently. It will not be easy for us in America, each of us must find our own way." Masao's words and the stern inflection of his voice instantaneously snapped Kenji out of his depressed state, and back to the moment. Kenji realized that Masao was not the cause of his false hopes, but since it was too late to take back his question or to apologize, Kenji responded to Masao with a quick, "*Hai!*" ("yes, I see"), followed with a nod of his head. This was the closest to an admonishment that his trusted *tomodachi* ever gave him.

Upon reflection, Kenji realized that the signs that Masao alluded to were always right in front of him. From day one, Kenji had dismissed the constant complaints and uncertainties discussed amongst the Issei laborers as idle chatter of beaten-down workers who lacked the discipline and foresight to stash away their earnings. Taking Masao's advice to heart, Kenji listened and observed fellow Issei, seeing how each individual prepared to deal with the fact that returning back to Nippon and a hero's homecoming was a pipe dream.

Individuals varied in their views on the prospect of an extended or infinite stay in America. Overall, Kenji found two prevailing schools of thought among the Issei. A small but increasing number of the immigrants resigned themselves to the fate of never returning back to the homeland, destined to live their remaining years on foreign soil. Within this group, some questioned the idea of returning when work opportunities in Japan were scarce with little family support. Their overall outlook was pessimistic; they did not view starting a life in America as an opportunity, rather it was a choice between the lesser of two evils. Their prevailing attitude was to live for a moment's pleasure—many blew their meager earnings on alcohol, gambling, or "short time" relationships with pale-skinned women of ill repute. These excitements and vices were readily available. Like clockwork, on the monthly payday, Chinese entrepreneurs would visit the labor camp with a traveling entourage, offering games of chance, alcohol, and a variety of prostitutes of all skin colors. This traveling festival never missed a payday and was never short on paying customers.

The second philosophy, adopted by the majority of the young Issei, viewed their predicament of being stranded in America as a temporary setback. Upon the realization that slaving for the Pacific Northwest Railroad Company was not the way to riches as promised, they began planning for the future. Their plans gave them a ray of hope, something tangible to grasp onto during tough times. After fulfilling their labor contracts, they planned to find work compatible to their backgrounds. They looked forward to venturing on their own to earn the type of money that would enable them to fulfill their vision of returning home with wealth and stories about life in a place called America.

This optimistic Issei group refused to surrender their belief of someday returning home to Nippon. They sought out information needed to develop plans for tomorrow. While this group still enjoyed a drink or two, played games of chance, and every so often, paid for a short time with a woman with a painted face, they did so in moderation.

Kenji's *tomodachi*, Masao Iwata, did not fit into to either group. Masao was neither optimistic or pessimistic about his future. His life experience had shaped him into a pragmatist. At sixteen, Masao left his village to find work in Hiroshima, where he worked as a laborer performing a multitude of different jobs. He was paid low wages, often just enough to sustain himself, so finding work during hard times forced him to sharpen his wits and hone his survival skills. Masao learned to appraise situations and to make decisions without letting emotional attachments cloud his judgment. When Masao signed his employment contract with the Pacific Northwest Railroad Company, he had no illusions of returning back to Japan a wealthy man. Upon arrival in America, Masao attentively listened, learned, and weighed all available options before planning his next move. Masao concluded that his best option was to create a new life in America.

Masao was the third son of six siblings. In his early youth he lived with his family in a seaport village on Shikoku, an island off the southeast coast of the main island of Honshu, Japan. It was his familiarity and comfort with the sea that would guide him to a place called Terminal Island, located near San Pedro, California. He heard from other Issei that Terminal Island was a fishing port with work available for Issei in the canneries or as boat hands and dockworkers. Another important factor in Masao's decision to try his lot at Terminal Island was that he is *samugari* by nature (a person sensitive to the cold) and he heard that the California climate was warmer than that of the cold Pacific Northwest seaports.

The labor camp had its own grapevine, the Issei willingly sharing news and information about different geographic locations offering work. Job opportunities were available depending on the type of work being sought. In America's Pacific Northwest, from Seattle up to Alaska, cheap labor was needed for the fishing industry at canneries, as deckhands loading and unloading ships, and in lumber camps. Issei with farming backgrounds migrated to California's Central Valley, to places like Fresno, Reedley, Hanford, Tulare, and Visalia, where land was plentiful, fertile and seasonal agricultural pickers were in demand. City boys, coveting business opportunities, gravitated to small pockets of "Japantowns" that were sprouting up and down the coast. With the influx of Japanese immigrants on the West Coast, cities like San Francisco, Fresno, San Jose, Seattle, and Los Angeles were building *Nihonmachi* (Japan towns), with Issei entrepreneurs operating small cafes, boarding houses, barber shops, general stores, bars, and even red light districts. The largest one, aptly coined "Little Tokyo," was in downtown Los Angeles. The Issei were building their own community, a temporary home away from home.

Two years after migrating to America, Masao Iwata was nearing the end of his labor contract with the Pacific Northwest. Finally, he would be free to leave the base camp to venture out on his own. He was fully aware that there was no guarantee that work would be available when he reached Terminal Island, and knew his struggle for survival in a hostile alien country was to begin. However, he maintained a strong sense of independence and pride knowing that he was no longer a piece of property that was owned and controlled by the Pacific Northwest Railroad. He understood that as physically demanding the work on the railroad line was, his next work opportunity would demand even more. The major difference was now he would work for himself.

Masao's only trepidation was leaving behind his *tomodachi*, Kenji. Their friendship had been forged through sweat and struggle. They supported each other and knew each other so well that they could finish each other's sentences— something generally not necessary because their friendship was not built on words.

To celebrate Masao's last night at the base camp, Kenji purchased a fifth of whisky. They both knew that Kenji's decision to party with Masao late into the night would exact a heavy toll on his body the next day, but neither was concerned— without expressing it they knew that this could be their last time together.

The night was special; both got happy drunk. A few hours before Kenji had to report to work, Masao rested on his cot. He did not remember when he fell asleep, but when he awoke the sun was up and Kenji was gone. He would miss his *tomodachi*, but once he reached Terminal Island and settled in, he would write to keep in touch. Masao could not believe that last night while they were celebrating, Kenji had brought out his savings and insisted that he take a portion of it. Masao was equally persistent, explaining to Kenji that it was not necessary or practical, because Kenji would need it for himself next year. Although Kenji knew that Masao would never accept his generosity, Kenji still insisted that he accept it as a gift. He, too, would miss his trusted *tomodachi*.

A few days later, during his trek to Terminal Island, Masao bedded down for the night in a small inexpensive hotel that catered to Japanese and other Orientals in downtown Fresno, California. When he unpacked his travel bag and pulled out a clean plaid shirt, he discovered a lump inside the breast pocket. Masao reached into the depths of the garment and brought the foreign object into the light. In his hand was a bundle, a wad of money.

Kenji's final year in fulfilling his labor contract was the hardest. It had little to do with the work load because his body had hardened and he was used to the combination of hard labor and long hours. His turmoil was caused by feelings of isolation and anxiety. Despite being surrounded in the company of other Issei, no one filled the vacuum and loss of Masao's friendship. During lonely moments he remembered Masao's advice, "to think and act independently." In a small way he was even grateful that Masao was not here with him at this juncture in his life, because his presence could have made it easy and convenient just to tag along and follow him to Terminal Island. Seven months after Masao left the base camp, Kenji received a letter. Masao wrote about his new life at Terminal Island. His work effort earned him a position of deckhand on a fishing boat and he shared a bungalow shelter with two other Issei deckhands. He told Kenji that if he decided to join him at Terminal Island that he would find him a job. As tempting as Masao's offer was, Kenji turned it down because what he knew best was farming. His plan after fulfilling his contract, was to pack his travel bag and head in the direction of the agricultural belt in Central California.

SAN JOAQUIN VALLEY

Armona, Califonia

CENTRAL CALIFORNIA, an agricultural belt, produces fresh fruit, vegetables and dairy products to feed America. This vast fertile area stretches over 350 miles, north from Elk Grove, a rural community outside of Sacramento, to small agricultural towns in the south. Most of the produce is grown in the southern part of the San Joaquin Valley by large growers and small independent farmers in small rural communities like Reedley, Porterville, Tulare, Visalia, Delano, Porterville, Hanford, Kingsburg, Lemoore, and Armona. The central hub in the San Joaquin Valley is a developing area named Fresno. Year-round agricultural duties of soil preparation, planting, cultivation, pruning, and harvesting, required hired help. The farmers and growers in Central California are always in need of efficient cheap labor. In the early 1900s, hundreds of immigrant Issei migrated to the agricultural belt of Central California with hopes of improving their lot.

The summer of 1900, found Kenji picking peaches alongside other Issei laborers in Armona, California. He came into this job by talking to other migrant Issei workers during his travel to Central California. The grower he was picking for was a small independent farmer. Picking peaches required a keen eye and quick hands. One had to develop an eye to pick only peaches that were not quite ripe but would ripen in a few days, when displayed at markets and fruit stands in the big cities. Kenji's farming background made him a quick study in spotting and picking soon-to-ripen peaches at an accelerated pace. Pickers were paid a daily wage predicated upon the number of peach crates they filled. By the end of his first week, Kenji had the third-highest earning amongst the harvesters. At the end of the second week, the field foreman stopped checking Kenji's crates for overripe and under ripe peaches, because Kenji had proven that he knew what he was doing.

Following the peach season, grapes needed to be picked. Again, Kenji's farming background and determination set him slightly apart from the other field hands. Kenji knew that his chances of making it through the upcoming winter months would greatly increase if he was hired by a local *hakujin* (white) farmer to work as a year-round helper.

Following the peach and grape harvests, watermelons needed to be pitched. Pitching watermelon was different from picking apricots, peaches, grapes and figs—it required a team effort. A watermelon-picking team consisted of nine men, plus a cutter. The cutter was the senior and most experienced man of the team. A

26

cutter would arrive at the watermelon acreage early in the morning before the rest of crew. He would select, then lop from its vine, the watermelons to be pitched that day. The cutter's job was to ensure that the selected melons would be firm and fresh at the time they were displayed at the markets and fruit stands.

At the crack of dawn the rest of the crew arrived. A flatbed platform, pulled by tractor, was placed on the field. On each side of the platform were three pickers standing side by side. The picker farthest away from the flatbed, would start the process by stooping down to shovel pass a lopped watermelon to the middle man who would catch it and in the same motion, pitch it to the third man standing closest to the flatbed. The third picker would toss it up to where the worker standing on the flatbed could catch it and shovel it to the last recipient who completed the process by catching and stacking the watermelon on the platform. This activity would simultaneously take place on both sides of the flatbed. The picking team had to develop a collective sense of timing and rhythm to minimize the number of watermelons bruised, cracked, or shattered.

When all of the lopped melons were picked from an area, the flatbed moved to the next area to repeat the process. Pitching watermelon required strong arms, backs, legs, stamina and teamwork. Some of the work stations were more physically strenuous than others. The outside picker, who did the most stooping, had the most demanding job. The team rotated so by the day's end, each member had worked all positions.

The watermelon crew worked from sunup to dusk. After all the melons were picked, the work crew followed the flatbeds into the unloading area and using the same chain line method in the opposite direction, unloaded the watermelons from the platforms into truck bins for overnight delivery to towns and cities. This workday was repeated until the end of the watermelon season.

Even Kenji, who prided himself on being in good physical condition, found pitching melons taxing on his back, shoulders, arms and legs. He learned to lift objects by using his legs instead of his back muscles. If he wasn't always so tired and sore, he probably would have been more concerned that no one yet had offered him a permanent job.

Late one afternoon, as the flatbeds were being positioned next to the delivery trucks, Kenji spotted Tanaka-san in the distance, waving him over. Tanaka-san was the crew's foreman. He was the senior member of the team and had the responsibility to select and lop the watermelons. Tanaka-san was noticeably older than his Issei counterparts. He was said to be one of the original Issei that migrated to Central California and had taught himself enough broken English to possess a working vocabulary. The local *hakujin* farmers valued him as their go-between messenger, able to communicate their commands to the young, non-English speaking Issei. Tanaka-san was one of the few Issei in the area to have a Japanese wife and children. He had three children: his two boys attended a local *hakujin* school during the winter and worked in the fields during the summer. His daughter, still a toddler, had just started taking her first steps. The young Issei in the area respected and admired Tanaka-san and would comment, "Imagine having a wife and kids, here in America!"

As Kenji approached Tanaka-san, he became aware of a *hakujin* man standing next to him. With the watermelon season nearing its end, Kenji hoped that he was not going to be laid off. In *Nihongo* (Japanese), Tanaka-san told Kenji that the man next to him was a local farmer, Mr. Whitman. He said that Mr. Whitman owned a small orchard grove and that he was looking for a permanent worker.

Kenji could not believe his ears; inside he was filled with jubilation, but outwardly he did not change his expression and continued to listen to Tanaka-san. Mr. Whitman was looking for a permanent worker to replace his Issei worker who had left after he received an offer to work for a large grower in Fresno. It was a mutual parting with no ill feelings because Mr. Whitman knew that he could not match the offer of the large grower. Mr. Whitman proposed that Kenji pick Mr. Whitman's apricots during the harvest season and between harvest and picking seasons, he was to cultivate and prune the orchards on the Whitman farm. Kenji would receive the standard rate during the harvest season but would not be compensated between harvests. Since the Whitman farm was small, Kenji was free to work for other local farmers when his work at the Whitman farm was done. In exchange for his labor, Kenji would be provided living quarters and a garden plot to grow his own vegetables. When Tanaka-san finished explaining this arrangement, Kenji agreed to it by saying, "*Hai, dozo,*" ("Yes, go ahead"). He then shifted his attention towards Mr. Whitman and said, "*Domo arigato*" ("Thank you") and bowed his head. Mr. Whitman responded by extended his open right hand to Kenji. Kenji knew that the clasping of hands was how the American *hakujin* greeted one another. Sometimes, while among themselves, the Issei would enjoy a moment of levity by mimicking this white man's gesture. Kenji would merely laugh along but would not participate because he saw no need to, but also, grasping another man's hand made him feel uncomfortable. Kenji's momentary inaction brought a confused expression on Mr. Whitman's face. Sensing Kenji's awkwardness, Tanaka-san loudly cleared his throat, snapping Kenji back to the moment. It was Tanaka-san's way of telling Kenji, "*Baka*, grasp his hand." Kenji reached out and offered his right hand, Mr. Whitman smiled then shook Kenji's hand up and down, sealing their arrangement.

Two weeks later, at the end of the watermelon season, Kenji moved into his new home. Bob Whitman owned two acres on the Hanford-Armona border. In Japan, such a tract of land was equivalent to possessing an empire; in Central California, Bob Whitman was just another small grower. He had a wife and two children; an eight-year-old son and a five-year-old daughter. Kenji had no reference point with which to estimate Mr. Whitman's age, in Kenji's mind, all of the *hakujin*, especially the ones in charge, all seemed to be old. This was one American custom that Kenji could understand because in Japan, the elders were always in charge.

Kenji's new living quarters was more a shack than a home. It was hidden from the rest of the property in the middle of a clearing in the apricot orchard, near an irrigation ditch.

On one side of the box-shaped shack was a small space for a garden; on the other side was a fire pit, encircled by steel bracings to elevate and secure a large barrel-shaped wooden tub directly over the fire pit, to be used for bathing. The shack's interior was partitioned into three rooms, having a bedroom in the back, a tiny front room and a smaller combination kitchen and eating area. It had neither indoor plumbing nor electricity. The *benjo* (toilet)was an outdoor outhouse near an irrigation ditch. Although Kenji's new digs was less than 200 yards away from the main house where the Whitman family lived, any comparison between the main house and Kenji's concealed shack were continents apart. None of this mattered to Kenji; he now had his own home, with an opportunity to work and earn money for himself. He had finally arrived in America!

Kenji made the most of his opportunity, working from sunup to sundown, seven days a week, and picking up a few side jobs from other local growers. He was one of many Issei men in the San Joaquin Valley. The Issei of Hanford-Armona, Kings County, made it their priority to become acquainted. They worked side-by-side in the fields and orchards, and when time permitted, they visited each other. They planted their roots in the Central Valley and considered this area their home. They depended upon each other for their economic and social survival in America. They organized, each Issei agreeing to contribute a small portion of their wages to a fund which would eventually be used to purchase a small parcel of property on the outskirts of Hanford. Because only American citizens could legally own land, the title to their collectively-owned parcel was to be placed under the name of Tanaka-san's oldest son, Tetsu Tanaka, who was born in America and possessed American citizenship papers. They used any spare time they had to construct, paint, and carve with fine detail, a large wooden structure—the first Buddhist temple in Kings County, California. The Buddhist Reverend Matsumoto, from the northerly Fresno Buddhist Temple, traveled to their temple twice a month to hold religious services. The Issei now had their own temple to practice their religious beliefs and to burn incense to honor their deceased relatives back home. The Buddhist temple also served as their community center, a place where social events and holiday gatherings were celebrated.

For all *Nihonjin* (Japanese people), whether rich, poor, from a village, city, or rural area, New Year's Day is the biggest event of the year. The New Year was celebrated with equal gusto by the Issei in America. On the morning of New Year's Day, the entire Issei community congregated at the Buddhist temple for service, paying homage to the past and also celebrating a cleansing of the mind and spirit, in anticipation for a prosperous new year. Following the morning service, the congregation was served a bowl of *soba* (buckwheat noodles) with fish cakes and diced green onions in a tasty broth. Upon finishing the *soba*, the Issei went home and returned to the temple later that afternoon, with dishes of traditional Japanese food for their New Year's festivities. For this day they prepared food that replicated the delicacies served back in Japan. They made *tsukemono* (pickled cabbage), *kinpira gobo* (finely sliced, seasoned burdock root), *teriyaki* chicken, fish steamed with vinegar, *shoyu* and black beans, country-style *nishime* (stew made with simmered vegetables), *mochi* (pounded steamed rice formed into rounds), *mochigashi* (mochi filled with sweet red or white bean paste), and gallons of potent homemade *sake* (rice wine). On this day, everyone celebrated, ate heartily, and the *sake* flowed. Towards the end of the evening, drunken off-key voices sang traditional Japanese songs that filled the room.

As the years passed, Kenji became an established Issei resident in the area. He always looked forward to the annual New Year's celebrations where he started noticing more and more Issei men accompanied by a Japanese wife. He was aware that their wives came to America through a *baishakunin* (go-between) who, for a fee, negotiated an arranged marriage through mail. Kenji and his *tomodachi* Masao kept in touch through yearly correspondence. In Masao's last letter, he reported the good news of finally having his own wife. Having a young Japanese wife was the ultimate status symbol for the Issei men. It meant that one was doing well enough to be able to support a wife and start a family. As time marched on, Kenji began to see more wives, kids and babies at the New Year gatherings.

Year after year, at the festive occasion, Kenji and other single Issei counterparts would get stink-faced drunk. By the end of the night, with their arms draped around each other, holding one another up, they would sing melancholy *Nihon* (Japan) love songs. At the end of the festivities, they returned home to an empty bed—tomorrow would be just another work day, the start of another work year.

NAGATA FAMILY IN AMERICA

FROM THE OUTSET of the of the Issei immigration, America tolerated the migration of Japan's young virile men because of their willingness to work the type of jobs that even the most economically deprived American worker was unwilling to undertake for the meager wages it paid. It never occurred to the American public that the overwhelming majority of the Issei men were here to stay. By limiting the work opportunities to only the Japanese men, it eradicated the unimaginable threat of this non-Christian yellow mongoloid race perpetuating itself on American soil by breeding a next generation.

By the time Kenji reached his late thirties, he had lived in America over half of his life. He no longer viewed his secluded shack amidst the Whitman's apricot orchard as a temporary home away from home, for Kenji it was now just plain "old" home.

During Kenji's tenth year in America, he received a letter from his *niisan* (elder brother) informing him that *Otoosan* had unexpectedly passed away. Immediately, Kenji began to make arrangements to return to Japan so he could help care for his *okaasan* (mother). He understood that once he left, returning to America would be difficult—in recent years the United States government had tightened its restrictions on Issei immigration. The few newly-arriving Issei that migrated to Central Valley, reported that Japan's economic outlook was still dismal. Kenji's plan was to wait until the apricot harvest was picked, in order to fulfill his duty to Mr. Whitman. Just before the upcoming apricot harvest and nearly three months after he received the letter from his *niisan*, a second letter from Japan arrived. Kenji took the news hard when he learned of his *okaasan*'s sudden, unexpected death. His heart was heavy with sadness, and he wished he could have been there for both his *otoosan* and *okaasan*, Kenji also knew that with the passing of his *otoosan* and *okaasan* there was no reason for him to return to Japan.

Time marched on, and other significant changes occurred. Mr. Whitman had aged considerably, and he no longer oversaw the day-to-day farm operation. His son, Travis, was now in charge. Truthfully, Travis had very little to oversee except to purchase supplies, for during the past decades, Kenji tended to the daily pruning and maintenance of the orchard grove, making sure that whatever needed to be taken care of was done.

A few years ago, for the first time, Mr. Whitman invited Kenji to his home. He told Kenji that there was an important matter he needed to discuss with him. For his visit, Kenji put on his special-occasion dress clothes. Invited inside the Whitman home, Kenji found it to be even more spacious than it appeared from the outside.

It was stylishly furnished, with window draperies, carpeting, electricity and indoor plumbing. The furnishings and tapestry were decorative and comfortable. Kenji found the house to be even more impressive than he ever imagined.

Over the years, out of necessity, Kenji had taught himself enough English to understand a little of what the *hakujin* were saying. Kenji understood them the best when they spoke directly to him using simple words in a slow cadence and utilized hand gestures to emphasize an important point.

Kenji sat in a comfortable chair in the parlor, directly across from from Mr. Whitman. Mrs. Whitman had served them a cold glass of water with lemon peel. After she left the room, Mr. Whitman explained to Kenji that he was planning to "retire" in a few years. Upon seeing a confused look on Kenji's face, he explained to him that retirement meant he was going to stop working. Kenji tried to grasp the message, hoping that this did not mean that Mr. Whitman was planning on dying because everyone he ever knew stopped working only when they died. Mr. Whitman told Kenji how much he appreciated his hard work all these years and then said that in the future, if he sold his farm or a part of it, he would first offer the lower one-half acre of the property to Kenji, if he were interested.

Kenji's ears perked up—he was sure that he heard Mr. Whitman correctly and he immediately said "H*ai*, thank you!" and bowed his head. Mr. Whitman returned the smile and stuck out his right hand. This would be the second time in his life that Mr. Whitman offered Kenji his hand but this time Kenji needed no prompting. As they clasped their strong calloused hands together, this time it was Kenji who vigorously shook it up and down.

Before he left the Whitman house, Kenji used all of his basic English skills to tell Mr. Whitman about his plan to bring a wife over from Japan. Mr. Whitman seemed genuinely happy for him and replied, "I was wondering when you would get around to it, I see more and more of you Jap workers getting hitched-up this way. I don't blame you a bit, it must get mighty lonesome." After Kenji finished his cold drink, he excused himself because he had work to finish.

Actually, Kenji was well pass the planning stage of his "picture bride" negotiations. He had already contacted a *baishakunin* who had facilitated communication between Kenji and a family interested in a marriage arrangement for their youngest daughter. During the past six months, Kenji had corresponded with a Matsuno family from Saijo, Japan. Kenji could tell from their letters that they had a country background similar to his own, and they were concerned about their youngest daughter's future. In his letters, Kenji described his situation and status in America. His letters must have impressed the Masuno family because his courtship with Sachiko Masuno had reached the final stage where Sachiko and Kenji exchanged their pictures. Upon Sachiko's and her family's approval, the only distance between their arranged marriage was the Pacific Ocean.

For, Kenji the letter-writing process with the Masuno family was troublesome. Until now, the extent of his penmanship skills was writing occasional letters to his family and a yearly letter to his old friend, Masao Iwata. Kenji was acutely aware of the importance these letters were to his life. If his letters impressed Sachiko and her family, his loneliness would finally come to an end. If they did not, odds were that he would live and die in this foreign land a lonely old man. To describe his lofty status in America, Kenji wrote about owning his own home in the country, being the person in charge of a farm operation, and described how Central California was populated with Japanese families, and they even had their own Buddhist temple.

Most of the half-truths that Kenji described in his letters did not trouble him as much as concealing his true age. When he received Sachiko's picture, she was so young and pretty that he instantly knew that she would never agree to marry a old man like himself. It was at that moment when Kenji decided to conceal his true age and send a picture of himself that was taken at a New Year celebration fifteen years ago. Kenji forgot who took the picture and why it was taken, but he was glad that he had kept it. Looking at his youthful appearance in the picture, combined with the thought of Sachiko, almost made him feel young again.

In September of 1918, Sachiko Masuno nervously stood next to her large travel trunk at the Port of San Francisco. Countless times, during the past eight months, she had envisioned in her mind this exact moment. Up to the very last instant of her departure, she possessed doubts whether she was making the right decision. All she knew about the man she had agreed to marry were from his letters and his picture that she now clutched in her hand. After a month-long boat ride across the Pacific she felt weary, but she nervously looked forward to finally meeting her new husband and taken to his home in the country. Never being intimate with a man, Sachiko's plan was to pretend that she was very tired for the first few days, and perhaps her new husband would allow her to rest up, which would give her time to become acquainted with him, before he took her as his wife. On her journey, she befriended fifteen other Japanese picture brides, all destined to meet their new husbands. This common destiny became their bond. They were all young, sharing the same anxieties, fears and nervous sense of adventure. When the steamboat finally docked in San Francisco Harbor, they all dressed in their finest kimonos. Looking at her traveling companions for perhaps the last time, Sachiko knew that she would miss her newly acquired friends.

During their sea voyage, as they became familiar and comfortable with one another, they confided in each other and even shared pictures of their soon-to-be-met husbands. It was during these picture-sharing exchanges that Sachiko's reservations about Kenji Nagata began to lessen. As her new friends passed around Kenji's picture they would comment on his youthful good looks. When Sachiko viewed the pictures of the men her companions were about to marry, she realized how fortunate she was because Kenji Nagata was noticeably younger than the other men and the other women were right, their men did not appear as strong or as handsome.

When the steamboat finally docked, many of the Issei men were waiting at the dock to meet and take away their new brides. The few left remaining on the dock were slowly picked up by their husbands, until only Sachiko remained. Many of the men who arrived were she recognizable because Sachiko had already seen pictures of them. It was strange that except for a few of these men, most of them appeared older than their pictures.

As the docks cleared, Sachiko began to worry that maybe something had happened to Kenji Nagata. From a distance, she couldn't help but to notice a man dressed in western style clothing looking at her. Every time she glanced towards his direction, he continued to gaze at her. Sachiko became tense and anxious and started resenting her new husband for not being there on time. She now was alone, with only a picture in her hand. She noticed that the man still standing in the distance was the only other person in the receiving area. Then he started walking in her direction. For some reason, Sachiko stared back at the man as he approached her. Shocked, her body went numb; all her anxiety, adrenaline and energy dissipated as the man now stood in front of Sachiko and reached for her trunk. Sachiko covered her face with both hands and cried.

Throughout the seven-hour train ride from San Francisco to Fresno, Sachiko refused to look or speak to the old man. They disembarked at Fresno, then hitched a ride on the back of a supply wagon from a local grower who was heading back to Armona.

Upon being dropped off at the Whitman farm, Sachiko saw the big house and was pleasantly surprised but did not to show Kenji Nagata any approval, fearing he might misinterpret her reaction. Oddly, the old man carried her baggage past the house and walked along a path into a dense orchard tree area. Having no choice but to follow him into the orchard, she thought, "What a strange man." When Sachiko saw the shack in the midst of the orchard grove, she would have cried again if she had any tears left inside.

It was a three-room shack with two windows. A small front room had two chairs, and a log-fed stove for cooking and keeping the shack heated during the cold winter. The second smaller room in the front contained an ice chest to keep perishable food from spoiling, and a bench table for eating. The back room was used for a bedroom. Sachiko angrily thought about how she was tricked into traveling this great distance by an old man living in a small shack and became determined to return home at the very first opportunity.

The next morning, Sachiko wrote a letter to her *otoosan* and *okaasan*, exposing Kenji Nagata as a fake and imposter. To his credit, he slept in the front room and Sachiko slept in the bedroom. Up to this point they had not exchanged a single word with each other.

By the end of the first week, Sachiko had still not spoken to Kenji, nor did she plan to. At times she felt her resolve weakening because she had no one else on the farm to talk to. The *hakujin* people that owned the farm were friendly to her but even if she was able to communicate with them, she would have felt uncomfortable doing so.

Sachiko Matsuno was the youngest of five children, and as she grew older, her siblings still called her the *"akachan"* (baby) of the family, and they were probably right. Sachiko could do things that her parents would overlook; however, if her siblings did the exact same thing, they would get punished. Her brothers and sisters accused her of being pampered, stubborn and spoiled. Sachiko would only admit that she was stubborn. She knew that her family did not have the money to purchase her a return ticket home so she concluded that she needed to earn money to buy her own ticket. This is when she finally broke down and spoke to

Kenji, telling him that she wanted to work in the fields. Kenji found her domestic household and cleaning work for *hakujin* families, at two nearby large farms. Sachiko was glad to work for it kept her out of isolation and helped occupy her mind with thoughts other than being homesick. Sachiko met other Issei women who worked on these properties. These women had lived in Central California for years and even given birth to children born here. When Sachiko confided to them about how Kenji Nagata tricked her into coming to America by lying about his age and status, she was shocked that these women were unsympathetic and did not even pretend to side with her. Instead, they tried to tell her what a good man Kenji Nagata was and a few even laughed as they told her how the same trick had been pulled on them. Sachiko could not believe what she was hearing—she was not like these beaten-down women! She would be here only a short while until she earned enough money to return home. She decided that until then, she would keep her plans to herself.

Months passed and still there was no letter from home. Sachiko had saved nowhere near enough money to purchase a ticket home. She continued to write to her family, telling them not to worry, and that she was determined to return home.

Finally, a few weeks before the start of the New Year, a letter from Japan arrived. Even if the envelope did not contain money for a ticket, just hearing from her family telling Sachiko how much they missed her and that they understood how she felt, would be enough motivation to keep her resolve until she had saved enough for a ticket home. Upon opening the letter, her body stiffened and then went numb and cold. If she had not already been seated, she would have collapsed. In the letter, *Otoosan* instructed her not to return home; she was to stay in America to honor her *shujin* (husband). Sachiko could not believe what she was reading. She suspected that just maybe, from the beginning, her *otoosan* and *okaasan* had known about and even silently approved of Kenji Nagata's deceit. For the second time since her arrival in America, Sachiko cried uncontrollably.

On New Year's Day, Sachiko and Kenji went to the Buddhist temple for a morning service followed by the afternoon festivities. Although Sachiko felt as if she was still in mourning, she could not conceal her delight when she saw all the Japanese food and delicacies. Everyone was in a festive mood and after a while she, too, felt herself relaxing and even beginning to enjoy listening to and watching the Issei men let down their hair, singing traditional songs with toasts of "*Kampai!*" (Cheers!) as the sake flowed.

That night when Sachiko and Kenji returned to the Whitman farm, something changed. Perhaps Sachiko's prolonged feelings of isolation and loneliness, finally resigned her to the fact that she was here to stay, and combined with the effects of drinking too much sake prompted Sachiko to call out and ask Kenji, already bedded down in the front room, to join her in the back bedroom.

In mid-September, 1920, Sachiko Nagata gave birth to a baby boy, Jiro. With the birth of a son, Kenji considered himself the most fortunate man alive. He now had a wife and a son to carry on the Nagata lineage. His son, an American-born citizen, could hold legal title to family property under his name and in a few years he would have saved up enough money to place a down payment on the half-acre of land promised to him by Mr. Whitman. Life was good!

Kenji and Sachiko continued to work and save. Jiro grew, took his first steps and was now a walking toddler. Soon, Sachiko was expecting another baby. Unexpectedly, tragic news of the sudden death of Mr. Whitman arrived—Kenji was never told what caused his demise.

A week could pass without Kenji and Mr. Whitman conversing. Despite their ethnic and cultural differences, over the passage of time, they had forged a bond based on mutual respect. Mr. Whitman was an honest man who did not say much, but he was a man who lived by his word.

Out of respect to the family, Kenji waited to approach Mr. Whitman's son Travis, who was now the head of his family, to discuss the arrangement of purchasing the half acre of land that his father had made with him. Knowing Mr. Whitman, Kenji was sure that he told his son, Travis, about their handshake agreement.

A month after Mr. Whitman's service, Kenji felt that it was time to speak to Travis. The timing was right because in a few months, Sachiko would be delivering the new baby. There would be enough time for Kenji to start preparations for building a new house for his family on his own half-acre of land.

On a Sunday, for the second time, Kenji went to the Whitman house, but this time it was without an invitation. Kenji chose this day because he knew that the *hakujin* did not work on Sundays.

Travis was surprised to see his worker Kenji, wearing his dress clothes, standing on his front porch. Throughout the years, he hardly spoke to Kenji because he just considered him his father's worker. Kenji was not invited inside, so he and Travis stood and talked on the porch. Kenji told Travis about his father's promise to sell to him the lower half acre of farm land. For Travis, this non-irrigated lower land area, needed more work than he was willing to invest; even so, there was not a chance that he was going to sell the parcel to his father's hired worker. If he ever did decide to sell it to Kenji, he could imagine hearing friends and neighbors calling him a "Jap lover!"

Travis told Kenji that his father had told him about their agreement, but it was never put in writing. He had plans for that plot of land and had no intention of selling it to Kenji, or to anyone else.

Kenji left the Whitman's porch feeling angry and betrayed. He wished that he had finalized the handshake arrangement with Mr. Whitman when he was still alive. Walking away, he uttered under his breath, "*Shikataganai*" (nothing can be done about it). Within his heart, Kenji knew that his remaining days on the Whitman property were limited. He refused to work for a man who did not respect him and could not trust.

TERMINAL ISLAND

IN THE 1890s, a cadre of Japanese immigrants came together to put their knowledge of the ocean to profitable use. They shared a common background, having all been raised in fishing villages along the southern coast of Japan. They combined their resources to start an abalone cooperative in the east bay of San Pedro—this area was later to be called Terminal Island. Their venture was successful and it attracted other Issei with fishing backgrounds to migrate to Terminal Island in search of similar types of work and opportunities. Before long, several hundred former Japanese fishermen now lived in Terminal Island. Soon, the Southern Fish Company and Van Camp Canning Company opened plants on the island. Rows of single-story houses were built by the canneries, to quarter their labor force. As the work opportunities grew, so did the Issei population of Terminal Island. Initially, Terminal Island was an all-male community but the number of women and American-born children slowly increased. Eventually, Terminal Island became known as the Japanese fishing village on the West Coast, having a population nearing three thousand men, women and children. Their streets were aptly named: Albacore, Cannery, Terminal Way, Tuna and Pilchard Streets. Tuna Street was the main business center—mom-and-pop markets, dry goods stores, barber shops, hardware stores, cafes, confectionary sweet shops, and a pool hall, were among Issei-owned-and-operated businesses. Terminal Island residents erected a Buddhist temple and a Baptist mission. To hold gatherings for their community activities and cultural events, the Issei built Fisherman's Hall, located on Terminal Way. Many of the cultural and sports activities such as judo, kendo, sumo, Obon Festival and Boy's Day and Girl's Day were celebrated at Fisherman's Hall. Japanese remained the main language on the island—the churches offered Japanese language instruction for the children of the Issei parents that would counterbalance their American training and education.

Terminal Island evolved into a tight-knit, self-contained Japanese community with over ninety percent of the residents consisting of Issei and their second generation (*nisei*), American-born children. The children growing up on Terminal Island enjoyed an idyllic experience. While their parents worked on the boats, docks and in canneries, they were free to play and explore in a safe environment. Families would feed and look out for each other's children. When children became of school age, they attended public schools across the bay and progressed through elementary and junior high schools, followed by enrollment at San Pedro High School.

In the fall of 1924, Kenji Nagata made a life-altering decision to relocate his family to Terminal Island. Having been raised on a rice farm in Japan and now having spent the past two decades toiling in the fertile fields of Central California, his was not an easy choice. He knew that this decision to forgo everything he knew about agriculture and start anew to learn about the fishing industry would be difficult. Once Kenji made up his mind to leave the Whitman farm, he knew that hardship awaited. If his decision only affected himself, Kenji would have merely moved further north in the Valley to find seasonal work, but he knew that his wife Sachiko and two sons, Jiro age three and newborn Takezo, required more than his sharecropping background could provide. Kenji Nagata's decision to move his family to Terminal Island was influenced by his longtime *tomodachi*, Masao Iwata.

Although two decades had passed since Kenji and Masao had last seen one another, they stayed connected through annual correspondence. Their writing kept them current on milestones and changes affecting each other: their jobs, promotions, wives, children and family matters. Kenji's most recent letter to Masao revealed that he planned to leave the Whitman farm, his home for over twenty years. He planned to find work further north near Fresno, where the larger farms and growers always needed Issei workers. Masao immediately wrote back to Kenji, strongly encouraging him to consider relocating his family to Terminal Island. He told Kenji that he could find him work as a deckhand on short-range and eventually long-range fishing boats, and he had discussed the matter with his wife Keiko— they both insisted that Kenji and his family stay with them until he was able to find his own place. He told Kenji "*No shimpai*" (no worry) because he would teach him all that he needed to know about deckhand work and fishing. He was confident that with Kenji's penchant to work hard, it would only be a matter of time before he was promoted to a job having greater responsibility and higher pay. Masao's letter described Terminal Island's growing *Nihonjin* community, along with American educational opportunities for Kenji's kids.

Kenji still had no concrete plan when he received Masao's letter, the only thing he was sure about was that he could no longer stay on the Whitman property. The timing of Masao's letter and in his family's best interest, Kenji was willing to sacrifice his comfort level—to start from scratch as a novice fisherman's apprentice. With the Terminal Island community offering his children better educational opportunities, he also knew that it would please his wife Sachiko to be part of a *Nihonjin* community.

YAKUDOSHI

August 19, 1938
Terminal Island, San Pedro, California
5:30 a.m.

LIKE CLOCKWORK, Kenji was the first up in the household, practicing his deep breathing meditation. Kenji never deviated from his early morning discipline. It didn't matter where he was situated—whether a peaceful pre-dawn quiet village in Japan, in Montana on a freezing cold, starry morning, arising in Central California to warm stagnant summer air, or now, to a brisk salty ocean breeze at Terminal Island—he continued his life-long practice.

Kenji remained under the sheet and blanket in the bedroom at his small, well-kept wooden house in Terminal Island. He lay still, quietly and evenly inhaling air through his nostrils, to circulate through his lungs, internal organs, before settling in his *hara* (located two inches below his belly button). Then the breath was evenly exhaled through his mouth. The rhythmic flow of his breathing emptied his mind of thoughts, worries, anxieties, and other needless clutter. It was in this relaxed, but focused, mental state that Kenji began each day.

There were no fishing boats scheduled to depart or arrive at the Terminal Island dock for the next two days, so Kenji did not have to report to work until Monday. Today, Kenji had difficulty relaxing and calming his mind even after he finished his morning meditation. He was fully aware of the source for his anxiety: today was to be his surprise *yakudoshi* celebration! He closed his eyes, savoring the moment, recalling the only other times he felt this level of nervous energy—after his wife Sachi gave birth to each of their children, Jiro, Takezo, and Sumi.

It was still dark outside, and Kenji was now fully awake. He tried not not to stir under the covers, because he did not want to disturb Sachi's slumber. He figured that today, she would need all of her energy to prepare for his surprise.

Kenji's eager anticipation for his surprise celebration was well deserved. There were moments when he had difficulty comprehending how a country boy from Japan, knowing little except hard work, now had a family of five, owned a home with title held under his eldest son's name, and was a respected elder in the Japanese Terminal Island community. These milestones were the results of his sacrifice, endurance, and having a *tomodachi* who believed in him.

When Kenji arrived at Terminal Island, Masao Iwata was a crew chief, supervising the Issei deck hands and scheduling them on commercial fishing boats. Utilizing his influence, Masao found a job for Kenji working on the dock. Over the next decade, through effort and by paying close attention to detail, Kenji had also been promoted to crew chief, and was now a dock supervisor. His new position earned him a bit more money. Being a dock supervisor meant that he no longer left port for long extended fishing expeditions, sometimes chasing schools of fish all the way to the southwestern coast of South America. No longer being part of a boat crew meant that he had more time to spend with his family, and less wear and tear on his aging body. There were moments when Kenji missed being far out on the Pacific Ocean, watching a morning sunrise or an evening sunset, and feeling a sense of calm and stillness that could only be described by being there. What he missed the most was the teamwork and camaraderie of working with his Issei crew mates. Kenji found the Terminal Island Issei to be hard-working, fiercely independent, strong-willed, fun-loving, loyal men and women. Kenji had found a home.

Slowly, rays of daylight shined through the curtains inside Kenji's bedroom window. Kenji lost track of how long he lay under the covers of his bed. He looked over at Sachiko, who was still asleep. Unlike Kenji, she would wait until the very last minute before rising. After all the passing years, looking at his wife peacefully resting in the early morning, still brought feelings of pride, joy, and an ever so slight smile on Kenji's weather-beaten face.

August 19, 1938 – 11:00 a.m.
Japanese dialect but English translation

From the kitchen, Sachiko called out in a loud voice, "Papa, Masao is outside, don't keep him waiting!" Upon hearing his wife, Kenji located his favorite brown fedora hat and headed to the front door, replying, "Okay, Mama!" "Don't forget to stop by Kimura's Hardware and pick up our package." Again, Kenji replied, "Okay, Mama." Outside, Masao was waiting for him in his pick-up truck, parked in front of the house. As Kenji took the passenger seat in Masao's rebuilt Ford truck, they exchanged greetings by nodding their heads to one another. For old *tomodachi* like Kenji and Masao, a nod of the head spoke volumes.

As Masao cranked the engine and began pulling away from the curb, Kenji finally asked, "Masao, where are we going?" Masao replied, "We're going to stop by Miyamoto's Garage. I told Shig that I would bring you by; I thought that you might be interested in looking at an engine he is rebuilding. After that, lets go eat at Mitsura's Grill." Kenji knew it was Sachiko's plan, to have Masao drop by and get him out of the house, so that she and the three kids could begin preparing for his surprise 60th *yakudoshi* celebration. Kenji felt that he had no choice but to play along so that he wouldn't spoil their "surprise." "Okay, but on the way back, Sachiko wants me to stop by Kimura's Hardware to pick up a package."

Whatever little free time Kenji had, his priority was to spend it with Sachiko and the kids; but, if was asked who his next choice to spend a leisurely day with would be, he wouldn't have to think twice, it would be Masao.

Next to Sachiko, Masao was the most influential person in his life. He not only found him a job, but also helped Sachiko find work at a local cannery. It was Masao who introduced him to the Terminal Island Issei neighbors and helped smooth his family's acceptance and transition into the community.

Kenji thought about how busy Sachiko and the kids, Jiro, Takezo, and their youngest daughter, Sumi, must be preparing for his celebration. Sachiko and his kids made Kenji's passage to America permanent and complete. Kenji purchased a small Terminal Island house by having his eldest son Jiro, hold title to the home. Kenji vividly remembered the first day when his family moved into their new home. Sachiko turned on all the lights inside the house. Next, she opened the water taps to the kitchen sink, bathroom tub and outside faucet. She then sat down in the middle of the house and listened to the water flow through the pipes to all the open taps, as tears flowed freely from her eyes. After a lifetime of not having the luxury of electricity or indoor plumbing, Kenji fully understood her emotions.

There were still moments when Kenji felt a distance between himself and his wife. At first, he thought it was because of his initial deceit; then surmised that it must be due to their difference in age, and as years passed, he gave up trying to figure it out.

Sachiko's initial resentment toward the deceitful old man had almost totally disappeared. It was true that if he had been honest in his correspondence, she would have never agreed to their paper marriage. She knew that due to her stubborn nature, in her heart she would never totally forgive and forget, but she came to realize and appreciate that Kenji was hardworking and kind. Unlike some of the other Issei picture brides in the community, she was fortunate that her husband did not drink excessively, womanize, gamble or abuse her.

Kenji interrupted the silence in the car, "What kind of engine is Shig rebuilding?" Masao, lost in his own thoughts, replied, "He said that the owner at the salvage yard was going to junk it as scrap. Shig told him that even though the car's body was unrepairable, he could restore its engine, so he bought it." "If you're not interested, I might ask Shig to put it in my truck before this engine gives out and dies of old age." Kenji chuckled, "Masao, your truck has lasted forever. You'll die of old age before your engine does!" Masao replied in his typical manner, "Ha!" and kept driving.

Terminal Island – 4:30 p.m.

By the time Masao pulled up and parked in front of Kimura's Hardware Store, most of the day had passed. They had spent the entire morning in the back office at Miyamoto's Garage. The back office was a local gathering spot for Issei men. Today, a gathering of local Issei men were engaged in a penny-a-point gin rummy game in the back room. Usually, both Masao and Kenji were either too busy with some type of house repair or family activity to leisurely pass time at Miyamoto's Garage. Since Kenji knew that Sachiko asked Masao to keep him out of the house until the arrangements for his 60th *yakudoshi* party was ready, Kenji was free to enjoy the day.

For Kenji, having a leisurely day to himself was a present in itself. It was nice to socialize with his Issei friends at Shig's. Lately, it felt like the only time he got together with his Issei *tomodachi* was at their Nisei children's school activities, sports games, judo tournaments and more recently, at wedding ceremonies for a son or daughter.

Today, the back room at Shig's was interested in hearing Kenji's opinion on the Terminal Island Dojo's chances in winning the upcoming annual Southern California Judoka Tournament. Kenji was one of the senior *sensei* (instructors) at the Terminal Island Dojo. The community took pride in the competitive reputation and fighting spirit that Terminal Islander Dojo was known for. Without boasting, Kenji knew that as long as his middle son, Takezo, remained focused and injury-free, the Terminal Island Dojo could hold its own against the other dojo. Takezo, his second son, was the more athletic and competitive of his two sons. Even as a toddler, Takezo displayed a strong competitive nature and did not like to lose in any type of competitive activity. There were moments when Takezo's temper would get the better of him, As both his *otoosan* and martial arts *sensei*, Kenji knew that he needed to discipline and temper his middle son's fighting spirit—an undisciplined temperament can be a source of pain and hardship in ones life.

What his older son, Jiro, lacked in athletic ability was greatly outweighed by his academic achievements. He was a top student at San Pedro High. As the Nagata family *chonan*, it was important that Jiro strive, achieve, succeed and perpetuate the family lineage. Sumi, his youngest daughter, was already demonstrating an ability in *odori* (Japanese dance), at least that is what her *odori* instructor, Mrs. Tanabe, told both him and Sachiko.

After leaving Shig's Garage, they ate a late lunch at Mitsura's Grill. Masao ordered the pot roast special, served with rice, brown gravy, and *tsukemono* (pickled cabbage). Kenji ordered his usual favorite, *nabeyaki* udon. After finishing their meal, Masao ordered a slice of Mitsura's famous apple pie, topped with a scoop of vanilla ice cream. Kenji was tempted to order the same, but decided to save his appetite for his birthday celebration.

By the time they finished talking to Kimura-san at the hardware store, and picked up the household items that Sachi had ordered, it was close to five o'clock. On the drive home, Kenji sensed that something didn't feel right and realized that Masao had not given him even a slight hint about today's surprise *yakudoshi*. After knowing Masao for such a long time, he thought that he could always read and sense what his close *tomodachi* was thinking, but not today! Kenji thought, "Oh well, Masao is even better at keeping a secret than I ever imagined." When Masao stopped at the curb in front of the house, he did not turn off his engine, or make a feeble excuse about having to come inside to use the *benjo* (toilet) in order to enter the house with him. Topping it off, the curtains inside the house were wide open and from the curb he could see inside the front room of the house, and it was empty. Now Kenji was confused—maybe his *yakudoshi* meant more to him than it did to the rest of his family. Even though his kids were learning American ways at their schools, he thought that their Japanese home training would have been enough for them to realize how special this day was and to honor him. As Kenji walked into an empty house, he thought, "How could I have been so foolish? *Baka*!" He placed the package on the kitchen table. There was not even a note left for him on the table. Maybe Sumi had *odori* practice today, and the boys were probably off visiting their friends. How life in America had changed their ways. Dejectedly, he decided to get some fresh air and stepped outside into the small backyard to smoke tobacco.

Kenji opened the back screen to the yard, to a loud greeting, "Surprise!"

SHIKATA GA NAI

"JAPS BOMB PEARL HARBOR"
Los Angeles Times headline

December 8, 1941

TAKEZO NAGATA quietly squatted, directly facing the RCA radio in the front room. He deliberately sat in close proximity to keep the volume down, not wanting to wake up his *okaasan* (mama), *niisan* Jiro (older brother) and *imooto* Sumi (younger sister). He wasn't worried about waking up *Otoosan* (Papa), because he knew that Papa was probably already awake. Ever since he could remember, every morning, rain or shine, Papa was always the first person up in the house. Today, Takezo woke up extra early and for the first time ever, he was not sure whether he had risen before Papa. Ever since yesterday afternoon, Takezo, called Tak by his second generation Nisei friends, was unsure about a lot of things.

For the Terminal Islanders, yesterday started off as a typical Sunday morning. It was a day off for the Issei fishermen and cannery workers, and a welcomed weekend break for second generation Nisei students. However, for Tak Nagata, Sunday would be just another training and conditioning day, at least until the San Pedro High Pirates finished their football season. Tak was a starting cornerback for the San Pedro varsity football squad. Despite being one of the smallest and lightest players on his team and in the entire conference, Tak made up for his lack of size with quickness, speed and tenacity. These attributes were developed and cultivated through countless hours of training and discipline he received at the Terminal Island Dojo. His judo instruction taught Tak how to handle physical contact and play with an aggressive, attacking style on the gridiron. On the preceding Friday, the San Pedro Pirates beat Franklin High, 7 - 6, in a hard-fought contest. With only two games remaining on their schedule, the Pirates had an opportunity to not only to take their conference, but also to go undefeated. At mid-season, Tak and other seniors on the team were determined to make their exit special, realizing that this would be their last season of playing football. They committed themselves to each other, which included practicing even on days off. Despite still feeling sore from Friday's slugfest, Tak along with Kenzo Nakahara, the only other Nisei player on the varsity squad, took the late morning ferry from Terminal Island to meet with their teammates at the San Pedro High School football field.

By the time Tak and Kenzo arrived at San Pedro High, most of their teammates were on the practice field. Although school was officially closed on Sunday, the crusty old custodian, Mr. Papadakis, had opened the gate to the practice field for the players. Rumor had it that Mr. Papadakis was the first and only custodian for San Pedro High since its opening. Mr. Papadakis was the son of a Greek immigrant, and while he never said much during Tak's three years at San Pedro High, he had a passion for football and was protective of the players on the football team. Mr. Papadadis stood on the sidelines and never missed a football practice or a home game.

Eventually, all 35 members of the varsity team showed up for their player-only voluntary work out. The three team captains, Richard Kolmisky, Jerry Bustamante and Tak Nagata, led them through their warm-up exercise routine of jumping jacks, knee-benders, and push ups. The practice was spirited as they all counted in unison. After warming up they ran one mile. After they finished the run and while everyone was catching their breath, Mr. Papadakis came scurrying onto the field and spoke in a loud voice, asking the team to gather around him. The entire squad became concerned because no one had ever heard or seen Mr. Papadakis act or talk this way before and immediately everyone formed a semi-circle around him. Mr. Papadakis, with a pained expression on his face announced, "Japan attacked our Navy fleet in Hawaii. That's all I have heard so far, all of you better go home." For what seemed like forever, no one said anything or moved, until he repeated himself, "All of you need to go home, now!" His repeated demand snapped everyone out of their initial shock; they went to gather their belongings and headed out of the gate. As Tak and Kenzo headed toward the gate, Mr. Papadakis intercepted them and asked, "Do you boys want me to go with you?" to which Tak replied, "Thanks, Mr. Papadakis, we'll be okay." Everyone left in a hurry without parting goodbyes; at the time, Tak was not aware that this would be the last time he would be together with his teammates.

Tak had traveled the same route from home to the ferry station, then to school, so many times that he practically memorized the color of every house, parked car, and even trees and shrubs on this route. That afternoon, for both Tak and Kenzo, the route back to the ferry station felt altogether different. People stood outside their homes, excitedly talking to neighbors. They even passed a few people who nervously stared at the sky. At first, Tak thought he imagined that these people were giving him and Kenzo angry, dirty looks as they passed by. After traveling a few blocks, Tak realized that it was not his imagination because people were angrily glaring at him. Without saying a word between them, he and Kenzo immediately picked up their gait. When they were one block from the station, Tak first heard and experienced it, "Dirty, JAPS!" The angry words coming from behind him sent a cold chill through Tak's body. He stopped dead in his tracks, frozen and unable to comprehend what had just occurred. Instinctively, he began to turn around to face his tormentor, but Kenzo immediately grabbed his arm and with a concerned look on his face said, "Not now, we need to get home."

Sachiko anxiously stood in front of the Terminal Island house, waiting for her son. When she saw Takezo from a distance returning home, she felt a weight being lifted from her shoulders. Of her three children, Takezo concerned her the most. Even though he was obedient and did what was asked of him, she knew how stubborn and headstrong he could be. She was thankful that he made it home safely.

Arriving home and being together with his family, Tak finally felt safe; however, upon observing the worried expressions on his parents's faces, the nervous tightness in his stomach returned. This scene was being repeated in Japanese households not only at Terminal Island but throughout the West Coast.

The Issei generation intuitively sensed that they were going to be singled out and blamed for the hostile actions committed by their mother country. Although they had lived in America for the majority of their lives, and their American-born children were naturalized citizens, they were still going to be viewed with suspicion. Not knowing what actions to take in order to protect their families, they gathered up their Japanese artifacts: family keepsakes, pictures, any items that could be misinterpreted and used to accuse them of being sympathetic and loyal to the Japanese Imperialist Empire. They burned and buried treasured silk kimonos, *Nihongo* (Japanese language) books and magazines, swords, family heirlooms, and in extreme situations, family Buddhist altars and shrines. By destroying their cultural artifacts, they hoped to appear less suspicious, less foreign, less Japanese.

The Nagata kids were typical second-generation American citizens: Nisei who were born, raised and educated in America, considered it home and had never set foot on Japanese soil. As in the case of all ethic second-generation American children, at home they spoke in the native tongue of their parents; were taught, practiced and participated in cultural activities of their ethnic culture, but outside the household they attended neighborhood schools, and made friends with classmates of different ethnicities. They participated in school activities and if asked, "What are you?" the Nisei would proudly reply, "I am Japanese American." For the Nisei, the term Japanese American was as non-threatening as their Caucasian classmates proclaiming and identifying themselves as Irish American, Jewish American, Italian American, or American of German descent.

Although Takezo Nagata had personally experienced a sliver of anti-Japanese hostility, he was confident that once the initial shock and hysteria wore off, people would come back to their senses and realize that the Japanese Americans had absolutely nothing to do with the bombing of the naval fleet, half way around the world. He understood his parents' concerns, but he felt that they were a bit too extreme, especially when Papa told him, Jiro, and Sumi that they were not to attend school tomorrow. As in all Japanese families, Papa's word was absolute.

Takezo remained fixed in front of the radio—he wanted to know more than the message, played all day yesterday on the radio, repeated over and over, "Japs sneak attack on Pearl Harbor!" His concentration was diverted from the family radio box when he heard the sound of a car stop in front of the house and within moments, heard the closing of car doors. Alertly, Takezo sat perfectly still. Next he heard footsteps pounding on the three wooden steps leading to a small porch landing in front of their house. He could tell by its sound, that there was more than one person standing on the small porch.

"Rap-rap-rap-rap." Takezo sprang to his feet and glanced around the front room. He was still alone and almost called out for his papa, but decided against it because if this early morning visitor was *hakujin*, the responsibility of interpreting and speaking for his parents would fall upon Jiro, the eldest son, or himself. For some unknown reason, Takezo didn't bother to look out the front window to see who was standing on the front porch, instead he went straight to the door and partially opened it.

On the porch stood two white men, both identically dressed in dark gray suits, ties, long coats, and medium brim fedoras. The larger of the two men, held out an official-looking badge, and said in a low intimidating voice, "We're from the Federal Bureau of Investigation. Is this the home of Kenji Nagata?" Takezo heard a small sound out of his mouth, "Yes." "Is he home?" Takezo heard his voice again, "Yes," and without asking for his consent, the two agents entered the house. Takezo considered himself a decent athletic and he was accustomed to feeling nervous energy before a judo tournament or an important game, but what he now felt was altogether different—for the first time in his young life he felt a dreaded sense of fear.

As if on cue, before the federal agents could ask another question, his papa entered the front room, while Mama stood behind him. Eerily, his papa was fully dressed, almost as if he had already sensed that government agents would be paying him a visit due to yesterday's tragedy that took place halfway around the world.

By now Jiro and Sumi, still dressed in their pajamas, joined the family in the crowded front room, but no one uttered a word. Takezo felt the family's palpable panic, hurt, shame and confusion. The FBI agent looked directly at Papa and asked him if he was Kenji Nagata. Papa slowly nodded his head and the agent said, "Come with us." They took Papa by his arm, led him outside and placed him in the backseat behind the driver, and the second agent sat next to him. Papa was unable to look out the car window to see his family standing outside. Then, without any explanation, they drove off, taking him away to the unknown. When the government car disappeared from their sight, Mama kept repeating in a panicked shrill, "Papa forgot his hat! Papa forgot his hat!"

That same morning, federal agents were busy rounding up other pre-targeted Issei men residing along the West Coast. In Terminal Island, Reverend Sugano, Tetsuo Yoshimoto, Kichigaro Yoshimura, Hujio Sumida, and Isao Ishikawa, among others, were picked up, detained, sequestered, and sent to various federal penitentiaries scattered throughout the United States. Kenji Nagata was imprisoned at a federal prison in Santa Fe, New Mexico. Most of these men were separated from their families for the duration of the war.

The names of the Issei on the list were provided to federal government agents through the cooperation of several Nisei (second-generation Americans) who were interested in gaining status and political favor with the United States government. It was evident that the government compiled its enemy alien subversive list, well before December 7, 1941.

The Issei men singled out by the government all had one thing in common— they were the elder respected leaders of the Japanese American community. Their leadership roles in the community were always transparent, and they were openly proud of their community involvement. Included on the government's subversive alien list were the community newspaper editors, business association leaders, Buddhist ministers, and martial arts instructors.

The suspicious behavior that placed Kenji Nagata on the subversive alien list was being a respected elder *sensei*, at the Terminal Island Dojo. For Kenji, judo was more than a sport—it was a mental and physical discipline where values of self-respect, and respect for others were taught through judo training. When his sons, Jiro and Takezo became of age, Kenji took them to the Terminal Island Dojo to start training. Kenji was asked to help train the novice judo class. He instructed his students using the same techniques that his *otoosan* passed onto him in Japan. As Kenji aged, he came to appreciate that his *otoosan*'s lessons went far beyond self-defense techniques—his rigorous judo training instilled within him values of balance, self-discipline, confidence, humility and respect. While Kenji was pleased that his kids were receiving an American education that would open opportunities that were unimaginable to the Issei generation, it was equally important that his children develop strong integrity, good character, and proper citizenship. As a *sensei* at the Terminal Island Dojo, he was able to influence and pass on these values through judo training. It was Kenji Nagata's passion and commitment to teach the youth of Terminal Island, the martial art practice and discipline of judo that branded him a subversive alien, a threat to white America.

Post December 7, the government imposed a curfew on all Japanese Americans living on the West Coast. Government declarations and yellow journalism fueled further suspicion and public hysteria directed towards the Japanese American community. Verbal and physical harassment and beatings of Japanese Americans in cities and in rural areas were reported. After December 7, fishing boats were no longer allowed to leave the Terminal Island port, resulting in the closure of the fish canneries. The Terminal Island Issei lost their source of income and livelihood. At night, a lights-out curfew was imposed on the Japanese American community. With the leadership voices of their community imprisoned and the combination of liberty restrictions, anti-Japanese propaganda, and no viable sources of income, the Japanese American community silently waited for the hammer to drop.

On February 19, 1942, President Franklin Roosevelt signed Executive Order 9066, authorizing the internment of Japanese Americans. This order empowered the government to "relocate" all persons of Japanese descent living in the West Coast to government concentration camps.

The sole qualification for concentration camp internment was showing that a person had Japanese ancestry. The government's requirement for proof was to show that the blood running through one's veins was one-sixteenth Japanese. Being of Japanese ancestry meant one could be sentenced and imprisoned without due process.

When Executive Order 9066 was signed, over two-thirds of the Japanese in America were second-generation Nisei citizens, and over half of the Nisei were children. No parallel executive order was enacted to remove and detain persons of German and Italian descent living in America. There was not a shred of evidence that the Japanese Americans posed a risk to American security. A group of Nisei, hand-picked by the U.S. government, were anointed as spokespersons for the community. This group was unwilling to voice any defense or protest on behalf of the Japanese American community regarding their unfair treatment. These hand-picked "leaders" took the position that the community's complete cooperation was necessary to prove their "loyalty" to the government, which could possibly result in receiving better treatment for crimes they never committed.

Within the Japanese American community, almost to a person, the only way that one could understand or rationalize the overt racism to which they were subjugated after December 7, was through a cultural attitude ingrained in the Japanese psyche—the concept of, "*shikata ga nai*." For centuries the Japanese, often farmers, villagers, and commoners, utilized this concept to silently and passively accept hardships due to Nature and mistreatment imposed upon them by abusive authority. The closest English translation of "*shikata ga nai*" is, "it cannot be helped." If you have no control over the situation, why complain—deal with it.

The signing of Executive Order 9066, gave the Japanese community a window of two weeks before they were to be "relocated." Each family member was authorized to pack a suitcase of their belongings—anything that could not fit into the suitcase had to be left behind. For the Japanese American community, intangible spiritual attributes of pride, dignity and hope would not fit in a small suitcase. These attributes were left behind; in its place, confusion, guilt and shame were crammed into the baggage.

News of the Japanese evacuation circulated and outside scavengers crawled out from under their rocks to capitalize on the community's plight. Opportunists canvassed the Terminal Island community offering Japanese families mere pittance for furniture, appliances, clothes, family heirlooms, and in some instances, businesses and homes.

During the scavenger feeding frenzy, Takezo Nagata stood outside his family home to watch over the family's furnishings and other items that needed to be sold or otherwise be left behind. A man drove up, stopped, and parked in front of the house. He began to examine the sale items. The *hakujin* man picked up Mama's favorite *chawan* set (tea bowl set), then told Takezo he would pay him fifty cents for the entire set. As the man started opening his coin purse, Takezo told him that the tea set was imported from Japan and purchased for ten dollars, but he could have it for three dollars. Upon hearing Takezo's counter offer, the man replied, "You're lucky I'm even offering you a half-a-buck, where you're going, money won't do you no good, anyway!" Reaching out, Takezo grabbed the teacup from the man's hand and threw it on the ground. The shattering of the cup brought Mama out of the house. The man looked at Takezo's angry glare, turned, and scampered back to his car. Takezo turned and noticed his mama's presence; her face looked worn and sad, he saw dampness in her eyes. Takezo felt torn; while it felt good to finally release pent-up anger and confusion, he was also sorry that his outburst hurt his mama. Standing in the front yard, he told himself, that for Mama's sake, he needed to control his temper.

MANZANAR

Eastern Sierra Nevada

THE WAR RELOCATION AUTHORITY (WRA) was established to oversee the imprisonment of over 110,000 Japanese in America. Ten concentration camps were built to intern them. The camps were scattered throughout the U.S., in Arizona, Arkansas, California, Colorado, Idaho, Utah, and Wyoming. They were named Poston, Gila River (Arizona); Rohwer, Jerome (Arkansas); Tule Lake, Manzanar (California); Granada (Colorado); Minidoka (Idaho); Topaz (Utah); and Heart Mountain (Wyoming). Although their names and locales were different, all of the internment camps were erected on desolate, isolated, non-irrigational terrain.

While the camps were under construction, the entire West Coast Japanese population was rounded up and detained at temporary locations most often racetracks and fairgrounds, and a few migrant camps. Families were herded into racetracks at Santa Anita in Southern California and Bay Meadows in Northern California—hygienic conditions were deplorable when crowded into former horse stables and tents. To endure, everyone had to cooperate. *Shikataga nai.*

The Nagatas and the Terminal Islanders were imprisoned at Santa Anita Racetrack. After weeks of detainment, they were shipped out to be interned at Manzanar on March 21, 1942,

Manzanar held over 10,000 detainees—it was the second-largest populated concentration camp. It was erected on the eastern side of the Sierra Nevada mountains, between the small town of Lone Pine and an even smaller town ironically named, Independence, the seat of Inyo County. The foundation of this armed, fortified prison was built on hard-baked desert sand, dirt and rock. When the desert wind kicked up, which was often, layers of top sand and dirt flew in all directions. Even with the majestic Sierra Nevada backdrop, one felt stranded out in the middle of nowhere.

Manzanar's 550-acre encampment grid was enclosed by barbed wire. Eight wooden guard towers were strategically placed around the barbed wire perimeter. Each guard tower had mounted machine guns pointing inward.

To house the 10,000 detainees, 800 wooden barracks were hastily constructed. The camp was divided into 24 grids, each grid having 15 barracks, with a separate communal mess hall, showers and latrines. Barracks were identified by a block number, a barrack row number, a barrack number, and finally unit number. A barrack housed as many as 40 detainees or eight families. The tiny, assigned

50

barrack space was to be a family's home for an indefinite duration. For privacy, the detainees used government-issued blankets as partitions for their designated areas. Over time, the blankets were replaced by drywall or whatever material the detainees were able to scavenge. The Nagata family's new address was Block 15, Barrack 5, Row 8, Unit 3, Manzanar, California.

The concentration camp experience marked the breakdown of the traditional Japanese family structure and changed the leadership roles within the Japanese American hierarchy. In pre-camp days, the Issei were the undisputed authority both within the household and in community affairs. Within the government-operated concentration camps, Issei control and influence over their community was undermined.

The Issei parents were opposed to the communal living structure and instructed their Nisei children to bring the food served at the mess hall back to the family barrack space, so the family could eat their meals together. As months passed, it became more common to see groups of Nisei youth sitting together at the mess halls, eating their meals in the company of their peers. Ambitious Nisei boys made the rounds to different mess halls to see if any of them were serving different food, and to check out the girls.

In addition to housing the detainees, barracks were used to maintain a sense of community. Some were turned into classrooms where *hakujin* contract teachers came from the outside to hold daily classes for Nisei students from kindergarten through high school. Certain barracks were designated to hold Buddhist and Christian services while others were used as medical infirmaries, recreational centers, barber shops, and community stores where one could purchase basic necessities. One even served as headquarters for the camp newspaper called the *Manzanar Free Press*.

For recreation, the Nisei transformed a barren desert area into a baseball field, a baseball diamond in the rough. They attached steel rims to wood backboards to play full court basketball. While playing baseball with the hard and unforgiving desert ground, sliding home was done at one's own risk, but for basketball, the hardness of the ground was a plus for helping the ball return quickly to the dribbling hand.

For their toddlers, they built a handcrafted playground, equipped with wooden swings and teeter-totters. An Issei group discovered an underground water flow and using their creative skills, collected large desert rocks, dug a deep channel that was filled by the water source, and built a Japanese garden pond in the middle of a desert. Creating something out of nothing, it was a Zen masterpiece—soothing water flowing through rocks and into a tranquil pond—it lacked only koi fish. By day, the Issei used the rock garden as a refuge, a place for temporary moments of tranquility away from the madness; at night, Nisei couples found the pond to be a romantic spot.

Organized sports competitions were a major camp event. Former Japanese enclaves like Boyle Heights, Fresno, Seinan, and Terminal Island fielded teams with players representing their old neighborhoods. These inner camp rivalries gave the detainees a break from the everyday monotony and provided all with moments of normalcy. The entire camp attended these games—everyone took the winning team's bragging rights seriously. In baseball, Takezo Nagata played centerfield and was a guard for the Terminal Island basketball Yogores.

Music was an important part of camp life. Manzanar had many talented Nisei musicians, many of whom had learned to play at their former schools—a few even brought their instruments to camp. They formed big bands and would practice and play contemporary swing tunes from Benny Goodman to Lionel Hampton. To earn the reputation of being a top-notch band required a group to perform at a Saturday night camp dance. A popular Manzanar band with such a distinction was the "Jive Bombers." The Jive Bombers packed the recreation room on Saturday nights, playing rhythms that inspired young Nisei to dance the "swing" and "lindy hop." A young Nisei vocalist was so talented that she was showcased by the War Relocation Authority. The WRA would escort her outside the confines of Manzanar to perform for white audiences at places like Stockton and Sacramento. She was dubbed, "The Songbird of Manzanar."

All camp activities required WRA approval. The WRA routinely rubber stamped approval for Nisei dances, talent shows, and athletic competitions. The traditional activities favored by the Issei generation, *odori* dance, *noh* performances, and martial arts competitions, were often rejected. Approval for these types of cultural programs and events were a rare occurrence.

The WRA favored and encouraged Nisei leadership and participation. The Nisei generation held all of the influential camp life positions, from mess hall chief, work crew supervisors, "elected" camp government seats, activities committees, to newspaper editor, and even camp barber.

The WRA recognized a Nisei group known as the Japanese American Citizens League (JACL), as spokesgroup for all of the Japanese detainees. Many detainees disagreed with that designation, with hardliners viewing JACL leadership as *inu* (dogs, traitors). They called them sellouts for the role they played during the evacuation and their prewar cooperation with the government. Bitter feelings toward the JACL came to a head when a respected worker at a communal mess hall, confronted and beat a JACL member who was suspected of providing names of disgruntled detainees to the WRA. The WRA arrested the assailant and confined him to a guarded barrack. When the word circulated about his arrest, hundreds of angry Manzanar detainees went to the holding barrack to demand his release. Armed soldiers were called to the scene and a riot broke out, resulting in a death of one of the protesters. Takezo Nagata was the only member of his family to participate in the protest. Following this incident, the WRA removed all persons listed on the disgruntled detainee list from Manzanar.

Many Nisei took advantage of the new camp hierarchy. For the first time in their young lives they felt liberated from their Issei parents' absolute control and Japanese way of doing things. It was evident that it was the Issei who lost the most personally, during the internment. As difficult as it was to lose one's earning power and livelihood, it was tragic for the Issei to witness the erosion of their status and respect. What hurt the most was feeling useless and invisible, seeing the young Nisei avoid their counsel and instead, seek approval from their concentration camp masters. Most of the Issei were at an advanced age where they felt "too old and too tired" to start all over again. Their views were generally devalued as being too "Japanese-y." Many Nisei now viewed their parents' cultural identity and value system as a liability, something negative that was instrumental in placing the Japanese Americans in this undesired predicament.

With the passage of time, Manzanar took on the characteristics of a small town. Like any close-knit community, it seemed like everyone knew everything about everyone else. The camp rumor mill churned out news and gossip, however relevant or inconsequential, on a daily basis. Gossip and rumors about who was cheating on who, and news regarding the war effort were typical topics for daily discussion.

A recent rumor causing concern and controversy among the camp detainees, was that the U.S. government was preparing to assemble a fighting unit comprised of inducted Nisei soldiers. For this to occur, all the detainees over the age of seventeen would be required to swear their allegiance to the United States government. The possibility of the government drafting Nisei soldiers to fight for democracy, while their families remained imprisoned and deprived of their Constitutional liberties, by the same government, created division among the detainees. For the Issei generation, the thought of their children being sent off to fight against their Japanese ancestors or relatives was a troubling concern. One segment of young Nisei men was prepared to prove their patriotism and loyalty to America at any price, even if it meant sacrificing their lives and fighting against their ancestors. A dissenting Nisei position was that their confinement was unconstitutional, in violation of their due process rights, and before they were sent off to fight for democracy, the U.S. government first had to demonstrate a reciprocation of loyalty, by releasing their families before their conscription into the armed forces. Stated simply, "How can we fight to preserve principles of freedom and democracy when our families are unjustly deprived of their democratic rights at home?"

The loyalty oath controversy was not restricted to Manzanar; discussions and divisions because of these concerns took place in all ten of the concentration camps. At the Heart Mountain concentration camp in Wyoming, young Nisei men formed a group calling themselves the Heart Mountain Committee for Fair Play and Justice. This group presented a document bearing their signatures to the WRA, stating that as long as the Japanese Americans and their Issei parents remain imprisoned in violation of their due process rights, it was unconstitutional for the U.S. government to induct them into the military. Without being granted a hearing to determine the merits of their concern, all participants of the Heart Mountain Committee for Fair Play and Justice were removed from Heart Mountain and sent to different federal prisons.

LOYALTY OATH

THE PAST TWO YEARS were a hardship for Sachiko Nagata. She did her best to keep the family together, but without Papa's presence, there were moments when she felt like she was waging a losing battle. Her eldest son Jiro, involved himself in camp life and affairs. His latest job was at the *Manzanar Free Press*, working as a reporter. He met a girl, Yoshiye Yoshimura, from Boyle Heights. When Jiro brought her to the communal mess hall to sit and eat supper with the family, Sachi knew that Jiro was serious about this girl. Jiro introduced her as Yoshiye Yoshimura, to which she replied, "You can just call me Yo-Yo, all my friends do." From that day on, Yo-Yo and Jiro were always together. Camp life for her youngest daughter, Sumi, revolved around her Nisei teenaged friends. Because her children were all on different schedules, the only time for the family to be together was at suppertime. Sachiko had her kids sit and eat together as a family. This was a rule that she insisted on; if not for this absolute rule, there would have been days when Sachiko would have hardly seen Jiro or Sumi.

The child that she was the most concerned about was her second son, Takezo, nicknamed Tak. Ironically, Takezo was with her most, and he was the most helpful. He would assist her by running errands and doing everyday chores. Takezo worried her because his short temper and stubborn nature, which got him into trouble as a little boy, still surfaced despite his growing older. With the exception of his papa, once Takezo concluded that he was right, he would not listen to anyone and would react without considering the consequences. Next to her, Takezo missed Papa's presence the most.

One evening, after finishing supper, the family returned to the barracks. In a hushed tone, Jiro told the family that at his reporting job, he heard that government officials were coming to Manzanar and anyone over 17 years, had to answer a loyalty questionaire. He said that there would be two important questions on the loyalty questionnaire that had to be answered, "yes, yes."

For Takezo, the idea of pledging his loyalty to the government was absurd and without mincing his words, he said, "After what they did to Papa, and keeping us locked up, they now want us to pledge our loyalty? Give me a break!" Jiro countered, "I feel just as bad as you about what happened to Papa, but don't make this out to be more than it is. If answering the questions means that we can get out of here faster, all the better!" Sachiko and Sumi sat in silence as the two brothers continued to argue; it hurt Sachiko because she felt that each of her sons was right in his own way. The argument ended when Jiro said, "I heard that in other camps, those who answered "no, no" were taken away to prison, possibly even sent to Japan."

Takezo sarcastically retorted, "When are they going to give this loyalty oath to the German and Italian Americans?" "Enough, I am your older brother and you better do what's right. Anyone who answers "no, no" will bring shame on their family." Sachiko thought, "If ever we need Papa, it is now."

Inside Manzanar, the news about the loyalty oath spread like wildfire. A few of Tak's Terminal Island friends made it a point to stop by to talk with him. They were concerned because they had observed him change from a popular, happy-go-lucky friend to a person that was now serious, sullen, and quick to anger. They told Tak that they heard that anyone who answered, "no, no" would be deported to Japan. They told him they understood how he felt but now was not the time or place to bring trouble onto himself and his family, that this entire ordeal was a *shikataga nai* situation They concluded by saying that the Japanese Americans must move forward. Tak knew these *tomodachi* his entire life; they were his neighbors, classmates and teammates, and he was grateful for their sincere concern. It was out of their friendship that Tak chose not to argue or try to persuade them otherwise. He knew that what was right for him may not necessarily be right for others. Tak did his best to make his friends feel comfortable, he even found himself laughing from his *hara* (gut) when the conversation shifted and they reminisced about past judo competitions, sporting events, and girls from the neighborhood. Before they left, Tak thanked them for coming by and told them that he would "think over" what they talked about.

On the day the Loyalty Oath Questionnaires were finally passed out, Tak sat alone inside the empty mess hall, as he continued to stare at the ink on the paper:

Number 27: Are you willing to serve in the armed forces of the United States on combat duty wherever ordered?

Number 28: Will you swear unqualified allegiance to the United States of America and faithfully defend the United States from any or all attack by foreign or domestic forces, and foreswear any form of allegiance or obedience to the Japanese Emperor, to any other foreign government, power or organization?

Tak was aware that the majority of the detainees had already filled out and turned in their questionnaires. They viewed this process as an exercise in futility, a way for the government to "save face." They had no problems answering "yes, yes" to question 27 and 28. For the government, answering, "yes, yes" to the loyalty questionnaire was a political necessity. The detainees that the government now wanted to conscript into an all-Nisei combat unit were the same classified enemy aliens who were evacuated from their homes, detained in concentration camps, and stigmatized with a 4-C draft classification, that of enemy alien status, a threat to the national security.

For an instant, Tak thought that maybe Jiro and his *tomodachi* were right after all, that the best way to gain *hakujin* trust was not to resist and to prove our loyalty, at any cost. Tak's dilemma was that he agreed with the position taken by the Heart Mountain resisters, that they would be the first in line to fight for America, provided that the government reciprocate loyalty by releasing the Japanese people from their illegal detainment.

What totally irked Tak was that this loyalty questionnaire did not provide any space to qualify his answer. Feeling like he was on the verge of losing his temper and remembering his papa's advice, Tak inhaled and held in a deep breath as he tried to clear his mind.

When Tak first arrived at Manzanar, he too, believed that by enduring all hardships, everything would work itself out. He recalled how he faithfully believed that it would only be a short matter of time, before the U.S. government would release his papa from the Santa Fe Federal Prison, in New Mexico and allow him to return to the family at Manzanar. He maintained his optimism as he participated in camp work crews and activities. He was promoted to a team leader on his work crew. Seven months after arriving at Manzanar, his belief system abruptly changed overnight. It happened on the day his family was summoned to the WRA barrack. When Tak and his family entered the WRA Office, he sensed that something was not right but the family was totally unprepared and devastated when the uniformed *hakujin* official informed them that "Kenji Nagata had passed away at the Santa Fe detention facility on October 11th." They were told that their papa had a severe abdominal appendix condition and all medical efforts to save him were taken, but were unsuccessful. As Jiro interpreted for Mama, she winced but otherwise remained still. Acting as Mama's interpreter, Jiro asked the WRA Official when her husband's body could be brought to Manzanar for cremation and a Buddhist service. The family was told that this is not possible because he had already been buried and put to rest at a cemetery in Santa Fe, following a Christian service. He told Mama that they were not equipped to handle cremations and that he was truly sorry for the family's loss.

From that day forward, Tak viewed his camp surroundings and the camp authorities with a suspicious eye. He also knew that he needed to keep his emotions in check. The lesson his papa taught him at home and at the dojo—to maintain his focus by not allowing emotions to control his actions—now needed to be internalized in his everyday existence. Tak was not always able to contain his anger, especially when someone blindly advocated loyalty and patriotism, but overall he managed his anger and contempt. He even noticed a change within himself; in the past when his anger surfaced, after "blowing off steam," immediately he felt better. Lately, even when he found an outlet to vent his anger, his anger never went away. Tak became quiet, sullen, and less willing to accept "*shikataga nai*" to explain life's injustices.

Tak's mind continued to race as he stared at the questionnaire. A thought entered his mind, "Since they won't give me any space to explain my answer to their question, I won't give them any satisfaction by answering it the way they want me to." Hastily, he leaned over and wrote "No, No" and added "with an explanation" to Questions 27 and 28. For the first time in a long while, Tak felt the weight lifted from his shoulders; he was also aware that there would be consequences for his actions.

Tak's feeling of relief was short-lived. Two days later, Tak and others were summoned to the WRA headquarters. They were told to pack their belongings and effective immediately, they were being sent to the internment camp at Tule Lake, in Northern California. Tak's biggest regret was knowing that the person who would be hurt the most was Mama. He only hoped that in her heart, she understood his decision.

For the past two weeks Sachiko had been gathering ingredients to bake a chocolate cake for Takezo's upcoming nineteenth birthday.

Part II

Nisei

Nisei, pronounced (nee-say) is a combination of two words, "*ni*" meaning two, and "*sei*" meaning generation. Nisei is the name given to the second generation—sons and daughters of the Japanese who immigrated to North America.

NISEI

On August 6th, and then on August 8,1945, the United States of America unleashed atomic blasts of radiation on Hiroshima and Nagasaki. The catastrophic effect of the radioactive mushroom blasts, resulted in the deaths of 120,000 men, women, children in Hiroshima. Two days later, another 80,000 people perished in Nagasaki. In each city, only a small fraction of the death toll were Japanese military personnel. Not calculated in the casualty count were those badly burned, mutilated, or the future generations of deformed infants or those with health abnormalities resulting from exposure to atomic radiation.

Japan unconditionally surrendered on August 10, 1945, after accepting the terms of the Potsdam Conference. On August 15, 1945, Emperor Hirohito broadcast the news of Japan's surrender to the Japanese people, and on September 2, 1945, representatives of the Japanese government and Japanese armed forces signed a document on the U.S.S. Missouri, formally surrendering, and the War in the Pacific was officially over.

Los Angeles
1945 – 1950s

STATISTICALLY, one-fourth of all eligible draft-age Nisei answered Questions 27 and 28 on the Loyalty Oath Questionnaire, "No, No" or they left the answers to the questions blank, while others tried to qualify their answers with a written explanation. Anyone answering the Loyalty Oath Questionnaire in such manner was branded and stigmatized by the WRA as being a "No-No Boy." Removing and isolating the No-No Boys by placing them at the Tule Lake Concentration Camp was a tragic, yet effective, implementation of governmental divide-and-conquer tactics.

Over 14,000 draft-age Nisei answered "Yes, Yes" and seventy-five percent of them either enlisted or were drafted into all-Japanese American combat units, the Military Intelligence Service or the 442nd Combat Regiment of the 100th Battalion.

In 1944, following basic training, the 442nd, comprised of Nisei from Hawaii and the mainland, were sent to fight in Italy, southern France and Germany. Their courage and valor was symbolized by their motto, "Go for Broke!" Considered expendable by the military brass and given the most dangerous assignments, their losses and casualties were disproportionate to that of other combat units. The 442nd amassed 9,486 Purple Hearts, twenty-one Medal of Honor recipients and remain the most highly decorated military unit in the annals of United States military warfare.

On the home front, labor was needed to sustain the war effort which prompted the government to offer the Nisei that remained in camp an opportunity to leave their confinement. The condition for release was to find an employer located in the Midwest or East Coast that would sponsor a work release request—no Nisei were allowed to seek employment on the West Coast. The majority of remaining Nisei left camp, and were on their own for the first time in their young lives. They left behind their Issei parents and younger siblings to become part of America's work force, contributing to the war effort. They found employment at plants, factories, and offices in places like Chicago and Seabrook, New Jersey, where Seabrook Farms made a concerted effort to recruit Issei and Nisei workers for their farming and processing business.

When the war officially ended, all remaining concentration camps detainees were now free to leave their confinement. The majority of them were Issei, either too old or not willing to start over again. The rebuilding of a Japanese American community was placed on the shoulders of the Nisei generation.

Most of the detainees returned to the West Coast. America still harbored strong anti-Japanese sentiments and unwritten racial restrictions were practiced. Many communities prohibited renting, leasing or selling homes to a Japanese American. Not in a position to challenge institutionalized racial bigotry, the Japanese Americans relocated to areas of safe haven. Returning to Terminal Island was not an option—after the Japanese Americans were ousted from their enclave, government bulldozers razed the housing, businesses, churches and temples—all that remained of a once bustling Japanese American community was a barren flat tract of land.

Santa Monica, Westchester, San Fernando Valley, and Culver City were areas that would not lease or rent to the returning Japanese Americans. The majority of the Issei returned to Little Tokyo in downtown Los Angeles, the pre-war hub of the Japanese community. Nisei found affordable living quarters in the Boyle Heights area of East Los Angeles. The largest Japanese American post-war settlement on the West Coast was established in southwest Los Angeles, in an area called "Crenshaw," referred to as "*Seinan*" by its Japanese American residents. Seinan, meaning Westside, was a low-income blue collar working class community. It became the new post-war hub of the Japanese American community.

Seinan stretched from Olympic Boulevard on the north, to Slauson Boulevard on the south; Western Avenue on the east, and La Cienega to its west. Crenshaw Boulevard was its main artery, the entire area was roughly five miles by five miles.

A large concentration of JA families within Seinan settled in the Jefferson Boulevard area. Many of the streets intersecting Jefferson Boulevard were numbered avenues, ranging from 2nd Avenue to 10th Avenue. The Jefferson Boulevard pocket of the Seinan JA community was referred to as the "Avenues."

At the close of the war, the government had yet to decide what actions to take against the Japanese American resisters and No-No Boys. Deportation to Japan, continued detention, or unconditional release were options considered. Finally, the government determined that the positions taken by these young men did not violate federal law and their responses to the Loyalty Questionnaire were protected under the Constitution. Forcing imprisoned detainees to answer a loyalty oath constituted additional violation of the right to due process. After recognizing that the draft resisters and No-No Boys had the legal and constitutional right to follow their conscience and beliefs, the government eventually set them free.

Takezo "Tak" Nagata was part of the last group of detainees released by the United States government. At the time of his release, his older brother Jiro had already moved Mama and his sister Sumi to Los Angeles where they found affordable housing on 8th Avenue, off of Jefferson Boulevard.

Starting over in a hostile environment was going to be a the challenge for the young Nisei. Regardless of their abilities, aptitude, prior training, and past educational level, the only jobs open to them were service-connected. Out of economic necessity, many young Nisei men became gardeners. Nisei women worked as seamstresses in garment factories, domestics, or if lucky, as secretaries. White folks coveted young, hard-working Nisei gardeners. Soon, it became an everyday occurrence to see fleets of gardening trucks heading to work or parked in front of their homes throughout the Avenues. The gardening trucks were neatly organized with tools of the trade: gas mowers, edgers, rakes, shovels, water hoses, clippers, fertilizer sacks, and potted plants for landscaping jobs.

Upon his release, Takezo reunited with his family in Los Angeles. It had been almost two years since he last saw them and was pleasantly surprised to see how his younger sister, Sumi, had grown. However, Tak was saddened by how much Mama had aged. She was no longer the strong, determined woman who singlehandedly kept the family together during the internment. She now appeared old and tired, even allowing her children to provide for her care.

Jiro had borrowed money from a community *tanomoshi*, (an informal neighborhood version of a credit union). With the borrowed money, Jiro purchased a used gardening truck and gardening equipment. By the time Tak was released, Jiro's gardening route had enough customers to keep them both busy. Tak welcomed the opportunity to be gainfully employed and immersed himself in learning his new trade.

For the next few years Tak adhered to a sunup-to-sundown, six-day-a-week work routine and eventually was able to start putting money aside. When able, he purchased a gardening truck and equipment to build his own route.

Jiro married Yoshiye, his sweetheart from camp, and the cramped 8th Avenue family home added another member. A few months later, Jiro announced that they were expecting their first baby. It was a time for the family to celebrate their good fortune—even Mama's energy and spirit were uplifted.

Tak moved out to make room for the expanding family, renting a small back house just a few blocks away on 4th Avenue. Slowly, Tak began to integrate himself into the developing JA community. He joined the Seinan Dojo where he worked out with other senior belts, two nights a week. On Sunday, his one day off, he attended service at the Senshin Buddhist Temple. It was at Senshin where he met his future wife, Kiyoko Matsunaga.

The next year, 1947, eventually turned bittersweet. It started out with promise, when Tak and Kiyoko married in early January, followed by Kiyoko's pregnancy.

Tak was now self-employed, married, and an expectant father. For Tak and the rest of his Nisei generation, their lives were finally taking a turn for the better. Then came Mama's sudden passing. It came as a shock, for Mama's energy and spirits had returned since the birth of Jiro's first-born son, named Kenji Robert Nagata, in honor of his grandfather. During the day while Jiro and Yoshiye worked, Mama cared for baby Kenji whom she adored, finding a renewed purpose in life. What was initially diagnosed as a bad cold, developed into a deep cough in her lungs. Despite bed rest, medicines, and a doctor's care, her tired body was no longer able to keep pace with her strong spirit, and she was finally laid to rest. With the passing of Papa and now Mama, the Nagata Nisei were on their own.

Much like the transition taking place in the Nagata family, the JA Seinan community reflected the passing of the old and the start of a new way of life. Sprouting businesses, owned and operated by Nisei proprietors kept pace with a growing JA population in the Crenshaw district. Most of the shops, markets, offices, garages, cafes, and restaurants were located on Jefferson Boulevard between Crenshaw and Arlington Avenue. Some of the Nisei establishments had Oriental names: Enbun Market, New Moon Fish Market, Saki's Liquor, Koby's Pharmacy, Kokusai Theater, Tak's Hardware and Lawnmower Repair, Kashu Realty, and Koy's Barbershop. Other JA businesses operated under mainstream names: Paul's Kitchen, Sam's Auto Repair, Ham's Gas Station, David's Watch Repair, Gilbert's Meat Market, Rosie's House of Dimes, and Grace Pastry. Colored businesses, churches, and storefronts were also part of Crenshaw's commerce, with Bard's Theater, Ed Burkes Clothing, Leo's BBQ, Fords 2nd Avenue Billiards, Flash Records, and Golden Bird Chicken to name a few.

In the late '40s, and early '50s, the *Sansei*—third generation Japanese Americans—exploded onto the scene. They were the post-war baby boomers. Most Nisei parents wanted to raise their Sansei children as "American" as they themselves felt, determined to shield their children as much as possible from the type of suspicion, hardships and racism they experienced.

They gave their Sansei children Anglo names like Michael, Gregory, Nicholas, Patrick, Gary, Carol, Jane and Barbara. Instead of traditional Japanese names like Kenji, Shoji, Keiko, Akemi, or Hiromi, those names were given to their newborns as middle names, if they were given Japanese names at all. The Nisei wanted to resume their "American" lives and move forward. They felt that the military service of Nisei soldiers spoke for itself—we are not white, but we are trustworthy, loyal Americans who want a better life with opportunities that their parents were not given. The stage was inadvertently set for Asian Americans, especially of Japanese descent, to become known in the future as the "model minority."

The Nisei started Cub Scout, Boy Scout and Girl Scout troops. To keep their kids active and out of trouble, a social group of young Nisei men calling themselves the "Has-Beens" created a Community Youth Council Sports League for Sansei kids. Many of the Has-Beens were excellent athletes before the war, and now had families and kids of their own. They wanted their Sansei children, many who lacked the size or talent to play on their school teams, an opportunity to play organized sports. The Community Youth Council ensured that all Sansei youth regardless of their skill level would be provided an opportunity to play organized basketball in the winter and baseball in the summer. Above any recreational activity, school and good citizenship was paramount.

While the Nisei were building a JA community, replicating American virtues and values, the older Issei now were the *jiichan* (grandfathers) and *baachan* (grandmothers) to the Sansei (third generation). Unless the Sansei attended a Japanese language school, the only time they heard *Nihongo* spoken at home was when their Nisei parents communicated with the Issei grandparents, or when Nisei parents spoke between themselves regarding private matters to which they did not want their Sansei children to be privy. *Nihongo* had become a foreign language in most JA households. Because of the language barrier, communicating with their *jiichan* and *baachan* took too much effort for the Sansei, even though it was evident that their Issei grandparents cared deeply and made efforts to reach out to them. As the Sansei became older, they found it easier to just give their grandparents a nice smile, a head nod and be on their way.

Three cultural activities survived the war: attending the small scattering of Japanese language schools, judo dojos, and the annual summer *Obon* (memorial to honor ancestors) festivities held by Buddhist temples. But prior to the war, the Nisei Week Japanese Festival had become a highlight festival for downtown Little Tokyo. During the Great Depression, a group of young Nisei men convinced the Issei business and community leaders in Little Tokyo that a festival to showcase Japanese culture could bring needed economic stimulus to the area. The event, which was organized by volunteers, brought together the entire Southern California Japanese community for a weekend of activity and celebration which included a queen competition, fashion show and sports and cultural events. The outbreak of World War II and the breakup of Japanese communities in California halted the festival. But within a few years of the end of the war, the annual event was reinstated in Little Tokyo and is still being presented today.

As the JA community forged ahead, looking back was not an option. The concentration camp experience was rarely open for discussion in individual households or in the JA community at large. Their camp experiences were swept under the rug, as if it had never happened. Aside from recounting the war exploits and bravery of the 442nd Infantry Combat Unit, other issues concerning their loss of property, denial of basic constitutional and human rights were not topics discussed among themselves or with their Sansei children.

The Nisei exhibited a characteristic common among oppressed ethnic minorities whose members were pitted against each other, divided, then conquered. An issue sensitive to the Nisei generation concerned how one answered the Camp Loyalty Oath Questionnaire. Many Nisei, including the JACL and some 442nd leadership, adopted the self-righteous position that it was due to their personal sacrifices and heroism that the Japanese Americans were able to earn back the trust of white America. Anyone who did not adhere to their patriotic beliefs, undermined their contributions—in essence, they were making reference to the No-No Boys, and Takezo Nagata was a No-No Boy who fell into this classification.

It bothered Takezo that some of his Nisei peers who knew about his concentration camp decision, held it against him. It was unfortunate and he felt powerless to change their attitude. Takezo had moved on with his life, and placed his bitterness aside. He recognized the losses and sacrifices of others, but he felt that the entire Japanese community paid an unprecedented price for a crime they never committed, one for which the government unjustly found them guilty. Takezo's conscience was clear, he felt that neither he nor the JA community needed to further prove their loyalty to America.

By the early 1960s, Takezo and Kiyoko had four children of their own. They had moved from the back house on 4th Avenue and were now living in the front house. They were making mortgage payments on their modest three bedroom home in the Avenues—with their grown kids, even this home felt cramped.

It was a special time for Takezo and Kiyoko—they could see all their hard work paying dividends through their kids. The eldest son, Shoji, had just graduated with honors from Dorsey High and he was accepted for admission at UCLA. Tad, their second son, was about to start at Dorsey and was expected to follow in his older brothers footsteps. Akemi, was the daughter, and Renbo, the youngest, was the "baby" of the family.

They were all good kids: the two older boys played basketball and baseball in the JA youth leagues. The kids complained about attending Japanese language school on Saturday, however, Kiyoko insisted they attend, except for Tadashi who rebelled and was caught one time too many ditching Saturday language school. To teach their second son a lesson, Takezo and Kiyoko had him get up early on Saturday mornings to spend the entire day helping his pop on the gardening route. While his siblings learned to speak *"sukoshi" Nihongo* (a little bit of Japanese) every Saturday, Tadashi woke up before sunrise and worked til sundown with his pop. His parents found it strange because until he reached high school age, Tadashi never once complained.

Judo remained an integral part of the Nagata family tradition. Takezo became a judo *sensei* at the Seinan Dojo. Three times a week, he took his boys, Shoji and Tadashi to the dojo for martial arts instruction. The Seinan Dojo practiced old-school training. Workouts were not fun, they were rigorous with the intent to teach and instill self-discipline and a competitive fighting spirit. Takezo noticed that it was not his disciplined and academically bright son Shoji that excelled on the mat, rather it was his free-spirited second son, Tadashi, who showed the most promise. Takezo was fair but he was also hard on his own kids—he was short on handing out praise and encouragement. In private, Kiyoko told him that although his children respected him, they were also afraid of him. Takezo replied that his *otoosan* had taught him in this same manner and his responsibility to his children was to be their papa rather than their friend.

Part III

Sansei

Sansei, pronounced (sahn-say) is a combination of two words, *san* meaning three, and *sei* meaning generation. Sansei is the name given to the third generation—grandsons and granddaughters of the Japanese who immigrated to North America.

SANSEI

The Japanese numerical system, "ichi," "ni," "san," as translated, is one, two and three, which explains how the term "Sansei" describes and categorizes the third generation of Japanese in America.

THE MAJORITY OF THE SANSEI were born after the Japanese American concentration camp experience. Those born during the internment were too young to have a distinct memory of camp life, and those who possessed a faint recollection of the camps, learned through their Nisei parents that it wasn't a topic to be discussed.

The Nisei rarely shared their camp experience with their children, and with the language barrier making meaningful communication difficult with the aging Issei generation, the Sansei were left clueless about their identity as Japanese in America.

The Nisei believed that their children needed to do better than the next person to advance in post-war America. Being equal to whites and other minorities was not enough, the Sansei children had to be better. This collective attitude was stressed in most JA households and within JA community institutions.

The Issei passed onto their children the need to educate themselves to create a path to a better life. In turn, the Nisei emphasized to the Sansei that excelling in the classroom was the key to success. Good grades, honor roll recognition and merit awards often became the measurements of one's worth. Anything short of academic achievement was disappointing.

Takezo and Kiyoko Nagata's firstborn son, Shoji, exceeded his parents' expectations. He was an honor student, vice president of his senior class, and he ran hurdles for the Dorsey High "B" classification, Southern League Champion track team. In contrast, their second son, Tadashi, was an average student at best; his parents couldn't understand why he did not excel like his older brother. He was equally bright, but Tadashi possessed a laid-back, easygoing nature that his parents could not change, no matter how hard they tried. Despite their admonishments, lectures, and punishments, he would not take school seriously. In junior high, after continually bringing home mediocre report cards, Takezo and Kiyoko stopped trying to motivate their carefree son who was oblivious about his future. For the sake of family harmony, they finally came to accept that their number two son was not academically inclined, but at least their oldest son would make the family proud. It was now time to make sure that the two younger children, Akemi and Renbo, followed in their eldest brother's footsteps.

From his earliest recollection Tadashi Nagata knew that his older brother, Shoji was gifted. As a toddler, Shoji would stand out and shine in a structured group setting as if he instinctively knew what the adults in charge were asking for and happily oblige them. His intuitive perception combined with laser-focus discipline, was Shoji's formula to achieve and succeed.

An outsider could surmise that Tadashi stopped trying to achieve because the expectations placed on him and the weight of his older brother's success were too great a burden. In reality, from day one, Tadashi did not like how being sent to school made him feel. Being forced to sit still for long stretches of time and being expected to learn by listening to a teacher lecture was not his idea of fun. Tadashi would fixate on the clock on the classroom wall, counting down the minutes, anxiously awaiting the ring of the afternoon school bell so that he could finally be free to leave. Even at an early age, rather than to go to Japanese language school for a half day, he chose to go gardening all day Saturday with his father.

Despite his easygoing and fun-loving nature, Tadashi was also inquisitive and headstrong. He lived for the moment and enjoyed playing sports. When he discovered an activity that captured his interest, his focus and concentration were intense. His priorities in life were playing ball, having fun, and hanging out with his Avenue pals. Unlike his older brother Shoji, the lessons that were important to him, were not taught in a classroom.

Like many JA families, both of Tadashi's parents worked to make ends meet. They trusted that their Sansei kids would come straight home after school to start their homework assignments. When the parents returned home after a hard day's labor, they still had to cook, clean, and get ready for tomorrow. This left very little quality time to spend with their kids.

Thrice weekly, Takezo took Tadashi and Shoji to judo practice, and Tadashi gardened with him on Saturdays; but the only communication between father and son consisted of listening to his pop lecture him, telling him what to do. Tadashi wasn't bothered—other than his pop caring about his school progress, there was little else for them to discuss. On the other hand, he and his friends always had plenty to talk about.

For a young, fun-seeking Sansei, growing up in the Avenues was righteous. The neighborhood was predominately "Colored" and "Oriental" blue-collar working class families. Throughout the neighborhood, Tad had friends with whom to play sports, hang out, and even get in trouble. Everyone in the Avenues knew one another or knew something about each other. In the neighborhood, Tadashi was known as plain old "Tad."

The Avenue kids attended Sixth Avenue Elementary School. The school was fifty-five percent colored, forty percent JA, and five percent "other." The Avenues had only a scattering of whites and other ethnic minorities. The young colored and oriental kids affectionately called themselves and each other "bloods" and "buddhaheads."

At Sixth Avenue, the top students and overachievers were Sansei, with a handful of colored students part of this elite group. Seated in the back of the classroom was where the underachieving buddhaheads and their blood partners sat. Tad Nagata sat in the back of the class with his Avenue partners.

Tad's Avenue partners were close in age—they hung out together, shared similar interests, and as they got older, fought and got in and out of trouble together. Like other low-income ethnic communities, "machismo" and being "bad" were admirable traits. Growing up in a close-knit ethnic enclave meant that everyone knew each other so well that when a person pretended to be something that he wasn't, he would be dealt with for "fronting off." Minor transgressions could result in a verbal putdown or be allowed to "let slide." However, a person busted one too many times for being "all show, no go" would take an ass-whipping. There was no shame in fighting to the very end and still take a whipping—this showed "heart" but talking "shit" without being able to back it up was the mark of a "punk." At an early age, Tad learned the importance of having "heart."

Not having any spending money didn't prevent Tad and his Avenue partners from having a good time. They just needed themselves and a ball to play year-round competitive games. In the winter, after-school football was played in the street. Fire hydrants, lampposts or parked cars were their goal lines, and three completed passes were a first down. On weekends, serious Sansei athletes from different parts of the Westside met at the grass archery field behind Dorsey High to choose sides for tackle football games. The game would start in the afternoon and last until the sun set. The competition was tough—busted lips, bloody noses, and even broken bones were part of the game. Tad relished playing in those games but he could only play on Sundays since he was busy gardening with his pop on Saturdays. Outdoor pick-up basketball was played on the blacktop. These games were easier to organize because fewer players were needed for a game and if alone, he could work on his shot. In the summer, they hopped the fence and played baseball on the schoolyard diamonds. On weekends, Tad and his partners combined their loose change for one person to pay admission at Kokusai Theater, the local Japanese movie house. Once inside, the one who paid admission would open the theater's rear door and the rest of them sneaked inside. There they watched samurai warriors defend their honor and bloody their enemies while upholding the *bushido* code, the way of the warrior.

Upon turning thirteen, Tad and his friend Davey got a paper route, delivering the *Herald Examiner*. Davey owned a bicycle, and after school, they folded, banded, and packed the newspapers, then took off on Davey's bike. Davey pedaled and Tad, sitting on the handlebars, would reach into the delivery bag and throw the folded papers onto the customer's front door step. The Avenue kids also earned money by hawking sodas, hot dogs and programs at the old Wrigley Field, home of the minor league baseball team, LA Angels. Tad bought sports equipment with his money— white Chuck Taylor high tops and a nylon basketball were his prized possessions. When Tad had extra pocket change, he would treat himself to a cherry coke at Holiday Bowl.

Located on Crenshaw Boulevard, Holiday Bowl was a JA-owned, state-of-the-art bowling alley, which opened when Tad was in the fifth grade. Holiday was a one-stop adult and family playground, possessing fifty highly polished bowling lanes, a billiard room with eight Brunswick tables, and a 24-hour coffee shop. The popular coffee shop served a diversified menu of Japanese, Chinese, and American food, along with local favorite concoctions, like Tad's favorite: "Beachboy Delight," a mixture of Portuguese sausage, green onions, eggs, scallions, with a special sauce, served over a bed of rice. It had a sushi bar with an imported Japanese sushi chef. Nisei singles or married spouses, looking for some side action, frequented the Holiday Bowl bar. Save for the brightly-lit bowling alleys, Holiday Bowl was dimly lit with an interior decor that featured a red carpet. From the moment it opened, Holiday Bowl was the JA Westside mecca.

When Tad and his buddhahead partners reached junior-high age, they began to emulate the older Sansei "cool" dudes in the Avenues. These cats dressed with style, walked with a swagger called pimping, talked shit, and didn't take shit. They were always in the center of any excitement worthy of conversation, plus they had the foxiest chicks. The conservative JA community did not look favorably upon them. To the Nisei they were *yogore*. For the Issei generation a *yogore* was someone who did not adhere to the strict code of Japanese niceties and could be loud and boisterous. The Nisei used *yogore* to describe a person that shames the community; someone to ignore or marginalize. *Yogore* now had a gangster connotation and was getting used like an English word to describe them.

To begin their apprenticeship Tad and his partners started combing their hair back into a pompadour—it was important to have tight "fronts." Using gobs of Murray's thick hair gel and sleeping while wearing a nylon stocking cap trained the hair to lay back as it grew longer. Afterward, the gooey Murray's was replaced by hair spray to kept the front in place. A righteous front added at least six inches to ones height.

With his front finally in place, Tad was ready to get his threads together. The "yogore" transformation required a head-to-toe makeover. PF Flyer and Chuck Taylor tennis shoes, blue jeans, and tee shirts were replaced with pointy French-toed kicks, khaki pants, slacks, and stylish Sir Guy shirts.

Tad viewed the older "cool" cats as modern versions of the samurai warriors that he romanticized. Learning to walk with a cool, exaggerated, slow cadence, conversing in street lingo, Tad was capable of throwing down from his shoulders and kick ass if necessary. What he did not like was when the "yogores" used their street status to intimidate and bully those they considered to be lames or squares.

On a hot summer day, before Tad and his partners were to enroll at Mount Vernon Junior High, word circulated on the Avenues that the Uyemura brothers were calling a meeting to form a gang, and anyone who wanted in should show up. Of all of Tad's partners, Gary Uyemura was the logical person to start a gang. Five years ago, he and his older brother, Richard, moved from a rough neighborhood in Oahu to the Avenues. After their arrival, even by Westside standards, their family was considered poor. Gary was short but strong, built like a pit bull and had a mean streak. If he didn't know you, or worse yet, if he didn't like you, he would take your money or whip your ass—sometimes both. His older brother, Richard, who could be just as cold, was already attending Mount Vernon Jr. High. For some reason, Tad and Gary got along from the beginning. Tad made it over to Gary's place to hear what the Uyemura brothers had to say.

When Tad arrived, most of his "I-don't-give-a-shit," sit-in-back-of-the-classroom partners were already there: Crazy Willie, Hawkeye, Suga, PeeWee, Lawrence, Yosh, Steve, and Davey. Tad was glad to see a few of their blood partners, Mike, Paul and Arthur, at the meeting.

Richard Uyemura kicked off the meeting by telling them what to expect at Mount Vernon. He said that at Mount Vernon, being a buddhahead meant that you were going to be in the minority and would be tested and challenged.

Tad knew that the majority of the buddhaheads living on the Westside would attend Audubon Junior High, the other junior high in the neighborhood. Audubon and Mount Vernon was separated by the railroad track on Exposition Boulevard. The neighborhood south of Exposition where Audubon drew its students was predominately white and Japanese American. With the exception of the Avenues, the surrounding area north of Exposition that fed into Mount Vernon was predominately colored. Metaphorically, Crenshaw residents living north of Exposition Boulevard were viewed as being from the wrong side of the tracks.

As Richard continued talking, he hadn't said anything that the group there didn't already know. What drew Tad's attention was Richard speaking about the blood gangs at Mount Vernon. He said that there were a lot of cliques and wannabes, but the three strongest sets were the Bachelors, Belquans and Bartenders from Vineyard. He said these thugs would shake people down to make them pay "protection" money and they would fire up and even stomp on somebody just out of general principal, or GP. Richard said that a few times they even fucked with him and he had no choice than to go down "toe to toe" to maintain respect. Tad knew that if these fools would fuck with a bad dude like Richard, then as sure as shit, he was going to be tested.

He said that with the exception of a few cats, most of the Mount Vernon buddhaheads avoided trouble by ducking and dodging confrontation; many even took roundabout ways home if they spotted trouble in their direct path. He said that some buddhaheads even gave up their lunch money rather than to fight back, and finished by saying, "Punks like them make it harder on the rest of us."

Richard said that he was glad that his brother Gary and his partners were coming to Mount Vernon because he knew that we weren't punks. Henry, he and a few others, were tired of being the only buddhaheads willing to throw down.

By late that afternoon, everyone at the meeting agreed to be a part of the new gang for they all understood the concept of strength in numbers. Because it was the Uyemura brothers' idea to start a gang, they began the initiation process by challenging the biggest cat at the meeting, Arthur Washington, to get up and to throw up his hands. As soon as Arthur slowly stood, Richard and Gary were all upside him, pounding away; Arthur did his best but he took a beating. Next, the three of them chose out the next victim and another whoopin' took place. Tad was not spared from a righteous ass-whippin' but he managed to get a few licks in of his own. He knew that if he grabbed one of his assailants and applied a judo choke, he could have taken at least one of them out, but he decided against it because everyone there was a partner, and that whatever bruising he endured was worth it. He was now a member of the gang.

The initiation served to unify them; they felt tighter than before. The next order of business was to decide what to call themselves. A lot of names were suggested; after a vote was taken they were now the "Little Gents."

The Little Gents was one of the first post-WWII, Japanese American gangs. Older Sansei buddhaheads had formed social clubs—members of these cliques would hang out together, organize social parties and activities, play sports together, and hit on the chicks, with fighting and backing each other up secondary to their social functions. In contrast, the Little Gents was formed for self-preservation and protection; social benefits would be a secondary bonus. There was no denial that the Little Gents was a gang.

WESTSIDE

ON THIS SWELTERING *hot summer evening, 7:05 to be exact, at the intersection of 116th Street and Avalon Boulevard, many of the residents in this South Central enclave were already hanging out on the street, seeking a reprieve from their oven-hot tenements, hoping to catch a whiff of a cool breeze, anything to beat the heat.*

At this time and location, a motorcycle CHP officer pulled two young brothers, Marquette and Ronald Frye, over to the curb, claiming to have observed an erratic driving pattern of the car driven by Marquette. Once on the sidewalk, the CHP officer conducted a field sobriety test on Marquette. When completed, he concluded that Marquette had been driving while under the influence. Marquette was handcuffed and placed under arrest for DUI. The CHP called in for a back-up patrol car to transport Marquette to the 77th Division Police Station.

The arrest took place a couple of blocks from where the brothers lived. A neighbor witnessing the arrest, immediately went to tell their mother, Reyna Frye what was going down. When Ms. Frye arrived at the scene, the LAPD was getting ready to transport her son to the station, and she questioned officers about the treatment of her son. The officers did not appreciate the aggressive tone in her voice and she, in turn, did not appreciate the hostile attitude of the police. Ronald came to the defense of his mother. The crowd, gathered on the corner, witnessed this routine arrest, could relate to Reyna Frye's anger and empathized with her frustration. The police officers did not appreciate what they perceived to be a public demonstration by the mother of a perpetrator, challenging and disrespecting their badge of authority, and they placed both Reyna and Ronald Frye under arrest. Reyna was in no mood for what she considered their nonsense and she defiantly challenged their attempt to place her in their custody. By now the crowd on the corner had increased in both size and its anger. Sensing the tenseness of the situation, LAPD called in for additional back up. What started off as a routine arrest on a hot summer night, ignited into an all out racial uprising.

Oddly, on this night, the LAPD's actions were no different than how their "business" in the "colored" community was generally conducted. What differed on this night was the colored community's militant response to generations of institutional racism, injustice, and police brutality. Sociologists hypothesized that the community's eruption could be attributed to racism, unemployment, inadequate housing, inferior education, and a lack of opportunity for upward mobility. The police commission placed the blame on outside agitators and neighborhood gangs. However, the everyday cat on the corner knew that his people's rebellion was fueled by daily feelings of frustration, anger and loss of hope. When a group of people are systemically excluded from participating in the "American Dream," deprived of a sense of hope, and backed up against a wall, they can either play the "Uncle Tom" role and passively accept the abuse, or "come out swinging." Tonight, the community came out swinging. As the City of Angels went up in flames, the Magnificent Montague, a popular disc jockey on local soul station KJLH, broke it down the best as he shouted, "Burn, baby, burn!" over the airwaves that resonated throughout the city.

The intersection of Crenshaw and Jefferson Boulevards was located less than eight miles from 116th and Avalon. In this ethnic neighborhood, Oriental and Colored families lived side by side. They worked and provided services for each other, sent their kids to the same neighborhood schools, and their kids in turn, attended classes, played, and grew up together. Overall, everyone got along and racial bullshit and tension between the Westside Orientals and Coloreds was an exception and not the rule.

The JA businesses on Jefferson Boulevard were mostly mom-and-pop operations. The owners of these shops lived and raised their families in the Crenshaw community. During the Watts rebellion, not a single store on Jefferson Boulevard was set ablaze or looted; neighbors both yellow and black were physically prepared to protect these shops from outside looters and malcontents.

Courtesy Liquor Store, on Washington Boulevard, was located one mile north of Jefferson Boulevard. It was at this store where Eugene Saito, a young 16-year-old was gunned down by the LAPD when he and his blood partners attempted to flee from the store when the police arrived at the scene. Eugene was unarmed, caught seven rounds and died instantly. He was one of the thirty-four people killed in the Watts Rebellion.

THE AFTERMATH of the Watts Rebellion witnessed a massive white exodus from inner city Los Angeles. White folks couldn't get out of "Dodge" fast enough. They moved to the sprawling suburbs of the San Fernando Valley and to the perceived safety of the rapidly-developing Orange County suburbs—even economically advantaged JA families moved from the inner city to a new developing area outside LA called Gardena. No inner city area was immune from white flight, Crenshaw included.

The Westside contains an area surrounded by blocks of apartment units in the proximity of Santa Barbara Avenue and Buckingham Road. Prior to the Watts Rebellion, Anglo and Jewish families rented ninety-five percent of these apartment dwellings. Because the area's landscape was dominated by tall African palm trees, it was dubbed "The Jungle."

At the time of the Watts Rebellion, Tad had just finished his first semester at Dorsey High, and was attending summer school, making up credits. For Tad and his Avenue *tomodachi,* many changes had taken place.

Four years had passed since the Little Gents formed. When the Gents started attending Mount Vernon Junior High, Richard Uyemura's prophesy was fulfilled. On his second day at Mount Vernon, Tad stood next to his hallway locker, when four older thugs approached him. These older dudes were making the rounds,

introducing themselves to incoming students to collect protection money from
them before other rival gang members hit them up. Fortunately, his partner
Davey was nearby and when he saw what was about to go down, he went to Tad's
defense. The older antagonists were surprised because they were not accustomed
to buddhaheads, or anyone else for that matter, stand up to them; plus these young
cats looked, dressed, and acted differently. They did not exhibit the "deer-in-
the-headlights" bewildered look that usually accompanies their "mark." When it
became evident that these two buddhaheads were not about to give up their pocket
money and were defiantly defending their space, the blood dude nearest to Tad
reached out and grabbed him by the shirt. Quicker than you could say *"Ippon"* Tad
executed a hip throw which he had practiced and perfected during endless hours of
training at the Seinan Dojo. The other three cohorts immediately attacked Tad and
Davey, driving them back against the lockers, but they managed to stay on their
feet and get in a few blows of their own. Like most scuffles at school, the pre-fight
posturing and bravado lasted longer than the actual fight. Tad, ended up with a
slightly raised welt on his left cheekbone and a torn pocket on his shirt, but he held
on to his money and kept his pride.

This incident was far from isolated; the heart and mettle of the Gents were
challenged and tested both individually and as a group. Most fights took place
on school grounds and were usually quick and violent confrontations. Other than
an occasional busted lip, darkened eye, body bruises and shredded clothes, no
one on either side was seriously injured. Establishing a reputation required a
willingness to throw down from the shoulders upon the slightest provocation,
whether real or imagined. Having your polished Florsheim kicks accidentally or
intentionally stepped on, not digging the way someone was looking at you, or any
verbal challenge, set into motion a heads-up or group throw-down. Going down
from the shoulder to kicking some ass, was the ultimate display of heart. Every
bad cat possessed a unique fighting style—generally the big dudes would use their
superior size and strength to overpower smaller opponents, and the smaller cats
relied more on their quickness and agility. The baddest dudes, the cats that no one
in their right mind challenged, fought with style, passion, and reckless abandon.
What separated these elite few from the rest was they actually seemed to "get off"
when they fought, combined with a "don't give a fuck!" mentality. The streets had an
unwritten code: anyone pulling out a shank or gun to defend himself was a "scary"
dude, someone who was weak, and lacked the heart to go straight-up. While the
Little Gents could not claim that they always got the "best" of their scuffles, it was
secondary to sending out the statement message, announcing to everyone that
they were not to be fucked with.

It did not take long for the other gangs at Mount Vernon to notice their presence.
The Gents marked out their own territory in the school's courtyard where they
congregated during nutrition and lunch breaks. Unlike the other buddhahead
students, they wore their hair pompadour-style, and dressed no different from
the bloods. They were organized, walking to and from school in groups and were
seldom caught off guard. Two distinct advantages that the Gents had were that
Richard Uyemura was part of their clique and he had already earned a reputation

at Mount Vernon; and the Gents had the backing of their blood partners from the Avenues, Mike G., Paul White and Arthur Spalding, in particular.

The intimidation and feeling-out phase for the Little Gents came to a head when Steve Saito—not a member of the Gents but an Avenue friend—was jumped while walking home after school. He was rat-packed and badly hurt: two of his teeth were dislodged, fourteen stitches closed an ugly open gash below his chin, had facial swelling, and had to stay out of school to recover with bed rest. All eyes were now directed toward the Little Gents, waiting to see how they would retaliate. The identity of the attackers was no secret, the shot-caller of his assailants was a dude named Shelton. Shelton was muscular, heavy set, and carried a "baad ass" reputation—a person not to be fucked with. There was a chickenshit side to Shelton for he liked to hurt weaker people just for the fuck of it. The problem was that no one was bad enough to place him in check.

The Gents knew that Shelton and his crew had to be dealt with; the difficulty was finding an opportune time to vamp on them. The first two days after Steve Saito's beat down were tense. Shelton and his boys strutted around the Mount Vernon campus in pompous arrogance. However, after school they were nowhere to be found. It was on the third day that the Gents decided they needed to take immediate action. At the afternoon lunch break they headed en masse to an area by the hash line, occupied by Shelton and his crew. As the Gents approached, Shelton and his partners rose from the benches, ready to take on the younger Gents. Upon arriving, the Gents spread their ranks, and the numbers were about even with each side ready to get down. Shelton spoke first. He said coolly that he'd been expecting them, and suggested that they settle this beef by going one-on-one with him and whoever the Gents decided to match against him. The only logical comment out of his mouth was, "Why should all of us get kicked out of school, when just two of us can squash this after school behind Ralph's?" The Gents hadn't anticipated Shelton's one-on-one challenge and before having a chance to regroup, Gary Uyemura took it upon himself to accepted Shelton's challenge. He told Shelton that he best be there and not punk out. Shelton, who was noticeably bigger than Gary, looked slightly down at his young adversary, merely smirked, turned his back, and sat back down on the bench as if it was no big thing.

The word quickly spread about Shelton going heads-up with a little buddhahead cat. When the bell rang ending the school day, a circus-like atmosphere of eager, excited anticipation filled the air. All the gangsters, thugs, wannabes, and curious onlookers headed to Ralph's Market on Washington Boulevard. The consensus of the mob was that they wanted to see how long it was going to take Shelton to fuck up the little buddhahead dude.

After school, Gary's older brother, Richard, called a meeting. He said he wasn't worried about Gary, because he could take care of himself—what concerned him was Shelton's boys jumping in while Gary was getting the best of Shelton. To ensure that they were not caught by surprise, a few of the Gents concealed tire irons, chains and screwdrivers. Richard's belief in his brother's fighting skills boosted the Gents' confidence—up to now, many of them did not even want to think about what it was going to take to whip Shelton's ass. What Richard knew, while many of the Gents were unaware, was that growing up in a poor, tough section on the island of Oahu, Gary was raised to fight. With only a few buddhahead families living in their neighborhood, Richard and Gary had only each other to depend on. They fought individually or together, taking on opponents bigger and tougher than Shelton. Richard knew that if there was one thing his younger brother knew how to do, it was to fight. When the Uyemura brothers moved to the Westside, they gravitated toward Tad and his partners because they saw in them, the same type of "don't fuck with me" mentality that they possessed. After they all became tight, if they weren't playing some type of ball, or getting into mischief, they would often be in someone's back yard, wrapping their fists with old tee shirts to soften the blows when sparring with each other. What evolved from these sessions, was a pecking order, with Gary Uyemura on top of the totem pole.

When the Gents arrived behind Ralph's Market, the back lot was packed. Shelton and his posse had a large crowd around him. He was enjoying the spotlight, acting his cocky self. In the meantime, Gary stripped off his shirt, to make it harder for Shelton to grab hold of him. Gary started to head towards Shelton, with Gents following behind. The crowd around Shelton dispersed leaving only Gary and Shelton facing each other. No words were spoken between them as they squared off. Their stances were different in style: Gary's fists were held chest high, while in contrast, Shelton's fists protected his temples, peek-a-boo style, with his elbows tucked in. Shelton initiated the attack, keeping his protective guard up and walking directly toward Gary. His movements were calculated and deliberate. He wanted to close the distance and force Gary to backpedal, which would maximize his superior reach and power, while his opponent would be forced to fight defensively while retreating backwards.

Just when Shelton closed into striking distance, Gary, who had not moved, much less retreated, quickly and adeptly moved to Shelton's right side, then sprang at him with a two-fisted attack. Gary's speed, agility, and mobility caught Shelton off guard, and he backed in retreat. Gary drove his fists at a furious pace, not allowing Shelton to recover his balance. Shelton's high-hand guard made it impractical for Gary to attack his head, so he attacked the center of his upper body. The crowd was in shock—it was obvious that Gary was getting the best of Shelton, who was not able to match Gary's fury and rage. Gary moved in fast, but he momentarily lost his footing as the soles of his hard shoes slipped on the graveled pavement, and this pause gave Shelton just enough time to regain his balance. The smirk had vanished from Shelton's face and was replaced with a grim, determined look. Again, Shelton moved forward to close the distance, slower and more cautiously this time, with Gary still standing his ground. Before Shelton could move into striking distance, Gary stepped forward with his left foot, moved his right foot in for balance, then aimed a waist-high side kick which caused Shelton to move back to avoid contact. Without skipping a beat, when Gary's left foot hit the pavement, he quickly pivoted one-hundred-eighty degrees, ending in the perfect position to execute a waist-high side kick with his right foot, striking Shelton on his upper right hip. The crowd let out a collective gasp; even Gary must have appreciated the beauty of his move because instead of rushing in for the kill, he calmly gathered himself to resume his stance, almost as if he wanted to prolong the fight. Shelton no longer looked cocky or determined; he now looked lost, without a plan, only instinct guiding him to keep up his guard. It was Gary who now had a small smirk on his face as he moved in for the inevitable. As Gary moved forward, Shelton moved backwards. When Gary saw that Shelton was intentionally keeping his distance by retreating and throwing out intermittent jabs with his left hand, he let himself go and rushed his prey. The force of Gary's attack drove Shelton backwards and Gary would have fallen right on top of him if Shelton hadn't crashed into an industrial trash bin behind the market. A thunderous noise resulted as everyone rushed over to see Shelton finally get his just due. He still managed to keep his guard up to protect his face, as Gary pummeled his open body. As Shelton's body began to slide in slow motion down the dumpster onto the pavement, Gary took a step back and then kicked Shelton dead in his face, right between his guarding hands. Shelton's entire body dropped to the pavement—all that he could do now was gather himself into a fetal position.

Shelton's crew had seen enough and they had no other choice than to step forward and come to the defense of their defeated leader. The Gents immediately stepped between them, blocking their pathway to the one-on-one affair; the posture and demeanor of Shelton's crew was more of resignation than confrontation. As Shelton lay sprawled out on the pavement, all eyes were on Gary, to see what he would do next. By now, Tad was standing next to Gary, protecting his back. He was close enough to feel the heat and intensity emitting from Gary's body, but even he was not sure what was going to happen next. Surprisingly, Gary dropped his guard, turned around, looked at the mob of onlookers, muttered, "Fuck this punk!" and slowly walked away with the Gents at his side. He put his shirt back on, straightened his front, lit a cigarette and took a deep drag.

Not by any stretch did the Ralph's Market whippin' resolve gang intimidation and bullying at Mount Vernon, but what it did accomplish was that buddhaheads were no longer viewed as open game or easy prey "just because" they were buddhaheads. While the Gents had established their street credibility, the true winner of this outcome was the typical striving JA student—the number of incidents of harassment they endured previously was drastically reduced. By becoming the beneficiaries of the work put in by the Little Gents, many of the Gents figured that it was only just that some of these uppity-acting lames and squares pay them for protection—ultimately they had to give it up anyway, so it might as well be to them.

Other than the academics and daily class work, Tad dug everything else about Mount Vernon; it was a time for fun and experimentation. To placate his competitive nature, Tad joined the after-school sports program. The winter months were for playing flag football, in the spring was baseball. Tad enjoyed the competition, testing his skills against many of the top athletes in the Westside, many who would later become his teammates at Dorsey High.

There was always something new to try, the to-do list was endless: smoking cigarettes without getting dizzy, then learning how to blow smoke rings, dropping someone with a six inch punch, making one bleed with a twist of knuckles, playing the dozens, hot-wiring cars, mixing cherry Kool Aid with cheap wine making it potable, scoring nickel bags, rolling joints, taking aspirin while drinking Coke, getting high on cough syrup, learning the steps to dance Hully Gully, Slauson Shuffle, and on and on.

Then there were the stone foxes, fine mamas, babes, broads, chicks, and bitches. Whatever name they were called, all the young dudes wanted to make it with a loose chick, the finer the better. Girls were placed in two categories: good girls and rowdy chicks. The majority of JA girls fit the good girl category—getting good grades, following the rules, and acting proper, whatever that meant. It wasn't as if they were standoffish or snobby, most of the good girls were well-adjusted, secure, cute, and friendly. They just were not interested in deviating from their good-girl routine and lifestyle. In contrast, the rowdy chicks were the female equivalent of the Gents. They were defined by their style, dress and attitude. They wore short, revealing skirts, nylon leggings, blouses unbuttoned just enough to show a peek of a bra. They caked makeup and powder on their face, and covered their eyes with long artificial eyelashes and dark painted-on eyebrows. Their lips glistened with gloss lipstick, and they wore their hair high, beehive-style. The Eastside *"ese"* chicks were known to conceal gang members' weapons in their high-styled hairdos. Many of the rowdy chicks were as game or gamer than the dudes. Big Vicki and Molly were tough enough to intimidate even some of the dudes. If a horny young cat had the fortune of going around with one of these girls, it meant hours of French kissing, hickeys, finger banging and if lucky, copping some pussy.

It was a rowdy girls clique whose exploits and reputation traveled throughout JA communities in California. The girls in this group attended Dorsey High School, and called themselves the *"Ichibans"* (number ones). What made the Ichibans infamous far beyond Seinan was their initiation into the group, which required having sex with a Colored boy. When word about the Ichibans spread their behavior was considered blasphemous and the Ichibans became the talk of the conservative JA community. Tad had a partner whose sister was a member of the Ichibans, she was always super cool to Tad.

By the ninth grade at Mount Vernon, the final year before graduating and moving on to Dorsey, the Little Gents had grown in size and reputation—they were now an established gang in the Avenues and on campus. It was in the ninth grade that a major change began when a new yogore cat enrolled at Mount Vernon. Rumors had it that this cat was from an area known as J Flats, and that he had already been kicked out of four junior high schools in the Eastside. It was said his parents enrolled him in Mount Vernon to get him into a new environment. His name was Ricky Yamada, a short, stocky dude with a huge head. He had a dark complexion, sunken eyes and dark heavy eyebrows—he looked like a Japanese clone of Boris Karloff. He knew a few JA students at Mount Vernon and immediately joined their clique. Because he was backed by a notorious older J Flats gang, he pimped around like his shit didn't stink. The Gents did not smell it this way, and gave him a nickname, "Bowling Ball Head." By the end of Bowling Ball Head's first week at Mount Vernon, Gary called him out. Ricky, who was no punk, said that he would fight Gary but only on his own terms. His condition was that each would be backed by only one person and the fight would take place in two days after school, at a long alleyway between the railroad tracks and Rodeo Boulevard. If Gary showed up with more than one person, the fight was off, and Ricky would spread the word that the Gents were too chickenshit to fight him heads up. Gary agreed to the arrangement. Gary chose Tad to be his second.

On the day of the fight, Gary and Tad walked to the designated alleyway. Upon arrival, no one was there, so they waited. Tad knew Gary well enough to know that he needed to focus on what he was about to do and did not want to talk. For fifteen silent minutes they waited for Ricky to show, finally Tad said, "Bowling Ball Head ain't showing, let's split." As they started walking out of the alley, they saw and heard a stream of cars from the opposite open end of the long alley caravanning toward their direction.

Tad's initial instinct was to beat feet and hightail it out of there—it was a set up and if they didn't split quickly, they were going to be trapped. Against his better judgment Tad followed Gary's lead and remained. Three carloads with older J-Flats yogores, pulled up and emptied out into the alley. When they saw only Gary and Tad waiting in the alley, their mood was jovial and nonchalant. They immediately circled them and were lightheartedly talking amongst themselves. Ricky got out of the lead car and he was standing next to one of the badder looking thugs, nodding his head up and down while listening to the older cat's instructions. Gary still hadn't said shit but just waited for Ricky. When Ricky finally entered the circle, he immediately was showered with words of encouragement, "Kick his ass Ricky!" "Fuck him up!" "He ain't shit, Ricky." There was nothing that Gary needed to hear from Tad; besides, Tad was too busy trying to figure out how he and Gary were going to get out of this mess and so far he hadn't come up with an exit plan.

Ricky didn't waste any time and he charged at Gary, who met him head on as they both let go of their hands and punched at each other. Ricky's punches were wide and flailing while Gary's blows were short and direct. Two of Gary's blows bounced off of Ricky's hard head, causing him to pull back from the initial skirmish. With Ricky now at the ideal distance for Gary's patented double spin kick, he executed it to perfection. Before Ricky could move, Gary's backspin left foot kick caught him in the stomach and doubled him over. Gary followed up by driving his fists upside Ricky's head, despite having his back turned to Gary's onslaught. Gary drove Ricky back into the reaches of his outside back-ups. Sensing what was about to take place they shielded Ricky, leaving Gary no other choice than to step back or fight them all. Gary stepped back. The outer circle helped Ricky regroup, gave him additional encouragement and sent him back out to fight. This time Ricky charged at Gary even more recklessly with his head down and arms flailing. Gary's accurate, straight punches stopped his charge and again drove him into the arms of the outer circle who rescued Ricky for the second time. This time, while the older cats were talking and trying to pump Ricky up, Tad could see Ricky shaking his head, although he couldn't hear what they were saying. The mean-looking dude who was talking to Ricky when they first arrived in the alleyway stepped towards Gary and said, "That's it, its over." Tad felt elated inside, thinking, "Gary not only kicked Bowling Ball's ass, but we're going to get out of here unscathed!" Then Gary spoke for the first time, probably all that day, "Where I'm from, if a dude quits, it means I get the last hit." Everyone, including Tad, was stunned not knowing whether what Gary said was true or not, but the older shot-caller did not challenge this defiant young junior high schooler. Instead, he turned to Ricky and said, "It's true." Ricky looked at him with chastened eyes but stepped forward. When the older cat told Ricky to stand in front of Gary, everyone there was on edge. Ricky took his position directly in front of Gary and even jutted out his chin. Gary stepped back, looked at Ricky and said, "I'm going to let you slide, just don't forget who kicked your ass." Ricky look relieved, the outside thugs slowly broke up the circle and headed back to their cars. Tad and Gary headed back to the Avenues.

WESTSIDE TOMODACHI

THE OUTSIDE YOGORES that witnessed Gary's demolition of their homeboy Ricky, returned to their neighborhood with news about an up-and-coming Westside buddhahead gang called the Little Gents. An older, multi-ethnic gang from J-Flats called the Black Juans became interested in absorbing the Little Gents into their set. The Black Juans had a history and reputation for violence and criminal misconduct; many of its members were serving or did time in the California penal institutions. The Black Juans was comprised of older hardcore buddhaheads, Chinese, Filipino, and Latino gangbangers. When the Gents were informed that the Black Juans wanted them to join their set, they understood that this was not an offer, it was a demand. The Gents held a meeting to discuss their options. The consensus at the meeting was that they were opposed to taking orders from shot-callers from the Eastside. They knew that they were not capable of taking on the Black Juans and since they were close to graduating anyway, the most practical course of action was to disband the Little Gents. They figured that when the word spread that the Little Gents had disbanded, the pressure on the Gents to merge would dissolve, since there was no longer a gang to absorb. However, they left their meeting with a long-term plan, which was to wait until after summer and when the former members of Little Gents entered Dorsey High, they would start a new gang with the same Avenue *tomodachi* under a new name. When they entered Dorsey, the former Little Gents regrouped and now called themselves the "Ministers."

At Dorsey, Tad's first assignment was to "educate" the Dorsey High faculty that despite being Shoji Nagata's younger brother, last name was all that they had in common. Shoji, three years older than Tad, graduated from both junior and senior high at the same time Tad was making his grand entrance. Shoji was a tough act to follow. He graduated with high academic and achievement honors, and teachers would assume that Tad was his older brother's clone. Tad understood that because of genetics, teachers would automatically assume that he was going to follow his older brother's path. He was proud but never envious of Shoji's honors and achievements; but his teachers failed to recognize that although he and Shoji possessed many of the same attributes, the big difference was the priorities they chose. Shoji's laser beam focus was directed towards academics in preparation toward a successful future. Tad, however, lived for the moment and focused on activities outside of the classroom. He possessed the intuitive ability to size people up and make quick decisions in stressful situations. Tad was not interested in sacrificing a moment's pleasure for the promise of future success; his only concern was about "now." On his first day at Dorsey, teachers greeted Tad at roll call, with a smile, asking, "Is

Shoji Nagata your brother?" By the end of the second week of class, they would usually inquire, "Are you sure, Shoji's your brother?" It was at this moment Tad knew he had "educated" his teachers. Tad was not disruptive in class so he didn't think that he had a problem. His view was that if there was a problem, it belonged to other people because he was perfectly fine in doing what he was doing—doing just enough to pass and get by.

Mount Vernon and Audubon were the two junior high schools that fed into Dorsey High. Bloods were the majority at Dorsey, followed by a large percentage of buddhaheads; whites numbered less than ten percent, with a sprinkling of Hispanics. Tad looked forward to attending Dorsey—it meant meeting different foxes from other parts of the Westside and having a wider variety of food from which to choose in the outside hash lines; specialties like popcorn smothered in oil and melted butter, hamburgers, fries, and frozen chocolate malts. Dorsey also offered Tad an opportunity to play high school ball in the mighty Southern League against the top athletes in the city.

Tad tried out and made the Dorsey High "B" football squad. The lower division sports teams at Dorsey were well represented by buddhahead athletes. Dorsey had a reputation for fielding championship lower division teams. In Tad's first year, the Dorsey Dons "B" football team took Southern League with its defense led by two all-Southern League cornerbacks who hailed from the Avenues: Ronald Booker and himself. With the first season under their belts, Tad and Ronald Booker made a pact: by their senior year they would both be the starting defensive backs on the Dorsey High Varsity.

At Dorsey High, the Ministers gang grew in strength and numbers. Dudes from different parts of the Westside were jumped into the gang. The Ministers' leadership and its most-feared members were the cats from the Avenues. By the time they entered Dorsey, the former Little Gents, now the Ministers, had adopted a street code. Their rules were simple but absolute: always back up your partner at any cost; never side with outsiders against another Minister, even when he is clearly in the wrong; misunderstandings between Ministers are to be resolved internally; and the last, but number one rule, was never snitch anyone out.

By now, Tad and his Avenue *tomodachi* had forged a bond of trust. Tad felt tighter with his homies than he did with his own family. They'd stuck together through thick and thin and were there for each other when push came to shove. They knew each other's true nature and character so well that they could acknowledge a person's strengths and weaknesses without being judgmental. In the classroom, they were the troublemakers and underachievers; outside the classrooms on the streets, they were the overachievers that demanded recognition and respect. They were the element in the JA community that the Nisei parents warned their own kids not to associate with.

Gary, Victor, Willie, Ats and Yoshio were a few of Tad's tight Avenue partners. On a mano-a-mano, kick-ass pecking order, Gary was top dog. He was small in stature but possessed superior strength, quickness and balance to overpower bigger opponents. Gary excelled in contact sports; he played linebacker and returned punts for the Dorsey Varsity football team. Some dudes loved getting good grades, others loved to play sports, a few loved getting "high," and slick cats loved to mac on the bitches—Gary loved to fight and kick ass. When Gary was engaged in a fight, which seemed to be often, others misinterpreted his combat facial expression as a mean scowl—those who knew him well, recognized that he was really smiling.

Victor was the most affable of the Ministers; he had a knack of getting along with almost everyone. He was a good listener, possessed a curious nature and was always seeking new experiences and adventures. Victor had a gift for explaining complex stuff by making it sound interesting and fun—his partners nicknamed him, "The Professor." If you were a part of Victor's inner circle, he would never let you down, but if you disrespected or betrayed his trust, then payback was a bitch. Victor was the first *tomodachi* to cop a real gig: he pumped gas on the weekends. One Saturday while at work, an older thug, Richard Taragawa, pulled into the gas station and told Victor to fill up his tank. Victor complied, cleaned the windows and opened the hood to check the water and oil. Richard told Victor to put in a quart of motor oil. When Victor asked him what kind of motor oil, Richard told him to put in the most expensive one. When Victor finished adding the oil and closed the hood, Richard stuck his head out of the car window and told Victor to put it on his tab. Victor knew that the owner did not take credit, and he politely told Richard, "You don't have a tab here." Richard, glared at him and said, "Look punk, don't make me get out of my ride and kick your ass! I said, put it on my fuckin' tab!" Victor, was left with only two choices, to let this thug play him for a chump, or to stand up to the older gangster and deal with the consequences. Victor said in an even voice, "Look Richard, you don't have a tab." Richard, hopped out of his car and angrily demanded Victor to meet him behind the station. Victor knew exactly what was on Richard's mind. Richard Taragawa had a reputation for shanking people with a screwdriver, and when he exited his ride, Victor looked for and saw a screwdriver sticking out of Richard's back pocket. Victor wished that his co-worker Stewart had shown up because with Stewart there, none of this bullshit would be going down. Without having anyone to cover his back, he headed behind the station with Richard Taragawa following. Fortuitously, Victor saw and picked up a piece of lumber in back of the station, and before Richard could make his move, Victor swung it at him. He missed Richard's head but smacked him on the shoulder with Richard letting out a loud yell of pain. Victor knew that it was on, with no turning back. If it had been Gary instead of Victor, Richard would have been history because Gary would have immediately followed up his initial blow with more heavy wood, but that was not Victor's nature and he waited to see how Richard would respond. Richard was pissed and went into his back pocket and pulled out his screwdriver but, armed with his plywood, Victor stood his ground. "Hey, what the fuck's going on?" The voice belonged to Stewart, who finally showed up at work. When Richard saw Stewart, he dropped his guard. While Richard acted like he was crazy in order to intimidate and bully people, Stewart didn't need to act like he was crazy; all he had to do was to be himself. Stewart was a cat that no one fucked with, not the gangster buddhaheads or bloods. Stewart could be seen driving up and down the Avenues with the Japanese rising sun flag attached to his front antenna, wearing a *hachimaki* (cloth headband) tied around his head, and was known to have a samurai sword stashed in his trunk. People who didn't know Stewart couldn't make any sense of him and kept him at arm's length. Those from the Avenues accepted him as being a taste eccentric, but having a big heart. Stewart, who was Dirty Willie's older brother, was not a bully and he would look out for his younger brother and his friends.

Stewart didn't hesitate; he rushed Richard, lifted him up by his shirt, slammed him against the wall, and pummeled him with his fists. The next time Richard Taragawa saw Victor was at Holiday Bowl. Victor was again alone, and didn't know what to expect. When Richard walked by, they made eye contact and Richard high-signed him with a head nod and walked off. Victor celebrated in his mind, as he thought, "Hell, yeah!"

Dave would have been the class clown, if he went to class. Since he ditched school regularly, he settled for the title of "neighborhood fuck-up." He was unpredictable and would come up with antics that would even make his Minister partners shake their heads in disbelief. When the mood struck him, Dave would hop on a crowded bus and walk down its aisle with his tongue sticking out of a corner of his mouth, point his eyes in opposite directions, loosely dangle his right hand over a limp wrist, all while walking with a spastic gait. It wouldn't take but a hot minute before a Good Samaritan-type got up and offer Dave his seat. Dave would gladly accept the seat, tilt his head sideways and loudly stutter, "Th-th-thaank you," while all of his partners on the bus could only pretend that they didn't know him. Out of all the Avenue cats, Dave was the most talented natural athlete. If he applied himself, he could have excelled in any sport, but Dave was not interested in sports because playing team ball required too much discipline for his taste. At times, even Tad thought it was a damn shame to waste so much ability.

Mas and his partner Art were the only Ministers that lived outside the Westside. They were both from J-Flats. In the eighth grade they showed up at Mount Vernon for summer school. The Gents immediately planned to jump them, that is, until they witnessed them defend themselves by taking on other thugs. Eventually, the Gents backed up Mas and Art when they were spotted surrounded by a pack of wannabes ready to rat-pack them. The Gents felt that if anyone was going to fuck up these outside cats, they had first dibs. Following this incident, things cooled off and Mas and Art in turn, even backed up the Gents on the schoolyard. They started socializing and hanging out together, and by the end of the summer they joined the Little Gents. Mas and Art spent all of their free time on the Westside with their Minister partners.

"Dirty Willie" earned his name by being a cold mothafucka. Dirty Willie's older brothers were Stewart and Myron: while Stewart was a loner that nobody fucked with, Myron was a hardcore gangster who exclusively ran with the blood gangsters. When Willie fought, what he lacked in style was made up in ferocity. He attacked "balls first," as if his life depended on it—being the younger brother of Stewart and Myron, this was to be expected. If Willie couldn't whip you heads-up, he would beat you with a stick, tire iron, or even a hard cast. Willie broke his right hand in a neighborhood tackle football game and his hand was placed in a rock-solid hard cast. Armed with his new "weapon," he went to a dance where he sneaked up on dudes he had a grudges against and *wham*, cold-cocked the suckers with a hard cast blow to the head. Through Myron's connections, Willie always had a stash of weed and the latest drugs on the street. Tad copped his first nickel bag from Willie which, after sifting out all the excess stems and seeds, had just enough of the product to roll only three joints—Dirty Willie!

Yosh was a FOB buddhahead (fresh off the boat). He was nine when his family left Japan and ended up on the Avenues on the Westside. Immediately, he was picked-on at school due to his FOB accent and lame clothes. Normally, it took a concentrated effort to understand what Yosh was saying but when he became excited and rambled, it was next to impossible to understand him. Tad and his partners took a liking to him because he stood up for himself and wouldn't take shit from anyone. In reality, it was like misfits gravitating toward each other. Yosh was a misfit and after he was jumped in by the Little Gents, it became his lifetime ambition to be a gangster. He developed an exaggerated gangster pimp swagger, talked out of the corner of his mouth, wore exclusively black clothing: black shirt and slacks, pointed black French-toed, side-zippered half-boot, and a black hip-length trenchcoat. Some even said that Yosh had a black belt in karate. He never said anything to either confirm or deny the rumor. One morning, when Tad and Yosh were in front of Dorsey smoking a morning cigarette before reporting to homeroom, their partner Greg rolled up in a red Corvette convertible that he hot-wired the previous night from a parking lot in Inglewood. Tad and Yosh squeezed inside the car and they decided to head out to the beach. First, they made a liquor store stop and got a wino standing in the front of the liquor store to buy them three quarts of Colt 45 and threw him out with enough change to buy himself a short dog. Next, they drove to Dockweiler Beach in Playa del Rey. Everything was cool, the sun was shining, the beach was vacant and drinking Colt 45 on an empty stomach provided a mellow buzz. When nature called, they headed to the public restroom. The trio walked by a group of white surfer-looking boys, one of whom was with a white chick. As they passed, Yosh looked over at the white chick and said with a FOB accent "Baby, you shor lookin' fine." Tad merely shook his head and mumbled under his breath, "Fuckin' Yosh." They stepped into the bathroom, each occupying a urinal to whiz. Before finishing their business, the group of white boys, along with the white broad, entered the bathroom; two of them blocked off the entrance. Slowly, Yosh, Tad and Greg turned around and faced the white boys—not counting the chick, there were seven of them. The one with the white chick said, "You need to apologize to my girlfriend for disrespecting her." Being away from the Westside, outnumbered, and knowing that Yosh was not going to apologize for shit, Tad knew that the doo-doo was about to hit the fan. In an excited Japanese accent, Yosh blurted out, "Fock yu!" and he immediately broke into a karate stance. Greg, standing between Tad and Yosh, assumed the same karate stance. Tad knew for a fact that Greg didn't know karate. Tad thought, "Fuck it" and did his best to imitate them. He bent his knees, squatted down into a horse stance, cocked his right fist next to his right hip, bent his left elbow and extended out his left hand around chin high as a protective guard. When the white boys did not immediately rush them and got quiet, Tad sensed that they were scared. Finally the white boy said, "Man, just say you're sorry, and we'll let you pass." Yosh shot back, "Fock yu! Modhafocka!" Greg and Tad correctly interpreted Yosh's response and said in belligerent voices, "Fuck you!" The trio in their karate stances remained locked and loaded. The two cats blocking the entryway were the first to exit the public shitter which took away any resolve left in the group, and they slowly filed out the restroom. The Ministers followed the humiliated group outside and watched them walk to the parking lot, leaving the beach. Yosh, with his Westside-Japanese accent, "wolfed" on them non-stop until they were out of hearing range, calling them all kinds of ponks, beetches, puusies, and modhafockas, in his FOB Westside gangster accent. Karate that, motherfuckers!

YOGORE

BEFORE THE CONCENTRATION CAMP EVACUATION, the Issei that migrated to Southern California settled in different geographic areas in Los Angeles County. Generally, the location where an Issei settled was determined by his upbringing and in some instances, past ties going back to Japan.

Issei with fishing backgrounds gravitated to Terminal Island in east San Pedro. Many of the Terminal Islanders' roots could be traced back to the Japanese coastal fishing villages of Wakayama and Fujioka. San Fernando and Imperial Valley attracted Issei seeking agricultural-related work. "Little Tokyo," on the outskirts of downtown Los Angeles, was a magnet for Issei with entrepreneurial aspirations and those preferring service-related work in an urban setting. In each community, a shared community outlook, value system, and in some locales, a distinct dialect evolved.

When the entire Japanese West Coast population was involuntarily uprooted from their respective communities and commingled in American concentration camps, they were not a homogeneous population despite having common Japanese heritage. Through observing mannerisms and listening to manner of speech, internees could often distinguish from which pre-war community another person originated.

It didn't take long for the internees at Manzanar to take notice of the rugged mannerisms and distinct gruff dialect exhibited by the Terminal Islanders. Those outside their inner circle viewed them as cliquish, unpolished, cocky and tough. The Terminal Islanders had a *yogore* reputation amongst the other internees. *Yogore* was a term used to describe a person that was "rough around the edges."

At the close of the war, the JAs needed to find new areas in which to settle. The Nisei found pockets of safe haven in the Crenshaw and Boyle Heights areas, known as the "Westside" and the "Eastside." What distinguished the Westside from the Eastside was that the Westside had a strong Colored influence, while the Eastside was predominately populated by Mexicans and Central Americans and the remnants of a Jewish population slowly moving or dying away.

By the late 1950s and early 1960s, the term *yogore* took on a new meaning. Being labeled *yogore* now meant that one was a lowly hoodlum type of person that other Sansei kids should not bring home or associate with. The Nisei applied this term to the young rebellious Sansei who dressed, walked, talked, and acted differently from the "good kids."

For the rebellious JA youth, whatever label the Nisei chose to call them did not matter—they had never solicited Nisei approval from the get-go. Many even viewed the *yogore* label as a badge of honor, a term distinguishing them from the lames and squares. Their priority was establishing a reputation of having "heart." To do so, one had to prove himself not only amongst his peers, but also with the older thugs in the neighborhood. For a young dude striving to become a part an "elite" group, he had to accept traditions passed on by the OGs as undisputed truths. On both the Westside and Eastside, all aspiring "yogores" were indoctrinated with the belief that yogores from the other side of town were enemies.

What started the Eastside-Westside rivalry is unclear—interpretations varied depending on who was telling the story. But as long as Tad could recall, Eastside and Westside buddhaheads never got along—this was a fact of life. Growing up on the Avenues, Tad and his partners had minimal contact and run-ins with cats from the Eastside, but that all changed once they entered high school. High school meant knowing cats with wheels and having the mobility to check out house parties, dances, summertime church and temple carnivals, throughout the city. These discoveries were not isolated to the Westside JAs, it was simultaneously occurring in JA communities on the Eastside and Gardena. When the yogores from different parts of the city ended up at the same house party or dance, the end result usually was an Eastside-Westside fight, or gang throw-down fueled by preconceived misconceptions about each other, combined with false rumors, liquor, drugs, high testosterone, and a few agitators thrown into the mix.

The Ministers' beefs with the Eastside started with petty shit, like giving or receiving the stink eye, accidentally or purposely stepping on someone's shoes, hitting on a chick who happened to be a younger sister of a member of the rival set, or worse, making a play on a rival's ole lady. At first, these types of slights were handled as personal matters and were either shined-on, verbally resolved, or settled by one-on-one throw downs. Soon, over zealous dudes from either side started jumping into the mix causing the Eastside-Westside feud to escalate to another level. Eventually, it reached the stage where a weekend event without having a Eastside-Westside confrontation was a rare occurrence.

The Ministers viewed their confrontations with the Eastside as merely carrying on a long-standing tradition like a Hatfield-McCoy feud which one was born into, and was an accepted way of life. A few of the more aggressive members of the Ministers actually looked forward to and thrived on the chaos. Cats like Tad, accepted the confrontations as something that had to be dealt with in order to party and have fun. Every Saturday night one JA youth group or another hosted a dance, usually at one of the popular venues such as the Roger Young Auditorium, Aeronautical Institute and Parkview Women's Club on the Westside. Featured Sansei and Latino bands as Carry On, Somethin' Else, and Thee Midniters, played fast dance tunes and slow-dance grinding music. An open bar rarely, if ever, checked for ID. The chicks wore short hemlined, stylish dresses. Ratted up hair and heavy makeup was the style of the day. They were looking fine, and the stone foxes already knew it. The dudes were decked out in suits, slacks, sports coats, creased shirts with narrow ties. Stylish cats topped off their rags with stingy brims. There were so many chicks, so many dudes, and so little time to waste. There was a different dance or house party to check out every weekend.

In the early summer, before Tad's 11th grade-year, an incident occurred that changed the nature of the Eastside-Westside feud. A Sansei girls social club, called the Jeanues, hosted a house party. Other than the Jeanues being the self-proclaimed foxes of the Westside, it was just going to be a typical house party. Tad and his partners passed on checking it out—from past experience they knew that the club's older advisors would be there to chaperone, watching over their flock like mother hens, making sure that no hanky-panky happened and that the gig stayed lame. Willie was the only Minister who went.

What should have been just another Saturday night on the Westside ended in a scene with the LAPD in attendance, and a county ambulance rushing Willie to ER. Those who attended the party were in shock. Describing what went down, they said it happened real quick. Three carloads of Eastside yogores crashed the party, apparently looking for Willie who put a big hurt on an Eastside cat at a dance a few weeks prior. They bogarted their way inside the house and found Willie rapping to a mamma in the kitchen. Since the party was held deep in the heart of the Westside, Willie was caught completely off guard and cornered by the Eastside. This type of predicament usually resulted in a righteous stomping with fists and shod feet. Instead, two of the bigger dudes grabbed Willie and wrestled him to the ground where another cat pulled out a knife and stabbed Willie in the chest. Willie went limp and the intruders split the scene, leaving Willie on the kitchen floor, lying in a pool of his own blood. By the time the Ministers heard about what happened to their partner, Willie was en route to County General Hospital. It turned out that the knife missed puncturing Willie's lung by an inch—Willie survived and after a brief recovery, he was back on the set, acting as crazy as ever.

After Willie's stabbing, both sides became more guarded and vigilant. What started as youthful exuberance and bravado had escalated into deep feelings of mistrust, paranoia, and hatred. Afterwards, to be on the safe side, whenever the Ministers went to a dance or party they brought along "protection"—switchblades, brass knuckles, lead pipes and tire irons. Every so often, someone would get caught napping without backing and take a righteous ass-whipping. The beatings went back and forth, resulting in missing teeth, busted eye sockets, broken noses, busted lips, sutures, and concussions, with one side momentarily boasting of having the upper hand, only until the other side rendered a payback.

One Saturday night, towards the end of the long, hot summer, Tad ran into Willie at Holiday Bowl. Willie devoted a lot of his time selling weed during his recovery and apparently business was good because he had just bought a used Volkswagen bug. Willie asked Tad if he wanted to go for a ride, Tad obliged, and they took off. Willie didn't say where they were going, but when Willie shot up Crenshaw Boulevard, hopped on the Santa Monica Freeway heading east, Tad figured that Crazy Willie had something on his mind. When Willie took the Adams Boulevard exit, Tad knew that Willie was going to the Roger Young Auditorium, where a dance was being held. Willie parked in the Roger Young lot, then told Tad that he was going to fuck up the cat up who shanked him, and opened his glove compartment which looked like it contained a bunch of metallic kitchen knives. Willie grabbed the one with the longest blade and concealed it under his clothing. Asked whether he wanted to go inside with him or wait in the car, the only thing that came to Tad's mind was to ask Willie where all the knives came from. Willie explained that the dude who sold him the car gave him the knives for a bag of weed. Satisfied with Willie's explanation, Tad picked out the second-longest blade and they both exited the car. Ignoring the girls at the reception table, they walked right past and entered the large, dimly-lit auditorium. Once inside, Willie spotted his adversary and made a beeline towards his target. Tad almost had to sprint to keep up with Crazy Willie. The unsuspecting dude was casually conversing in a small group and before he knew it, Willie was right up on him, directing his knife blade in a downward motion right at his chest. Everyone, including Tad, froze while they watched the knife make contact with the victim's suit jacket. Instead of witnessing the expected, they saw the metallic knife bend sideways upon impact. While it surely hurt its intended victim, it did not cut through the clothing and penetrate his skin. The dude, just having seen his life slip away, did not move, nor did his partners. Willie had given it his best shot—he and Tad sprinted back to the car and took off before the enemy could regroup. On the way back to Holiday Bowl, all Crazy Willie talked about was how he going to beat the mothafucka's ass for selling him those cheap-ass knives.

For the first time in his young life, Tad looked forward to a new school semester to begin. Returning to school meant the start of a new football season—the real reason for his enthusiasm. It was time for the Dorsey B squad to defend its Southern League title. During the football season, the daily after-school practices and Friday games dominated Tad's life. Once again, Tad and Ronald Booker were the mainstays of the team and voted co-captains by their teammates. During the football season, Tad even took his academics a bit more seriously because he was aware that he had to maintain at least a "C" average to remain academically eligible to play on the team.

Dorsey was a special place where instead of just tolerating and co-existing with one another, the bloods and the buddhaheads were tight. This was not surprising because most of them grew up together in the same neighborhoods and they judged one another by their actions rather than their skin complexion.

On the home front, older brother, Shoji, was starting his sophomore year at UCLA. He worked over the summer and saved up enough money to move out with two other roommates to live closer to the UCLA campus. He continued to make his parents proud. Sister Akemi was attending Mount Vernon and was a "good girl," popular with her classmates and excelling academically. Renbo, to his Pop and Mom's dismay, was beginning to worry his parents because his elementary school teachers would comment that he wasn't a bad kid, but he lacked focus in the classroom. Tad's folks had resigned themselves to accept that Tad lacked motivation, discipline, and had to learn life's lessons the hard way with little they could do to change him, but they certainly didn't expect another son to follow in his footsteps.

Just as he anticipated, the Dorsey High "B" football squad not only repeated as Southern League champs, but went undefeated. For the second straight year, Tad and Ronald Booker were unanimously voted to the all-conference team by the Southern League coaches. Tad and Ronald were on track to fulfilling their pact, that next year—their senior year—they were both going to be the starting cornerbacks for the Dorsey High varsity. Tad was righteously enjoying himself, playing ball, partying, and hanging out on the weekends with his Minister partners. Another significant development that leap-frogged to the top of Tad's priority list was Nancy. Nancy Domoto was a grade below Tad, and he noticed her the moment she arrived at Dorsey. Nancy lived in a different part of the Westside, an area that fed into Audubon Junior High. She was a stone fox, had a petite, shapely figure with nice long legs, big eyes and a cute, sexy smile. Nancy possessed a natural aura of freshness—even without caked-on makeup and eye shadow, she still looked fine. Tad invested a lot of time and energy scheming on how they were going to get together. It paid off and by the end of 11th grade, he and Nancy were going around together. Tad looked forward to the upcoming summer, spending time with Nancy, and hanging out with his partners. Life was good.

During this time, Tad was so much into doing his own thing that he failed to notice changes taking place in the neighborhood. For starters, a new generation of yogores arrived on the scene, both in the Eastside and Westside. The wannabe gangsters had already started their own gang, calling themselves, the Ministers II. They emulated the OGs, extorting lames out of their money, hot-wiring and stealing cars, and waging battle against the Eastside. A major difference between the younger dudes and the OGs was that the young dudes loved to get high. The more stoned they got, the braver and more belligerent they became. They dropped all types of downers (barbiturates), red devil F-40s, yellow jackets, tuinals, pink ladies; they sniffed glue and drank cheap wine. When they were finally fucked up and half way out of their minds, they stumbled out on the streets and terrorized. When the older Ministers saw the Ministers II stumbling about the neighborhood with bloodshot, glassy eyes, slurred speech, and unkempt attire, they took them aside to talk to them. The OGs quickly saw the Jekyll-and-Hyde dichotomy effects that drugs had on a person. When the young dudes were straight, they were respectful and at least gave a pretense that they were listening to their counsel; however, when they would see them fucked-up, high as kites, the slurred words coming out of their mouths were, "Fuck this" and "Fuck that." As high as these dudes were, they weren't insane enough to say "Fuck you" to the OGs. Eventually the Ministers decided that these knuckleheads were too hardheaded to take their advice and were going to do their own thing. They learned to never try to reason with a loaded person—it doesn't work. Regardless, the OGs were still protective of the Ministers II. Tad christened them the "Revells" after a brand name on a glue tube.

With the Ministers II arriving on the Westside scene, a new yogore gang on the Eastside gathered momentum. They called themselves the Buddha Bandits and had the backing of the Aliso Village *Eses*. The Buddha Bandits even managed to recruit a few strays from the Westside, into their ranks. A primary concern regarding the arrival of the new generation of yogores was their cold-blooded mentality. They settled beefs with guns. Earning a reputation by showing heart and throwing down from the shoulders was replaced by getting high and popping caps while in a drug-induced stupor. Many of the new breed of yogores would not hesitate to bust a cap on your ass if they felt they were disrespected.

Even though Tad knew that there would be slights and fights between the Ministers and the Eastside, he was determined to not allow the bullshit to ruin his summer. Yet an incident at the beginning of summer spoiled his plans. It happened on a night when Tad and Yosh drove to Gardena to check out a house party. At the party, they stood outside rapping to a couple of Gardena chicks when a car pulled up and parked across the street. Tad looked across the street and recognized three Buddha Bandits who were now standing by the trunk of the car. Tad was confident that they wouldn't fuck with Yoshio and him because he thought that they knew better. Besides, he and Yosh were there to enjoy themselves, and as long as no one fucked with them, everything would be cool. After that momentary pause, Tad returned to his conversation when next he heard someone shout, "Buddha Bandits!" He looked across the street and heard loud, sharp, capping sounds, *pow, pow, pow, pow*. In an instant, he and Yoshio dove behind the manicured bushes in the landscaped front yard. He heard a two more shots fired and saw clumps of grass around him fly into the air. Finally, he heard car doors slam and the sound of screeching tires. He and Yoshio dusted themselves off and headed back to the Westside.

They drove straight to Holiday Bowl to regroup and sort out the shit. Even though Tad and Yoshio could identify their ambushers, they knew very little about them. At Holiday, they ran into Dave Sogi and told him what had just gone down. Dave was a permanent fixture at Holiday—he knew just about everybody and everything that went down on the Westside and what Dave didn't know, was probably irrelevant from the git-go. Dave listened as Tad and Yoshio gave a description of their attackers, and told them that the two cats they described were Eiji Takata and Steve Iwaki. He wasn't sure where Steve lived, but said that Eiji was an FOB that lived nearby on Victoria Road. Tad went to the pay phone booth and looked up and found a number for a Takata listed on Victoria. He dialed the phone number and after a few rings it was answered:

"Hello."

"Put Eiji on the phone!"

(Pause) Tad heard whispering in the background.

"Eiji no here."

"I can hear him, put him on the phone!"

"Eiji, no home."

Tad was pissed and yelled, "Tell your son he's dead!" as he slammed down the receiver.

The three drove to Yoshio's house where Tad and Dave waited in the car while Yoshio went inside. Within minutes, Yoshio returned to the car carrying a 12-gauge shotgun that he "borrowed" from his father's closet. He hopped back into the car, handed Tad the shotgun and pulled out a box of shotgun shells. As Yoshio drove, Tad loaded both chambers. They drove westbound on Coliseum Street, hung a left on Victoria and stopped in front of the address belonging to Eiji's house. Armed with the 12-gauge, Tad stepped out of the car while Yosh kept the engine running and Dave remained in the back seat. All of the lights in Eiji's house were turned off and Tad had no idea which room belonged to Eiji so he decided to blast out the largest two windows in the front of the house. *Blaam*! Glass shattered, neighborhood dogs started barking, and the shotguns recoil nearly threw Tad off balance. Again, Tad took aim, *blaam*! He looked over at Yoshio and told him to toss him the ammo box but Yoshio yelled, "Get in car, let's split!"

Late afternoon, the following day, Tad and Yoshio were kicking it at Holiday Bowl, when they spotted Eiji walking through the front entrance. Tad immediately stood up and dug into his pants pocket and gripped the switchblade he now carried everywhere he went. They waited as Eiji walked towards them. Eiji stopped and faced them from about the same distance where he stood last night when the Bandits shot at them. Eiji lifted up both hands and showed them his empty palms. He slowly walked closer, still showing his empty palms, stopped and quietly said, "I'm out." He stood there waiting for a response. Tad looked at him and saw resignation on his face. Yoshio didn't say anything but nodded in his direction. Eiji then put his handsdown, turned around, and headed back towards the door. Tad looked over at Yoshio and said, "Let's find out where Steve lives."

During the long, hot summer months, tensions mounted as fights between the Eastside and Westside escalated. It was not surprising to witness that the Japanese American community chose to ignore this problem. Their denial of gangs, violence, and drugs in their community denied the existence of an alarming number of rebellious Sansei youth. No Nisei leadership group or individual reached out to intervene. As far as the Nisei were concerned, these youth were nothing more than no-good yogores casting shame on the JA community, and not their problem.

The Nisei were too busy directing their efforts in showcasing and promoting the academic achievements of the top Sansei students. Another major event that promoted the Japanese American community in the most favorable light to *hakujin* outsiders was the annual summer Nisei Week Japanese Festival. This event took place in downtown Little Tokyo—a weeklong festival of cultural exhibits, displays and demonstrations that included tea ceremonies, calligraphy, *bonsai, ikebana* (flower arrangements), Japanese cooking, karate, and judo. The highlight of Nisei Week was the weekend carnival followed by the Sunday parade.

The Nisei Week carnival was a magnet for JA youth of all ages and all areas. The carnival offered rides, food and game booths. Pitching a dime on an elevated tilted glass plate gave older youths an opportunity to win stuffed animals for a main squeeze. Toddlers won small prizes and live goldfish in plastic bags filled with water. For the yogores, the Nisei Week carnival was an opportunity to step out in public, daring someone or some group to fuck with them. In the past, when trouble jumped off at the carnival, the situation would immediately be squashed by vigilant hired security, and beefs were settled outside the carnival. This summer, the word on the street was that cats were coming to the carnival, packing heat. Just in case these rumors turned out to be true, the Ministers packed their hardware, and kept it in the trunks of their cars.

The Ministers—over twenty-strong—caravanned to the Nisei Week carnival. After arriving, the Ministers enjoyed themselves, congregating at the dime pitch booth where many of them either brought or met their ole ladies at the carnival. Just as they felt at ease, the Eastside showed up with over thirty members, including a few partners from Aliso Village. They set up camp next to the kiddie ring toss, directly across and facing the Ministers. Within their contingent was an *Ese* dude named Richard; he was stocky, muscular, and scary to look at. Richard had the reputation of being more than capable to throw down from the shoulders.

Gary, who was with his ole lady, was a smaller version of Richard, and as the two stood across from each other, surer than shit, they began to mad-dog each other. Before anyone could avert the inevitable, Gary bolted towards Richard and all hell broke loose. They locked in like two pit bulls, trading blows, toe-to-toe, with everyone from each side jumping in, swinging, kicking, stomping. Chicks from the Eastside yelled out, "Go get the guns!" Someone else shouted, "The cops are coming!" Richard and Gary were just getting started and they had to be pulled apart, clothes torn; each was bleeding with neither satisfied with the outcome. Everyone sprinted in different directions to their cars, the Westside shouting out, "Meet us at Holiday Bowl!" and the Eastside yelling, "Bring it to Shatto!"

The Ministers were livid. Word spread that the bullshit was going to be settled once and for all, Saturday at Shatto. The following weekend, close to a hundred Ministers and Westside associates met at the back parking lot at Holiday Bowl and caravanned to Shatto Park, located on 4th Street and Vermont. Next to the park was Shatto Bowl. They went inside and took over Shatto Bowl, waiting for the Eastside to show. Everyone wore red *hachimaki* (head cloths), because they knew it would get crazy once the shit hit the fan and the headbands helped to identify those on your side. Everyone was aware of the likelihood that tonight's beef with the Eastside would probably be settled by bullets rather than with fists.

The adrenalin rush became palpable when a lookout came running into the bowling alley shouting, "They're here!" Everyone rushed to the exits and scurried to the park's open tennis court area. From the corner of 4th and Vermont, Eastside opened fire, the sound of gunshots and the sight of hot flames coming from gun barrels filled the air. The Ministers saw bullets hitting the ground around them. They ran to nearby trees for cover and returned fire. What probably lasted less than two minutes felt like an eternity as they emptied their chambers. Before reloading, chaos took over with people from each side yelling and running in all directions. The Ministers ran to their cars parked next to the tennis court area and retreated back to the Westside.

Tad was awakened the next morning by a phone call from Richard Uyemura who asked excitedly if the police had been over to his house to talk to him. Tad didn't know what he was talking about until Richard explained that early that morning, LAPD detectives had come to pick him up along with Gary, Willie, Mas, Greg, James, Lawrence, Danny, and Dave, and take them to the Wilshire Division station. By the time he and Gary arrived everyone else was already there. Since they had all been arrested separately and placed in different interrogation rooms, the Ministers didn't have a chance to talk it over and get their story straight. Richard said that someone snitched because before he was even asked any questions, the detective already knew who was at Shatto, who drove what car, and who the shooters were. The detective even mentioned Tad's name and asked him for his address, but Richard had replied that he didn't know anyone named Tad. He concluded by saying that after questioning, everyone except Gary, Mas, Lawrence, and Greg were released from the station.

It turned out that two people from the Eastside were shot, but no one was killed. In the aftermath of the shootout, Mas was sent to adult state prison as he was over the age of eighteen. Lawrence and Greg, who were still legally considered minors at the time were sent to camp. Within weeks of the shootout Victor, Art, and Davey enlisted in the Air Force. The Shatto Park shootout marked the breakup of the original Ministers. The torch was handed to the Minister II druggies to uphold the honor of the Westside.

For Tad, things were not the same. With many of his partners incarcerated, in the service, or laying low, his youthful exuberance of living for the moment and the thrill of "whatever happens, happens" diminished. At the start of his senior year, he felt lost and alienated from his classmates. He totally lost focus and at the five-week progress report, he was declared academically ineligible to play sports and was dropped from the varsity football team. Without sports he started skipping class and regularly ditched school. Tad got high everyday, and his "fuck it" attitude worsened, and finally he broke up with Nancy. By the winter break Tad was expelled from school for getting into a fight and cussing out a teacher.

As Tad continued to stagger home in a loaded stupor, his folks were no longer able to communicate with him and became concerned about his negative influence over their youngest son, Renbo. Renbo had just entered Mount Vernon and was at an impressionable age. They worried because they sensed that Renbo looked up to Tad more than to Shoji, the eldest brother. Tad was given an ultimatum—straighten up by either getting a full time job or enroll at another school and graduate. Faced with these choices, Tad chose option number three: he left home.

BUSTED

August 5, 1967
Los Angeles, California

BY MID-MORNING, it was already too hot, smoggy, and muggy to move about. Tad was crashed out on an old tattered couch that doubled as his bed, dead to the world. His mind and body was on total shutdown, wasted from last night's drug binge. Even in a comatose state, he was not immune from the day's summer heat wave, as evidenced by his moist, sticky body.

Suddenly, at 11:00 a.m., George Ozaki, his roommate, woke him up. "Tad, get da fuck up, time to make some money!" Being a heavy sleeper, Tad ignored George's wake-up call. He turned his body to face the opposite direction and was now stretched out facing the back cushion. Undeterred, George stepped over to the front window of their upstairs one bedroom apartment and with a quick arcing swipe of his right hand, yanked off a thick wool army blanket that was draped over a curtain rod. The thick blanket served as a buffer, keeping their apartment in a darkened state day and night, and helping to separate them from the outside world.

Instantly, the bright sunlight trespassed and exploded into the apartment's cramped and cluttered front room. Tad could not handle the sudden brightness of the sun's rays. It felt like laser beams were penetrating his skull, as if someone placed his brain inside a vise and was tightening its grip. He contorted his face, tightly squeezed his eyelids, and cupped his face with both hands.

Keeping his eyes shut for as long as possible, Tad tried to orient himself to time and place. It felt like an out-of-body experience when he heard raspy involuntary words escaping from his stale, cotton mouth, "Shit, what da fuck, what's wrong wid you?" George ignored Tad's morning greeting and walked over to the portable record player, where he placed a stack of vinyl .45 discs on the turnstile, then pushed the "play" knob.

To the rhythm of "Baby Love," Tad ever so slowly regained consciousness. He pulled himself up into a sitting position and began to pry open his eyes. Still groggy, but now semi-awake, he rubbed his eyes a half-dozen times while scoping out his immediate surroundings. Sprawling out before him was the dump they called their "pad." Along with a tattered couch, the other furnishings and appliances in the front room were comprised of a bent frame aluminum folding chair, two milk crates overturned and stacked to use for a table, a miniature TV with an 8" screen, a portable record player and a hot plate to warm up water for instant coffee. They inherited the couch, folding chair, and milk crates from the previous tenants who left those items behind when they skipped out without paying their rent. The TV and portable record player were "hot." A threadbare, faded green carpet and dirty yellowish walls completed the pad's interior décor. Scattered between the sparse furnishings were empty Colt .45 malt liquor cans, 40-ounce bottles, paper food wrappings, Silver Satin and Ripple Red short dog bottles, overflowing ash trays, greasy soiled brown paper shopping bags filled with empty fast food takeout containers, plastic plates, and stale uneaten food. A growing pile of Tad's pants, shirts, socks, t-shirts, and drawers, was in a corner of the front room. The pad's funky odor was a mixture of tobacco, perspiration, dirty laundry, stale food, and desperation. Thoughts of "What the fuck am I doing here," or "How did I get here?" never entered Tad's mind—as far as he was concerned, he was at "home." Tad's stomach felt cramped, and the inside of his head ached, but he focused his attention on his most immediate needs: a cigarette and a cup of java.

The .45 turntable was scratching out its fifth song of the morning, the beat of Baby Washington's "That's How Heartaches are Made," when the cobwebs in his head began clearing up, his vision becoming more focused, and his body responding to the scratchy rhythm sounds, playing on the portable record player. "Yo, George, got a square?" George was sitting on the metal chair, his undivided attention locked onto the eight-inch TV screen that sat on the carpeted floor. George was zoned out and useless in addressing Tad's cravings. Ever so slowly, Tad got up, moving about, hoping to find a pack of Pall Malls. He recently switched over to Pall Malls because it was non-filtered and longer in length compared to any other cigarette brands, so the smoke tasted stronger and the cigarette lasted longer. Shit like this had become important to Tad's day-to-day existence. Tad mumbled aloud to himself, "Yeah," as he found an opened pack of Pall Malls in the pocket of a shirt laying atop his pile of clothes. He went back to the couch, sat down, fired up, and sucked in a deep drag of smoke. As he inhaled the hot tasting smoke, his lungs let out an involuntary deep, "Ughuuhg, uuugh." That first drag in the morning was always a killer. With his free hand, he reached out and grabbed a jar of Yuban instant coffee off of the milk crate. The jar was empty, "Fuck!"

George looked at Tad. Satisfied that he was awake, he shook his head in disgust, rose from his chair, and headed back toward his bedroom, which was even smaller and more cluttered than the "living" room.

Tad hooked up with George Ozaki about four months ago through a mutual acquaintance. However, even before Tad was formally introduced to George, he already knew who he was. Around six years ago, every yogore and thug in the neighborhood had heard about George Ozaki. In the late 50s, at an annual Nisei Week Parade, George shot and killed a person he mistook as a rival Westside gang member. Within the Japanese American community, this incident was so incomprehensible and so "out there" that the community as a whole, chose to "shine it on," ignoring it as if this tragedy had never taken place. As far as the JA community was concerned, it was an aberration that law enforcement was responsible to deal with. On the streets, Tad and his partners congregated and rapped about what went down at Nisei Week. They came to the only logical conclusion that made any sense to them, "George Ozaki is a crazy mothafucka!" For his misdeed, the court sentenced George to a California state penitentiary. At the time, Tad was getting ready to attend Mount Vernon Junior High.

Seven years later, George made parole and was released from the joint. George made a half-assed effort to rehabilitate. He found a warehouse gig and slowly reconnected with his old neighborhood partners in crime. It didn't take him long to realize that after seven years, he and his partners now had very little in common except for shared battles and escapades in the past. Many of them had married, were holding jobs, making mortgage payments, and some had kids—a few were even back in school. While they were all genuinely glad to see George, and were truly happy that he was released, the truth was that they had moved on with their lives and now had very little time, if any, to hang out with George. The few that had all day long to hang out and reminiscence with George about the "good ole days" had very little to offer him, except for hard drugs. It wasn't long before George found himself out of work, without an income, in violation of his parole, and mainlining heroin.

By the time Tad hooked up with George Ozaki, they were both idling on empty. For the previous six months, Tad existed day-to-day, meal-to-meal, and at night he crashed at the pad of different partners and acquaintances until his welcome wore thin and he was asked to move on. Tad managed to find and hold down a job at a small neighborhood liquor store. Although the gig paid less than minimum wage, he didn't complain because he needed the cash and they paid him under the table so taxes were not deducted. The gig was easy but at the same time, monotonous and a dead end.

James Miyo, whom Tad happened to be staying with at the time, introduced him to George Ozaki. On the day he met George, Tad and James Miyo were kicking back at Holiday Bowl. They occupied the swivel chairs facing the bowling lanes, watching nothing in particular. They were both high as kites, wasted on F-40 barbiturates—downers called "reds" or "red devils" because its deadly, potent, white powder was contained in a digestible red capsule. They were enjoying their buzz when from a distance, they noticed a dude entering Holiday through the electronic Plexiglass rear door which let out to the parking lot. Looking toward the back entrance from where they sat, the combination of the backdrop of the sun's glare and their barbiturate-induced blurred vision prevented them from seeing anything but a silhouette, power-walking towards them.

It was neither advisable or intelligent for an outsider to come pimping into Holiday Bowl, trying to impress and be "baaad." The few who tried were too loaded to know better or were straight-up stupid. Neither reason was a valid excuse. Westside yogores took intrusions into their territory as a personal affront which usually ended in a beat-down if the intruder was lucky; or if unlucky, a trip to ER. In any event, Tad and James needed to check out this dude.

"Mister Cool" continued to pimp down Holiday's carpeted aisle that led to its coffee shop. To reach it, he had to walk directly past Tad and James, which would give them the opportunity to size him up and figure out how to deal with him. As he drew closer to where they sat, he slowed his gait, and when even with them, stopped to make eye contact. This cat was no longer a silhouette—he was on the short side, had a medium build, thick shoulders, and buffed guns. From top to bottom, his hair was dark and slightly wavy, cut semi-short but just long enough to maintain a front. His tight-fitting black nylon wife-beater undershirt was tucked inside sharply-creased khaki pants. Over his black tank top, he wore a brown plaid Sir Guy short sleeve shirt. On the inside of his left bicep was a jailhouse-looking dragon tattoo. His kicks were half-length black boots, French-toed with a side zipper. Judging from his appearance, this cat was definitely from the "Eastside."

His facial features were more angular than round or flat, his complexion somewhat ruddy and dark, all accented by a thick, dark mustache. He had OG written all over him and emanated an aura of confidence. His dark, piercing eyes were his most mesmerizing facial feature. Unlike the brown eyes that most buddhaheads have, this cat's pupils were a deep, dark brown, damn near black. As the eye contact continued, Tad and James simultaneously stood up—they were now face-to-face with their adversary. Tad knew that the shit was on! Just as he was about to blurt out, "What the fuck you looking at, punk!" then rush him, the dude looked directly at James and said, "Ain't you Kenny's brother?"

Back in the day, James' older brother, Kenny, ran the streets with George Ozaki. Being Kenny's brother, gave James street credibility. After George identified himself, the tense situation was diffused and James then introduced Tad to George. Tad realized that the dude that they were about to challenge was "George Ozaki, the crazy mothafucka." Tad remembered as a kid, seeing George Ozaki at the Crenshaw Square and Nisei Week carnivals. The image in the back of his mind was of a dude a whole lot bigger than the George Ozaki now standing before him. But Tad already knew that the smaller dudes were usually the gamest, acted the craziest, and started the most shit, almost as if they had something to prove, and generally they did an outstanding job of proving it. Tad felt relieved knowing that he and James didn't have to defend the honor of the Westside by throwing down against George Ozaki. With that settled, Tad sat back down in the swivel chair and quietly listened as George and James continued their conversation. James ran down how his brother Kenny got popped on a drug sales beef and was now locked down at the County and had been fighting his case for the past four months. George didn't even flinch, his response being, "That's a bitch." George related how he was paroled from Folsom three months ago, how he tried to go straight, but the square life wasn't for him and he was now in violation of his parole. George continued, saying to no one in particular, "I don't ever want to go back to the joint, but I got to admit, there are moments when it feels like it was easier being in, than on the outs." Tad couldn't help but glance over at George, who momentarily lost his look of confidence. George's comment either flew over James' head, or maybe he just didn't give a shit because all James replied was, "Yeah, it's a bitch." Not knowing George well enough to say anything, Tad felt that it wasn't his place to say shit. George reached into his shirt pocket, pulled out a pack of Kools, flipped open his Zippo and lit up a cigarette. Between drags, he asked them, "Anyone holding?" When James was unresponsive, Tad refocused his attention on George where any prior look of doubt or uncertainty was gone—and his dark, confident, piercing look had returned. Tad said, "Yeah, I got some RDs." George said that he was short on cash but he would appreciate it if he could hold a roll and that he would straighten Tad out later. Tad dipped into his pants pocket and with a closed fist, pulled out a tin foil bindle of reds and cupped it over to George's open palm where in a single motion, he instantly transferred the bindle into his own pants pocket. Tad said, "No sweat, consider it a welcome home gift." George thanked him, then asked him again for his name; they all exchanged hand shakes. Before leaving, George asked Tad if he knew where he could score some "horse." Tad replied that he wasn't into that, but word had it that Togo was dealing and that he stayed over on 39th and Degnan. Upon that, George turned around and headed back toward the rear parking lot door.

Tad next saw George two weeks later, again at Holiday Bowl. This time Tad was by himself; George remembered him and they started rapping. George seemed to be a lot mellower than the first time they met. His speech pattern was slow and deliberate, his dark shades concealed his eyes, but because the lighting at Holiday was always dim, it was a dead giveaway that George was fucked up. George asked him if he had any money. Tad told him not only was he busted, he had gotten fired from his gig two days ago for stumbling into work loaded on reds. He asked where he had worked and Tad replied, "Oaks Liquor over on 5th Avenue." George asked if it was the same liquor store that the Sakamoto family owned, and Tad said it was, but the family sold the store a few years ago, after the riots. Since then, the store had changed ownership a few times and was now owned by two young Korean dudes who were known in the neighborhood as "the ugly brothers." George said in a direct, matter-of-fact way, "Let's go knock it off." Tad didn't think it was a good idea because they knew who he was and besides, they had a piece behind the counter. George asked what kind of gun, and Tad said it was a .38 six-shot revolver. George quickly lifted up his shirt and exposed the butt of a pistol grip sticking out from his waistband asking, "Like this?" Tad replied, "Yeah, just like that."

Tad recommended a safer plan. On weekdays, when the store closed at 11:30, they could park a car behind the store, directly below a refrigeration unit that jutted out from the wall. This unit kept items cold in the store's refrigerated room; but if the unit could be dislodged from the wall, and if someone could make himself small enough to squeeze through the tiny open vent then, bingo! If they made it inside, he knew the location and combination to the safe. The safe would contain start-up money for the following day and the .38 revolver. The downside to the plan was that even if they managed to get inside the store, the safe's combination may have changed since he had just recently been fired. Even if the combination hadn't been changed, it usually contained only fifty dollars in different denominations for making change. George said, "Fuck it, it's better than nothing."

Late that night, they executed Tad's plan. The stars in the universe must have been favorably aligned because everything worked according to plan. The combination to the safe hadn't been changed, and it contained not only the next day's change but also money that should have been deposited in the bank from previous days' profits. "Hot damn! Ugly brothers, be slippin'! Fire me, mothafucka! Shee-it!"

They made off with a case of Hennessy cognac, a swivel display rack holding chips, pork rinds, cookies, and assorted candies, boxes of Slim Jim Beef Jerky, and a few bottles of wine—the type that had to be expensive because they were sealed with a cork as opposed to a twist-off cap, and the fancy French names on the labels couldn't be pronounced. After loading up the trunk of the car, they drove straight to George's pad to settle up. They split the cash and since George already owned a piece, Tad kept the .38 revolver. They celebrated their score by kicking back, drinking cognac and getting high. That night was the first time Tad had ever seen someone mainline heroin. By the time George nodded out on the metal folding chair, Tad was wasted on barbiturates and cognac, compliments of Oaks Liquor. Tad spent the night crashed out on the couch in the front room at George's pad and he has been there ever since.

Tad's planning and organizational skills must have impressed George, because after that night they became a team, partners in crime. Their main boogie was residential burglary. They would canvass and case out different neighborhoods throughout the city, and only when they were confident that they knew a resident would not be at home, would they break in. George needed his daily heroin fixes and Tad was getting strung out on barbiturates. His deepest fear was getting busted and going to jail. He did his best to talk George out of taking unnecessary risks because going to jail was not an option to Tad; he couldn't vision himself as jail material.

By the time Tad finished smoking his second cigarette of the morning, George reentered the front room. He had changed into his gardening, or "G-Man" outfit of weathered work boots, strong-corded work pants, and clean white tee shirt. Due to it being so hot that day, neither George nor Tad wore the long sleeve, khaki gardening shirt. The main difference in appearance between the genuine Nisei gardeners from the "fake-ass" Sansei gardeners was that no respectable Sansei would ever muss up his front by wearing the Nisei gardener's trademark on his head: an African safari-style, metallic gardening helmet. The only lids that touched Tad's head was a stingy brim or a football helmet; nothing else was going to fuck up his front.

Taking George's lead, Tad went over to his pile of clothes and found a pair of grubby grass-stained jeans. Continuing to sort through the pile, he dug up a white tee shirt. He was about to take off the tee shirt he was wearing, when the stale smell on the one he held in his hand made him change his mind. He asked George, "Yo, you got an extra clean tee-shirt?" Taking George's non-response as a "no" he tossed the tee shirt back on the pile and made a mental note to cop some new tee shirts, socks and drawers at JC Penney after their next score.

Tad didn't have any work boots so he wore dirt-stained white Chuck Taylor high tops instead. Before George could complain and tell him to "Hurry the fuck up," Tad made it over to the *benjo*. Once inside, he closed the door, threw some water on his scruffy unshaven face, lowered his head to the faucet tap and took in a long swig of water. Upon raising his head, he tried to ignore the reflection that confronted him from the bathroom mirror. The image that stood checking him out was a sorry-looking dude with bloodshot eyes, oily skin, yellow-coated tongue, and ashen pock-marked complexion. Thinking, "Damn, what the fuck happened to me," he didn't wait to answer his own question but tried to change the image that mad-dogged him. He focused on his mussed up hair—it needed immediate styling. With his hairbrush, comb, hairspray, and blow dryer all within reach, he proceeded to straighten out his front. Tad lost track of how long it was taking, but eventually he was satisfied that his pompadour front was together enough for him to step out in the public. Returning to the front room, he found that George had resumed sitting on the unbalanced metal chair and was staring down at the eight-inch TV screen. Tad returned to the couch and looked over at the tiny TV screen. It tripped him out to see George intently watching a Mighty Mouse cartoon! It tickled him to think that if he told his Avenue partners that "crazy, badass George Ozaki is into Mighty Mouse cartoons" they would have thought he was bullshitting. Tad saw that George was so locked into the toons that he didn't even notice that Tad reentered the room and was ready to split.

Being together with a person 24/7 forces one into familiarity with the other person's idiosyncrasies, moods, likes, dislikes, attitude and temperament. Tad had now been around George long enough to understand his nature and to read his intent. He could tell when George was merely bullshitting or playing around as opposed to being in a deadly serious, "don't fuck with me" mood. When a TV commercial interrupted the cartoon show, Tad's words snapped George out of his Mighty Mouse fixation, "Yo, let's book already, we ain't got all day." George flashed him the evil eye, and in a slow deliberate tone, said, "Man, I ought to waste your ass." Tad knew that he had busted George, caught him off guard, but he could also tell that George was just "talking shit" so he retorted, "Yeah, if you waste me, then who's gonna keep the pad clean?" George mumbled something under his breath, got up from the metal chair and headed toward the door. They left the apartment, the Mighty Mouse cartoon show and the portable .45 turntable playing Little Anthony's latest cut, "Going Out of My Head."

They hopped into the '56 Chevy that George had "borrowed" from an acquaintance when he just got out of the joint, and never bothered to return. On the way to their score, Tad put two reds in his mouth and dry-dropped them without taking any water. He was at a point where he maintained a buzz all night and day.

George drove to a house that they cased out the day before; it was a two-story duplex located in a nice neighborhood in the Mid-Wilshire district. Upon arrival, George parked the car in front of the duplex. They knew the resident was on vacation and the house was unoccupied. Their operation was simple, but so far, effective. During the day, when people were at work, they would drive around different neighborhoods, looking for houses that exhibited signs that the home had been uninhabited for a while. Telltale signs like a front porch light turned on during daylight hours on consecutive days, mail and newspapers not being picked up, and curtains and venetian blinds being tightly drawn during the day—these were some of the more obvious signals they hunted. If a house exhibited these types of signs for three consecutive days, they would return on the fourth day and if no neighbors were outside, George would park in front of the house. Tad would go up to the door and ring the doorbell. If no one answered and if he felt confident that no one was inside, he would signal George who'd be sitting in the car with its engine running. George would immediately drive into the driveway and park as close as possible to the front door. They would break in and be in and out in a matter of minutes. Their next stop was to the fence to redeem their haul for cash.

So far, their routine was flawless. Even if they miscalculated and someone answered the doorbell, Tad would be standing there in his gardening outfit and politely ask, "Ma'am, do you need any landscaping or maintenance for your yard? I am looking for customers." Being a buddhahead and dressed in a "G Man" outfit roused no suspicion. In fact, a couple of people who had answered the doorbell actually tried to retain his services, but he put them off by telling them that he would come back the next day. As long as they didn't overwork a neighborhood, they foolishly thought that they would never get caught.

It was only two days ago, at this very duplex on Hudson Avenue where Tad now stood on the porch ringing its doorbell, that an elderly white lady answered the door. After Tad gave his spiel about looking for landscaping and maintenance work, she told him to come back in two weeks because she would be leaving town that night and wouldn't return for until least another week. Bingo!

Tad waited and when no one answered the doorbell, he felt confident that she had left for vacation and that the place was unoccupied. On his signal, George drove up the curved driveway and parked close to the front door. Tad was by the side of the house and quickly covered a side window with strips of duct tape until most of the glass pane was covered. He then pulled out his .38 from is waistband and with its butt end, hit the duct tape-covered pane with just enough force to crack the glass. The duct tape kept the noise level down by preventing the glass from shattering, thus eliminating a loud crashing sound. Tad pulled off enough of the duct taped cracked glass to enable him to reach inside and unlatch the window lock. He pulled up the window frame, then he and George climbed through and made their way inside.

Even with the reds he dropped starting to kick in, Tad had enough of his wits to go up the stairs and find the master bedroom. It was this room where they usually found jewelry, money and other valuables. George remained downstairs and was busy placing electronic equipment and small appliances next to the front door that they could quickly load into the car. They had perfected their routine and would be in and out of a crib in less than 15 minutes, often with enough stuff to keep their habits and "lifestyle" going for at least another week.

As Tad was busy rifling through the dresser and drawers in the master bedroom, he heard George downstairs saying just loud enough so that he could hear, "Fuck, Tad, the cops are outside!" Tad rushed to the window, peeked through the curtains and saw three black-and-white police cars parked in front of the duplex. George came running upstairs, panicky because they were both packing heat and he was in violation of his parole. Tad's reaction was to do like they did in the movies: he moved a bedroom dresser against the door and went back to the rear of the bedroom and sat down in a chair facing the door with his .38 in his hand. Tad thought, "Here I am, with crazy George Ozaki. This is what we got to do." George watched Tad, then gave him a weird look and said, "Fuck this shit, I'm giving myself up!" Now Tad was thinking, "Fuck, I thought this cat was supposed to be crazy!" George walked down the staircase, opened the front door and shouted, "I'm a hype, don't shoot!"

Tad was still upstairs, but now he was at a complete loss at what to do next. Any thoughts about shooting it out with the cops disappeared when George gave himself up. Beads of sweat began to appear on his brow, he was scared; the worst of his fears was coming true—he was going to prison and he knew that he was not jailhouse material.

He heard the police downstairs asking George, "Is there anyone with you?" George said, "No." Tad opened the bedroom closet door and hid behind the long dresses and coats hanging inside. Tad's instincts told him to ditch his gun which he did by putting his .38 inside the pocket of a coat hanging in the closet. He remembered that he was still holding a roll of reds so he took it out of his pants pocket, opened the tin foil bindle, and threw them all in his mouth and swallowed.

Cops came upstairs to look around and one entered the bedroom. Tad, hiding in the closet, peeped between the clothes and through a crack in the closet door, could partially see what was going on. The cop looked under the bed; next, he opened the closet door wide, looked inside but did not spot Tad who was concealed behind the long dresses and coats. When the cop finished checking out the room, Tad heard him walking out the bedroom saying, "It's all clear."

Tad thought, "Ooh, shit yeah, I'm going to walk!" Another cop from downstairs loudly shouted, "If anyone is in here, come on out!" Under normal circumstances, Tad would have cracked up, but he held his mug because this was serious business. He then heard someone else with an authoritative voice say, "Check the rooms one more time and then we'll leave."

The same cop reentered the room, again he looked under the bed, then opened the closet but this time his search was more thorough as he took a step into the closet and started pulling hangars apart. Then he separated the hangers where Tad was hiding—*busted!* Tad stood frozen, face-to-face with LA's finest. Instinctively, the cop jumped back and nervously fumbled with his holster. While he was trying to unlatch his holster to pull out his gun, he shouted at the top of his lungs, "Don't move or you're dead!" Finally, he pulled out his gun and all Tad saw was the barrel of a gun pointed directly at his face. Tad wanted to cover up and flinch, but something told him not to move because the cop was just as scared as he was and any movement could cause him to panic and shoot his ass. Tad didn't move and he thanked Buddha that he had stashed his .38 because if he had it on him, he didn't know what would have happened. Police back-up rushed into the bedroom, guns drawn, and they all shouted at Tad, ordering him to put his hands over his head and slowly step out of the closet. Tad obeyed and no sooner than he stepped out of the closet, he was immediately jumped on, taken face down to a flat prone position and handcuffed.

By the time he was taken downstairs and placed in the back seat of a patrol car, George was nowhere in sight. By now, Tad was feeling the red devils kicking in and was getting sleepy. He was asked questions but they had a difficult time understanding him because he was slurring his words. His wallet was removed and they checked his ID to figure out who he was. The combination of being loaded, tired, and disgusted, was too much for Tad to handle, he closed his eyes and crashed out.

He didn't know how long he nodded out, but awoke when a police officer entered the front passenger side of the patrol car, slammed its door shut and told the cop sitting in the driver's seat, "Change of plan, we're dropping this one off at Eastlake instead of the County." The driver said, "But Eastlake's for juvies." His partner responded, "This punk lucked out, he turns 18 in two days." Despite being fucked up, Tad knew that he'd caught a break. The ride to Eastlake was quiet and uneventful until the cop riding shotgun turned around and with a sneer on his face asked, "Are you Oriental?!" The tone of his voice sounded more like an accusation than a question, so Tad shined on the cop. When the cop figured out that Tad wasn't talking, he said, "We don't get a lot of your kind, what happened to you?!" Again, Tad refused to take the bait and remained silent. The cop wouldn't turn back around in his seat but continued to glare at Tad. Finally, Tad reacted with a hostile glare of his own. He could tell that the cop was getting worked up as he leaned over the front seat and with a sadistic smile said, "What's wrong boy, no speakee English? I bet your family's really proud of you!" With that, Tad broke his silence and for the second time today, heard involuntary words coming out of his dry, raspy mouth. This time the words were slurred, "F-f-fuuck yuu, yuyuyur mmmaama!"

Tad's words struck a nerve in the cracker's psyche; his face and neck turned red like dick on a dog, he torqued his upper body and now directly faced Tad. Tad felt his angry words, hot breath, and wet spittle all hit his face at the same time, "Fuckin' Jap!" In a split second, the redneck's fist headed towards Tad's face, his right fist crashed into Tad's upper left cheekbone, everything went dark.

Part IV

Tad's Story

SANSEI – TAD'S STORY

August 6, 1967

LIGHT ENTERED through the slits of my eyes; I was groggy and oblivious to where I was, how I got here, and how long I had been out. The only thing I knew was that my body ached all over. The very last thing that I remembered was getting fired-on by the redneck cop. I tried to remove the crud caked on my eyelids and panicked upon discovering that I couldn't raise my hands to my face. Quickly I propped my head up and saw that I was laid out, dressed in a County blue smock with my arms and legs immobilized by straps fastened to a metal bed. A needle, attached to a long tube connected to an IV bottle, pierced a vein in the bent crook of my right elbow.

The room I was in was empty except for two other unoccupied beds. It had no windows; the faded institutional white walls and the scuffed linoleum floor gave the small room a cold feeling. A massive brownish-red, locked, steel door with a large key slot in place of a doorknob, and a small, thick, wire mesh-embedded glass window meant that I was in deep shit.

My mind started to race—how did I get here? What happened to George? What were they were going to do to me? Since I couldn't come up with any answers, I tried to focus on something positive that would slow down my panic attack. It took an effort, but all I came up with was, "Fuck it, at least I'm not dead!" Even though I could not see or touch my left cheekbone, I knew it was swollen because it throbbed when I moved my mouth, however slightly. I also felt a sharp pain at the back of my throat when I swallowed or breathed through my mouth. This was strange—I knew why my cheekbone hurt but had no clue what caused the pain in my throat.

Helplessly strapped down in this supine position, I thought that I'd better figure out what I could say to get me out of this mess. *I'll tell them that I was going door-to-door, trying to line up gardening jobs, when I went up to this house with its front door wide open. I heard a lady's voice calling out for help, so I went inside! Now it was starting to make some sense. When I went inside, it looked like the house had been ransacked. I went upstairs to see if someone needed my help. That's when I heard the noise downstairs and I got scared because I thought the burglars had returned, so I hid inside the closet. By the time I realized that it was the police, I knew that I should have come out of the closet, but I panicked because I didn't know if they would believe me. That was stupid of me!*

Mentally I was ecstatic. *Hell yeah, I just might be able to bullshit my way out of this because they didn't find shit on me, and I know that George isn't going to dime*

111

me out. If my throat didn't hurt so bad, I would have started yelling to get someone over here this very instant so that I could explain what happened and clear up this misunderstanding. Then it hit me, I needed to explain why I was loaded when I came out of the closet.

Before I could think up the second part of my alibi, I heard a jingling noise coming from the lock on the steel door, then the door swung open. In walked two men, the more distinguished-looking one was an older white man, dressed in a white smock, with a thin build, wearing wireless framed glasses, toting a clipboard and wearing a stethoscope wrapped around his neck. The other dude was an overweight white guy, with a ruddy complexion, dressed in a wrinkled loose-fitting powder blue denim short-sleeve shirt with a law enforcement-looking type of badge pinned over its right breast pocket. They walked over to my bedside and peered down at me. Seeing that I was awake, the medical guy placed two right fingers on my secured wrist and read my pulse. Upon finishing, he scribbled his finding on the clipboard, and they turned around and headed back towards the steel door.

I didn't want them to go away without telling me what was going on, so I tried to call out. Upon doing so, the insides of my throat hurt so bad that all I could muster was a soft garbled, "Scuse mee." Fortunately, this was enough to get their attention. They turned around and stepped back to my bedside. The security guy looked at the doctor and said, "Doc, I thought this one wasn't going to make it." The doctor looked at me and said, "Don't talk, the pain in your throat is because we placed a tube down your throat to pump out your stomach. You were unconscious when you arrived here, and we wanted to make sure that you didn't overdose. You've been out for over twenty-four hours." The rent-a-cop chimed in, "Yeah, lucky you didn't die because if you did, we'd still be filling out paperwork on your sorry ass!" I ignored this fool and concentrated my effort on communicating with the doctor. I looked at him and forced out a sentence asking him where I was. Before he could respond, the cop blurted out, "You died and woke up in hell!" Most likely, the doctor was used to working with Mr. Personality Plus. He said in a calm voice that I was at the LA County Hospital jail ward unit and I would remain under observation for one more night, and tomorrow, I would be transferred to County Jail. I nodded my head, to indicate that I understood. I then shook my wrists, which brought a small smile to his face, and he told me that some time this morning I would be unbound and transferred to another cell. Satisfied, I nodded in acknowledgement to the doctor. Off to the side I heard his sidekick say, "I'm glad you're up because my buddies who brought you here told me all about your bad attitude and asked me to personally see to it that you enjoy your stay here. I'll be back later to pay you a visit." With that being said, they left the room.

Later that morning, two orderlies removed the IV and bindings and I was then transferred to a smaller cell. Even though my head ached, my body was stiff and sore, and I couldn't speak without pain shooting from my throat, it still felt good to be back on my feet. Now I had to prepare for whatever was going to happen next.

I was bummed because the doctor mentioned that they were sending me to the county jail. Man, I hoped that he was mistaken and meant Eastlake. I knew that I better start working on my strength and reflexes, because wherever I was going, be it Men's Central Jail, or Eastlake Juvie Hall, I best be ready to defend myself. I thought about the fat pig who promised to pay me a "visit" before I left. I promised myself the very instant he got physical with me, that I would smack him dead on the bridge of his nose. If he goes down, I could apply my judo choke hold, but if he doesn't go down, then anything goes.

The night passed without incident and the following morning I was handcuffed and removed from my cell. Fortunately, the loud mouth rent-a-cop who threatened to do me bodily harm was a liar who failed to make good on his promise to pay me a visit.

Silently, I was damn near praying that I would be taken to Eastlake. I knew if I ended up at County, that I had no choice than to go psycho on the first cat that fucked with me—it was either that or end up someone's punk. I learned from listening to older cats from the Avenues who did county or joint time, that being a buddhahead in jail was a bitch. They said that in jail, we are a minority of one—not accepted by the bloods, *ese*'s, or gray boys. They emphasized to never depend on others to cover your back, and do not rely on the guards or anyone else for protection because it comes with a price. Finally, never accept any property, favors or gestures of friendship until you first established your credibility as a person who is not to be fucked with. Until then, keep to yourself, trust no one, and send the first cat that challenges you to the infirmary.

My obvious preference was to be sent to Eastlake. A lot of my partners put in time at Eastlake before they were sent to road camps or the California Youth Authority. Even though Eastlake was a war zone in its own right, with gangs, racism, violence, and intimidation running amok, I knew that I'd be better off there than at County. Eastlake was located around the corner from County General Hospital, literally in walking distance. On the other hand, County Jail is situated across downtown, over by Union Station. I figured that if my transportation escorts put me in a car, it meant that I was going to County, because if I was being sent to Eastlake, in the time it would take to walk me to the parking lot, secure me in the police car, and drive two blocks to drop me off, we could have already walked to Eastlake.

I was escorted out of the hospital by two LAPD cops. We took a back elevator leading to a secured County General parking lot, and as I approached the patrol car, I thought, "Oh shit, I'm going to County." After being secured in the back seat of the patrol car, we took off. Leaving the parking lot feeling depressed, I accepted my fate. Arriving at the first stop sign, instead of turning right in the direction of the Santa Monica Freeway, they turned left. I thought maybe they were taking a back way to the County that only cops knew about. Then I flashed—we were headed towards Eastlake! The drive was over in an instant as the patrol car turned into Eastlake Detention Facility roadway. Beyond my wildest imagination, I never thought I'd ever be so overjoyed to be locked up at Eastlake Juvie Hall.

Eastlake is run by the LA County Probation Department so I was surprised to see that the probation officers didn't wear uniforms and were dressed casually. Another observation was that the majority of the Eastlake probation staff was made up of minorities and these dudes were buffed. Most wore tight knit short-sleeve shirts that showcased their biceps and guns. They were advertising the obvious,

"Behave, and act right, because if you don't, I'll knock you out!"

While being processed through intake, my throat felt a bit better and by speaking slowly I was able to answer their questions. When asked, I told them that I had no gang affiliations and did not use drugs. A probation officer read the LAPD Arrest Report, looked at my bruised right cheek and snickered, commenting aloud, "I bet they're going to charge this one with resisting arrest." Next, I was medically examined and cleared, then given a juvie county uniform, a pair of bluish gray pants, two white tee shirts, a hand-me-down faded powder blue sweat shirt inscribed with county markings, two pairs of white socks, and black tennis shoes.

By the time I was taken to my unit, it was a little before noon. I was assigned a cot and instructed to wait for lunch formation. The room was large enough to house thirty, it had fifteen cots on each side with an middle walkway aisle. I placed the county-issued property, clothes, towel, toothbrush, soap and shower shoes in the footlocker next to my cot. I sat on my cot awaiting the arrival of my "roommates." Before I could get comfortable, three *ese* entered the unit and just like that, they stopped in front of my cot. The dude directly facing me looked older than the other two flanking his sides; he was a little bigger than me and carried himself with more confidence than his two tag-alongs. I detected sarcasm in his voice as he asked, "Chino, where you from!?" I should have stood the moment these chumps entered the room; I was now at a disadvantage, sitting on the edge of the cot. In response to his verbal challenge, I looked him in the eye and our eyes locked. For whatever reason, he didn't take advantage of my vulnerability to rush me, instead we continued mad-dogging each other, waiting for the other's next move. Finally he blurted out, "What's up Chino, no speak Englas!" Sick and tired of this "no-speakie shit," I jumped to my feet, and said, "I got your Chino, *ese,* what's up!" The two wannabes spread out maneuvering to my blind spots. I focused on the older cat in front of me—if I was gonna get fucked up, I would make sure there was two of us that were gonna get hurt. Before anyone made a move, the youngest-looking one of the trio said, "*Ese,* let's fuck him up later, that way we won't get caught." Now, I knew these chumps were fake; if they were for real, we already would have locked ass. I continued to stare down my adversary and said, "Yeah, you best to listen to lil man, before I fuck you up!" I knew that with this challenge there was no turning back, the next move was on him. Being lunch time, wards began to trickle into the unit, and whether this saved his ass or mine, I'll never know. Still looking at me he said, "Chino, I'll see you on the yard," then he and his flunkies left the room.

Our unit marched to the cafeteria; I was so hungry that I disregarded the lingering pain in my throat and scarfed down a bologna with American cheese sandwich, cup of fruit cocktail, an apple and carton of milk. After eating, we marched out to the main yard. There must have been at least five hundred delinquents on the yard, and not enough probation staff to keep track of us. Like in all institutions, the population is segregated by race. The blacks claimed a grassy area away from the main building, the Latinos congregated over by the handball court, a minority of whites sat on bleachers by the fence, I even saw a couple of Orientals who were Chinese but they walked by without acknowledging my presence. I located an empty bench off to the side and sat by myself—my nerves were shot, and I was tired, but my adrenalin was still running on overdrive.

When I noticed a group of bloods were headed my way, I thought, "Fuck, now what!" This time, I wasn't going to be caught off guard and immediately stood. I tried my best to act nonchalant, I didn't look in their direction even when they stopped a few yards in front of me. When I finally looked, I knew I was in trouble: they were lined up two deep, the four cats in the front all looked to be around my age, or older, with two of them outright big enough to probably even give the probation officers a good "go." I knew that there was no way I could take on these dudes and if I was taken down, I'd better cover up and protect my head and family jewels. I said, "Fuck it!", balled up my fist, stepped back and planted my fight foot, hoping to get in a few good licks of my own. From the back of the group came, "Yo buddhahead, you gonna beat us all up wid your jujitsu shit?" For some reason it sounded more like a joke than a threat. Two big dudes standing in front of me, slid to the side, and stepping through the opening was Ronald Booker, my partner from the Avenues! I was never so glad to see a friendly face—if I didn't have to maintain my "cool" I would have hugged him. I stepped forward and we exchanged the neighborhood handshake. He told me that he just heard about a crazy-acting Chinese dude that punked three wannabes in Unit E. He said that he had a hunch that it just might be one of his old buddhahead partners from the Avenues, so he decided to check. He introduced me to his crew, telling them the two of us went all the way back to grade school, and played ball together.He finished up by telling them that I was one of those crazy buddhaheads that he grew up with.

After the introductions, Booker's partners returned to their yard area, while Booker stayed so we could catch up with each other. Booker was always straight with people; a natural born leader, both popular and respected, who carried himself with a lot of confidence. We met at Sixth Avenue Elementary School and grew up playing a lot of ball together. We were the same age, and while he was a taste faster than me, I always felt that I was quicker than him. When we played against each other, we competed our hardest, trying to get the better of the other—he won his share of the battles and I mine. Through it all, we developed a sense of mutual respect and realized that when we were on the same side, we were a deadly combo. Booker and I had more in common than just sports; although we were both capable of doing well in the classroom, we were drawn to the streets. Many of our same teachers, administrators, and adults viewed Booker and me as wasted potential.

We ran the streets, bullshitting and partying, fighting, strong-arming chumps for their money, thieving, hitting on bitches, getting high, and hanging out with the thugs. For us, school and academics were for "lames" and for squares. Booker ran with the bloods, and I with the buddhaheads, but our lives paralleled each other, and our bond stayed strong.

Booker told me how he felt like crying when his mom gave him the news that his family was moving from Crenshaw to South Central because the Firestone plant on Imperial Highway was hiring. He said the big-time disappointment was that he had been working out during the summer because it was finally going to be our time to shine on the varsity football team. His transition was smooth when enrolling at Jordan High, because his cousin of the same age also attended Jordan. His cousin was a member of the Imperial Court Gang and Booker cliqued up right from the gate with them—it was just a matter of time before he was jumped into their set.

Booker told me that this was his second go-round at Eastlake, and on his first trip here, he hooked up with Billy Cooper from the Avenues. Billy told him that Marcus Henry, John Desmond, and Sherman Davis, three cats from the neighborhood, had all died from drug overdoses. I told him that I heard about Marcus and John OD'ing, but now hearing about Sherman is a mind-fuck. I knew that Marcus and John were druggies and headed that way, but Sherman was the least likely cat from the neighborhood anyone would ever imagine OD'ing. The Sherman I knew was a straight-A honor student, top-notch athlete, popular, good-looking, and respected by both thugs and squares alike. The last I heard was that a college in Northern California had offered him a baseball scholarship. Booker said that he, too, was stunned when Billy dropped the news about Sherman. It turned out that Sherman and Barbara Kaneko, an Oriental girl who lived by Audubon had a thing going with each other. This didn't surprise me at all, because they were both smart, popular, class officers, shit like that. Barbara wasn't fine, fine, but she was nice to look at. Both being smart, they ended up taking a lot of honors classes together, and it was probably just a matter of time before the romantic thing kicked in. They were a perfect couple, but when Barbara's parents found out that she was involved with a "colored" boy, they freaked out, and not only forbid her from seeing Sherman, they transferred her to a Valley school. For Sherman, this was his first and last wake-up call. He learned that despite good grades, academic honors and achievements, there are people that don't give a shit, and to them you'll always be just another "nigger." Billy told him at first, Sherman was confident that once Barbara's parents met him and got to know him, they would come to their senses. He tried contacting Barbara but she didn't return his phone calls or letters. Barbara was Sherman's first love—he really dug her, and it bothered him to such a point that he told a close friend of Barbara named Patty, to tell her that he was coming to her house that weekend to talk with her parents. He thought that since they both dug each other, there was nothing her parents could do to keep them apart. Before the weekend came, Patty hand-delivered a letter from Barbara to Sherman. No one knows what was in the letter, but afterwards, Sherman was not the same cat. He became a loner, almost to the point of being anti-social. Eventually, petty shit that never would have bothered the Sherman of old, started to get the better of him. He got into an argument with the baseball coach and thrown off the team. He finally quit going to classes, started dressing differently, his neat short-cropped hair being replaced with a high red-processed front. He started running and getting loaded with the fuck-ups—the rest is history.

As Booker related the particulars surrounding Sherman's OD, it felt as if a dagger pierced my heart. I met Sherman at Mount Vernon; he was cool with everyone and spent a lot of time hanging out with the buddhaheads. It wasn't like he was uncomfortable with the color of his complexion or had an identity hang-up, it was about people getting along and liking each other. Out of all of us, Sherman was hands-down the smartest and arguably the most athletic. By high school I stopped hanging out with Sherman, mainly because he was into school, good grades and doing things the right way, while I gravitated to people that didn't give a fuck. I wished I had ten minutes with Barbara and her parents to put some evil on them so that they could feel the same pain that Sherman felt because of their racist beliefs. It pissed me off thinking about how some buddhaheads actually think they're better than other people—mothafuckas act like they white! I was doubly disappointed in Barbara, because she seemed like a sweet, down-to-earth girl. This only reinforces my belief that being an honor student doesn't necessarily make one a person of "honor."

Booker read my funk and drew me out of it by asking, "Yo, blood, how's your pop doing?" His question threw me for a loop because it had been a while since I last saw or even thought about my family. I told him that I hadn't seen Pop in a while but I guess he was doing okay. Booker said that when he was growing up in the Avenues, my father was one of the few people in the neighborhood who scared him. He reminded me of a time in junior high when he was at my house and my pop took him along with me and my brother to our judo workout. He remembered seeing him transform from an everyday mind-your-own-business gardener, into a no-nonsense, hardass, old-school judo *sensei*. He recalled Pops saying very little but everyone in the dojo, from the little kids to the older brown belts all acted different when Pops came around to correct their techniques. He talked about our classmate, Ronnie Suenoda, clowning around when he should have been working on his technique. He said that my pop immediately put an end to Ronnie's fun by pairing off against him and with ease, maneuvered Ronnie in any direction he pleased, as if he was a puppet—he flipped and tripped him, over and over. Finally Ronnie had enough and lay helplessly on the mat. That's when Pops stood over him challenging him to "Get up," and every time Ronnie tried to stand, Pop would sweep his feet out from under him causing Ronnie to lose his balance and fall back onto the mat. It seemed like this went on forever before Ronnie quit and stopped trying to get up. That's when Pops really got on him, telling him to get up and kicking him lightly with his foot until Ronnie got so frustrated t he looked like he was going to cry. My pop didn't let up until Ronnie finally squirmed, arched his back and desperately tried to fight his way back up. When he finally figured out how to maneuver and get himself up, Pops stood facing him, telling Ronnie to straighten his *gi*. They faced each other and bowed from the waist. Pop walked away searching for the next student in need of instruction. I reminded Booker about my pop asking him on the ride back home from the dojo if he was ready to start his martial art instruction and how he told Pop that his mom wanted him to concentrate on his schoolwork. I remembered laughing to myself, listening to Booker make up lame excuses. Pop ended the conversation by telling Booker, "Yes, studies are important, maybe you can start in the summer when school is out."

Booker said, "Man, I'll never know how you were able to keep going back to the dojo all those years, that was some mean shit they taught over there." I said, "Yeah, at first I didn't have a choice; I hated it, but I got used to it. Believe it or not, right before I quit judo, I actually started to look forward to going, to test my skills against the black belts." Booker asked me when my court date was, but I told him that I didn't know. He said that once you're arrested they have three days to get your ass to court. He added, "Don't be surprised if your folks show up at your court hearing because our people are notified about our court hearings." This was news to me; I hoped my folks couldn't be located because I didn't want them, especially Moms, to see me like this.

Booker said that he got busted on a humbug. I said "Yeah, that's what they all say, some other dude did it." He replied, "Check this out, square business, this Valley white boy drove a cherried-out, metal flake, candy apple-red GTO convertible with mag rims, into the projects where me and my homies were chillin'. He shouts out asking us where he could cop some downers. My homies walked up to him and the next thing I saw was that he was outside the car, running out of the hood. Since none of my partners knew how to operate a stick shift, that's where I came in. I knew I shouldn't have because I was still on probation but the temptation was too great; I got a hard-on, just thinking about opening that baby up. The plan was to take the ride over to someone's cousin's place, drop it off and get paid. On our way there, I saw police lights flashing behind me, I took off but wasn't able to shake them, I made a wide turn on 59th and Avalon and crashed the car. I lucked out because the white boy didn't pick me out of the lineup, so they pinned a GTA on me." Booker said that he had already been to court and his public defender told him that if he pled, he could guarantee that he would be sent to camp for six months. If he fought the case and lost, he would be looking at the Youth Authority because he was already on probation and this would be his second offense. He said that on Wednesday, he's going back to court for sentencing and the sooner they sent him to camp, the sooner he would be out.

He said he lucked out because his case was in front of the lady judge in Department 203, and if his case had been sent to Department 201, he would have been looking at the California Youth Authority because the judge in 201 is a redneck who doesn't cut anyone slack.

It was getting late in the afternoon and the wards were lining up in formation. Before splitting, Booker asked, "If you don't mind me asking, who busted up your cheek?" I said, "Ain't you heard, I was jumped on by the baddest gang in LA." Booker said, "That's bullshit, the Imperials is the baddest gang, and we shor didn't do you like that!" I laughed, "No man, you the second-baddest gang, LAPD be the first." Booker grinned, "You got that right partner, they some stone thugs. I got to book, catch you later." We exchanged the handshake, and he went into his cool pimp walk, heading back to his homies. It was righteous spending time with someone I could relate with. I knew that being identified with Booker and his partners meant that I wasn't going to have any more problems dealing with fools.

That night, before lights out, a probation officer came into our unit and read off a list of names that were scheduled to go to court tomorrow. Accompanying each name was the department where the case was going to be heard. He read off, "Nagata, Department 201." I went to sleep knowing that my lucky streak had come to an end.

The Eastlake Courthouse is a fortified brick building, separate, but located directly in front of the Eastlake Juvenile Detention Center. The next morning, those of us having court appearances were chained together and marched to the rear of the courthouse. Once inside we were put in a large holding tank, unchained and instructed to sit and wait until our name was called. We were monitored by a slew of probation officers, most of them sitting at their desk drinking morning coffee. There were twelve of us cramped together, sitting on a hard-ass concrete bench, waiting for our name to be called.

Throughout the morning, the probation officers unlocked the cell door, called out names and escorted wards through another door that most likely was a rear entrance to a courtroom. It was a little after ten when my name was called. Instead of taking me through the rear courtroom door, I was put into a small private conference room. They had me sit on one of two chairs that were directly facing each other separated by a sturdy metal table. After sitting down, the probation officer left the room and locked the door.

Shortly, the door clanked open, and a young Latino dude in a charcoal gray suit, carrying a small stack of manila files, and a red calendar book, stepped inside. He started talking the instant he sat down, "My name is Robert Govea, I am your court-appointed attorney." He extended his hand and I shook it. He looked down at his paperwork, "So you're Tadashi Nagata. Let's see, they're charging you with two felonies—residential burglary and assaulting a police officer—and two misdemeanors: being under the influence of a controlled-substance and resisting arrest." He started reading aloud the LAPD Arrest Report describing how George and I broke into the house, how I jumped out of the closet and attacked the police officer, and how they used reasonable force to fend off my attack. When he read the reasonable force part, I started to snicker and shake my head. He heard my reaction, stopped reading the report, and said, "From the look of your cheek, I'd say that they popped you good. That's why they have to justify their actions by saying that you attacked them first, otherwise, they would have to explain how your face got busted up. I see this kind of stuff everyday." He asked me to tell him what really happened. I was now at a point where I was tired of bullshitting and felt that no matter what lie I could conjure up, it didn't matter because the redneck judge was going to nail me anyway. I just wanted to start doing my time and get it over with. I told my attorney what the cops wrote down was basically true except for the part that I attacked them, and I told him how the cop fired on me when I was handcuffed in the back seat of the patrol car. After I finished telling him my side of the story, he said that I will be going into court in a few minutes and at my arraignment today, I will deny the allegations and the case will be set for a trial in three weeks. He said that I am in front of a hard judge who even sends first-time offenders to camp or the California Youth Authority. He mentioned that a major problem with my case is that I just turned 18 and detention camps don't accept anyone over 18 years of age, which only left the option of the Youth Authority. He said he would try to keep me out of the Youth Authority and after explaining my legal situation he left the interview room.

A short while later, a probation officer escorted me into the courtroom. Department 201 looked nothing like I imagined—it had a small classroom feel to it with the distinct difference that instead of a teacher's desk in front of this room, there was an elevated, wooden podium bench. On the wall directly behind the podium hung a large, circular, gold-colored symbol, with an inscription which read, "Seal of the State of California." The Seal was flanked on each side by an American flag and the Bear Flag of California. My attorney was already seated in a chair behind a long wooden table that faced the podium. I sat down next to him. Seated to our far left was another suit, probably the DA. Behind the attorney table was a desk where a bailiff sat. I looked at the elevated podium and on the podium's platform was a nameplate, "Michael Axel, Judge Pro Tem." My attorney whispered to me that the judge is in his chamber and will be coming out any minute. He then asked if I knew if my parents were here. Before I could answer, he turned around and asked the bailiff if anyone had checked in. The bailiff responded, "His mom and dad are here, I'll page them." He picked up an intercom and spoke into it, "Parties for Tadashi Nagata, please report to Department 201."

I hadn't seen my folks in over six months; suddenly I was more concerned about seeing them than I was of facing the redneck judge. I stared at the door leading to the front entrance of the of the courtroom, hoping that a mistake had been made and that my parents were really not here. That's when the judge entered the courtroom and the bailiff had us all stand until he sat down in his elevated perch. I looked at the judge and he did not strike me as anyone special, he looked like any other white person I was used to seeing in a position of authority. What made Judge Axel special was that he sat in a high seat, looked down at me, wore a black robe and had control over my life. I was not going to act stupid and try and stare him down. Behind me I heard the bailiff say, "Please take a seat." I turned around and saw my mom and pop seated in the back of the courtroom. I looked at them, we made eye contact and I tried to convey with a small smile that I'm okay and not to worry. They did not return my smile, instead they nervously focused their attention on the judge seated on his throne. The judge, my attorney and the DA started talking legal-ese, while I sat there, not really listening. My thoughts were on how hard this must be on my folks sitting through this. I really wished they hadn't come, but in a selfish way, I was glad they did. After the judge and the suits finished with their legal mumbo-jumbo, the judge asked my attorney, "Who is seated in back of the courtroom?" My attorney said, "Your honor, they are the minor's parents, Mr. and Mrs. Nagata. I felt like turning around to see their expressions, but I remained facing forward. I noticed that the judge was looking intently at my parents, and then he shifted his focus and stared directly at me, as if he was trying to look through me. He made me feel uncomfortable, and even though I had already told myself I had to be cool, something inside me snapped and I met his gaze with my own angry glare. This person was no longer an all-powerful judge that I had to kiss up to, now he was just another person in my life that was about to fuck me over. I guess that the judge got tired of looking at me because he returned his attention back to my attorney and the DA, telling them that he wanted to see them both in his chamber. I was confused; Judge Axel stood up and exited the courtroom without saying another word. The bailiff escorted me out of the courtroom and back to the interview room. Before leaving the courtroom, I caught a glimpse of my parents who were also being excused from the courtroom.

I took the way the judge stormed out of the courtroom as a bad omen. I thought,

"Shit, he's probably one of those people who lost a family member in World War II, and hates Japs! Man, why couldn't I have gotten the lady judge!" It felt like forever before my attorney came to talk to me. When he reentered the room, I swear to God, I detected a bounce in his step. He sat down and told me what Judge Axel said during their back room conference. "It was strange, Judge started talking about how hard his job was, seeing lost kids come in and out of his courtroom every day. Then he talked about his duty to protect the public even though there are times a kid may be deserving of a break. He said that kids today lack discipline, and if he gave a kid a chance without understanding consequences, it would be setting that kid up for failure in life. For some reason, your parents struck a nerve in him because he started talking about how he lack direction when he was young, and how he found it by enlisting in the Army. He told us that the Army helped mature him and when he was discharged, he joined the police force, got married and eventually went to law school at night. In the last twenty minutes, I learned more about Judge Axel than I have appearing before him the past nine months." He continued, "Anyway, remember how I told you that I was going to keep you out of the Youth Authority? Well, Judge Axel worked it out for you. He said that since you just turned eighteen, you can enlist in the military without your parent's consent, and if you agree to enlist, he will dismiss your case. What do you think? I suggest you make a quick decision before he changes his mind." Man, I didn't know what to think, going to jail was one thing but the military, damn! I told him that I need to think about this and asked him if he could arrange it so that I could talk this over with my parents. He said he'd try and pull a few strings to arrange it. We shook hands, I thanked him and he left the room.

Alone, with nothing but my thoughts, I knew the time had arrived to face my parents. I felt nervous and guilty—how could I have slipped so far? During the past few days, I was so absorbed in my survival, I even forgot about my birthday! Eighteen fuckin' years old and my folks have to see me like this! As tempted as I was to just say, "Fuck it I don't give a shit!" I knew that my folks deserved better. Even though I have been a disappointment to them, their showing up today, meant a lot. I wanted to tell them how much I appreciate everything they ever did for me, and that the mistakes I've made, are mine and mine alone, with no reflection on them. I wished that they could just see me and accept me for who I am, but I know that it's asking too much.

A probation officer brought my pop into the interview room. After Pop sat down across from me, the officer said, "Mister Nagata, when you're finished with your visit, knock on the door and I'll let you out." Pop thanked him, and the door was closed, leaving just the two of us. His face did not show anger or disgust, instead he looked serious. Before I could even say "Hi Pop", he began conversing, telling me that he did not want Mom to come into the room because it would have been too hard on her; he said that she was nervous even entering the courthouse. I told him that it was okay and that I understood. I told Pop about the deal that the judge offered me. I expected my pop to tell me that I was getting a break and that I should enlist. Instead, he said nothing and covered his forehead with his left hand and rubbed it as if he had a headache. I asked, "What's wrong, Pop?" He didn't answer and just sat quietly. Finally, he removed his hand from his face and looked intently into my eyes. I thought to myself, "Damn, something ain't right, I hope the judge didn't renege on his offer." In a controlled but calm voice, Pops spoke, "When I was your age, my *otoosan,* who you never met, died alone in a federal prison. Right after Japan bombed Pearl Harbor, the FBI came and took him away; that was the last time I ever saw my father. When he died, I became angry and blamed the United States government. I still do, but after all these years, I think that maybe what happened to us *Nihonjin* had more to do with a terrible and confusing time that affected everybody. People were angry, scared and wanted revenge, and someone had to be blamed, so white America took it out on us Japanese people, even those of us born in America. While I was at camp, the government gave us a loyalty oath questionnaire, but I was angry about my father's death and I didn't answer the questions the way that they expected me to. I ended up being sent to a camp where they put all the so-called troublemakers where I stayed until the end of the war. I was angry, felt betrayed and felt pain whenever I thought about my father dying alone."

Whoa! I wasn't ready for this! I asked, "Why didn't you tell me about this before?" For a brief instant, Pop looked down, then his eyes returned to mine. "After the war, I was still bitter, and then I met your mom and had you kids. Slowly, things started to change and after a while, I didn't feel it was necessary to tell you kids that your old man did time in a federal prison. Maybe I should have." For the first time in my life, Pop looked old and tired. I tried to lighten his mood, and said, "That's okay Pop, it's a relief to know that I'm not the first Nagata to get in trouble." He was not amused, so I asked in earnest, "Pop, what should I do?" He said, "I can't make this decision for you, because you're the one who's going to have to live with it. All I know is what I read and see in the news. We're at war, and if you enlist you'll be sent to Viet Nam. If you choose not to enlist and go to jail, your mom and I will support you either way." His voice cracked as he finished his thought, "I lost my *otoosan* because of a war, and I don't know how it would affect your mom to lose her son." His eyes became moist, he glanced away.

We talked a little more about the family; he told me how much my kid brother, Renbo, missed me and how much Mom worried about me. Just when I was ready to tell him how much I appreciate and miss my family, I was interrupted by the locked door opening and the probation officer saying, "The judge needs you back in court." My pop stood and placed his hands on my shoulders and gazed into my eyes, no further words were needed.

Even though I still hadn't made up my mind, I felt more confident and better about myself than I had in quite a while. Everyone, including my parents and the judge, were already seated when I arrived in the courtroom. Upon taking my seat next to my attorney, he turned his head to the side and asked me in a soft voice, "Are you going to take the deal?" I said, "I'm not sure." The judge must overheard our "private" conversation because he looked down at me and directly asked, "Well, Mister Nagata, have you made up your mind? We haven't got all day." I looked up at him, knowing that whatever split-second decision I was about to make was going to change my life. I said aloud, "I'll enlist." Immediately, my attorney patted me on my back and the judge tried hard to suppress a smile. I sat there as the DA said that his office would dismiss my case upon showing proof of enlistment in the military. With the exception of my folks, everyone else in the courtroom was in a celebratory mood. Before I was escorted out of the courtroom, I turned to see my parents who were standing in the back of the courtroom, give me the look that parents have when they wish that they could help their kid, but are helpless to do so. All I could do was to raise my right hand and wave them a simultaneously "hi" and "goodbye." I gave my mom a small smile, trying to let her know that I'll be all right.

The next day, I was allowed to change back into my regular clothes and a probation officer took me to the induction center on Broadway and Ninth Street, in downtown LA The front section of the induction center quartered military recruiters from all the different branches. Each recruiter wore immaculately pressed, brass-buttoned uniforms. Directly above the right breast pocket, they showcased their medals and brightly colored ribbons. Their shoes were spit-shinned and reflective like a mirror. I spent the entire morning listening to different recruiters trying to convince me why their branch was superior to the rest. The Army, Navy, Air Force, and Coast Guard recruiters talked about occupational specialties, and duty station assignments they could guarantee, along with available benefits upon discharge. The only branch that interested me was the Air Force; they offered a diverse range of job training and interesting overseas duty assignments. The problem was that they wanted a six-year enlistment—no fuckin' way! Except for the Marine Corps recruiter, none of the other branches even touched upon being sent to Viet Nam. The Marine Corps recruiter said that no matter what branch I chose, at some point I will be sent to Viet Nam, and the Marines prided itself in preparing one for combat. Even though I knew this was bullshit, at least the Marine recruiter was honest and the Marines were the only military branch that offered a two-year enlistment.

After listening to all the recruiters, the one thing I knew for certain was that there was no chance in hell that I planned to make a career out of the military. The Army had the next shortest enlistment, that being three years. If both enlistment terms were equal, I would have signed up with the Army because the Marines had a reputation for having the hardest training and always getting the worst fighting assignments; however, I was anxious to get this all behind me and serving an extra year in the military was out of the question. Besides, I knew that no matter what branch I chose, my yellow ass would eventually end up in Viet Nam, so I might as well be trained by the best.

That afternoon, I went back to the Marine Corps recruitment desk. The recruiter seemed surprised to see me back at his station. He nervously filled out my enlistment papers, and when he finished typing in the information, I signed the bottom line committing myself to a two-year enlistment contract. After signing, the recruiter told me that I could delay my reporting date up to three months or I could start as early as Friday, which was only two days away. I looked in the direction of the probation officer who trailed me all morning and now idly occupied a chair behind me. When he caught me looking at him, and before I could say anything, he said, "No way we're going to let you go home and party, you still belong to the County!" I looked back at the recruiter and asked, "What time on Friday?"

The next day, back at Eastlake, three days had passed since I had been out on the yard due to my court appearances and recruiting outing. I returned to the same spot where I sat on my first day on the yard. I looked around for Booker, but did not spot him. I remember him mentioning something about being sentenced on Wednesday; I hoped it went okay for him. When yard time ended, as I headed back to formation, I was waved over by one of the big dudes who had been with Booker. As I was walking up to him, he extended his hand and introduced himself as James. He told me that when Booker went to court, the lady judge gave him Camp Gonzales. He said Camp Gonzales is the most lenient of the senior camps and if Booker runs a tight program, he'll be back on the streets in six months. He said that before Booker left, he was looking for me and was concerned about my outcome. I told James that I felt bad that I missed Booker and told him about enlisting in the Marines. James shook his head and replied, "Watch your ass, brother man, niggas be dying over there. Word is that blacks and browns are sent to the front lines and the white boys stay in the rear, drinking beer." We shook hands and parted company. I walked away knowing that Booker would be home before Easter, and I wondered what my Easter egg hunt in the jungle of Viet Nam was going to be like. I thought, "If only I got the lady judge, instead of that redneck psycho burnout, I could have been home in time to help plan Booker's welcome home party—ain't that a bitch!"

MARINE CORPS RECRUIT DEPOT

August 1967

IT WAS EARLY FRIDAY MORNING when my probation escort stopped in front of the Selective Service Induction Center on Ninth and Broadway. When I stepped out of the county vehicle, I realized that he was still behind the steering wheel with the engine running on idle. He reached over, lowered the front passenger side window and asked if I had all my paperwork. I told him that I did, and still leaning over, he said, "Good luck, and don't forget to duck!" Before I could get in a word he left the curb and was gone. Damn, it felt good to be free from being watched and confined. I knew that my freedom was going to vanish, the moment I set foot inside the induction center. A thought flashed through my mind about calling up one of my partners to come pick me up so that I could have one last fling in the neighborhood. As tempting as this was, I knew that if I made that phone call, one thing would lead to another thing, and I probably would end up AWOL, before I even got started. Fighting off my instincts, I entered the induction center.

Once inside, I spotted my Marine recruiter seated behind his desk. I ambled over and stood in front of his desk. He was reading a document and was either too occupied to look up, or he was ignoring me. I waited a few moments before saying, "Sarge, who am I supposed to give my papers to?" Without looking up he lifted his left hand and pointed towards the direction of the large adjacent connecting room. I thought, "Fuck this! Only four days ago this same pooh-butt white boy had all the time in the world for this buddhahead, telling me about *esprit de corps*, all-for-one Marine Corps bullshit, and damn near cum in his dress blue pants when I signed on the bottom line. Now he won't even look me in the eye!" I felt myself getting hot, and continued to stand in front of his desk. He raised his head, looked into my eyes, and immediately lowered his head and said in a quiet voice, "When you enter the processing room, you'll see a registration table. Put your papers in the basket, and then wait for them to call out your name." I looked at him with contempt, shook my head and headed to processing room.

It was late in the afternoon when I finished my physical, completed my paperwork, and was sworn in. My ass now belonged to the U.S. government. After swearing us in, they instructed us to be seated and wait for further instruction. Looking around the overcrowded seating area, every metal folding chair was occupied by an inductee. I estimated there were probably over three hundred of us awaiting departure. Most of the inductees were Army draftees and headed off

125

to Fort Ord. The rest of us were split between the Marines, Air Force, and Navy. The room was half empty by the time the PA system announced, "All Marine Corps inductees, immediately report to the front of the building and board the Greyhound bus for departure." About two dozen of us simultaneously rose and headed towards the door. I won't swear on it, but it felt like when we all stood, the rest of the seated inductees, either started to snicker, rolled their eyes, or shook their heads. Their facial expressions and body language suggested that they were saying, "You all fucked up!" I walk out of the induction center with a stupefied feeling, the kind one gets when you finally figure out that all this time everyone knew what the deal was except you. I boarded the bus and took a seat in the back. I tried to rid my mind of negative thoughts, telling myself, "Fuck 'em, they don't know shit!"

By the time the bus left the induction center, every seat was occupied by either a Marine or Navy recruit because their boot camps are both located in San Diego. Even though today felt like it dragged on forever, I knew that my day really wouldn't begin until the bus arrived at Marine Corps boot camp—what a depressing thought. I started thinking about all of the changes that happened to me in the past week-and-a-half, going from a junkie-thief to a wannabe Marine; what a mind-fuck! These last few days, my body was starting to get some of its strength and energy back, and at times I even noticed that my thinking was getting clearer. Actually, the past ten days were the longest I stayed clean in months.

The Greyhound had air conditioning and soft, comfortable seats. Without traffic, LA to San Diego is a ninety-minute drive; since we left during rush hour, there was no telling when we'd get there. I was in no hurry—I was officially on military time. It had been such a long day my eyelids were starting to droop, but I tried not to nod out since I didn't know when I'd be back and I wanted to take in the sights of LA for the last time. Finally, my eyes gave into their weight, my mind relaxed for the first time in ages, and I started to drift…I didn't fight it, I let myself go.

The loud commotion woke me from my deep slumber. It was pitch dark outside; the bus had parked with its dim interior lights turned on. The last thing I recalled before I nodded out was hopping on the Harbor Freeway. Now I didn't know where I was and what the fuss was about. That's when I saw the reason for the uproar—strutting down the aisle of the bus was a Marine Corps drill instructor. He wore heavily starched and creased green fatigues; he wasn't tall but a Smokey the Bear hat atop his head gave him a taller and wider appearance. Truthfully, the LA probation officers looked more physically imposing than this funny-style clown. The moment he opened his mouth, I knew that I miscalculated him. He commanded, "All you Marine maggots, get off the bus, NOW!" At this moment, it wasn't his size or uniform that concerned me—what spooked me was the tone in his voice. He wasn't suggesting or asking us to get off the bus, he was *ordering* us, and by his commanding voice, I knew he wasn't bullshitting! I slowly got up from my seat to exit the bus. Three rows in front of me, this cat said aloud, "I sure am glad I enlisted in the Navy, so long suckers!" Having had his say, he let out a hearty laugh. Before the seated Navy recruit even finished laughing, the DI flew down the center aisle and stood directly over him. He shouted at his face, "What did you say, you fucking squid faggot!" He didn't even give the Navy recruit a chance to reply and punched him in the face. That was my cue to quickly maneuver around this madman, and bolt off the bus. Apparently, everyone felt the same, as we all made a mad dash to the exit. We started to stumble over each other and I dodged a few bodies to exit the bus. I made it out unscathed and saw others that were not as lucky, thrown off the bus compliments of the Marine Corps boogeyman.

It was dark outside and we were not the only recruits to arrive; others were already here, too many to count. Outside the bus, were other DIs, all having similar authoritative voices, shouting commands at us: "Line up at the parade deck! Place your feet inside the yellow footprints! Don't move a muscle! Shut the fuck up! Look straight ahead!" Too much was happening all at once. I followed everyone else as we ran over to the area where the other recruits were standing stationary. Once there, I saw sets of painted yellow footprints on the pavement and placed my feet inside a set. The footprints were lined up to place us in a formation. Standing in the footprints, I scoped out the area and saw that I was confined in a fortified military base. I also noticed that we were close to an airport because periodically I could hear and see planes coming and going from a distance.

All of the DIs dressed identically to the one that chased us off the bus. They shouted at us, got in our faces, slapped us, and every so often punched someone. The yelling and abuse was nonstop; I felt like they had me surrounded. They kept reminding us, "You cocksuckers better keep looking straight ahead, don't move a muscle, if I catch you eye-fucking the area, you will be dealt with!" I told myself to freeze and to quit trying to sneak peeks in. I thought, "You stupid buddhahead, I shoulda just done the time!"

I lost track of how long I stood frozen in this position, but I knew that I couldn't last much longer. My muscles were starting to tighten up, causing involuntary twitches, everyone surrounding me was squirming and doing the same. The DIs were having a field day, handing out tongue-lashings, slapping people upside their head, and using us as their punching bags. It must have been over an hour before the rest of the buses arrived. I wasn't sure of the time, but it felt very late. Finally, one DI went to the front of the yellow footprint formation and shouted, "When you hear your name, answer with a loud, 'yes sir' and step forward!"

The DI stopped taking roll after approximately eighty names were called out. This first group of recruits were herded off by a trio of drill instructors. Roll call resumed, more names were called, but my name, Private Nagata, had yet to be called. I had no idea how many of us were still standing in formation because I didn't want to look around. The DI then called out "Private Charlie Chan!" I thought, "There's another Oriental here, Charlie Chan! Damn, his folks sure did him cold!" The DI called his name out again, "Private Charlie Chan!" Still no answer, then out of the corner of my eye, I saw the DI moving briskly in my direction. He stopped within inches from my face, so close that I felt the brim of his Smokey the Bear hat touch my forehead. He shouted at me, "Private Jap, I'm talking to you!" My body stiffened, and out of habit, I looked him dead in his eyes. That was a no-no and he shouted at me, "Boy, are you eye-fucking me!" I was pissed off and confused all at the same time, and I heard myself say, "No sir." He must have chilled out because instead of swinging at me he yelled in my face, "Move your slimy ass out of here!"

I left the formation to join the other sorry-looking recruits and we all waited to see what was going to happen next.

When our group became large enough, we were the second group of terrorized recruits to be marched off by three abusive drill instructors. They took us to a different part of the base where we were placed in a long single file line, then stood at attention next to a building. We entered the building in groups of threes. As I got closer to the entrance, I heard buzzing sounds. When it was my turn to step inside the building, I was ordered immediately to sit on one of three barber chairs. Behind each chair was a butcher, disguised as a barber holding a hair clipper. Surrounding the chairs were mounds of hair—so much hair encircled my chair that it completely covered the linoleum floor. All I saw was hair: black, brown, yellow, straight, curly and kinky, all mixed together on the floor, looking like a psychedelic art collage. As soon as I sat down, the barber went to work. With six long strokes and two half-side-strokes to remove my sideburns, I was transformed from, "Mister-don't-step-out-the-pad-unless-my-front's-together," to a Mr. Clean, skinhead fool. After my "haircut" we were taken to a supply room, where I was issued a green canvas sea bag, three sets of green fatigues, four sets of green wool socks, and two lame-looking green caps with Marine Corps insignias. The only dress items not green were two pairs of black clodhopper boots with black lacing, four white tee shirts and drawers, two khaki canvas belts, and two brass belt buckles.

After receiving our threads, they took us to a large room that reminded me of the Dorsey High School locker room, because of its similar funky, damp, musty odor. It had concrete flooring, dim lighting, and a large back shower area. We were ordered to strip out off our clothes, then they told the eighty of us, "I want every swinging dick to to get your slimy civilian ass into the showers, scrub yourself clean, and wash out your dirty civilian assholes." While giving this instruction, two DIs were already inside the showers, turning the cold water knobs on full blast. Upon command, we all scrambled into the shower area. This shower area only had twelve shower sprays, and was not built to accommodate eighty of us plus three drill instructors. We were packed in, elbow to asshole tight, with rabid drill instructors, shouting, "Hurry the fuck up you slimy turds," "Wash out your assholes, you fuckin' maggots." After three minutes, we were ordered out of the showers. Upon exiting the showers, I saw that half of us never even got wet, myself included.

We stood in front of our property upon reassembling in the dressing area. Towels were handed out and we were ordered to dry off and to put on our skivvies. I got anxious because I didn't know what skivvies were! My anxiety eased when others around me started putting on their government-issued drawers and tee shirts. We were now sitting in a kneeling attention-position, when a cardboard box with a shipping label affixed to its flap was distributed to each of us. We were ordered to place our slimy civilian clothes inside the box, and then write down our home address on the shipping label.

After we stacked up the boxes in the corner of the room, we were told to put on our green fatigues and socks. Next, the DI showed us how to lace up and tie our boots. After dressing, we put the remaining clothing items in the green canvas sea bag, and stood at attention next to it. The drill instructors walked around the room to inspect us, one of them stopped in front of a recruit and asked, "Where is your cover?" The recruit replied, "Sir, I don't know, sir!" Immediately, the DI slapped the recruit upside his freshly-shaven head, giving off an open-hand-to-skin sound that my ears were becoming all too familiar hearing. "You dip shit turd, this is your COVER—you never step outside without wearing your cover, and you never wear your cover indoors." With that, he handed the terrified recruit his government-issued Marine Corps hat. Nervously, the recruit took his hat, I mean cover, and put it on top of his head, and in an instant the DI punched him in the stomach. "You fuckin' turd, I said never wear your cover indoors!" The recruit was doubled over, gasping for air while the DI hollered at the rest of us, "You all got that shit!" In unison we shouted, "Sir! Yes, sir!" His next command was, "All you maggots, pull out your covers!" Before he finished his command we were all frantically rifling through our sea bag looking for our hats, I mean covers. Just my luck, mine was at the bottom of my sea bag!

We picked up our sea bags, went outside, put on our covers, and marched to a different supply area. We were now back outside, kneeling at attention, while the supply people placed in front of us, additional government-issued gear. We were told that this would be all the gear we would need for our basic training: two sheets, a blanket, pillowcase, two towels, two washcloths, canteen, helmet, cartridge belt, writing stationery, soap, foot powder, toothbrush, shaving cream, razor, toothbrush, toothpaste, shower shoes, sewing kit, and brass polish—everything plus the kitchen sink.

They demonstrated how to pack our property into the canvas sea bag. By the time all the gear was packed, it easily weighted over eighty pounds. They put us back in formation and ordered us to lift up our sea bag and place its carrying strap over our right shoulder.

Our formation was four lines, with the four standing abreast ordered to lock their arms. Upon doing so, the DI commanded, "Forward march!" None of us knew what the fuck to do but we stepped at the same time. Just trying to walk with locked arms, four abreast by itself takes teamwork, coordination and practice. Add into the equation an eighty-pound sea bag on your back with its strap digging into your shoulder blade and collarbone, it became an impossible task. We walked and walked; the DIs never let up, continuously yelling at us with each and every step we took. No one dared to stop walking, even though we all wanted to. Every so often, I managed to shift the position of my laden sea bag so that the pressure of its strap would cut into a different area of my collarbone.

Finally, I heard, "Platoon halt!" We had stopped at an isolated area on the base; all I saw were military corrugated steel Quonset huts, surrounded by fields of dirt. Before we could catch our breath, the four lines were ordered into separate Quonset huts. A row of double bunk racks ran along two inner corrugated walls, with the opening between the two rows of bunks creating a long narrow walkway through the middle of the hut.

By now, we were all traumatized, terrorized and tired, and our fatigues were soaked with sweat. The sight of a bed never looked so good to me—I was exhausted and desperately wanted to lie down and shut eye, but I knew this wasn't about to happen. We were told to gather around an empty cot, where the DI proceeded to grab someone's sea bag and emptied all of its contents on the floor. He picked up the sheet, blanket, and pillowcase. In less than two minutes he demonstrated how we were supposed to fix our rack. Upon completion, the bunk's thin mattress was neat and tight, all corners of the sheets and outer blanket were tucked in at forty-five degree angles. The DI pulled a quarter from his pocket, flipped it atop of the mattress, and it literally bounced off the tightly tucked sheets and blanket. He said that this is how our racks are to be made from this moment on. He then told us that we had three minutes to make our racks. He looked down at his watch and started the countdown, we all ran back to our sea bags frantically searching for our blanket and sheets. I found my sheets, blanket, and pillowcase and tried to duplicate what he just showed us. At home, I used to make my bed, but never with a forty-five degree tuck. I was tugging on the blanket trying to make it tighter, when the DI called out, "Time!" We stood at attention next to our racks for inspection. I was nervous—even though my rack looked tighter than most, it was nowhere near his finished product. He went down the row, inspecting the racks, pulling sheets and blankets off mattresses and tossing them on the floor, yelling at each recruit, calling us, "cocksuckers, maggots, turds, and assholes." When he got tired of yelling at us, he started socking some of us. When he arrived at my rack, either my rack was half way presentable, or he was just tired of yelling and beating on us. Without even looking at me, he pulled out the corner tucks from my mattress and said, "Do this right!" I shouted back, "Sir, yes sir!"

When he finished his inspection, we were all wide awake. He told us that reveille was at oh-five-hundred. He said, "For you civilian turds, this means five a.m. Upon reveille you will have five minutes to dress, make your rack and be outside lined up in formation." He continued, "Any cock sucker who doesn't have his rack properly squared away, will answer to me! You got that shit!" We responded in unison, "Sir, yes sir!" He retorted, "I can't hear you, ladies!" Again we shouted it louder; this back-and-forth game went on for at least a minute. He finally stopped and instructed us to strip down to our skivvies and stand at attention next to our rack. Next, he shouted, "Hit the rack!" It took but a second to jump on the top bunk and lie at attention. His next order was, "Out of the rack." We hopped back to a standing attention position. He kept repeating these commands, but instead of getting frustrated and slowing down, we kept up with his demands. By the time he was finally satisfied, we were all breathing heavily, laying down at attention on top of our racks. He turned off the lights, and warned us, "There will be no talking. You will not fuck around like you did in civilian life. Those days are over with and if I hear any people playing grab-ass, I will be back and you all will be in a world of shit!" With that, he slammed the door as he left our hooch.

With the exception of a cough or two, we remained as still as possible—no one wanted mister crazy fuck to return. Seconds became a minute, and minutes became longer. Finally, I started to relax thinking that even fuckhead had to sleep too. A loud fart broke the silence, followed by nervous muffled laughter. I had held in so much since I arrived at this insane asylum, I found the mere passing of gas to be a moment of hysterical relief. A voice from within the hut said, "Shut the fuck up." A voice from a different part of the hut, said, "You shut the fuck up." This disagreement was quickly squashed when someone said, "Both of you shut up, go to sleep. I don't want him coming back tonight." This was the first logical thing I'd heard since I was rudely awakened on the bus.

All around me, recruits were silently creeping out of their rack, trying to fix their mattresses the Marine Corps way. I got up and finished tucking in the edges of my mattress. When I was satisfied that my sheets and blanket were tight enough to pass morning inspection, I climbed back atop of my rack. Many changed back into their fatigues and fell asleep on top of their blanket, not wanting to mess up their finished product. I heard others quietly cursing as they relieved themselves by pissing into their canteens.

I was exhausted, but I knew that the worst was behind us; it was their job to try and scare the shit out of us before we start our real training. I've experienced this don't-fuck-with-me-I'm-crazy routine before.

DEAR MOMMA

September, 1967
Sunday morning – MCTF

OUR PLATOON—all eighty of us—sat at attention on our foot lockers, all eyes focused on our Senior Drill Instructor, Gunnery Sergeant Minnifield, awaiting further instruction. While our other two drill instructors, Sergeant Bryant and Corporal Manlove were sadistic mothafuckas in their own right, from the get-go it was unconditionally evident that Gunny Minnifield was the main man, the baddest of the bad. Like many things in life, looks can be deceiving. This adage applied to Gunny Minnifield, with his neatly cropped military cut, processed hair, razor-trimmed mustache, angular facial features, and light cocoa complexion. I swear to God at first glance, I thought he was Harry Belafonte.

I have now been at the Marine Corps Recruit Depot, MCRD, for three weeks—the longest three weeks of my life. From the very first morning when I stood in formation, nervously waiting to begin our basic training, it has been nonstop torture of the mind, body, and spirit. That first morning, DIs Manlove and Bryant picked up from where they left off the night before, yelling, harassing, and hitting us. At the time, I still believed, "enough already, you all made your point last night when you terrorized us, now chill so we can start our training!" It still hadn't registered that this abusive shit was our training, and this wasn't even the tip of the iceberg! Suddenly, Bryant and Manlove stopped fucking with us; they stepped to the front of the formation, and stood at attention. That's when out of the corner of my eye, I saw Gunnery Sergeant Minnifield. He walked out of a billet that I later learned was the drill instructor's hooch. He confidently strutted to the front of our formation—he knew he was the star of this show and had a captive audience. He was a bit older than the other two drill instructors; I'd estimate him to be in his mid-thirties. The other DIs wore Smoky the Bear hats, starched dark green fatigues, and spit-polished boots that were entirely exposed because their starched fatigue pants were bloused directly above the top of each boot. In contrast, Gunny Minnifield wore a dressier light tan short sleeve uniform, more like a business outfit compared to the DI's work threads. The stripes of his rank was sewn on the upper sleeves of his pressed shirt, above his right breast pocket he wore numerous Dentine chewing gum-sized pins, each bearing different marking and colorings. The only commonality of his uniform dress with that of the other DIs was the Smoky the Bear hat.

He wasn't more physically imposing than the other DIs because they all carried themselves with an intimidating LAPD look and attitude. What distinguished him was his cocky sense of confidence and how the other DIs deferred to him. When I first laid my eyes on him, if this wasn't so damn serious, I would have been tempted to whistle Harry Belafonte's banana boat song, "Dayo." The moment he opened his mouth, he sang a different tune. "My name is Gunnery Sergeant Minnifield. I am your Senior Drill Instructor of Platoon 358, your other drill instructors are Sergeant Bryant and Corporal Manlove. You will address us at all times as "Sir." You will obey all our commands. The commandant of the Marine Corps has instructed me to turn you worthless slimy maggots into Marines. You are worthless civilian faggots, your mamas have coddled you all your miserable lives, and now you want to join my Marine Corps! You cocksuckers make me wanna puke. Marines are the baddest fighting machine on the face of this planet. We do all the dirty work that allow you slimy civilian turds to grow your hair long, smoke dope, disrespect the flag, and finger bang your girlfriends on Friday night. Looking at you cocksuckers makes me sick. Your longhaired hippie days are over; you got that shit!" We followed his welcome to MCRD speech, with a rousing, "Sir, yes sir!" Gunny Minnifield had worked himself into a rage—any thought that this was just an act had vanished. This shit is for real!

What is hard for me to comprehend is how they have managed to cover up and get away with this abusive shit all these years. I knew a few cats from the Avenues that were in the Marines, and as far as I know, they never told anyone about this shit. I was now pissed at them for not saying anything. The first chance I got, I was going to drop a roll of dimes on this place and shut this bad boy down!

Today, being a Sunday morning, I estimated that it was around eight o'clock, or oh-eight-hundred in military time. If I was back home, I would either be sound asleep, or if Saturday night was a happening, I would just be dragging my ass home. Today, I already did physical exercise, passed a billet and rifle inspection, ate chow, and am now sitting on my footlocker, waiting for Gunny Minnifield's next order.

Gunny Minnifield was now ready to speak. "Secure your Marine Corps writing gear. This morning you will write a letter to your mommas." After retrieving my writing gear, we were ordered to write down his dictation word for word on our stationery:

September 13, 1967

Dear Family,
I am sorry for not writing to you sooner but I have been very busy. Everyday I train hard, leaving me little time to write. My training is challenging and I am learning what it takes to become a Marine. My health is excellent, and my drill instructors are firm but they are also fair.

I miss the family, but don't worry about me because I am fine. The Marine Corps provides me with everything that I need. Even though I miss your home cooking, the food here is healthy and tasty. Please do not send me anything from home because the Marines provide me with everything I need.

Gunny Minnifield then interjected, "Does everyone have this written down so far!" We responded with, "Yes, sir!" He said, "Now finish your letter with:

I am sorry that this letter is short. I have an inspection today that I must prepare for, I know you understand.

Your Son,"

Gunny Minnifield finished by saying, "Sign your letter, address your envelope, put your letter in the envelope without sealing it." Then he ordered the squad leaders to pick up the letters that will be sent out after they are inspected. I signed my name at the bottom of "my" letter.

After the squad leaders picked up our letters, Gunny Minnifield said, "The commandant of the Marine Corps has issued an order, saying that all you churchgoers have the option of attending Sunday service. The rest of you non-believing atheists will remain in the area and will use this time to clean your rifle, polish your brass buckle and square away your gear." This surprise announcement was music to my ears. This was going to be my first break since I got off the bus. Man, I never thought that I would live to see the day when I would be so thrilled to sit on a hard wooden foot locker, at eight in the morning, polishing a belt buckle, and boots. I thought, "And I volunteered for this shit!"

Around fifteen recruits from our platoon were marched over to the base chapel for Sunday service. The rest of us kept busy, cleaning, polishing, and shining our equipment. We weren't allowed to talk, so the only conversations taking place, was the silent dialog taking place within our minds. Sitting on my footlocker, using a patch of cloth and Brasso, to shine my belt buckle, I started to think about the bullshit letter I just wrote. I began to mentally draft the letter that I intended to send; here it goes:

Dear Mama,

Help! The people in charge of this asylum are sadistic and deranged. I know I have messed up in the past, but I have never complained about the punishment or price I had to pay for my misdeeds. Well, this is the one exception. No one deserves this type of physical and mental abuse. From the moment we get up (5:00 a.m.) to lights out at the end of the day, it's non-stop harassment. They call us every filthy derogatory name imaginable, and when they run out of names to call us, they make up some more. We are slapped, punched and even kicked by our drill instructors. Unlike the John Wayne war movies where all the soldiers are middle-aged, everyone here is around my age, and from what I am finding out, a lot of us were in trouble with the law and the Marines was the alternative to jail. Even though we all volunteered, we did not sign up to take this type of abuse.

Pop and Yuji Sensei taught me the true meaning of training and discipline at the Seinan Dojo. What they do to us here has nothing to do with discipline—it's brainwashing through abuse and torture. They have mastered the art of "divide and conquer." With each passing day, I see more and more fellow recruits start to mimic the attitudes of the drill instructors. This week in my billet, a pack of vigilante recruits waited until "lights out," then tip-toed up on another recruit and gave him a "blanket party." When it was over, this recruit was beaten and bloodied but he could not report it because it was dark and he couldn't identify anyone because he was covered with a blanket when he was beaten. I know for a fact it was the drill instructors that instigated his beating. The guy who was attacked is constantly picked on and singled out by the DIs. I don't know his real name but everyone calls him "Private Shitbird" because that's what the DIs call him. He struggles to keep up with the strenuous exercises; personally, I don't blame him because there are moments that I am so fatigued that I am close to dropping due to exhaustion. Whenever someone can't keep up, falls behind, or drops from exhaustion, the DIs make the entire platoon start over from the beginning and then we are told that we are being punished because of the shitbirds who don't give a fuck. Those who can't keep up are excused from the group punishment inflicted on the rest of us by the DIs. The shitbirds are ordered to stand in front of us, smile and forced to drink swigs of water from their canteen, while the DIs continue to torture the rest of us with endless exercise drills. It's usually the same people who are the weak links or shitbirds. This week it came to a head when a hit squad made the rounds and threw blanket parties on all the shitbirds. The irony is that after the blanket parties, the shitbirds stopped lagging behind and now keep up with the rest of us. Life is strange.

We are divided into three platoons: each platoon has eighty recruits, three platoons make a company. Within the company, the three platoons compete against each other. The competitions are serious business. Our first competition was a physical fitness test, where we did a whole bunch of push-ups, chin-ups, ran an obstacle course, stuff like that. My Platoon 358 did not win the competition; the winner was Platoon 360. After the contest, my attitude was, "We did our best, better luck next time." Our head drill instructor, Sergeant Minnifield, didn't share my view—he was righteously pissed off and he punished us. Our billet area is surrounded by dirt, and when we returned to our quarters, he made all of us swim in the dirt. For the next hour we did the backstroke, freestyle, and breaststroke. After finishing our "swim" he made us do squat thrusts, which is a killer on the knees. He commanded, "Squat thrusts until your nose bleeds!" Over and over, up and down, down and up, we did squat thrusts until I was getting dizzy and thought that I was going to pass out. Finally, we stopped because a recruit's nose actually started to bleed! He still wasn't finished with us. We were all drenched in perspiration and caked with dirt. He told us that looking at us made him want to puke, and we looked like fuckin' pigs. He made us lie face down in the dirt and roll back and forth, while "oinking" aloud. When he finally allowed us to get up, he laid down the law. "Platoon 358 will not lose any more competitions." He told us to look to our right, the area where the winning Platoon 360, is billeted. Their platoon was sitting down on top of their water buckets and smoking cigarettes. As he continued to insult and berate us, he said that they were laughing at us. Somewhere in Gunnery Minnifield's ancestry, there must have been some chameleon blood mixed in, because that day I saw him change colors from light cocoa brown, to red with anger, to white with rage. After he finished punishing us, I was so pissed off, tired and dizzy that I didn't care anymore; all I felt like doing was hurt somebody.

In our platoon, I am the only Oriental, in fact I am the only Oriental in the entire company. Everyday, I am reminded of this. I have been called racial slurs that I never knew existed. "Gook" is the name they call the enemy we are fighting in Viet Nam, whose leader is Ho Chi Minh. Along with the regular racial slurs, "Jap," "slant-eyes," "slopehead," and "Chink," the DIs also call me "Gook" and "Ho Chi Minh." Since our platoon leader is a Negro, he rarely uses the word "nigger," however, he uses just about every other derogatory racial slur. It's just harder for me because I am a minority of one—I have never felt so isolated.

I had a lot more to "write" in my mental letter to home, but the churchgoers just returned so I better get my mind focused back on the bullshit. However, I still had enough time to sign off.

Miss you all, and wish I was there,

Tadashi

KILL

Boot Camp
November, 1967

DI MANLOVE bellowed out loud, "Lift your head and hold it high!" *Clomp, clomp, clomp*, without breaking our stride, we echoed in unison, "Lift your head and hold it high!" DI Manlove continued, "Three-fifty-eight is coming by, sound off!" Again it was our turn as we shouted, "One-two," *clomp, clomp*. Manlove continued the "running" dialog "Sound off, one-two," to which we ended the mantra, "Three-four, three-four!" *Clomp, clomp, clomp, clomp.*

I've lost track how long we've been running, but judging from the sticky wetness inside my fatigues, it has been way too long. Where we were running to, and how much longer Corporal Manlove could keep up his grueling pace never entered my mind. I was totally focused on the rhythm of my breath and the timing of my steps, making sure that I stayed in stride with the rest of the platoon, *clomp, clomp*.

Manlove shouted out, "I don't know but I've been told!" *Clomp, clomp*, here we go again, we answered, "I don't know but I've been told!" He finished off, by shouting, "That Eskimo pussy is mighty cold, sound off!" *Clomp, clomp*. Still in stride I thought, "That one was half-way funny," *clomp, clomp.*

Actually, Manlove's intermittent lame rhymes and pre-scripted mantras helped to keep our platoon in one rhythmic harmonious step. The thundering sound, created by the soles of seventy-four pairs of combat boots, all hitting the ground in perfect timing as we ran, was music to my ears, *clomp, clomp, clomp, clomp*. It felt good knowing that our shit was getting tight.

A thought flashed through my mind: I remember seeing a picture in a *National Geographic Magazine* of geese in a tight V formation, flying south for the winter. If that same flock of geese was flying over us, and checked us out, they would be impressed by our tight formation! *Clomp, clomp, clomp*. To distract myself from my aches and pains, and to keep my sanity, at times I would momentarily let my mind drift. This very moment, if I dwelt on my pain, how with each stride my rifle and backpack straps dug deeper into tender sore crevices on my shoulders, the heat and sweat emitting from inside my steel helmet making my head light and my vision blurred, it would be intolerable. Our fatigues, buttoned down from the top of our collar to the wrist buttons, trapped our body heat, creating a sauna-like effect. At times like today, when the sun was beating down on me, I felt my trapped body swishing about in my sweat-drenched fatigues. *Clomp, clomp, clomp.*

Some of the shit I tripped on to distract when I was near the brink of exhaustion was far out, like flying geese!! Shiiiit! One area that I absolutely forbid my mind to drift off to is anything having to do with home. My first week of boot camp, I made the mistake of constantly thinking about anything and everything that reminded me of home. By the end of the week I was so miserable that I felt like I was going to crack. Right then, I told myself that if I was going to make it through this bad mothafucka, I better get my mind right and quit thinking about the Avenues. Ever since I let go of the neighborhood, boot camp became more of a daily challenge, and less of an intolerable torture. *Clomp, clomp, clomp.*

Don't get me wrong, the DIs still slapped, hit, yelled, insulted, and harassed us, sunup to sundown. The bullshit never let up and even got worse, but a funny thing happened. As training got tougher and more demanding, as a platoon, we got tighter. Without having it said, we all came to the same conclusion that the only way we were going to get out of this bad boy in one piece was by working together.

From the moment we stepped off the bus, it was hammered into us that our platoon is only as strong as its weakest link, and if one person failed, we were all punished. Peer group pressure is a bitch and these mothafuckas are PhDs on the subject. Ever since we were punished for losing the first intra company competition, Platoon 358 has won all the ensuing competitions: we kicked ass on the obstacle course, bayonet stick fighting, close order drill, and inspection. I got to admit, I tried like a mothafucka to win each competition and I did my part. After we won the drill and inspection, Gunny Minnifield told us, "You turds are starting to resemble a mean green fighting machine." I suppose that this was his sadistic way of paying us a compliment. I still hated the DIs, but it sure felt good after each company competition victory, to strut in cadence back to our billets, then sit on our buckets in front of our hooches with Gunny Minnifield proudly announcing, "The smoking lamp is lit!" After a resounding, "Aye, aye sir!" I chained smoked for the next hour, one cigarette after another until my head got dizzy. It's been a long time since my head caught a buzz, and it felt good, anything for a cheap high! I even felt a sense of pleasure, watching the two losing platoons get punished for losing to Platoon 358. *Fuck it, better them than me!*

Private Well, a countrified white recruit from Wyoming, broke the rhythmic silence, singing out, "I don't know but it's been said!", after we repeated these words, he followed up, "that Indian pussy is might red!" *Clomp, clomp, clomp*, his improv was welcomed because it broke up the monotony and got us focused back to the moment. Manlove was directly to my immediate right, and I swear to God, for the very first time ever, I could hear him breathing deep. "Mothafucka's getting tired!" *Clomp, clomp*. My aches and pains no longer mattered. I am prepared to run til I die, I will not quit, I will not lose to this cocksucker! I was in a position to feel Manlove's presence—I had been picked out by the DIs to be one of four squad leaders in our platoon. I don't want to have anything to do with their Marine Corps, but I was too chickenshit to tell them, "Thanks, but no thanks!" Being a squad leader did have an advantage because now when we marched or ran in formation, I was in the front row of the formation and could see where we were headed to, whereas before, all I ever saw was the back of the head of the recruit in front of me.

Clomp, clomp, clomp. Finally, directly ahead and slightly to the right of the dirt road, I saw a clearance with empty wooden bleachers—to me it looked like an oasis. Manlove began to slow down the pace of our formation as if we were a bus and he was its driver. He gently eased on its brakes, and slowed our engine to a slow trot, then idling without turning off its engine. To his command of, "Mark time, march!" we high-stepped in place. We were all relieved to see the wooden bleachers and looked forward to resting our raggedy asses.

Before sitting in the bleachers, we stacked our M-14s, took off our helmets, cartridge belts, and backpacks, then we were allowed to take a swig of water from our canteen. Man, in less than two minutes, I dropped over forty pounds, and quenched my thirst—life is good! In the bleachers, we sat at attention and waited for the other two platoons to finish their run and join the company. It is nice being the lead platoon of the company because at times like this, we had a few extra minutes of rest before the other platoons joined us for our next indoctrination session.

By the time the other two platoons were seated in the bleachers, my new challenge was keeping my eyes open. Judging from my internal clock, I figured that it must be late mid-afternoon, because before our run, we had eaten noon chow, marched back to our billets, put on our combat gear, and it felt like we've been running for at least an hour; anyway, I'm fuckin' tired. After a day of grueling drills and exercise, having to sit at attention for a bullshit indoctrination class without nodding out, is impossible. As long as we are on the go, our bodies and minds function on adrenaline and overdrive and I have no problem staying awake. It's when we come to a standstill that both my body and mind want to shut down. I swear to Buddha, there are moments that I dozed off for a few seconds with my eyes wide open.

Kerpow! I recognized the distinct sound of a DI's open hand, slapping the shit out of some unsuspecting recruit's skinhead. *Kerpow!* This one was close, might even have been someone from my squad. The sadistic DIs lived for these moments, knowing that it is humanly impossible for us to sit at attention and remain awake. They got their rocks off by creeping up on tired-ass recruits, nodding out with heads bobbing and weaving, eyes closed trying to catch a quick catnap, then smacking the shit out of them, bringing us back to their reality. *Kerpow!* I thought, "Man, I hope Viet Nam ain't this bad," when out of nowhere appeared a training instructor. Each combat training indoctrination class is taught by a different Marine Corps instructor. I wonder what load of bullshit this cat was pushing.

He stood in front of the bleachers, facing over two hundred of us, "Good afternoon recruits." We answered, "Good afternoon, sir!" "My name is Staff Sergeant Lilly. Today, I am going to tell you about your enemy, Victor Charles. He goes by other names, VC, plain old Charlie, or as I prefer to call him, "Gook." Sergeant Lilly cleared his voice and continued, "Victor Charles lives in the jungle and can live on a bowl of rice for over a week. He does not believe in God, and places no value on human life. He believes in reincarnation and he is not afraid to die because it is his mission to die and come back reincarnated as a water buffalo." I tuned out because this is the same type of crap that I've heard before. He continued, "Before I tell you more about your enemy, I want to show you what a Gook looks like!" Wow, now he had my undivided attention; I wanted to see for the first time what my enemy looked like. I thought, "Damn, these fools are so organized, they even captured a Viet Cong and brought him all the way back for us to see!" I eagerly waited to see the live Gook prisoner. Sergeant Lilly made no order or motion to bring the prisoner front and center, instead he stayed in the same spot and scanned the bleachers as if he lost something. I thought, "Man, what's up?" That's when I saw his eyes lock in on my face—he wasn't looking me in the eye but surer than shit he was locked in on my face! He pointed at me and said, "You, Private step forward!" My entire body went numb like someone drained my blood. I felt a cold chill run through my body; "Mothafuck," I was singled out. I hesitated, but knew that this bullshit had no exit ramp. Slowly I stood, my legs feeling weak and rubbery, and I stepped forward. I could barely feel my legs move and everything felt like slow motion. When I stopped in front of him, he said in a commanding voice, "Private, about face, now face the bleachers!" From that moment on, I don't know how long I stood in front of the company. I felt one-hundred-ninety pairs of eyes riveted on my face, etching it in their collective psyches. Sergeant Lilly exclaimed, "Gentlemen, this is what the enemy looks like. Remember this face, because your life will depend on recognizing your enemy!" Finally, he said, "Private, you may return back to the bleachers." I went back to the bleachers; I could feel their eyes on me, I felt the hatred of their glares and I wanted to shout out, "I ain't no Gook, I'm one of you!" I bit my tongue; it was too late, the damage had been done.

As I worked my way back to my seat in the bleachers, I was no longer tired. I was on hypersensitive alert, acutely aware of everybody and everything surrounding me. I didn't have the luxury to feel sorry for myself, I knew there was going to be some fallout. I had no idea in what form or magnitude it would present itself, all I know is that I'm fighting the first mothafucka who pulls this "Gook" shit on me. I'm worried because there are too many ignorant-ass mothafuckas here and I'll probably be getting into beaucoup fights. I was straight with most of the minority cats in my platoon. With the exception of a few that were from the South, the rest were from big city ghettoes and barrios, places like Harlem, Chicago, Dallas, and East Saint Louis, Illinois. The ones that concerned me were the countrified white boys from the sticks—many of these yahoos never had contact with an Oriental. If they had, it was at a Chinese restaurant or from watching that punkass "Hop Sing" Oriental actor on the TV program, "Bonanza," selling out our collective Oriental souls, by playing his "Sing-Song Chinaman" role on the tube.

A few weeks ago, we were "educated" by a senior instructor at an indoctrination session on how filthy and non-human Gooks are. He said that when we get to the Nam, "Never fuck a Gook whore. They have incurable diseases, some so nasty that even penicillin can't cure it. It's called black syphilis and if you get it, they will put your sorry ass on a ship that circles the Philippines; you will remain on that ship until your dick rots off! The commandant of the Marine Corps will write to your family informing them that you are missing in action." "That boat circles the island with dipshits like you on board, people who didn't listen to me, sorry cocksuckers that will die on the USS Black Syphilis." At that time I thought, "Shit, I'll jack-off before I get the black syphilis!" The instructor was not finished, "Vietnamese women are not like white women, their pussies are even slanted like their eyes." I couldn't believe what this fool was selling. It meant that if Oriental chicks have slanted vaginas then my dick had to be slanted when I was getting some of it, and there is nothing slanted about my Sir Richard. The real problem is that some yahoo fool is gonna believe this silly mothafucka. Sure enough, that night a peckerwood in my squad asked me before lights out, "Naagouta, do Oriental women really have slanted pussies?" I glared at him and said, "Go ask your one-tooth momma, peckerwood!" No further questions were asked.

Until now, all the racial bullshit directed towards me was shit I could handle. I had one fight over the "Jap" shit. It ended so fast, I couldn't even call it a fight. A gangly, bucktooth, Gomer Pyle-looking hillbilly from somewhere in Missouri called me "Jap" during a Sunday morning church break. I was sitting on my foot locker when I felt the sting of his word. With no DI around, I immediately stood up to answer his challenge. Fool thought he could take me and charged at me with outstretched arms as if I was just going to stand there and let him snatch me! Instinctively, I stepped to my left, planted my right foot and tagged him with my right fist, dead center in his right eye, bullseye! Damn, it felt good! Sucka's feet went out from under him and he fell sideways into Hicks, a big blood cat from East Saint Louis. Hicks witnessed the entire event and said, "Get your ass off me!" and threw Gomer Pyle onto the ground. I sat back down and continued to polish my belt buckle. Blood was rushing through my veins, but it was all good knowing that I whipped the punk-ass chump. Hillbilly wore my blackeye all week. "Jap that, you peckerwood mothafucka!"

"358, put on your combat gear and line up!" Manlove's command shocked me back to my reality. Automatically, I rose and hustled over to our equipment stack. As I was strapping on my backpack, Hill, one of the eight blood recruits from East Saint Louis, approached me and spoke, "Don't worry, the brothers got your back." I looked at him and said, "Solid, I appreciate it." That took a little bit off the edge.

GRADUATION

MCRD
December, 1967

I STOOD IN FORMATION, listening to Gunny Minnifield, "At oh-eleven-hundred, I will dismiss you from formation, you will have the rest of the afternoon to visit your families and guests. At oh-fifteen-hundred you will muster back in formation on the parade deck, you got that shit!" We answered with a resounding, "Yes, sir!" He continued, "You are free to take your guests anywhere on base except to the restricted training areas. You can eat at the Enlisted Men's Club, or at the canteen; you can even take your families and shop at the PX, but under no circumstances are you to leave the base; if you do, you will be AWOL. You will not drink any type of alcoholic beverage. Do you hear me, ladies!" I shouted another "Yes, sir!" I was getting impatient, thinking, "Enough already, this control freak is gonna play out his bullshit to the end." His sermon lingered, "Tonight is your last night on MCRD. Tomorrow at oh-six-hundred, you will be transferred to Camp Pendleton to begin your advanced infantry training. During this training, most of you will get weekend liberty passes. After completing your combat training, you will have a two-week leave. I recommend that during your leave, you stock up on all the pussy you can get, and for you nasty white boys, eat all the pussy you can! When you come back from leave, you will be sent directly to Viet Nam. Many of you will die in the jungle, but I want all you swinging dicks to remember, *Marines don't die, we just go to hell and regroup!*" I belted out another, "Yes, sir!", and thought, "This fool's a regular Dale Carnegie positive-thinking mothafucka. If this pep talk doesn't fire you up, what will? Sorry ass mothafucka!"

He then let out a thunderous, "Platoon 358, ATTEN-HUT!" In unison, fifty-nine of us clicked the heels of our shoes together and shifted from an at-ease position into an erect stand-at-attention posture. Today we were styling, dressed in our formal tan khaki uniforms, spit-shined dress shoes, polished brass, glistening shooting medals hung over our right breast pocket, and formal uniform-matching covers with spit-shined brims topped our heads. It felt righteous to finally wear something other than the dark green fatigues and combat boots—this is the sharpest I felt since I got here.

"Platoon 358, forward march!" As trained, I stepped off in perfect timing with my left foot, realizing, "Mothafuck, it's time!" Today we weren't marching, we were strutting to Gunny Minnifield's cadence, "Oh-I-oh-I-oh-ioit!" All three platoons of the company, marched towards the parade deck for our graduation ceremony, with Platoon 358, the company's Honor Platoon leading the way.

I could hardly believe it; in less than an hour I will be spending the afternoon with my family. Everyone except my older brother, Shoji, was driving in from LA for my boot camp graduation ceremony. I felt disappointed when Mama wrote, telling me that Shoji wouldn't be able to attend my graduation because he just started a new job and hadn't been there long enough to ask for a day off. Shoji and I were never close—we had different values, interests, and friends, but the fact remains that he is my oldest brother. We are blood, and just maybe, this could have been one of those moments that brought us closer together; now we'll never know.

Looking back on the past fourteen weeks, there were moments when it felt like time had come to a standstill and that I was never going to get out of here in one piece. Never in my life had I experienced anything like this non-stop dark in the morning to dark at night harassment. Now that my boot camp training is coming to an end, I wonder, "Man, if the Nam is worse than this, I'm going to be in a world of hurt."

My emotions are mixed: I am eager to see and spend the afternoon with my family, but I'm also feeling confused and anxious. The cause of this confusion started fourteen weeks ago, the very moment I stepped off the bus. Back then, I made a promise to myself that the first chance I got, I was going to drop a dime on every last one of these demented sadists, exposing their game about the abuse and bullshit that goes on here. In less than an hour, I will be in a position to tell my folks about the abuse and racism I've endured. Maybe my folks could notify some organization like the JACL that is supposed to protect JA people like myself from racial prejudice. Better yet, maybe to silence me and get me to shut the fuck up, they'll work out a deal to give me my discharge papers and call it a wash. Deep within, I knew this was unlikely to happen because at the end of the day, buddhahead leadership and organizations like the JACL are too chickenshit and lack the balls to stand up and confront "the Man." All that would come out of it was that my folks, especially Moms, would internalize my pain and suffering and make it her's, as if carrying my burdens inside her will lessen my pain. Ever since I was a kid, this was how my folks always chose to deal with the trauma and changes I was going through. After a while I made a conscious decision not to tell them about difficulties and changes I was experiencing because it hurt to see them suffer for my actions—it was a burden and guilt trip that I didn't need.

"Pick 'em up, set 'em down, three to the left, three to the right, oh-i-oh-io-iowat," we continued strutting to Gunny Minnifield's cadence. We took a short cut to the parade field, marching through the main part of MCRD where the permanent personnel are quartered. I continued my train of thought, *So, if I wasn't going to tell my family about the personal racism I experienced, what will I tell them? Maybe, I'll start by showing them the Sharpshooter Medal I earned at the rifle range. Yeah, that rifle range was a bitch-and-a-half.* Nothing in my previous life prepared me for the rifle range; the physical pain and mental stress was beyond intense, it was all about blood and sweat, with no tears.

It began on the tenth week of our training when our entire company was transported up the freeway to Camp Pendleton for two weeks of rifle training. From the first day at the rifle range, until the final qualification test two weeks later, it was intense, serious business. It was made absolutely clear that if you do not qualify with your M-14, you are a failure and disgrace to the Marine Corps. On first hearing this bullshit, my initial reaction was, "I can live with that, maybe then they'll make me a cook instead of a grunt." However, they quickly captured my undivided attention on why I needed to qualify at the rifle range. On the first day at the rifle range, the DIs made a list of those who did not perform up to their standard of expectations. That night, the names on the list were called out and the recruits told to put all of their gear in their sea bags. Carrying their sea bags, they were ordered front and center to the open middle area of our barracks. Then the party began. It started with the DIs making them do close order drills, pretending that their sea bags were their rifles. Over and over DIs Manlove and Bryant barked out commands, "Left shoulder arms! Port arms! Sea bag salute." It is humanly impossible to handle and maneuver an unbalanced ninety-pound sea bag the same way you could a M-14 rifle. Every time someone dropped his sea bag, Bryant or Manlove immediately pounced upon him physically and mentally, beating him down until the poor bastard regrouped and picked up his sea bag again to resume the torture. This abuse went way beyond the typical ass-kicking shit we were all now accustomed to—judging from the beaten-down, desperate expressions on the non-qualifiers, I thought someone was going to get seriously hurt. Finally, the yelling stopped and the day's non-qualifiers, eight in all, were ordered into a small closet-sized storage room, sea bags included. I still don't know how they all managed to squeeze into that undersized space, but when they did, the DIs shut the door. It's hard enough to imagine eight bodies sleeping standing up, asshole to elbow with filled sea bags to boot, locked up in a small closet, if only it had stopped there. Throughout the rest of the night, Manlove or Bryant took shifts banging on the closet door, shouting insults and obscenities at the non-qualifiers, while they exhaled cigarette smoke through the open crack at the bottom of the door. The next morning when they were released from the closet, they all looked like they had died and been barely resuscitated back to life. I don't know how any of them made it through the next day.

At the rifle range, I would wake up every day with new aches and pains in different places on my body. Somehow, I blocked out the mental fatigue and physical pain and worked through it. I have to admit, the thought of spending the night in the closet kept me motivated.

After the first night at the rifle range, I promised myself that if there is one thing in life I will be, it's a rifle-shooting-qualifying motherfucker! From that moment on, my M-14 became my lady, my main squeeze. I became obsessive and possessive about my bitch—every chance I got, I took her apart, oiled and cleaned her barrel, trigger casing, bolt action, and magazine clips. I got to know my lady so well that I could take her apart and reassemble her blindfolded. I knew that if I took care of my lady, she would look out for me.

I was right on! My lady and I qualified every day for the next two weeks. Sometimes it was so close that my fate came down to my last few squeezes of the trigger, but I managed to do it. On the ultimate day, with the accumulation of two weeks training, I felt ready and confident that I was going to blast the shit out of the targets. When my final score was tallied, I missed an Expert medal by three points, but qualified as a Sharpshooter; more importantly, unlike a quarter of my platoon, I avoided spending a single night in the closet.

I am now one with my rifle. From a prone position I can place a grouping on a three–foot diameter bullseye target from a distance of five hundred meters—fuck, that's over five football fields. Do you know how small a three-foot bullseye on a target looks from that distance? I'll tell ya, it looks smaller than a dime. To bulls eye that chickenshit dot from that distance, your form, aim, breathing, wind calculation, and mental framework has to be one with your rifle. Any breakdown in mechanics, however slight, like anticipating the recoil of the rifle, flinching while squeezing the trigger, improper breathing, or a break in concentration is enough to make you miss the target, and if you miss too many times, it's closet time. Even worse, we were warned that if you do not qualify on the final day, you will not graduate with our platoon and will be phased back to a new recruit platoon to start your training back at week two.

To become one with our rifles, we had to condition our bodies by holding our rifles in different statue-like locked positions every day, hours at a time. The process of locking into the different standing, sitting, and prone shooting positions is called, "snapping in." Man, I used muscle groups in my body that I didn't know existed; at times my body felt so contorted that I could have passed for a yogi. The pain was big-time, but as days passed, I slowly felt I was getting the hang of it. My best shooting position was the prone position, which is not surprising, since lying down has always been my strong suit.

Looking back, I'd say that over 95 percent of what my instructors taught was total bullshit, designed to break me down, indoctrinate me, and get me ready to kill gooks. But I'll be the first to admit that they are on top of their game when it comes to teaching you how to fire weapons. Since I am on my way to Nam, and will get shot at, they did me a huge favor by teaching me how to shoot back and defend myself. Now, I can bust caps on anyone wanting to kill me, and I can do it standing, sitting, or laying down—I guess that makes me ready for Viet Nam.

"Eyes right!" Shifting my focus back to Gunny Minnifield's command, I saw we were marching straight through the base's permanent personnel area of MCRD; we rarely saw this part of the base because it is separate from the boot camp training area. We marched past the Enlisted Men's Club, PX, movie theater, post office, and barber shop—this restricted area is a little community unto itself and where I will spend the afternoon with my family. The reason Minnifield made us shift our heads and eyesight was that we were about to strut by a brand-spanking-new platoon of sorry-ass "boots" on our immediate right. Their pathetic sight got me thinking back to my first night in boot camp, how we didn't know shit from Shinola, how awkward and disjointed we were, locking our arms as we marched from one area to the next. I remember the awe and envy I felt whenever an advanced senior platoon marched by us, executing precise maneuvers and maintaining a tight formation. Back then, it was beyond my comprehension that our sorry-ass, locked arm-in-arm, non-marching selves would ever become such a disciplined unit. I sensed the new recruits' trauma from the deer-in-the-headlight look on their faces, their out-of-step clownish appearance, and their being yelled at while carrying their sea bags with arms locked together. "Eyes front!" We snapped our heads forward as we passed by the raw recruits. I asked myself what one piece of advice I would give them to help them get through what they were about to experience? It's weird because my mind is drawing a blank and I can't think of a damn thing. Maybe this is because I still haven't figured it out for myself, what I got out of my training. *Fuck it, the only thing that matters now is that I'm finally getting the hell out of here, going to spend the day with my family and I am one step closer to the Nam.*

All three platoons, a company of close to one-hundred-seventy soon-to-be-graduating Marines, marched toward the parade grounds, dressed in our winter finest, and strutting like we owned the place. From a distance I saw the portable bleachers that were set up on the parade ground to accommodate our families. My heart started to race, *It was time!*

As all three platoons entered the parade grounds, the public address system was playing the Marine Corps Hymn, the energy emanating from our formations palpable. We approached the bleachers where the base commander and his aides were seated in a middle VIP section. I wanted to look for my family but there were so many people seated in the bleachers, I wouldn't be able to spot them without breaking rank. We were passing the VIP section of the bleachers, when Gunny Minnifield ordered, "Eyes left!" On cue we snapped our heads toward the center of the bleachers as Gunny Minifield saluted the company commander as we marched. "Eyes front." We snapped our heads forward, still marching to the Hymn. We came to a halt about fifty yards from the bleachers, all three platoons, now standing at attention, facing our families and guests.

A booming voice on the PA system welcomed our families to the graduation ceremony and asked everyone to rise for the Marine Corps Color Guard and the Pledge of Allegiance. As the pledge was being recited, I still could not spot my family in the crowd, and a bummer of a thought entered my mind, "What if Pop had car problems and they were stuck on the 405; that would be a bitch." After the pledge, a full-bird colonel, who I had never seen before, stepped forward to address the audience, "Welcome to Marine Corps Recruit Depot. Today we are here to witness the young men standing before you, join the ranks in the United States Marines. They have been trained physically, mentally and spiritually to carry on our proud tradition." Quickly, I lost interest in what he had to say and zoned him out. With my head perfectly still, I have mastered the art of sneaking in peeks to help me to figure out my situation and surroundings. My eyes scanned the bleachers, looking for my family, but I still didn't know what I was going to tell them.

As the colonel continued to ramble, I thought about last night and the cold sense of calm I felt. For the first time in my life, I knew exactly what was expected of me—where I was going and what I needed to do. It happened right before taps and lights out when Gunny Minnifield assembled our entire platoon into one billet.We had already shit, showered and shaved and had on our skivvies and shower shoes. Once assembled, he ordered us to return to our billet and come back with our buckets and cigarettes. "Yes, sir!" We all scurried and reassembled, forming a circle around

Gunny. He ordered us to sit on our buckets and then he lit the smoking lamp. By now I had switched from Pall Malls to Camels because most of the time I wasn't allotted enough time to finish a whole cigarette; Camels are shorter in length and stronger in taste. I lit my Camel and enjoyed the taste of smoke filling my lungs. Next, Gunny Minnifield ordered someone to bring him a bucket. He sat in the center of the circle, and asked for a Kool. It was comical watching mothafuckas rush forward trying to be the first to give our tormentor a Kool. I was glad that he didn't ask for a Camel, because I wasn't giving him shit. We all sat sucking in and exhaling hot air but after Gunny Minnifield took a few drags of his Kool, he put it out and asked Corporal Manlove to bring him the orders. I wondered what the fuck was up on the eve of our graduation, I hoped it wasn't going to be bad news. It turned out that Gunny Minnifield had received our orders from the commandant general of the Marine Corps headquarters. It was on a single sheet of paper, alphabetically listing our names and our designated military occupational specialty, or simply put, our MOS.

Shit, this was going to be intense; this was our day of reckoning. Oh-three-eleven was the dreaded number that you didn't want connected to your name. Oh-three-eleven meant that you were assigned to infantry and would end up in "grunt" unit. Any combination of numbers other than "oh-three-eleven meant that while you were still in danger of getting hurt or killed, but your odds for survival had greatly increased. Gunny Minnifield didn't give us time to weigh the gravity of this moment—as soon as Manlove handed him the orders, he commenced, "Acosta, 0200, supply, you lucked out," and nervous laughter filled the room. "Adams, 0311," more nervous laughter. Gunny Minnifield stopped, lifted his eyes up from the paper, spotted Adams and merely shook his head. "Benitez, 0311." On and on, name after name, he continued. After a while, the dreadful announcement of oh-three-eleven lost its stinging impact, probably because up to now, well over half the platoon were given oh-three-eleven assignments. We now were laughing at, even booing, the lucky bastards who were assigned MOSs other than infantry, like office, supply, transportation. One white boy even got an embassy duty assignment, and while I even laughed at that one, deep down inside, I was worried. Finally, "Nagata, 0311." Gunny Minnifield spotted me and said, "*Sayonara!*" His stand-up comedy routine drew more laughter from his captive audience, however, I wasn't amused. Even though I thought I had prepared myself for this very moment, I still felt like I did when my *baachan* (grandmother) was diagnosed with terminal cancer and lived out the last two months at our house. At that time I thought I had prepared myself for her pending death, but when she finally succumbed to her illness, I couldn't shake the lonely empty feeling in my gut. I tried to think of something to make my feeling of emptiness go away, then I remembered a word folks used to say when a situation seemed hopeless, "*shikataganai*," which I interpret as, "Man up, and deal with it!"

Finally, the long-winded colonel wrapped up his speech; next they called MCRD's commanding general to the podium, to say a few more words. Still having a bit more time before reuniting with my family, I thought, "Why not make this a feel-good day, and just talk about the positives? I could tell my family about being in the best condition of my life, gaining fifteen pounds of muscle. I could impress them by telling them about my daily routine: getting up at five-thirty in the morning to shit, shower and shave, dress, make my rack, clean my area, then perform physical, all before morning chow at oh-seven hundred." *Man what's up with this oh-seven hundred chow shit! They sure did a number on my head, even got me talking like them. It's probably best that I just act and talk regular and let whatever happens, happen.* Satisfied with this approach, I started rescanning the bleachers looking for my family.

The general's speech was shorter than I expected; as he finished congratulating us, and started back to his seat, Gunny Minnifield and the other two head drill instructors took their positions directly in front of their respective platoons. It was almost over with, it was really happening! Even the families and guests sensed that this was the moment and the bleachers came to life. I felt my body tingle with nervous anticipation. Gunny Minnifield, standing before us, shouted out, "Platoon 358, dismissed!" I let loose at the top of my lungs, "Aye, aye, sir!" Unlike the movies, no one threw his cover in the air—I don't know why but we just didn't. Instantaneously, we broke rank and headed towards the bleachers.

It was mass humanity and it felt good just to be able to walk in any direction I damn felt like. From my immediate right, I heard, "Mom, Pop, I told you that was Tad!" I recognized Akemi's lovely voice and I looked in the direction from where it came. There they all were, headed towards me: Mom, Pop, Akemi and Renbo. I wanted to run to them but instead I just quickened my pace and made a beeline towards them with them stopping as I approached. Looking at their beaming faces and smiles, I could tell that they were in high spirits. I went straight to Moms and hugged her—she felt so good that I didn't want to let her go. From the peanut gallery, I heard Renbo, "What's up Tad, I thought Marines were supposed to be tough!" I let go of Mom, kissed her on the cheek, looked at Renbo, smiled and said, "So you bad now, huh!" He looked at me, tilted his head to the side and said, "Yeah, I even took over your room!" I laughed and gave him a hug, which he tried to shrug off. Sweet Akemi hugged me and asked me why my uniform had a stripe on my upper sleeve while most of the others didn't. Before I could say anything, Renbo interjected, "That's because he got in trouble and they put a demerit on his sleeve!" Mom said, "Renbo, stop; your brother got promoted, that's right isn't it Tad?" I said, "Sure, Mom, I run this place, I'm the head buddhahead in charge." Pop finally spoke, "It looks like you're the only buddhahead around here, right Tad?" Pops had given me an opening, a chance to tell them not only about boot camp but what it was like being the only buddhahead in the entire company. I felt a knot start to form in my gut and at that moment I realized that it would be impossible to tell them all I experienced these past four months: how it made me feel and how it changed me. It would probably come out all disjointed and confuse the fuck out of my family. I could tell by the look in Pop's and Mom's eyes that they knew that being the only Oriental must have been rough, but deep down inside, I knew that Mom did not want to believe that it made a difference. They all waited for my response, my verification that life is fair, but my silence must have made them uncomfortable. Finally Mom asked, "Tad are you okay?" I looked into her eyes and realized that those same eyes had seen in her lifetime, more racial bullshit than I can ever imagine, and yet they still radiated with warmth and love. Suddenly I realized, "Who the fuck am I, thinking that I need to educate my folks about racism? My shit is kindergarten next to the racist bullshit they endured in camp." The tension in my stomach started to drain away—I was starting to warm up and relax. I cleared my throat, "Yeah, Mom, everything's fine, I just missed you all a lot and it feels good to see you. Come on, let me show you around the base. I hope you're all hungry because I sure am!" Akemi said, "Mom, shall I go back to the car and bring out the chicken, potato salad, *onigiri* (rice balls), and *tsukemono* (pickled vegetables)?" Today was going to be a good day!

THE NAM

Republic of Viet Nam
March, 1968

ONLY A FEW HOURS AGO, at the Kadena Air Force Base in Okinawa, I boarded a C-130 cargo plane, my "ride" to the Nam. The C-130, is a far cry from the air-conditioned, single-seat, foxy stewardess-attended TWA jet that flew us from LAX to Okinawa three days ago. The C-130 is shaped like an industrial trash bin with wings. We were told that the flight from Okinawa to the Da Nang airstrip would take roughly nine hours; I hoped that this plane had nine hours left in it. I found an open area on the long, cold, steel bench riveted to the side of the C-130, and settled in.

Hours later, out of nowhere, "Mmmhmmmmmmmmhbbbmmmmmmmmmmmhm.

"Whoa! What the fuck! Pleeese, God, don't let me die!" I was surrounded by panicked voices and pleading souls, as a continuous deafening drone filled the inside of the cargo plane. The spine-tingling noise was accompanied by short spastic jolts. Suddenly, the plane lunged downward; the quick, violent drop felt like I was trapped in an elevator when its cable snapped. I was jolted out of my seat. I panicked—I wasn't ready to die, not like this. As quickly as the noise and tremors had started, it stopped! Seconds ago, forty Marines sat side-by-side on the long, steel bench inside of the C-130. Now, we all found ourselves sprawled out on the cargo plane's floor. I heard a few moans and groans, but I was too scared to move and get up off the cold steel floor of the plane. I had never experienced anything like this. I was clueless as to what just happened—whether it was over with, or if this was just the start. I cringed and prepared for the worst.

It was totally silent inside in the plane—no one moved. The first to get up off the plane's floor was a cat wearing metal sergeant's chevrons on his collar. I could tell by his rank and appearance that unlike the rest of us, he was not a "cherry." His camouflage jungle fatigues and jungle boots had a jungle rot look. His complexion was tanned and weathered, and he exuded a "been-there, done-that" demeanor. In contrast, the jungle fatigues and boots the rest of us had on, were fresh off the Okinawa supply rack. There was a coolness in the way he pick himself up and stretched his body as if he was checking to make sure all his body parts were working. Casually, he located his sea bag and retook a seat on the steel bench. Our eyes were all riveted on him; he didn't say a damn thing, we just imitated his actions. I picked up my sea bag and headed back to the bench. Someone finally asked him, "Sarge what da fuck was that?" Sergeant "Cool Breeze" didn't answer, but he could not help but notice thirty-nine pair of eyes all glued on him, begging for an answer to the question. A smirk emerged on his weathered face, he said, "We hit an air pocket. Some are worse than others; that one was crazy, even scared *me* for a moment." Someone else blurted out, "How come we didn't hit any air pockets on our flight to Okinawa?" Before Sarge could respond, a different voice answered, "You dumb fuck, the commercial plane that brought us was a high-class hooker that didn't even flinch when it hit an air pocket. This raggedy piece of shit for a plane, ain't nothing but a horny bitch, begging to cum, every time it hits an air pocket!" Even though I had no idea of what was just said, it kinda made sense.

The C-130 steadied itself and continued its flight to Da Nang. It hit a few more air pockets causing more noise and turbulence. Fortunately, none of them were as intense as the first; one clown even started cracking jokes that had us all rolling. When the plane hit an air pocket and started to shake and quiver, he yelled out, "Ooh baby! Yes! Yes! Make me cum!" The combination of the air pockets, continuous whirling buzz of the plane's turbo engines, intermittent rattling sounds of the nuts and bolts holding the C-130 together, and facing the reality that I was finally on my way to the Nam, made it impossible for me to relax.

There wasn't enough room on the long steel bench for all of us to stretch out and catch some Zs. A few slept in a sitting position, others found space on the floor to lay and crash out. I chose neither option, instead I started to reflect on all the shit that had happened since my boot camp graduation. I thought about my Advanced Infantry Training, or AIT as they called it, at Camp Pendleton.

AIT is an intense guerilla warfare crash course that lasts six weeks, the emphasis of AIT being different from boot camp. Boot camp was about adjusting our attitudes, getting us mentally prepared to kill; AIT taught us the specifics on how to kill, and survive in the jungle. We had endless forced marches, always equipped in full combat action gear: M-16 semi automatic, cartridge belt, ammo bandoliers, steel helmet, flack jacket, backpack filled with survival necessities, C-rations, canteen, folding shovel, bayonet with sheath, ground tarp, rain poncho, blanket, and anything else I failed to mention. During those weeks, I forgot what sleeping in a cot felt like. In full combat gear, our training unit constantly moved from training station to training station at a brisk pace—somewhere between a jog and a walk—they called it, "route step." Man, we route-stepped up and down the trails, hills, and mountains at Camp Pendleton. We crawled under barbed wire while live ammunition was fired over us as we snaked our way through the training course. We tossed hand grenades, shot .45s, machine guns, and learned how to coordinate return fire as a squad during a fire fight. Every day we fired off hundreds of rounds of live ammunition. I became proficient with my M-16; I learned to quickly reload a new magazine clip with minimal interruption in fire.

Our instructors were all returning combat vets. They said that unless we were assigned to a sniper platoon, actual combat wasn't anything like the rifle range—there wouldn't be time to lock in and aim at an enemy target; it was about spraying an area and finding cover. They said that unlike a Hollywood war flick, where you could just about finish a bag of popcorn before the battle scene ended, the majority of the skirmishes we would encounter were going to be brief, but deadly. Guerilla warfare was about chasing and pinning down Charlie in the jungle, mountains, and bushes in Viet Nam. They made it sound like a deadly combination of two kid's games: tag and hide-n-seek, but with a different set of rules. In tag you never caught Charlie, so you always remained "It." In hide-n-seek, the person hiding gets to plant booby traps on the seeker: traps such as explosives set off by well-concealed trip wire, razor-sharp pointed bamboo sticks with poisoned tips, land mines, stuff that might not kill you, but most definitely will fuck you up for the rest of your natural life.

Our AIT trainers made it clear to us that they were not drill instructors or lifers. They were returning Viet Nam combat veterans who were finishing out the remainder of their enlistment contracts. Most of them made it implicitly clear that their immediate mission in life was to finish out their enlistment and "get the fuck out the suck."

We were fortunate to be trained by experienced combat vets. If they had sent us to Viet Nam immediately after boot camp, a lot of us would have died needlessly—we were too gung go after boot camp, and our balls would have trumped common sense. Whenever an opportunity arose, many of us would pick the minds of any AIT instructor willing to talk about his combat experience. While they all had their own personal war stories, I found it interesting that not a one had any patriotic message to pass on to us. They preached survival, making it back with all your body parts intact.

The best part about being stationed at Camp Pendleton was going home on weekend liberty. On my first weekend pass, I left base and went to the Greyhound bus station in Oceanside. As I was nearing the bus terminal, a supercharged, canary-yellow, 1968 GTO pulled up in front of the bus terminal, stopped, and its driver got out to announce, "Anyone who needs a lift to the downtown LA bus station, hop in. It will cost you five dollars!"

I couldn't believe my eyes and ears—it was Harvey Yorimoto, a cat from the neighborhood! Harvey was a year older than me, and his family lived on Tenth Avenue, six blocks up the street from where my family stayed. I went up to greet him, "Harvey, what's happening!" He was surprised to see me; he extended his hand and we shook Avenue style. He said that he heard back in the neighborhood that I had signed up. Having said that, he looked at me and shook his head. Harvey told a white guy who had already jumped in the front seat of his ride, to take a seat in the back, and told me to ride shotgun. Everyone paid the five dollars and we took off. The ride to LA was nice—Harvey had installed a deluxe stereo sound system that was blasting out recent hits from his 8 track tape deck. I had been away from the civilization so long that I was hearing Smokey Robinson's new single, "Swept for You Baby" and "The Big Payback" by James Brown for the first time. Man, the music was so righteous that it touched my soul. Since Harvey had been raised on the Westside, we had similar tastes, the three white dudes in the back seat remained quiet and were probably thinking, "What's up with these Oriental guys, listening to this colored music?" I couldn't give a shit. As long as they didn't verbalize their ignorance out loud, the ride home was cool.

It took about ninety minutes to get to the downtown Greyhound station. After

Harvey dropped off the backseat riders, he asked me if I was going back to the neighborhood. I told him, "Damn straight," and he said that he'll drop me off at my folks'. On our way back, he took surface streets. After leaving the crowded downtown area, Harvey dug into his cigarette pack and pulled out a marijuana joint. He took it in his mouth, moistening the rolling paper so it would burn evenly. He fired it up, took in a deep drag, held it, then exhaled. Without saying anything, he passed it over to me, I took it from him, took a long deep drag, held it in, and exhaled. The first thing I felt was my shoulders relaxing, almost as if I had just unstrapped and taken off my heavy backpack. We continued to pass the joint back and forth. Between drags, I asked Harvey how short he was. He said, "Three more months and a wake up." He asked me what my MOS is, I told him infantry. Harvey quietly replied, almost as if he was talking to himself, "Ain't that a bitch." I asked him if he was a grunt, he said, "Yeah." He said that he returned back from the Nam five months ago and he was finishing up his time at Pendleton, working in supply. He then said, "Watch your ass because when you first arrive in country, they make the cherries walk point." He continued, "Yeah, I walked the point when I first got there, and on my third day, I walked into a VC ambush and drew fire. I was caught in an open area, and had no choice but to *di-di-mao* back to my platoon. Some motherfucker in my company saw me running back to cover, and thought I was a gook and opened up on me. I yelled, 'IT'S ME!' and dropped to the ground. I was caught in a crossfire, shot at by both sides, rounds flying all around me. I thought my ass was grass. When the firefight was over, I was shaking all over but I was more pissed off than scared. I went out-of-control looking for the cocksucker who tried to kill me—I was going to waste his ass. They grabbed me and took away my M-16. Everyone kept rapping, making excuses for the punkass that shot at me, saying that he was new in country. I wasn't going for it. Finally I calmed down enough to where I wasn't going to waste his ass anymore. I told them that I needed to talk to the dude who shot at me. They said that that might not be a good idea but I told them that sooner than later I'm going to find out anyway and I ain't gonna let it slide. They talked it over and brought his punkass over to me. Bitch was shaking like a leaf. I told him 'Look at my face real good, because if you ever shoot at me again, this is the last face you're ever going to see right before I blow your ass away.' Poohbutt white boy didn't say shit, he just held his head down and nodded. I told him to, 'Get the fuck away from me.' I was loud-talking, making sure that anyone within earshot heard me and I yelled, 'The same goes for anyone else making the same fuckin' mistake.' Harvey said after that, he never walked point again.

We were approaching Venice and Arlington, nearing the Avenues. The weed had me feeling real mellow. I told Harvey, "Damn, that's fucked up; if anyone shoots at me, I'll light him up. I don't care if the mothafucka's wearing government issue or black pajamas." Harvey replied, "Right on!" I told him that was some good shit we smoked, and he replied that the weed back home ain't shit, just wait 'til I get to the Nam; they got weed laced with opium, called "OJs" or opium joints, that will put you in another dimension. He said that the stuff we toked up was better than nothing, and it helps calm his nerves. Harvey pulled up in front of my house and I thanked him for the ride and smoke. We shook then he handed me another rolled joint. He said to look him up every Friday that I got liberty and he'd run me back to the Avenues.

My first few weekends back home felt strange. For some reason, I didn't feel like hooking up with friends or stepping out of the house. One reason was that many of my tight Minister partners had enlisted, were in jail, or otherwise laying low. I spent most of the time hanging out at the house, eating Mom's cooking, making late-night refrigerator raids, listening to the newest cuts and oldies on the turntable, or more often, I would just want to be by myself, thinking about nothing. Moms must have sensed something wasn't right, because she started to bug me about going out. Unlike before, when she used to get on my case for not being home enough, now, she worried because I didn't feel like going out and just wanted to hang out at home—you figure her out.

I was so lost in my thoughts that I totally lost track of how long we had been up in the air. It probably wouldn't be too much longer before I plant my first step "in country." If I am one of the lucky ones, I'll return back to "the world" exactly thirteen months from the day we flew out of LAX, but if something goes haywire, I'll be medivaced home sooner, hopefully not in a body bag. I sensed that all of us inside the C-130 were thinking similar thoughts, because with the exception of a nervous cough or two, it was totally silent. I never seriously thought about death—for the past month I consciously tried to block it out of my mind, because the thought of dying freaked me out. Sitting here, I'm going to make myself a promise: I'm going to look out for myself, control what I can control, and make it back alive. *I hope like hell, that I fulfill my promise.*

Someone from the cockpit came back to tell us that we are two hours out of the Da Nang airstrip and it will be early morning when we land. I still couldn't fall asleep. I thought about Lani, whom I met two weeks ago during my extended leave. Yeah, if circumstances were different, things could have worked out with us. I know that I would have been willing to give it a try. Lani was fine, a stone fox. We met when my partner Craig heard that I was home on leave and he needed someone to double date with because his girlfriend, Joanne, wanted to introduce her new friend from work to Craig's friends.

When Craig called and asked if I was game to meet Joanne's friend from work, I told him, "No thanks, blind dates ain't my thing." Craig knew better than to beg me, but he was persistent, telling me that it really wasn't a date, we would just be meeting Joanne and her friend at Paul's Kitchen for Chinese food. All I had to do was show up and chop, chop; afterwards, if I wanted to split, it was cool. He said that he promised Joanne that he would find someone to introduce her friend to. He said, besides, even if I wasn't interested in Joanne's friend, he wanted to catch up with me and treat me to dinner before I left for Viet Nam. Paul's Kitchen was on Edgehill Avenue and Jefferson, walking distance from my folks, so I decided to go. It will be nice to see Craig—he was a game cat that always had your back, plus he was a mac daddy with the ladies. Besides, by stepping out, even if only for dinner, it would make Mom happy and get her off my case for a bit.

The next evening, while walking to Paul's Kitchen, I still had doubts about this blind date arrangement and I contemplated turning around and heading back home. Before I could back out, I saw Craig's '58 Chevy parked in front of Paul's Kitchen. Fortunately, I was thinking more with my stomach and figured that if I went back home, my family would have already started eating and Renbo was probably stuffing his face this very minute. Knowing him, there ain't gonna be anything left by the time I get back. I thought, "Fuck it, Craig said all I had to do was show up, eat, then split, and I sure am hungry." Being a Tuesday, there were a lot of empty tables when I walked into Paul's Kitchen. I immediately spotted Craig and Joanne sitting at a table in the back. They saw me and waved as I headed towards them. Since it was only the two of them, I figured that Joanne's friend had backed out of the "arrangement."

Craig and I went through our homeboy handshake ritual and traded insults. He capped on my white sidewall, military haircut, and since I didn't have any comeback for this, all I came up with was a weak, "Yo mamma!" Joanne broke up our routine by coming up and giving me a big hug and planted a wet kiss on my cheek. I told her to be cool, because I didn't want Craig to find out about us. Craig played if off, saying, "You wish."

It felt so good to reconnect with friends that I was totally caught off guard when I realized that another person joined in our laughter. I turned to see who it was and it was Joanne's friend, Lani. I swear, I dug her from the moment I saw her. She had a smooth, tanned complexion, a knockout smile, clear lively eyes, long black hair, and even though she was wearing loose fitting casual clothes, I could tell that she had a healthy petite figure. Mamma be fine! I was momentarily stunned and at a loss for words. Joanne probably recognized my look and bailed me out, saying, "Lani, this is Tad, he's one of Craig's closest friends. Don't be scared by his rice bowl haircut, he's in the military." She then introduced me to Lani, "And this is my friend Lani. We work together; she's from Oahu." Lani took the initiative, and said, "Nice to meet you, Tad, sorry to sneak up on you like I did, but I was in the ladies room." I said, "All my military recon training and you're able to creep on me like that, you're good, girl!" She said "Really?" I assured her that I was serious and said, "For real." She finished off our introduction by saying, "Good, in that case, you can pay for our meal!" We all laughed, sat down and enjoyed the moment.

When we finished eating our delicious meal, no one was in a hurry to leave so we ended up pouring ourselves continuous cups of tea and talking until the restaurant closed. Outside, Joanne said that she and Craig were going to stop by Holiday Bowl for a while, and then go over to her apartment; she welcomed Lani and me to join them. At that very moment, there was no other person that I would rather be with and get to know more than Lani, but I didn't jump at Joanne's invitation because it was important for me to see what Lani's reaction was. Even though we just met, I could sense from Lani's reactions that she wasn't keen on the idea. I spoke up, "Thanks, but I gotta hit it, I need to take care off some last minute stuff." We spent a few more minutes outside the restaurant, saying our farewells. Craig and Joanne both knew that I was headed to Viet Nam next week, and Joanne gave me a sisterly hug, and told me to be safe. Craig said if I need anything, to write and he'll send it. I told them that I'll be seeing them before they see me and to take care. Lani was quiet and she gave me a hug before I left.

It was now dark as I headed home, and I thought, "Damn, I fucked up. Maybe if I took Joanne up on her offer, I'd be sitting next to Lani right now." When I reached the end of the block, a car pulled alongside, and upon looking over, I saw Lani behind the steering wheel. I said, "Damn, you good at sneaking up on people!" She said, "Hop in, lets go for a ride." In a Westside heartbeat, I was inside the car.

Since Lani was new in town, she asked me to drive. I asked her where she wanted to go and she said that she really didn't care, only she had to work tomorrow. I shot up Crenshaw, hopped on the Santa Monica Freeway, headed toward the beach. We talked and talked all the way up the coast. I finally stopped a little past Malibu, at White Sands Beach, a favorite perch-fishing spot for Nisei fishermen. On the other side of the highway away, from the beach, is a humongous slope of white sand—it looked like Mother Nature picked up a large scoop of sand and poured it over a mountain. Even though climbing to the top of the white sand crest took an effort, reaching the top was worth the effort because it was so far away from the city lights that you could see hundreds of stars twinkling in the dark night sky.

To my amazement, Lani was almost in better shape than me. She made it all the way to the top of white sands, only stopping twice to catch her breath. It was so, so nice to be alone with her at this romantic spot. Between my starting to really dig her, and at the same time feeling hornier than fuck, I wanted to be all over her fine self. She acted different than from other chicks that I had brought up here—other girls knew why I brought them here and what my intentions were. Lani was different: she was really into the stars, the sound of the ocean and the cool night breeze. She said that she hasn't felt this peaceful since she left the Islands. The more we talked, the more she told me about herself: how she needed a change and decided to come to the mainland after breaking up with her boyfriend back on the Island. She explained that growing up in Hawaii was nice, but she started feeling too confined and that life on the Island had become too predictable. I surprised myself by confiding to her, "I'm a little scared about going to the Nam. I don't know what's going to happen and how it will change me." I knew that I was taking a big chance telling a person I just met about my feelings and insecurities, but for some reason, it felt safe and natural talking with Lani.

We talked late into the night; finally I got the courage to make a move and to my delight, she responded. We spent the rest of the night on top of White Sands and Lani even dozed off in my arms. I realized that it was going to get light in a few hours so I woke Lani up. We made it back down the slope and drove back into town. When I told her that I better drop myself back home so that she can go to work today, she asked if I wanted to wait for her at her place, while she went to work. I inquired, "Where's home?"

I spent the last few days of my leave with Lani—we shared conversation, meals, hung out and made love again and again. We never talked about anything having to do with the future, I think we both sensed that topic was out of bounds. We talked about everything else, and for the first time in a long time, I felt at peace. When Saturday arrived, I had just two more days before I had to report back to Pendleton. That night we went out and ate Hawaiian BBQ; afterward, we went to Gung Hay, a nightclub near her apartment in Gardena. We had a few drinks and listened to a local band before we returning to her place. I told her that I'm going to have to leave tomorrow, because I had only one more full day and I needed to spend it with my family; I hoped she understood. Lani more than understood, she took my hand and we went into the her bedroom and stayed up almost all night, making love, enjoying what little time we had left together.

I wondered what Lani was up to, and… My train of thought was interrupted. A flight team crewmember came to the cargo area, telling us, "We'll arrive at Da Nang at oh-seven hundred." After a brief pause, "As we start our descent, in the event we take incoming, instead of landing the craft, the cargo hatch will be lowered and the craft will slow down but it will not stop. If this happens, I will be here to instruct you when it is safe to exit by jumping off the plane with your gear. After you all exit, the aircraft will lift off again without landing. It is important that you disembark only when I tell you it's safe." The crewmember returned to the cockpit, I thought, "Please, no incoming!"

It wasn't going to be long now, my time has come; I'm about to take my first step "in country." When the C-130 started its descent, we felt a sudden jolt. I gripped the lower part of the bench with both hands, waiting to see what was going to happen next. As we continued to descend, I kept my ears perked for "incoming." We must have been close to the landing strip because I heard and felt the plane lower its landing wheels. Suddenly, I felt a bump and heard the sound of rubber hitting a surface—it rattled and shook the inside of the plane as we came to a complete stop. The cargo hatch opened and immediately I felt the temperature inside the cargo area change from chill to warm and humid. I grabbed my sea bag and headed down the cargo ramp.

The hot, sticky, humid air all but made me forget about what it was going to feel like taking my first step in Viet Nam. The air felt moist and thick while I took in a few short breaths, trying to acclimate my breathing rhythm. Looking around, Da Nang airstrip looked more like an open work area than an airport. Even though it was early in the morning, a lot of activity was taking place: a few cargo planes were being loaded and unloaded, and mechanics were working on the engines. The personnel on the airstrip were either wearing Air Force or Army fatigues. After we all exited the aircraft, we stayed in a loose-knit group, waiting for someone to come and tell us what to do next. Finally Sergeant Cool Breeze threw his bag over his shoulder and headed in the direction of some bungalows—like lost sheep, we followed our leader.

I waited in a line outside the bungalow—once I got inside, I was disappointed to discover that it was hotter inside the hooch than it was outside. The only cooling system was a small noisy portable fan sitting on top of the processing clerk's desk, pointing directly toward him. When my turn came, I handed the clerk my orders and he told me that I was assigned to the First Division, Alpha Company and if I hurried to the motor pool, a convoy was pulling out this morning headed to my assigned unit. He kept one copy of my order, stamped the rest and handed them back. He said, to follow the row of bungalows and behind the last one, I would see the motor pool area, I couldn't miss it.

DAY ONE

Vandergrift Combat Base – Viet Nam
May 1968

IT WAS STILL EARLY MORNING when the convoy left the Da Nang Airstrip. Three other new replacements and I stood on a wooden platform in the rear of a military truck. Accompanying us were three seasoned grunts. Our vehicle was one of fifteen trucks and jeeps in a convoy that carried supplies back to the bush. We were told we would be motoring all day to reach our destination before dark.

The military transport truck resembled an open cattle truck, having detachable wooden side railings that slotted into the wooden floorboard in back. After sitting nine-plus hours on the rock-hard seating of the C-130, my butt was sore so I chose to stand by a side railing. I also wanted to take in the sights of my new surroundings.

Once outside Da Nang, the scenery and landscape quickly shifted from an urban city setting to an open rural environment. We drove past small villages with straw thatched bamboo hooches—I saw Vietnamese farmers, villagers and even water buffalo. As our convoy motored by these small, seemingly self-contained villages, I found it odd that other than small Vietnamese kids, not a single Vietnamese adult smiled, waved or acknowledged our presence.

The three grunts traveling with us kept to themselves. It wasn't like they totally ignored us, they asked what company we were assigned to and what part of the world we were from, but that was the extent of our conversation with them. I quickly assessed that they truly didn't give a shit about us. It was amusing to be in the presence of six white guys with the three new guys trying their damnedest to "fit in" with the seasoned grunts. They just didn't get it, even though they shared the same skin pigmentation with the hardcore grunts; the grunts didn't give a rat's ass about these "cherries." Stupid white boys!

As we approached a relatively large village, I saw a group of kids up ahead, standing on the side of the road. For the first time since we left Da Nang, the three grunts got up and stood along the side railing. One of the grunts asked us if we had any C rations on us, none of us did. Another grunt pulled out a metal can of government-issued crackers then handed it to the requesting grunt. He took it and as we neared the group of kids, said, "Watch this." He dangled his hand outside the railing, showing the kids the cracker container. The kids were obviously excited and shouted exclamations in Vietnamese. I thought, "this cat's cool." When the kids ran up closer to our truck, the grunt pulled his hand back, wound up like he was

158

Bullet Bob Gibson and threw the metal can at the group of kids. I saw the cracker can hit and bounce off a kid's head and the kid fell to the ground as the other kids scrambled for the metal can. Instinctively, I blurted out, "What the fuck!" but the grunts were too busy laughing amongst themselves to pay attention to what I said. "Yeah, I got that little gook good!" Man, I couldn't believe this shit. I thought, "Aren't these the people that we are supposed to be helping?" I told myself, "Don't even try to make any sense out of this bullshit." After we passed the village, I noticed that the three new guys start to gravitate more towards my direction, and now were trying to get friendly with me, stupid white boys!

Da Nang now seemed like a distant memory—we had been on the road most of the day, and slowly the sight of villages and villagers disappeared and the open country landscape changed into thick bush and dense terrain. I hadn't been issued a M-16; it made me feel defenseless and at the mercy of the grunts I was traveling with for protection. As the terrain changed, it dawned on me how easy it would be for someone wanting to ambush our convoy, to conceal themselves in these surroundings, and to take us out by surprise. With this disturbing thought, I started looking at my new environment with leery and cautious eyes. Suddenly, every plant, tree, and shadow became a ominous threat: a hiding place for Charlie, a booby trap waiting to be detonated.

After hours of travel, I suspected that we must be nearing the base camp for we were now slowly heading uphill on a sinuous single lane dirt road. The ride got so bumpy that even the grunts were forced to stand and hold on to the guard rails to balance themselves. From air pockets to mammoth pit holes, what a fuckin' day! The convoy didn't slow down and I wondered if it didn't want to risk being ambushed.

It had been at least a few hours since we passed the last village—we were now deep in the bush. For the life of me, I couldn't comprehend how anyone could build a combat base in this dense terrain, and even more perplexing, why would they even want to? We were in no-where's-ville, deep in the fuckin' boonies.

Soon, I saw the answer to the first part of my question. We approached a humongous area that had been leveled off and cleared of its natural vegetation. As far as my eyes could see, the area was enclosed by barbed wire—this had to be the combat base, because there was no other logical explanation for its existence. The convoy pulled up and finally stopped at the first barbed wire perimeter. Two sentries raised an entry gate and waved our convoy through. We passed another barbed wire perimeter before entering the combat base. The base was huge: it contained rows of wooden bungalows, a helicopter landing pad, sand bunkers strategically placed around the perimeter, and I even saw a flagpole in the bungalow area, waving the Stars and Stripes. My first impression of this military compound was that, unlike any other military base I have been on, there was a complete disregard for military décor and formality here. It looked like the old Wild West back in the cowboy and Indian days—I saw Marines strolling by with M-16s flung over their shoulders, some wearing flak jackets and helmets, others wearing jungle fatigues and some just wearing olive green tee shirts.

The convoy finally came to a stop at a motor pool area. The three grunts we rode with got off the truck and went their separate ways, leaving only a group of twelve new replacements from the entire convoy. We all waited until someone came by to escort us to the bungalow area. All the bungalows were identically painted a brownish-gray color. The one we were led to had a wooden sign attached over its screen door, which read, "VANDERGRIFF COMPANY HEADQUARTERS, 3RD MARINE DIVISION."

Hanging out near the bungalow was a group of black Marines; while they were Marines, it was obvious that these cats were from a separate tribe. They sported tight afros that protruded out from under their covers, some wore beads around their necks, and one even carried a stylish bamboo cane—for a hot minute, I thought I was back on Crenshaw! Within our group of twelve, two were black. We reached the bungalow, dropped our sea bags, and while we waited to be called inside, the two black dudes headed straight towards their welcoming committee, which formed a single file line. It was righteous watching the two new dudes walk through their greeting line, as if they were attending a wedding reception. One-by-one, they introduced themselves to each soul brother standing in line with a two-fisted power handshake, followed by casual conversation about where they were from in the world and whether they possibly knew anyone in common. The way the soul brothers embraced each other and had each other's backs was heartwarming to witness. They carried on as if the rest of us weren't there, nor did it really matter to them. This party was for their people and they didn't need anyone's permission to host it, nor was anyone about to crash it.

When we were finally summoned into the company office, we placed our orders on a desk. Seated behind the desk was an older man, tall and lanky, with ruddy leathery skin, closely cropped military-length hair and receding hairline, grayish sideburns, thick granny-style reading glasses, and a defining WC Fields-type bulbous nose. The nameplate on his desk identified him as Sergeant Major Guidry. After he finished scanning our orders, he raised his head, peered over his reading glasses, and spoke. By this time, I had heard so many people speak from different parts of America, I considered myself an expert at distinguishing where someone was from just by listening to their accents and mannerisms. Listening to his accent and slight twang, I'd bet money that Top Sergeant Guidry was a Texan.

I was assigned to Alpha Company; my unit was out on a patrol and wouldn't return for a few more days. In the meantime, I had to take a copy of my orders over to the supply hooch to get issued my combat gear and to report to headquarters every day for work detail assignments. . Top said to find a bunk at the transit barrack, and settle in, that chow is served at the enlisted men's mess hall at seventeen-hundred. He finished by telling me to report to the flagpole at eighteen hundred in my combat gear for tonight's perimeter watch.

I was the first one to arrive at the flagpole. Although I knew that I was early, I still felt anxious thinking, "Maybe there's more than one flagpole on the compound." Since leaving the headquarters hooch, I had gone to supply and been issued my helmet, flak jacket, backpack, canteen, folding shovel, poncho liner, soap, matches, insect repellant, foot powder, extra sox, under wear, mess kit and a other essential items. Next I went to the armory and was issued my M-16, and eight fully-loaded magazine clips, each containing twenty rounds. Since my company was out in the bush, I went to the transit barrack, where I found an open cot and placed my gear. Finally, I headed to the hooch that served up mess; there I picked up a metal tray and stood in line for supper. The shit was awful: powdered mashed potatoes, two slices of stale bread, canned lima beans, and leathery meat that I had to chomp on like bubble gum before it became soft enough to swallow. There was a large canister of Kool Aid for washing down your meal. Even though the meat gave my teeth a workout, I was so hungry, I ate every last bite.

I waited by the flagpole as this long day dragged on, finally turning to dusk. I was ready for perimeter watch: I had on my flak jacket, my cartridge belt and my M-16 flung over my shoulder, gripping its barrel with my right hand. I even filled my canteen with Kool Aid in case I got thirsty. I anticipated that my big problem tonight was staying awake—I'd been up for well over twenty-four hours.

Slowly, others assigned on tonight's watch trickled in. Listening to them, most of them were assigned to companies that had just returned to the rear area after being out in the bush for weeks. They were pissed off for having to pull perimeter watch on their first night back in the rear. They rightfully felt that it was unfair and questioned why they couldn't spend a well-deserved leisurely night at the enlisted men's hooch, playing bid whist, drinking beer, whiskey, smoking dope and unwinding.

By the time two transport trucks picked us up, there were forty of us for tonight's perimeter watch. We were divided into teams of three, the trucks took the teams and dropped us off at the strategically placed bunkers on the perimeter. Each group was given a radio, and infrared night binoculars.

Since I was not familiar with the layout of the compound, I had no idea what part of the perimeter I was protecting, nor did I know the other two dudes I would be spending a night with in the bunker. When the three of us were dropped off, it felt like we were far away from the main base camp. The bunker was a long rectangular pit dug into the ground, was lined with sandbags and built up an additional five feet above ground level. Inside, the enclosure had a full open view of the perimeter. Once we situated ourselves in the bunker, my two watch mates introduced themselves and we divided up the night shifts. Since it didn't get dark until around nine, we had some time to kill. It turned out that the other two didn't know each other, either. One guy was from Florida and he had been in country for about five months. All he talked about was his upcoming R&R to Sydney, Australia, and all the round-eye pussy that he was going to fuck and eat. The other dude was quiet and didn't say where he was from—he had that far away look that I was starting to get accustomed to seeing more and more; he volunteered to take the first watch. As darkness began to roll in, the dude from Florida pulled out a perfectly rolled cigarette from a plastic baggie. He fired it up, and took in a deep drag; I immediately smelled the odor of marijuana. He passed it to the other dude, who took a hit and then offered it to me. I knew that if the shit was as good as advertised, and with my energy level running on empty, the weed would definitely fuck me up, I said, "I'm good, I'll pass." They both gave me a strange look and they continued to toke up. I went to a corner of the bunker and pulled my helmet over my eyes.

I felt a tug on my fatigues, "Pssssst, get up, it's your watch." It took moments for me to register where I was. *Man, it's pitch black out here.* I couldn't see my own nose, and blinked my eyes a few times, making sure that they were open. I grabbed my M-16 while the quiet guy who just finished his watch found an open space in the bunker and crashed out. I positioned myself at the bunker's front and stared in the direction of the barbed wire perimeter. The problem was that it was so fuckin' dark, I couldn't see shit, not even the barbed wire. *This is fuckin' spooky.* After a while my eyes began to acclimate to the darkness, but I still only had visibility around twenty yards in front of me. I thought, "Damn, if Charlie's out there and creeping up on me, I wouldn't know it until he was dead on top of me!" This thought intensified my concentration.

The harder I tried staying awake, the heavier my eyes got. I knew that if I closed them, I was gone for the night. I kept talking to myself, forcing myself to stay awake. What was even worse than the darkness was the utter silence. It was so quiet and still, that all I heard was my thoughts racing through my mind. I wanted to smoke a cigarette but knew that a flicker of light would advertise our position like neon lights on a Vegas casino. Maybe thinking about home will help keep me awake.

I heard a sound, or thought I heard a sound—it was a swoosh type of noise. I told my heart to quit pounding because it was beating so hard, whoever or whatever was out there could probably hear it beat against my chest. I concentrated, listening to discover where the noise in front of me was coming from. Then I heard it again, *sssswissh.* I scurried over to my bunker partners and jerked on their fatigues. Before either could speak aloud I whispered, "Sssshhh, I hear something." Only the quiet dude got up, the other guy was dead to the world and didn't budge and we didn't have time to wake his ass up. We both went back to the perimeter viewing area. He was looking through the infrared binoculars, then we both heard the noise. He pointed the binoculars in the direction of the noise, dropped the binoculars and grabbed his M-16. He spit out, "They're inside the perimeter!" I aimed my M-16 in the same direction and we unlatched our safeties, and opened fire, *ratatatatatatata tatatatatatat.* I fired off twenty rounds and quickly changed magazines, when he said, "Be cool." We both were sweating, and had our trigger fingers planted, ready to fire. The dude from Florida stumbled over to us. He was panicky, asking, "What the fuck's going on?" We didn't say shit and my combat partner picked up the infrared binocs, and scoped out the perimeter. He handed them to me and pointed in the direction he wanted me to look. As I focused in, I thought I saw an outline of a body about a hundred feet in front of our bunker, but I wasn't sure. He told Florida to radio command post to report a possible kill. Florida grabbed the radio and we could hear command post instructing us to wait until there is no further signs of enemy activity, to go out to the area where we spotted the body to confirm the kill. I couldn't believe what I just heard, thinking to myself, "Mothafuckas are nuts if they think I'm stepping out there."

We stared out into the darkness from our bunker, waiting in silence. Finally, Florida said to me, "It's safe for you now to go and confirm the kill." I shot back, "Fuck you, I did my part, now you go out there and do yours!" The quiet dude didn't take my side, he just picked up the radio, calling command post and telling them we were having problems deciding who had to confirm the kill. The command post person, sounding pissed, said that he didn't care who the fuck went, but someone better get their ass out there unless the three of us wanted to be sent to the brig. He ended the transmission by saying, "Whoever's watch it happened on has to go out there, ASAP!" "Motherfucker!" I grabbed my M-16 and squeezed myself out of the bunker. I crawled on all fours as quickly and quietly as possible toward the direction where I spotted the body. As hard as I tried to make myself invisible and noiseless, I heard myself making the same crawling noise that I just opened fire on, "ssswissh." Man, I'm scared but kept crawling. Then I saw it, it was more than an outline of a dead body, it *was* a dead person. He was wearing a top and loose-fitting bottom black pajamas outfit, and had an AK-47 next to his body. I turned around, crawled back to the bunker, and told the other two dudes what I saw. We called back command post to confirm our kill, command post told us to bring the body back to the secure area. For some reason, this order did not seem to bother my two companions. The three of us crawled out to the body and dragged it back to the bunker area. We dragged it behind the bunker, the three of us were all huffing and puffing but we were now fully awake. The dude from Florida turned the corpse over onto its back, I could see a bullet hole in his chest area. The blood was dark colored and crusted over his clothing, caked with dirt and gravel. His face was contorted and his eyes were fully open. I flashed on Calvin Elliot, a classmate at Dorsey, that I saw die in his own pool of blood outside the school gym, stabbed to death by a gang member from Manual Arts High following an inner city basketball game—the difference was that I played no part in Calvin's death. The dead Vietnamese looked younger than me. The three of us looked at the same corpse but we all had different thoughts. Florida glanced at me and said, "Your first." I had no clue what the fuck he was saying, and since I didn't respond to his nonsense, he nudged me said, "Go ahead and pick." I thought, "The fucker's nuts!" I looked over at the quiet dude for my verification. Mister Quiet looked at me, and said, "Yeah, he's right, that's how we do, fuck, take the wallet!" I told them, "I ain't taking shit!" They didn't argue or try to persuade me otherwise, they began quibbling about who had next pick.

I watched the buzzards, my mind went blank.

GRUNT

Liberty Bridge, Republic of Viet Nam
October, 1968

MAN, I'M PISSED—fifty-one days in the bush; finally, we're back in the rear and no sooner than we drag in, strip off our back packs and combat gear, they tell us that we're pulling perimeter watch tonight! Chicken-shit, motherfucks! Just another reason why, but fuck it, at least I'm still alive! During the last fifty-one days, I've witnessed over twenty-one deaths, a lot coming from booby traps, 155s and box mines. Our platoon sergeant lost an arm and both legs, four days before he was going to go home. I've seen indescribable shit—bodies completely blown away, nothing but flesh hanging in trees and bushes. I've seen every human body part blown to shit. They medivaced one guy out in a C ration box, and that's not even taking into account the number of dead Vietnamese I've seen.

Three weeks ago while on patrol, we were walking alongside a rice paddy dike, nearing a village we were about to enter. All of a sudden, our point man gets shot, then a second man goes down, the rest of us all hit the ground and we call in an air strike. They came and napalmed the shit out of the village. When the dust settled, we went through what was once a Vietnamese village, all we found was body parts of kids and women. Half of their skulls were blown off. All I remember was seeing pieces of kids and old women, no one else. It fucked with me, picking up little arms and parts of little kids' faces. We didn't find any weapons. This is not the first time I've witnessed this scene. Usually when we destroy a village, I would secretly hope that we would find at least one male adult body and a cache of weapons; it would almost justify what we had just done—it makes no sense. Like all the other times, I placed this scene behind me, because tomorrow could be a repeat of the same shit, it just keeps happening.

I hate this place, and I hate the thought that after a few days of rest in the rear, our company will be sent back out to the bush for more of the same madness. It's hard for me to believe that I've been here a little over five months. I feel like I've aged fifty years during this time. A bit of good news is that my Gunny Sergeant told me earlier today that my R&R request to Japan has been approved and I'll get to go sometime next month—hell yeah! Since I have the rest of the day off before we pull line watch, I think I'll drop a kite to Rick, an old Minister partner. Rick recently sent me a letter, telling me how he lucked out and got assigned to an Air Force base, around Tokyo. He wrote about a fine mama-san that he's shacking up with, the

164

night life, and the blast he's having over there. Man, as fucked up as my situation is, I'm still happy for Rick, that skate mothafucka! It would be righteous if we could hook up when I take my R&R to the "motherland." Maybe his fine ole lady has a super fine sister! I better get busy—where did I put my writing shit?

Say Rick,

I got your letter—sounds like you're doing all right for your bad self. Getting your head bad and all, sounds like you're on a thirteen-month vacation!

I'm at Liberty Bridge, our battalion rear. After fifty-one days in the bush, we're getting a three-day break. This is when I try to unwind, and let me tell you, when it's safe, which isn't to often, I get righteously fucked up.

Last week, we were attacked by RPGs, B40s, and chi-cons, which about wiped out our platoon—talk about fear. I shook for about two hours after it was over. Anyways, I just want to get the fuck out, and TET ain't even arrived yet! They say TET will be one big bitch! I'd do about anything to get out. I don't think I'll be the same when I rotate—seeing guys yelling without legs, little kids blown away by air strikes. Things like that makes me do a lot of thinking. It's hard to believe I'm here, but what can you say.

My rotation date is in June. Unless I get three Hearts or two 40-hour hospitalizations, I'll be here for the long haul. I'm supposed to get a Purple Heart for taking shrapnel in my shoulder from a B-40—shit yeah, just two more!

Next month, I'll be out your way for my R&R. If you can swing it, let's try and hook up so that we can party together. It's been a long time, but I'm definitely ready to do my thing! I'll drop you a line when I get the exact date.

Gotta run, I hear a bid whist game calling my name.

Later,

I signed off, addressed the envelope and placed it in the outgoing mail bag.

Now it's time to find my main man, Wagner, and make some money. Wagner is a tough Italian cat from Chicago—he doesn't take shit from anyone, and nobody fucks with him. It took us a while to get tight, but once we clicked, we became inseparable. The more we learned about each other's lives, the more we discovered how much we had in common, and when under pressure, we even have tendencies to think and react alike. Out in the bush, your life depends on instinctive reactions of those around you. Wagner is the best radioman in our company. He is in my squad and whenever the shit hits the fan, he is right on my footsteps, right by my side. It's a known fact that we have the tightest squad in the company because no one gets killed.

When we rotate back to the world, we've already made plans to visit each other's neighborhoods. His Italian crew has the same type of mentality as my buddhahead partners, strong-arming chumps out of money, getting high, drinking wine, fighting, hitting up bitches, partying, even our jargon is similar. When it's safe to kick back and relax, we get loaded, and fantasize about a *mafia-yakuza* alliance we're going to form when we get back to the world.

The only positive thing about being assigned to a grunt unit is that we are truly family. We do not take part in any of the bullshit politics, racial shit, rank status and ass-kissing that happens in the rear. For us, the only thing that matters is that a person carries his own weight and is locked, loaded and ready to fire when the shit hits the fan. Anything beyond that, don't mean a goddamn thing. That's why Wagner and I will only use our secret bid whist signals and gestures to take money from the chumps permanently assigned to the rear— fuck 'em! Up to now, we're up over a thousand!

Walking over to the chow line, I spot Wagner, "Yo, ready for some bid whist?" He responded, "Yeah, but first I gotta get me some hot food."

The last time we were in the rear, Wagner and I cleaned up. The word must have circulated because we couldn't find a big money game to save our lives. We ended up playing a few friendly games with some of our platoon partners. Still, it was cool to kick back, relax, talk shit, and let the day leisurely pass by. It's a fuckin' shame we got perimeter watch tonight, because it kept us from getting our heads bad. We all chipped in and copped some opium joints; also, Smitty brought back a couple bottles of Scotch from R&R. Just got to wait til tomorrow to party.

1900

Staring out from the inside of my bunker, I never realized how huge this the base is, probably because of its airstrip. Anyway, I'm glad to be back in the rear, eating hot food and outdoor showers. Rumor has it that there is a large North Vietnamese Army build-up in this area, maybe that's why they put us on watch tonight.

0220

Baaaaaam, Baaaaaaam!!! "Where's that coming from!" "Fuck, I dunno!" Wagner got on the radio; we were told, "Sappers made it through the perimeter, they're in the headquarters base area! Get back here!" Wagner, me and the new cherry, di-di-mao'ed out of the bunker, flagged down an Amtrac, told its driver what was going down and to take us back to main base area. Upon arrival, everyone around the base area was rushing to different bunker positions. I spotted two guys from my squad. "Wagner this way," and we sprinted over to them. I asked, "How bad is it?" Flores said, "Gooks made it through the perimeter. They've killed six already and took out two of our big guns. Gunny told us to clear them out of the compound before they reach headquarters!" The five of us were huddled inside a bunker on the outskirts of the base area. We had to shout over the deafening sounds of M-16s, AK-47s and nearby grenade blasts. I shouted, "Don't split up, let's go to the artillery bunker over there!" All five of us ran towards the artillery bunker, but before reaching it, a NVA pops up and fires his AK-47 at us. Copeland goes down; we unloaded our magazines on the NVA. Mothafucka goes down! "Help me!" Flores helps me pick up Copeland and we make it to the bunker. Our second lieutenant was inside the bunker with a radio and two new guys, both whom were freaked out.

He immediately tells me, "See that bunker over there, take these two guys and hold it down. Our guys over there have been shot." I quickly figure ain't no one bunker safer than another, I look at Wagner and say, "Ready?" Second Looie says, "I need Wagner with me, I need an experienced radio to set up headquarters." Wagner looks at me with a "Fuck him" look on his face. Against my better judgment, I look at him and say, "Its cool." I look back at the second looie and say, "I still need a radio." He gives me one of the new guys with a radio. I waited and when I didn't hear any blasts or fire, I sprinted to the other bunker. When I got there, I saw two guys in the corner of the bunker, both were bleeding, but alive. A third person wasn't moving—I could tell by the vacant look in his open eyes that he was dead. I asked the two survivors if they could stand: one said he could and the other said he couldn't. I told the one that was bleeding from his shoulder to follow me. I knelt over and told the other guy to hop on my back. Cat was heavy, but I was able to place him in a fireman's carry and the three of us went as fast as possible back to the artillery bunker, with Wagner and Flores spraying cover for us. By now, I knew that the gooks were in front of us and not behind us. I knew it was best to defend ourselves by occupying both bunkers. I turned around and looked at the two new guys who were supposed to go with me the first time; they were both frozen. I glared at them and said, "You're coming with me to the other bunker and if I turn around and you're not behind me, I swear to God, I'm coming back to kill your ass!" They both stood up, I grabbed the cat with the radio, and pushed him out the bunker, the three of us scurried to the nearby bunker. Inside the bunker, I saw a M-60 machine gun, but no ammo canister—a fuckin' machine gun but no ammo! I found a M-79 blooper gun—great, I had a shotgun! I felt a pounding in my heart because it was now quiet outside, and I knew that sappers were creeping up on us. I loaded the blooper and fired round after round at the grass area in front of our bunker. About thirty yards in front of the bunker, I saw a head pop up, I blasted half a clip at him, and ducked my head. I moved to a new position in the bunker and he popped his head up again. This time I got a better look and opened up, *ratatatatat*. I wasted him! I heard shots next to me, it was the other two guys—both turned out to be all right. We kept firing rounds off into the night.

0500

It's starting to get light, and it's been quiet for a while. The silence is welcome, but it's an eerie silence, almost as if saying, "Don't get too comfortable, it might not be over yet." From behind our bunker I hear voices and movement. An officer and about twenty others come to our bunker area, talking shit, "Yeah. We got those gooks, good!" I left my position and told the other two guys to head back to the artillery bunker and I'll meet them there. In close proximity to our bunker, I saw at least six dead NVA soldiers, with the dudes from the rear encircling them and stripping their dead bodies for souvenirs.

I dragged my ass back to the command post bunker—no one is saying shit to me. The same second looie, who was barking out orders last night, sees me and has a concerned look on his face. I don't say shit to him but look for Wagner. The second looie, breaks the silence, "Wagner took a round and was medivaced." Before these words could register in my shell-shocked brain, Flores mutters, "Wagner's dead, man. He was making radio calls and took a round in the neck." "Goddamn, motherfucker!" I want to kill, hurt someone, but don't know who! I can't make my body stop shaking. The second looie says, "Nagata, you're going to get a medal for what you did." I tried to calm myself and will myself to stop shaking. "What the fuck are you talking about!" I walked out of the bunker, knowing that I was ready to go off. I didn't even get to say goodbye. I whispered to myself, "Wagner, even though I didn't know you very long, you are one of the closest people I'll ever know. We lived, fought, and dreamed of better days together. We slept in the same foxholes, shared our care packages from home, cakes and cookies, and even got to know each other's families. The one time we get separated by a fuckin' stupid ass lieutenant, you get killed. The one time we follow orders, you die! If only we stuck together, everything would have been cool! I will miss you my brother."

BACK TO THE WORLD

For the troops in Viet Nam, returning home was referred as, going back the
"world"

Da Nang Air Base
March 1969

"WHOA, HOLD TIGHT, this wasn't part of the deal! I ain't fucking getting in there! Hook me up with the next flight." Having said that, I thought, "Fuck this shit, I ain't getting on that plane, it's *baachi!*" (bad luck or karma).

Just a few minutes earlier, everything was money, I anxiously waited to board the next bird out of here. I am laid out on a stretcher on the tarmac with a medical clearance fit to travel. It was time to leave the Nam.

What screwed it up was when a cargo truck arrived on the airstrip and a work crew began unloading wooden coffins from its back platform. Then they started loading the coffins into my plane ride back to the world. Fuck that noise, I ain't riding with corpses.

The head person in charge is probably the cat with the clipboard, telling everyone what to do and how to do it. This dude was totally shining me on. Judging from his looks, I could sense that this clipboard-carrying fool had never experienced one second of combat. At this point, I was beyond caring about rank or anything else. In my loudest voice, I shouted, "I know you heard me!" He walked over to where I was laying on the airstrip, looked down at me and said, "Look guy, I don't have anything to do with shipment, they just hand me the papers and I make sure it's loaded up. I'm sorry about this but it's out of my control. If you don't want to be on the same flight with the stiffs, I'll scratch you off the manifest." I asked, "Yeah, so when's the next flight?" He said, "In two days, but there's no guarantee I can get you on it." He continued, "Look, it's going to take a while to secure these boxes down. By the time we finish, if you still don't want on, just say so, and I'll scratch you off the list, okay?"

Part of my reluctance was that I am sure that some of the bodies inside the sealed caskets are people I fought with just a few nights ago, and I don't want to deal with thinking about why I'm alive and they're not. The medics told me that when I get back to the world, I'll be going to a naval hospital to mend, probably the one in Long Beach. I lost so much blood, they want to monitor me for a couple of weeks; otherwise, disregarding the fragments of shrapnel in my chest, shoulder and back, I should be alright.

What happened was three nights ago, while I was watching lines, I saw dark objects running across the road. I looked across at the tree line and saw red dots—the VC were using infrared scopes and aiming RPGs at us! I refocused my eyes and I saw long weeds moving 50 feet in front of me—this gook was creeping up on us. I pulled out a grenade and threw it. It exploded, then all hell broke loose. All at once, their rockets hit our positions. The foxhole that I was in took a hit right outside of it, and upon impact, I was blown out of it. The ringing in my ears was deafening. My chest was bleeding and I saw a fragment of shrapnel sticking in it—I was laid out. I looked around and saw bodies on both sides of me; I saw three gooks running through the perimeter, sling-shooting grenades as they ran—even though I couldn't hear, I saw explosions everywhere around me. The blast that knocked me out of the bunker had hurt my leg, and I couldn't get up to retrieve my M-16, so I tried crawling to it. The guy next to me was shot in the stomach, and before I could figure anything else out, I looked up. Standing directly over me was a NVA. He looked directly at me—I'm dead! For some reason he hesitated and didn't kill me on the spot. Instead, with his free hand, he reached down, grabbed me by my fatigue collar and turned me face down. Helplessly, I lay face down, waiting to die; instead, I feel him rifling through my rear pants pocket. I close my eyes, contort my face, and tighten my body, waiting to be shot. I wait, then nothing. Instinctively, I turn my head, he's gone!

From a distance, I see Puff the Magic Dragons saturating the area all around us with Gatling-style machine gun fire. All I see is this red cone of firepower—it was one of the most beautiful sights I have seen in my life. The NVA started to retreat from the compound—I'm still alive!

At last the choppers arrive to medivac those of us who are injured but not dead. They tried landing but caught enemy fire and didn't come down. All around me, everyone is pissed because they won't land to medivac our wounded. Some of our troops are so pissed that they start firing rounds at the choppers. Our company commander went ape-shit and got us to stop firing. They finally come down low and land.

I am medivaced on the second helicopter and taken to the rear hospital area. My fatigues are soaked with blood but there are others around me that are a lot worse off. They lay me on a gurney and leave me on the floor with the other wounded, my ears are still ringing. Maybe that's not a bad thing because it allows me to drown out all the sounds of pain and suffering surrounding me.

While lying on the stretcher, every time I touch my body, I see blood on my hands. All the medical people are busy working on wounded Marines. I don't know how much time goes by, but I'm still lying on the stretcher in the same spot. My chest is starting to hurt more and I can feel my breathing become shallower; I hope I didn't lose too much blood. I'm doing everything in my power not to panic or pass out before they work on me.

I open my eyes and I'm the only stretcher left on the floor! Here comes an orderly, "Yo doc, what's up with this shit, you gonna fix me up or what!" Fucker's eyes got big, and the expression on his face changed from indifference to a startled concerned look, "Why didn't you tell us you was American?" My ears may be ringing, but I definitely heard that! Assholes thought that I was a South Vietnamese

Kit Carson Scout. Lucky for me that my wounds weren't so serious that I couldn't talk—they would have left me to die!

"Guy, what's your pleasure; you up to going home with the corpses, or you want to go back to the hospital?" Mister Clipboard snapped me back to the moment; right now all I want is a change in my reality. "Fuck it, load me up, at least I'll be surrounded by good company."

The loading crew finally lifted my stretcher and placed me on the cargo plane. When the cargo hatch was finally closed, it hit me, *I am leaving Viet Nam forever!* In my mind, I flashed on the image of the youthful face of the NVA soldier that spared my life but ripped me off for my wallet and identification. I'll bet he'll be surprised when he discovers I ain't twenty-one yet. If he sneaked into the USA, my ID won't even make him legal to buy a drink! A small smirk formed on my face.

HOMECOMING

Los Angeles, California
May, 1969

TAP-TAP-TAP-tap-tap-tap, "Tadashi, come out and greet your guests, don't be so rude." *Tap-tap-tap-tap-tap.* "Tadashi are you in there?" *Maybe if I don't answer, Mom will understand and make an excuse for my absence, then everyone can just eat and leave.* Deep down, I knew this wasn't going to happen because Mom didn't operate like that. She was doing her best to try and get me out of my bedroom. I wasn't ready to leave my room, so I said to her from behind the closed door, "Mom, start without me, I'll be out in a little while."

"Tadashi, you said that over an hour ago. All your uncles, aunties, cousins, and neighbors are waiting. Please come out, everything will be okay." Mom's voice no longer sounded demanding, it sounded concerned and sad, in trying to persuade me to come out for my homecoming party. As far as I was concerned, there was nothing more I could say. I continued to sit on the edge of my bed. I heard Mom's footsteps walking away from the other side of the bedroom door that separated my world from theirs. I could hear her voice, saying to our guests, "Tadashi's still getting ready, he'll be out in a few minutes.

Even though everyone on the other side of the door was important and special to me, something stopped me from opening the door to face everyone that I hadn't seen in over a year, acting like everything is normal and I have it under control. I hate to admit it, but I'm scared and I don't understand why, and where this feeling is coming from. Ever since I returned home from the hospital, I consciously avoided being around anyone other than my immediate family. Whenever the doorbell rang, I would retreat into my room before the door was answered. The few phone calls for me went unanswered. Man, I thought that this feeling would go away after a few days back home, but it didn't. In fact, it's getting worse, and at this very moment I'm sitting alone in the dark and perspiring. Something's not right and no matter how hard I try, I can't get myself to chill and relax.

Maybe, I'll just take down the window screen and sneak out, just like I used to when I was a kid. Shit, I have enough money to check into a motel room and stay there until I start feeling regular again. Maybe all I need is a few days to myself. Yeah, that's what I'm going to do, but I better pack a few items.

I went to my dresser and started to put my underwear and socks in my sea bag. I felt bad for my family—especially Mom because she had gone all out preparing for my welcome home party. She had been cooking all day, making my favorite foods: teriyaki ginger chicken, Hawaiian-style macaroni salad, Korean barbeque short ribs, shoyu-flavored string beans, and three cartons of shrimp chow mien from Paul's Kitchen. For Mom, this occasion was so special that she even purchased two rock cods from New Moon Fish Market; she steamed one with black bean sauce, the other with ginger and green onions. I better leave her a note at least—I hope she'll understand. Now, if only I can find something to write with; I can never find shit when I need it.

PAAT-PAAT-PAAT! That couldn't be Mom, because she doesn't knock that hard unless she's pissed. "Tad, it's me, I'm coming in!" It was my Uncle Charlie's voice. Good ole Uncle Charlie. "Uncle Charlie, not now, I don't feel good."

"Tadashi, I know you don't feel well, but I'm gonna come in anyway, for a few minutes, then I'll leave okay?" There was no use arguing because once Uncle Charlie makes up his mind, there's no changing it. He opened the door.

Uncle Charlie entered my room and to my surprise, he didn't say anything. He just sat down next to me on the opposite edge of my bed. Uncle Charlie is my mom's older brother and while I was growing up, he was the one family member I felt close to and looked up to. All my life, when I was getting in trouble, he was always there for me—even when I was clearly in the wrong, he never gave up on me. Like my pop, he worked hard to make ends meet. He was a self-trained body-and-fender man and word on the street was that Charlie really didn't hammer out the dents on damaged cars—he just filled the dents with plaster and sanded it to perfection. At the body shop, they affectionately called him, "Bondo Charlie"—everybody liked Uncle Charlie. The only time Uncle Charlie ever got pissed at me was when I was in junior high and got caught stealing a bag of pistachio peanuts at Adler's Market. By the time Charlie came over to the house to talk to me, I had already been yelled at by Mom and slapped upside my head by Pop. I was in no mood to hear another lecture. I remember acting disinterested when he was talking to me, when he suddenly exploded and said, "Boy, don't you ever roll your eyes when I'm talking to you. When you act stupid and hurt your mom, you shame the entire family—that's when your nonsense becomes my business!" Uncle Charlie grabbed me, lifted me up by my shirt collar, walked me over to the front of the house, and threw me into the rose bushes. By the time I untangled myself and got out of the bush, Uncle Charlie was already in his car driving down the block. I never again rolled my eyes when Uncle Charlie was talking to me.

I hadn't seen Charlie in over a year; it felt strange seeing him sitting on the edge of the bed, not giving me advice or cracking jokes. I broke the silence, "Look Uncle Charlie, I appreciate what you're trying to do, but I ain't leaving my room. I'm not going out there."

"Tad, I didn't come in here to make you come out of your room. You're a grown man and I don't have the power to make you do anything you don't want to do on your own. I just want to see you and see how you're doing, that's all."

"Uncle Charlie, I'm not feeling too good, it's nothing personal."

"Look, I know. A lot of my buddies were in the 442nd and they saw a lot of bad things that they couldn't talk about. What they saw and did, affected each one differently. If, years from now, you still don't want to leave your room, and I didn't have the courage to talk with you when I first had a chance to, I would never forgive myself. Do you understand what I'm trying to say?" My chest started feeling heavy, "Yeah."

"Tad, on the other side of the door is your family. We are more than your friends, and no matter what, we will always be there for you. I never told you this, but you and me are alike, we're both hardheaded. Being headstrong makes life more exciting, but it comes with a price. Tad, this time you paid your dues in full. You don't owe anybody anything—not your parents, not me, not the government. How I see it is the only person you owe something to is yourself. You can walk out this room and still be locked up in your own head the rest of your life and that would be no different than sitting here in the dark. Don't be hard on yourself; you did what you had to do. Tad, do you trust me?"

Uncle Charlie's words touched me; it reached a part of me that I had been resisting—my family's love. Softly, I replied, "Yeah, I trust you Uncle Charlie."

"Come on, let's go chop-chop, your mom made a feast." Charlie stood up and walked over to the light switch and turned it on. The light's brightness didn't bother me as it usually did. Uncle Charlie was now standing right in front of me. I lifted my head and our eyes met. I felt wetness in my eyes, but when I saw the same wetness in Uncle Charlie's eyes, tears involuntarily poured from mine. I stood and accepted his warm embrace.

When my breathing relaxed, Charlie and I sat back down on the bed. He transformed back into good ole' Uncle Charlie and he ribbed me about how skinny I got and I kidded him about how old-looking he got. To this, he said, "Bullshit, the women still fight over your Uncle Charlie!" I shot back, "Yeah, and I heard that the loser gets the booby prize and has to spend the night with you!" "Haaaarh!" Charlie laughed and threw a playful jab into my ribs.

"Hey you hungry?"

I thought about it, "Man, I'm starving, lets go eat, Uncle Charlie."

PART V

Serve the People!

ASIAN CONFUSION

In the annals of US military engagement, America's Viet Nam soldier was the only one sent into a hostile combat fighting zone, individually. In all other wars and conflict, American troops were/are deployed into a combat zone as a cohesive division, battalion, or company. An even greater challenge for the Viet Nam Soldier was returning back to the "World", alone. Yesterday, being in a bamboo jungle trying to stay alive, then overnight back home to a changed concrete jungle. The hardest part was coming back to a country that not only didn't appreciate your service, but was hostile towards it.

September 1969

KERPOW! I stiffened while raising my imaginary weapon to a ready position. Pivoting, I saw smoke emitting from a muffler on a backfiring stalled car. Damn! I thought this shit was behind me. It's been four months now, and I am still getting spooked. The last time it happened was late at night driving home, when a LAPD chopper shined an overhead spotlight on me. Between the sound of the chopper's whirling blades and the glaring light, I flashed; it felt like being medivaced all over again. I'm actually glad this occurred late at night when no other cars were on the road, I could have easily caused an accident.

One positive change is that I'm sleeping more soundly, ever since I bought a Browning 9 millimeter. Knowing it's under my pillow helps me sleep better at night. Before I copped my piece, I felt naked and vulnerable. I just make sure that in the morning, I stash it inside the closet so that my family is kept unaware.

I thank Buddha for my family—I don't know what I would have done without their support. They are sensitive and patient with me. I appreciate the personal space they give me, not asking a lot of questions and allowing me to figure things out at my own pace. I hate to admit it, but coming back to the "world" hasn't been easy.

It blows my mind seeing how the much the world has changed since I've been away. From fashion, attitudes, and even to street slang, everything is different.

Before I left the neighborhood, cats wouldn't dare to step out of the pad unless their slacks were creased, shirt pressed, shoes polished and fronts immaculate. Today, I see these same cats dressed in tattered jeans and powder blue work shirts. Open toe sandals have replaced polished French kicks. Gold chains and pendants are out and love beads are in. It's a rare sight to see someone with a pompadour front; the new trend is JC-style shoulder length hair or longer, tied in a pony tail.

Facial hair and goatees are new status symbols for being *down*. A dude's wardrobe is one thing, but what really irks me is a large number of the chicks sport the same fashion. Being a legman, I miss mini skirts.

Due to my military experience, I'm hep to the black power movement, and how "bloods" now call themselves "blacks" or "African Americans." Following their lead, other minorities have redefined themselves: *Ese's* are "Hispanics" or "Chicanos." Indians have changed to "Native Americans" or "Skins." But to find out that buddhaheads now call themselves "Asian" or "Asian American*," please*, what the fuck is that all about?! It goes on and on: dudes, cats, chicks and bitches are now everyone's "brother" and "sister." The government is "the Establishment," elected officials are "The Man," and the police are "pigs." The only constant is, "white boy" is still "white boy."

It's a trip to seeing people my age pissed off and protesting about one thing or another. There are so many different counter-culture groups advocating different agendas, that I lose track. The rebellious white youths refer to themselves as "hippies." Their hippie expression, "Far out!" describes it best.

Personally, I've rebelled against authority my entire life and I don't need to join any group or sect. Those days are behind me; the last group I joined shaved two years off my life and gave me two Purple Hearts. I have no beef with the hippies or anyone else so long as they don't disrespect my service and fallen comrades.

I do know that keeping busy and my mind occupied, is when I'm at my best. In early spring I went to sign up for my GI education benefits at the VA office in Westwood. I completed their paperwork and upon turning it in, the clerk asked if I wanted to meet with a VA counselor to talk about any trauma I may be experiencing. The muffler back-fire incident was still fresh in my mind, so I decided to give it a try. He gave me a numbered piece of paper and said to have a seat until my number is called. I waited so long that I dozed off before hearing my number called. I entered a small office and before getting comfortable in the chair, the shrink started talking, asking straight up, "What's been troubling you?" I said, "If I knew the answer, I wouldn't be sitting here!" But I did tell him that I still get nervous and anxious over stuff that I thought shouldn't bother me. He didn't ask for any specific instances, instead, he asked if I ever thought about hurting myself. I said, "Hell no!" Next he asked if I have trouble sleeping at night. I wanted to say, "Not since I copped my piece," but thought better of it. The shrink looked down and wrote something on a piece of paper. He handed me the paper, then told me to go across Wilshire Boulevard to the VA hospital, give them the paper and they'll schedule an appointment to see a psychologist. In the meantime I'll get a prescription that will help me sleep. I stood, looked at him, shook my head, left the piece of paper on his desk and walked out. My counseling session lasted less than three minutes.

On my way home, I felt stupid. *What a fuckin' waste of time; I don't need any sleeping pills, I can score some reds on my own, without having to go through this bullshit!* It's a good thing the shrink didn't ask me if I ever felt like hurting elitist pooh-butt bureaucrats!

TEACH

Spring, 1970

SLOWLY, I'm getting my shit together. With a portion of my military savings, I bought a navy blue VW bug with a sunroof top. I'm enrolled at LA City College and collect the GI Bill. It's time to get my own place. As righteous as it is, staying with my family and eating Mom's cooking, I'm ready to move forward.

Returning from classes at LACC, I can't resist the thick strong barbecue smoke that fills the air at the intersection of Crenshaw and Adams. I follow its scent and am drawn into the Leo's BBQ parking lot. While waiting to order a medium hot combination hot link, pork rib plate, I see Willie ahead of me in the take out line! We get our plates, sit in the parking lot eating BBQ, and catch up. Man, even Crazy Willie is changed—he's a full time student at Cal State LA, majoring in business, working part time at UPS, and he still sells weed to supplement his income. Willie says that every now and then he runs into a Minister partner. The Ministers are all scattered and everyone's doing their own thing. The brothers that did joint time, work in service trades, like plumbing, meat-cutting, and janitorial gigs. Gary, Mas, and Steve are hitched. Mas married Sumi who stuck by his rowdy ass, and they have a kid with another one on its way. Except for a couple cats strung out on drugs, everyone else is alive and getting by. I don't talk about my Viet Nam experience, but I tell Willie that it feels good to be back. Upon sharing my plan to move out, I find out that by coincidence, he is looking for a place, also. Business major Willie, calculates that if we combine our money to rent a two bedroom house, we'll pay less than if we rent solo for a smaller apartment unit. Getting to know each other isn't an issue because we grew up together; in fact, I bought my first nickel bag from Crazy Willie! I left Leo's parking lot with a full stomach and new roommate!

We found a small but comfortable two bedroom crib on St. Andrews Place— we're still in the Westside, a hiccup away from the Avenues.

Living with Willie is forcing me back into circulation. He knows me well enough to give me personal space, and out of respect he won't throw large gatherings at our pad. However, this won't stop Willie from having a few guests over for a relaxing night of weed, wine, music, conversation, and whatever else may follow. Often I join in their revelry where I meet people with different backgrounds and experiences; surprisingly, we usually find something in common to rap about. I dig my arrangement—if I start to feel uncomfortable or get too wasted, I don't have to drive home, I just get up, excuse myself, and go to my room to find my pillow.

Even better is meeting a "liberated" woman, game to share my bed with no strings attached!

Today, Willie tells me that Craig is dropping over to cop some weed. I hear Craig is attending Long Beach State and into the Asian American Movement thing. Lately, I've met a lot of people involved in the Asian Movement.

The last time I saw Craig was at Paul's Kitchen, right before I left for Viet Nam. The Craig I knew always had a super fine girlfriend and upon breaking up, he'd have an even finer one for his back-up. Smooth Mac Daddy!

When Craig stops by, he looks different from the Craig I remember. The old Craig was strictly a GQ fashion statement; this imposter has that hippified look I am getting accustomed to seeing. I'm curious what Craig has to say for himself. After killing a six-pack and smoking a couple of joints, our conversation loosens as Craig explains himself.

He got into Long Beach State through a minorities program, called High Potential, which pays his tuition and housing. He chose Long Beach because he heard that the finest ladies go there, which turned out to be true. He said by utilizing his Westside rap and attitude, he got over big time with the fine mammas. Because he was having such a blast, he almost flunked out. Needing to raise his GPA to keep his financial aid, he enrolled in two Asian American Studies classes. He was told that as long as you attend class, you're guaranteed to pass. He said early on, he intentionally distanced himself from movement people because he didn't want to be judged by them. Initially he resisted their rhetoric, but after putting that aside, he found the Asian American classes interesting. He said he's learning about things our folks should have told us, but never did because of their misplaced shame and guilt. He said that the more he's learning, the more he wants to know. He even views his past way of thinking as superficial and shallow.

After getting tight with the movement people, he realized that if anyone was pre-judging, it was he and not them. He's checked out political demonstrations and AA social gatherings and digs what is going on and how it makes him feel. Craig said that the unity he feels in the movement is sorta like what we had back in the Avenues, but different.

Listening to Craig, I notice that even his slang has changed: "bitches" are now his "sisters," and "dudes" his "brothers." It's new to me listening to a cat that you grew up and ran the streets with, now talking politics. Even though his appearance, friends and activities have changed, Craig still has his aura of confidence, like he's on top of the situation.

I don't spot a twinkle in Craig's eyes or the silly grin Jesus freaks radiate when they are "born again." But after all these years of knowing the old Craig, I'm skeptical that Craig's newfound interest in the Asian American Movement has more to do with scamming on the bitches, or as Craig put it, "Asian sisters."

Late into the night, before splitting, Craig invites Willie and me to a Long Beach Asian American Alliance Teach-In, followed by a house party next week. He said he'll even swing by to pick us up. I'm hesitant to attend a large gathering, but with Craig acting his persistent self and the weed and alcohol taking effect, I finally say, "Fuck it, I'll go." Willie declines saying that he's been missing too many work shifts at UPS and can't make the teach-in, but to leave him the address to the house party.

Next week rolls by and Craig picks me up. Our car ride doesn't start on a positive note because I finally get pissed at Craig for constantly referring to his new friends as brother-this and sister-that. I say, "Look man, the Ministers are the only *brothers* that ever had your back and we got the scars to prove it. When the shit hits the fan, the fools you now call your brothers are going to be nowhere in sight, and you can take that to the bank, *BROTHER!*" Craig gets quiet and I feel bad for raining on his parade. I extend my closed fist in his direction and Craig meets it with his own closed fist. I bring out a joint, fire it up and pass it on to Craig. Soon we're talking about old neighborhood stuff, and other relevant shit like how the Lakers are going to kick Boston's ass in the finals.

The teach-in is being held on campus, in a large room in the Music Department. We arrive early because Craig is one of the event organizers and needs to help set up. I take a seat in back of the room, near the exit, just in case I get uncomfortable and need to leave the room.

By the time the teach-in starts the room is packed with young Asian American students. I am impressed that Craig's group could pull in so many people, thinking, "Man, we could have used all these brothers when we was hassling the Eastside!" Finally, a member of the AA Alliance steps up to the microphone to introduce the featured speaker. I'm so busy checking out the people in the audience that I don't pay attention to the introduction until I catch these words, "This evening Sally Fuji will share with us her experiences as a member of the Third World Peace Delegation that was invited by the Provisional Revolutionary Government to North Viet Nam, where she witnessed the Vietnamese people's fight against US imperialism." Fuck! I'm tense, "Holy shit, she is for the other side!" Now, I am completely locked in—I even get up to move closer to the front.

Sally Fuji, standing in front of a large gathering of students, is a small, petite, older-looking Sansei. She has on a thin, white cotton top and bottom, the kind of outfit I saw Vietnamese village women wear. Her facial expression looks sad, but concerned; the kind of look someone has when they lose or misplace something important to them. Sally Fuji began to speak.

She starts by sharing her personal history that led to her to being chosen for the Third World Peace Delegation. She was raised in the Silver Lake area, a nice middle class area near Griffith Park. She graduated with honors at Marshall High and attended UC Santa Cruz where she became active in the student movement. After college she was a volunteer worker for the Democratic Party and worked in both Kennedy campaigns. She became involved in the Civil Rights Movement, but eventually grew disillusioned with believing that meaningful change could occur through the electoral political system. This led her to work in grassroots community organizations and eventually to her selection as a member of the Third World Peace Delegation.

She said the delegation included members from progressive grassroots community organizations as the Black Panther Party, Young Lords, and Chinatown's Red Guard, to name a few; it even included a celebrity actress. The goal of the trip was for the delegates to experience firsthand the Vietnamese struggle for their national liberation, and to take back and share what they learned with their communities. So far, I find her to be sincere and personal. I no longer feel like I am part of a larger audience; it feels eerie, almost as if she understands my source of confusion and is speaking directly to me.

Sally said that the Vietnamese people had been fighting for liberation against colonialist and imperialist nations for over two hundred years. Before US involvement, this tiny nation had resisted and defeated China, Japan and France. Viet Nam has rich natural resources of tungsten and tin, and is a potential source for cheap labor—all valued commodities for imperialist nations like the US.

She explained how the last four wars that America has fought, were against Asian nations and how racism against Asian people is institutionalized through the media and government politics and policies. She said institutional racism dehumanizes people of color and justifies white supremacy and racist atrocities. She used concrete examples: black slavery, Manifest Destiny, Trail of Tears, Wounded Knee Massacre, Japanese American concentration camps, Chinatown massacres, atomic bombs on Hiroshima and Nagasaki, My Lai massacre, on and on. She said that the people of Viet Nam do not see the American people as being their enemy, but they do hold the US Government accountable for this war of aggression.

Tonight I am learning more relevant history than I had when sitting in LA Unified classrooms for the past decade-and-a-half. It is not only the information that captivates me, it is the way it is presented. Sally Fuji displays no anger, edge or bitterness in her tone of voice; however, I detect a feeling of urgency from her voice.

I am surprised to learn that the Vietnamese translation for the word "gook," is "foreigner." I flash, "Wow, they weren't the gooks, *we're* the gooks!" She used this as an example how white skin privilege and supremacy manipulated a word by turning it into an object of hatred. Words like, "jap", "chink", "nigger", "spic", "wetback", and "gook", are all politically used to dehumanize people of color and to remind white supremacists that we are less than human.

She closed by saying that she understood that a student's priority was to get good grades to lead to a good job, to make good money. She said that college students have the luxury of getting immediate pleasure and gratification from things like ski trips, smoking dope, dropping acid and watching the sunset or sunrise. She emphasized that it was not her intention to guilt-trip anyone in the room but Asian brothers and sisters in South East Asia are dying because of America's racist war of genocide on the Vietnamese people. As Asian Americans, we have a responsibility to do our part to support the Vietnamese people in their struggle for national liberation and self-determination.

Damn, this is a whole lot to swallow in one big bite. Tonight is the first time that I ever understood that being Asian is bigger and more important than just being a buddhahead—it means that we are one with other Asians, especially Vietnamese. When I was fighting in the bush, it was life and death and I didn't have time to think of the "enemy" as "brothers" and "sisters," and if I did, I probably would have lost my mind. However, I can't blow off what Sally Fuji said, it was logical and made sense.

For the first time, I am able to see what I had gone through in a larger political context. The confusion about my participation in the war, now needs further clarification and investigation. If my suspicions are correct, then Uncle Sam played me for a chump. It meant that Wagner and all the other war casualties on both sides should have never happened!

I always equated strength with being physically dominant. Tonight, Sally Fuji showed me humanistic, compassionate strength, absent machismo bullshit. Teach Sister!

MINISTERS REUNION

THE SHATTO PARK SHOOTOUT which happened three years ago, marked the end of the Ministers. Going their separate ways, many chose their next path, but for an unfortunate few, their next stop was handed down to them by the California Penal System.

For his involvement, Mas served a bullet in County Jail. Lawrence, not quite 18 years old at the time of the shootout, was sent to a delinquency detention camp. Rick, Davey, Art, and Tad enlisted in the military. Ministers like Henry, Willie, Craig and Yoshio never left the neighborhood.

Five months after Shatto, Gary caught an "assault with a deadly weapon" charge, after he avenged a beat-down of his partner James. He knocked the crap out of Jame's assailant. His alleged deadly weapons were his fists and shod feet.

It started when James stumbled into Kabuki, a Westside nightclub behind Crenshaw Square. He was high as a kite and loud-talking. A long, lanky dude named Cliff took exception and punched James in the mouth, knocking out a front tooth. When Gary found out what happened, he went gunning for Cliff. He tracked Cliff down on Farmdale Avenue, directly across the street from Dorsey High. He put a big-time hurt on Cliff; when finished, he dumped Cliff head-first into a trash bin. This happened right when school let out and was witnessed by the Dorsey student body.

Cliff was hospitalized with a fractured jaw and a busted eye socket. His family pressed charges against Gary. Gary was arrested and locked down in County Jail, awaiting a preliminary hearing. Yoshio, the aspiring Westside gangster, went to Cliff's house and threatened the family if Cliff testified against Gary. The family reported this incident to the DA's Office and they tacked on an additional charge of witness intimidation. What's a brother to do without friends?! Eventually, Gary's case was plea-bargained down to two years in a state prison—he served his sentence at Soledad.

By now, all the former Ministers were back on the Westside. When they bump into each other, the vibe is always good, but everyone is busy doing his own thing. They exchange phone numbers and share the uptick and sightings of their Minister partners—through this neighborhood grapevine, they keep in touch.

With the exception of James, who was slamming heroin into his veins, the rest of the Ministers are alive, kicking, and doing all right. A few of the married cats have toddlers, some are back in school, and most have blue-collar gigs. There are even a few entrepreneurs: Kenny, Bobby, and Steve started a janitorial, furniture-repair service, and Art, a business order forms operation. Even though they were no longer running the streets together, they all take pride knowing that everyone is handling their business. As the saying goes, "Right on!"

"Are you still at Saint Andrews Place?" "Yeah," I reply, "You gonna try and make it?" Dave shoots back, "Be there, or be square, catch you later!" Willie and I watch as Dave slides into his car and leaves the West Adams Christian Church parking lot. Tonight is bittersweet. Sweet because for the first time in what felt like ages, all the Ministers are together. Bitter because we came here to support our Minister partner, Stan, and pay our respects to the family. Stan's kid brother Alvin, died of a drug overdose. It's hard for me to accept that Alvin's gone. I still picture him as a young kid, trying to tag along with his older brother Stan, whom he idolized. Word is, Alvin started running with some fuck-ups and graduated from dropping reds, to skin popping, and ultimately mainlining smack.

Willie and I are the last ones left in the parking lot. It's ironic because we couldn't wait for the service to end, but are waiting now for the reverend, to ask him a few questions that trouble us. Listening to the reverend's eulogy, it was obvious that he didn't have a clue who Alvin was and what his life was about. I wouldn't be shocked if tonight was the first time this reverend ever laid eyes on Alvin, as he lay stiff in his casket. His abstract religious terms sugar-coated Alvin's life; what made it even worse was the reverend saying that Alvin died of a heart attack!

"Yo Tad, it's getting late and I don't think he's coming out, he probably has a secret escape hatch, what do you wanna do?" I glanced over at Willie and replied, "Yeah, let's book." Leaving the parking lot, it bothers me to see a young life wasted. I'd like to think that Alvin's parting gift was bringing us together, giving us an opportunity to reconnect. Tonight we all agreed to get together the following Saturday at my pad, for a potluck. I'm looking forward to our reunion.

Saturday couldn't get here quick enough. We're all in a festive mood, feasting on Chinese food from Chin's and Paul's Kitchen, Leo's BBQ, Golden Bird chicken, and Mr Angelo's thin crust pizza. Not to be outdone, the married cats brought dishes prepared by their wives. Gary's wife, Cathy, made spam *musubi*; Mas' wife, Sumi, baked a chicken broccoli casserole dish; and Rick's wife, Keiko, who he met and married while stationed in Japan, made tofu salad. The tofu salad is so delicious that us single dudes keep bugging Rick, asking him if Keiko has any available sisters!

"Hey, Moose, word on the street is that in the Nam you got shot in the rectum. Don't worry, I straightened it out and told them, wreck-em my ass, damn near killed him!" Over everyone's laughter, I shouted, "Fuck you, Pencils!" It's been over three years since I've been called "Moose," a moniker bestowed on me by my Minister partners. Greg is "Pencils" because the top of his head comes to a point; Dave is "Blinky"—when he gets excited, his eyes blink a mile a minute. Dennis, whose mom is white and dad is Nisei, is "Buddha-Paddy." Chris is "Roach"—I nor anyone else can remember how that name originated, and I'm "Moose," due to my pronounced Adam's apple.

I haven't laughed, rapped, joked, and jived like this in ages. Everyone's here, except Stan and Yoshio. No one has seen or heard from Yoshio; we all hope he's okay. Earlier, when we talked about Stan's younger brother's funeral service, we concluded that even though he died of an overdose, he wasn't a weak or a bad person, nor did his folks fail him or have anything to be ashamed of. I remember how the youngbloods on the Westside, like Alvin, used to look up to us, the same way we admired the older thugs when we were up and coming. There were cats like the Nakano brothers, Big Clyde, Monkey Man—badasses who didn't take shit from anyone. A few of us feel a taste responsible—maybe there was something that we could have said or done for Alvin when he was alive.

In the midst of our reverie, Craig, "Mister Asian American Movement," changed the mood of our reunion by saying, "Crenshaw's changed a lot since we ran the streets. Today young Sansei are overdosing, and the *Rafu Shimpo* obituary section reports 'heart failure' as the cause of death." Dave chimes in, "Heart attack my ass, they all OD'ing on fuckin' reds!" We all know that Dave's getting worked up because he's blinking incessantly. Henry agrees, "Yeah, it's different nowadays; everyone is dropping downers. My neighbor's daughter OD'd last month. She can't be more than fifteen, and she ain't even the rowdy type." Mas adds, "Another heart attack!" Henry concludes, "She lucked out, she made it to ER on time and they pumped her stomach." The more we rap, the more it's apparent that everyone personally knows a young Sansei on the Westside who died of drug overdose. The kicker is that most of them were not *yogores* or hardcore dope fiends, but young school-age Sansei.

Gary says, "If you ask me, these kids are spoiled; everything is handed to them. What they need is tough love—get them so scared of an ass-whippin' that they won't even think of taking an aspirin for a headache." Craig shoots back, "Yeah, and after you whip *their* ass, *your* ass gets rolled up by your parole agent on a violation!" As hard as we were all busting up, we all know that Gary is stone serious because that's who he is—a straight ahead, old school brother. Henry adds, "The young dudes think that the more loaded you get, the cooler you are."

Now Art drops this bombshell, "Yo, dig this. Last week I was eating at Holiday Bowl and three young gangster types approached me, saying that they want to talk. I didn't have the foggiest clue what was on their minds, so I asked them to sit down. These cats didn't have the long-haired hippie look, they reminded me of what we looked like back in the day. I got their names: Steve, Danny, and Richard. They said that they knew that I was a former Minister. They said that they're holding down the Westside and have their own gang. Check this out, it gets better—they call themselves *Ministers III!* They said out of respect to us, they want our approval to use the Ministers name."

"Bullshit!" "No fuckin' way!" "Get the fuck outta here!" "Damn, I didn't even know there was a Ministers II!" We're all stunned. Craig says, "Man, I'd like to meet and check out these young brothers." He spoke for all of us. Art has their number and says he'll contact them and set up a meeting.

Henry comments, "Back in the day, if the older thugs we looked up to had taken us aside and schooled us, things might have turned out different." Dave replies, "Shit, back then the only advice we'd listen to was someone showing us how not to get caught!" Knowing Dave was right, I nod in agreement. But, I also know that times have changed—our time was about making a rep, making money, kicking ass, copping some tail, and getting a little loaded on the side. Now it's about overdosing deaths being reported as heart attacks!

It's hard to say; maybe because we're older, a bit wiser, or just don't want to see the youngbloods make mistakes like the ones we made, that brought us to this point. Something needs to be done to change this situation that our community chooses to ignore and cover up. We need to take action, and give something back. There will be no more Alvins, no more funerals, no more heart attacks!

YELLOW BROTHERHOOD

"TAD, ANY MORE ROOM in your ride?" I replied, "Yo, everyone move in, and make room for Kenny." Over the grumbling, we managed to squeeze six of us in my VW bug. "Where we going, today?" Acting irritated, I responded, "Man, I told you all last night after study hall, we're going to USC to hear about the concentration camps our folks and grandparents were locked down in." More grumbling. "Man, let's do something fun for a change!" Quickly I responded, "I guess you're telling me you don't want to get up next to all the fine sisters that will be there today?" Finally, "Naw, just asking."

Our eight-car caravan, all fifty of us, left the Centenary Methodist Church parking lot, heading to the USC campus to attend a teach-in, presented by the USC Asian American Student Alliance on America's concentration camps.

Everything has happened so quickly that it's a mind fuck to think back; it was only five months ago when we first met at Lawrence's parent's back yard. We chose this location because they lived on Muirfield Road, a hop, step and jump from Dorsey High. Only Craig, Lawrence, Art, Gary, and I were there to represent at this meeting. We figured that since it's a Friday after-school meeting, just a handful of youngsters would show. Damn, we miscalculated—by the time the meeting started we were outnumbered by close to a nine-to-one ratio. The backyard was almost too small to hold all the JA youth, with a few more that trickled in.

I'm glad we were semi-organized and had an agenda. After we introduced ourselves, we asked the young Sansei to say something about themselves and why they showed up. Even though this was time consuming, it was important that everyone have an opportunity to express themselves—plus it allowed us to check out the group's "pecking order." It turned out that most of them showed because Steve, Richard and Danny told them to come. Including those three, there were a dozen or so *yogore* types, with the majority of the JA kids being "dopers." It's not to say that the young thugs weren't getting high, but they came to hear about "gangsterism."

We knew that to organize them, we had to first earn the trust of their leaders; once this happens the others will follow. If they detect any bullshit, phoniness or weakness from us, it's over. To gain their trust we had to keep it real.

Keeping it real was never a problem for us. We talked about growing up as "outcasts" in the Japanese American community; how we never fit into the JA "good boy" stereotype. They expressed similar feelings about isolation, and rejections from the JA social clubs, honor societies, scouting troops, and even the JA sports leagues. We shared how being a Minister made us feel superior to the lames, squares, and goodie-goodies. Our intent wasn't to glamorize our past, so we talked about choices we made and consequences we paid. Gary spoke on how hard it was being the only buddhahead in the joint, and I surprised myself by sharing for the first time ever, a little about my military and Viet Nam experience.

That afternoon, we supported each other and spoke in one voice. I think our unity made a favorable impression on the JA youth. Our meeting lasted until supper time, and we all agreed to meet again on a Saturday, so all the OGs could attend.

Before the next meeting, we met with Steve, Richard and Danny at the coffee shop at Holiday Bowl. We shared with them our vision of starting an Asian American youth organization in Crenshaw for outcast JA youth that will have programs and activities they could relate to. I mentioned that without positive alternatives, gang-banging and ODs would continue. Gary added that he respects what they started but it's not our intention to help them become a bigger and badder street gang. We talked about how a group of street brothers in Oakland organized themselves into a militant community organization making revolutionary change in the African American community. I didn't see why we couldn't do the same in Crenshaw. Our sit-down was a success: Steve, Richard and Danny were game to give it a go.

With Steve, Richard, and Danny on board, the weekly meetings grew in attendance and participation. Our JA youth base was the *yogores,* dopers and fuck-ups. A few rowdy young sisters started showing up. Lawrence's family backyard became too small to hold our weekly meetings. It became clear that our goal was to work together and start programs and activities that would be positive alternatives to gang-banging and drugs.

With all of the OGs back together on the Westside, we see each other almost every day despite some of us going to school or working. We organized cells with each of us responsible for five young cell members, who in turn chose a cell leader. The cell leader checks on his group daily, then checks in with his OG sponsor. This helps us keep a finger on the pulse of the younger membership, to be able to douse any potential problem sparks before they burst into an open flame.

With our sponsorship program in place, Craig and I went to Dorsey High and met with the vice principal. We defined out goals to him: our intention and commitment to work with our targeted JA youth. The VP, Mr. Davis, was receptive and said that if he finds one of our members on drugs, ditching, or violating a school regulation, he'll call us before calling law enforcement, as long as the transgression is not overly serious.

Our next challenge was to find a facility large enough to hold our meetings and run our programs. We met with various Nisei leaders in our community: business types, Buddhist reverends, pastors—even the JACL—asking for the use of a community faculty for our youth programs. The Nisei didn't want to hear or acknowledge that drug abuse and gangs exist in the JA community. We got insincere smiles and lame excuses as they politely showed us the door. Feelings of resentment resurfaced and I realize that I still harbored some of my old anger within.

It's obvious that the Nisei establishment views us as troublemakers and unworthy of their support. Then we met the head pastor of Centenary Methodist

Church, Reverend Sano. He listened to us and opened the back room of his church, allowing us to use a site large enough for our after-school program and weekend activities. He even had us speak to his congregation on youth-related issues in the JA community. Reverend Sano is a beautiful brother who practices the Christian values he preaches. Finally our youth group has access to a facility.

We're a large youth group with a growing membership; our presence is felt as we attend and participate in community functions and events. Because of our strong presence, we're attracting attention in the JA community. It's cool to see the "invisible kids" in our community feeling pride in themselves, empowered, and feeling "unity."

My cell group is now in my ride as we head towards the teach-in at USC. "Man, I thought we'd never get here!" Backing into a cramped parking spot, I countered, "The ride wasn't that long." "Yeah, that's cuz you didn't have to sit here in the back cramped up with Kenny B and Big Glen." The best I could come back with was, "Haaaarh!"

The large lecture hall is packed with students, youth and a surprising number of Nisei and Issei. We're all seated together near the front, I'm glad we came because our members know very little about the concentration camp experience of our people. As a white professor type approaches the speaking podium, I only hope that what he has to say is brief.

Shit, Professor "White" been talking for ten minutes now and he ain't about to give up the mic, nor am I about to sit here all afternoon, listening to him lecture to us about "our" concentration camp experience. Glancing at Craig, Art, and Dave, without even having to say a word, we all stand simultaneously, and step to the dais. Politely I reach out and take the mic from Professor White, who hasn't said a word since we stood. "Thank you Professor, we'll take it from here." I hand the mic to Craig and he announces, "We came here today to learn about the camp experience from our elders, not from someone who read it from a book."

"Right on!" "Teach, brother!" is reverberating throughout the hall. Craig continued, "Will some of you Issei and Nisei who actually lived through this experience, please come up and share your experiences with us?" I'm a bit tense, but it quickly dissipates as I notice a stirring in the audience and individual Nisei and Issei stand and approach the dais. I thought, "Man, this is going to be a beautiful afternoon."

Following the program, grabbing a bite to eat at Holiday Bowl, our group occupied most of the coffee shop tables. While waiting for our food orders, Craig said, "Man, that was righteous. Today was probably the first time the Nisei and Issei shared their camp experience." Art chimed in, "After the program ended, I went to the head and while I was taking a leak, I heard a few students talking among themselves, "Who were those brothers who stormed the mic?" and a dude who was also taking a whiz said, "I think they're some type of brotherhood." Brent, a young brother blurts out, "Damn straight. We're the Yellow Brotherhood!" It's like the entire Holiday Bowl coffee shop reverberated with our laughter.

Yeah, that's who we are, the Yellow Brotherhood!

PRAIRIE FIRE

"A single spark can start a prairie fire."
Chairman Mao Tse Tung, Little Red Book

STRETCHED OUT on the manicured front yard lawn at 1227 Crenshaw Boulevard, and surrounded by my tight partners, I looked up at the mid-morning bluish-gray LA sky, feeling the warmth of the sun. I took in a deep breath, then slowly exhaled. Man, I haven't felt this relaxed in ages. I guess my homies feel this same contentment because no one is saying shit.

Breaking our solitude, Lawrence asks no one in particular, "Damn, how did this all come about!" Gary quickly responds, "The *Rafu Shimpo* article had a lot to do with it." Mas adds, "Yeah, but without our programs and the youth participation, there never would have been a *Rafu* article on the Yellow Brotherhood." My mind is now in retrospect mode: I recall how busy we got, immediately after Centenary gave us access to their facility. We outreached to college students in Asian American alliances to help tutor the YB members and we held a mandatory study hall every day after school. We monitored their school progress, and even though I felt hypocritical pushing the school thing, I knew from our past experience that ditching school and idle time is a dangerous combination. Before we started the tutorial program, most of the YB youth were habitually ditching school and those attending were barely passing. With sponsorship and tutorial programs in place, at the ten-week progress report, their overall grade point average was over a "B." Making sure that the brothers and sisters receive a "relevant" education, Asian American movement speakers were invited to discuss topics like, Asian Identity, Black Power, sexism and Third World unity.

We even entered the YB in the Westside Coed Volleyball League. Yeah, that was a trip-and-a-half! At first they all were reluctant to play that "sissy game." We convinced them to try it once and if they still didn't dig it, we'd drop out of the league. We didn't practice and just showed up and got killed! I think they were embarrassed, because on the ride back to Centenary following the slaughter, no one said a word—it was the quietest I've ever seen them. The following day, before I could submit our team registration, I drove into the Centenary parking lot where the young brothers and sisters were in a circle passing a volleyball around in the parking lot. They showed me "heart!" Every day after study hall we'd set up a makeshift net and practice. As the season progressed we improved and with a few breaks we made it to the playoffs. The volleyball gods looked upon us—we peaked at the right time and made it to the championship game. Our entire YB organization came and cheered us on to victory. I remember Richard, one of the young leaders, telling me, "Six months ago, if you told me that these gangbangers would be playing volleyball, I wouldn't have believed it! Man this is beautiful!"

Art returned my straying thoughts back to the moment, "I remember how we all got a kick out of the *Rafu* article. It was right in front of the community's eyes: the drugs, ODs, gangbanging, but they had to fuckin' read about it to believe it; please!" Davey adds, "All you had to do was to go to Holiday Bowl on a Saturday night and see all the young fools stumble around like zombies!" Davey stood, then stumbled around, perfectly imitating a drug-induced barbiturate walk—we all crack up.

Actually the *Rafu* article served as the catalyst to get the Nisei community to support the Yellow Brotherhood. The *Rafu Shimpo,* a Japanese American community newspaper consisting of English and Japanese language sections, has been in circulation since before World War II. Its subscription extends beyond Los Angeles and is the largest circulated JA newspaper in North America. For Issei and Nisei, the *Rafu Shimpo* is the truth. The article verified the existence of drugs and gangs in the JA community, and its effect on JA youth. It reported how YB's programs weres making a positive impact on JA youth in the community. The article chastised the Nisei for not acknowledging that problems exist, and for not helping the Yellow Brotherhood.

"Yo, Craig, has the Nisei Business Club invited you to their next meeting yet?!" Craig replies, "Actually, I called Yosh Kawataki's office a couple of times, but he ain't called back." Dave says, "As far as the Nisei businessmen are concerned, you're a devil, which makes us your disciples".

Believe it or not, Dave's comment has a lot of truth to it. My take is that as a result of the *Rafu* article and our strong presence in the community, the Nisei Business Association stepped up and offered to raise funds to purchase a two-story house on Crenshaw Boulevard, north of Pico Boulevard. Using their community ties and political connections they organized a massive fundraising campaign.

Everything was falling into place, until we had a major difference of opinion.

Their plan was to host a fundraising dinner, and to showcase the Yellow Brotherhood as a model self-help program. We were cool with this but what we objected to was that the association invited city government dignitaries, including Mayor Yorty, to speak at the fundraising dinner without consulting us. We explained to them that we are an autonomous grassroots organization, and we do not endorse any electoral candidate or party. As a matter of fact, we view the government, including local government, as part of the problem.

They blew a fuse, but we remained firm on our position and even said that if they went ahead with the fundraising dinner, that the Yellow Brotherhood membership will "picket" the event. That was the last straw for them, but just before the fundraiser was about to be cancelled, Reverend Sano intervened and proposed a compromise. He suggested that instead of having Mayor Yorty as the featured speaker, Senator Inouye from Hawaii, should be invited to speak at the dinner, and the YB will have an older and a younger member speak at the dinner. I recall that when we regrouped to discuss this proposal, for the first time in our history, we couldn't reach a consensus. One side emphasized that being Asian and having served in the 442nd Regiment Combat Team, Sen. Inouye should get a pass.

I sided with those who felt that despite Sen. Dan being Asian, he is still part of the electoral political system. He and other dignitaries would be welcome to attend, but should not be speakers. Our leadership body lacked a unified political awareness and methodology to resolve a disagreement of this type and so it was never fully resolved. Sen Inouye ended up as the keynote speaker at the fundraiser, Mas and Ronnie presented on behalf of the YB.

Craig finally breaks the silence, "I know that the Nisei businessmen still view us as hardheads, uncontrollable and ungrateful. I just want to tell them how much we appreciate their efforts and we are willing to continue to work with them or any other progressive group, as long as our principles of autonomy are respected." Dave replies, "Fool, they ain't calling you back, whatcha been smoking!"

The good news is that enough funds were raised to purchase our youth center. The YB house is a two-story wooden house, with four bedrooms, three bathrooms, a basement, and a three-car garage with an upstairs room built over it. To boot, it is freshly coated with yellow paint! We have a big backyard and the front-yard is landscaped, compliments of the Japanese Gardeners Association. As former gang members, we made a commitment to serve the youth in our community. What started out as a spark, spread like a prairie fire! I have a hard time comprehending that this all came together in a little over a year.

RISE AND FALL

Winter, 1972

THIS IS MY TIME; my time to relax, gather my thoughts and prepare for the upcoming whirlwind. For the next hour, I have the house all to myself that is, until school lets out and then it's on! Yeah, it's been quite a ride! From the moment the Yellow Brotherhood house opened its door, it's been a beehive—a center of activity for Westside Asian youth. The YB house is theirs and they claim ownership. Their energy, unfiltered edge, swagger, raw humor, compassion, and loyalty to each other motivates and inspires me.

With the other OGs working or otherwise tied up in the late afternoon, I adjusted my school schedule so that I can open the house and start the after-school study hall program. Probably, our daily YB routine may seem mundane from an outsider's perspective: after-school study hall, followed by a community activist guest who discusses relevant topics; in fact Brother Warren is coming today to talk on Asian American identity. After study hall it's time for a break and after supper we reconvene at the house. In the evening the older sponsors drop in and check on their cells. What keeps me going is that there is never a dull moment, something's always going down at the house: backyard winner-stay-on-the-court half court b-ball, shooting stick on the pool table in the recreation room above the garage, grooving on the latest .45 jams, talking smack, politics, or sweet talk with a sister you want to get up next to, or just plain hanging out and kicking it with your homies.

On weekends, we open up early in the morning and either do an activity at the house or attend a community event. The married brothers alternate their weekends at the YB house; regulars like myself are here around the clock. These past five months have given me the opportunity to witness the young YB members grow as individuals. With the YB structure in place, they no longer seem as lost and angry. This ain't to say that issues and drama still don't arise, because they do, but they are no longer life-threatening. With the Westside *yogores* in check, gang-banging in the JA community is a thing of the past, and substance abuse amongst young Asians is in check. I'm not naive enough to say that no one does drugs anymore, but the young people now have a choice, and the peer group pressure now tilts in favor of hanging out at the YB and participating in its program as opposed to running the streets.

Looking out the large front room bay window, I spot the first wave youngbloods walking up the driveway. Time for me to quit tripping and reminiscing, and get busy!

194

Spring, 1972

"Tad, did you read the article in *Rafu* on that young Gardena cat that we dropped in on last month?" All I could say to Richard was, "Damn shame!" and refocus my attention back on my writing assignment. Richard senses my reluctance to talk further about the matter, and quietly leaves the house study room to go to the backyard, where a group of the brothers were lifting weights and shooting pool.

Lately, I sense myself having less to say and getting irritated quicker than before. I definitely have to check myself, so that I don't bring my issues to the house. I guess, being here around the clock, dealing with everyone else's problems, not having time to adequately complete my own school assignments is beginning to wear on me. Like I already said to myself, "Get your shit together, Tad!" During moments like this, I fall back on what Pop taught me at the *dojo,* "Clear your mind, inhale deeply, hold it, relax, then, evenly exhale the same breath through the mouth." Whew, it still works!

The *Rafu* article Richard referred to reported the death of a young high school-age JA, from Gardena. Because of our accomplishments, the YB has gained a rep for being a grassroots, Asian American youth group. Asian youth groups are starting up throughout the West Coast. We've met and shared information with grassroots youth organizations in San Francisco, Fresno, Seattle, Sacramento, and Stockton. Locally, we receive phone calls from Nisei parents asking for assistance. The majority of the calls are from isolated Sansei youth seeking understanding and support.

Anyway, two months ago, I took a phone call from a young brother from Gardena. He wanted to rap with someone about the "changes" he was going through. Like many youth, he felt alienated, couldn't relate to school, and unable to talk with his parents, was now dropping reds. I took his name and address. Richard and I drove out to his Gardena address. He lived in an upper-middle-class area; all the homes on the block had immaculately sculptured gardens and pristine front lawns. We rang the doorbell, a Nisei woman answered. We introduced ourselves, and explained why we were there to visit her son. She asked us to wait a minute while she went to get him. She left the door slightly ajar, but not wide enough to peek inside. She came back alone and told us that her son was in his bedroom and not feeling well. She apologized for our inconvenience and offered me gas money. I said that I needed to see her son because he's the one that called and asked us to come by, but if he changed his mind that's okay too. I just need to hear it from him. She told us to wait, and that she will ask her son to come to the door—this time she shut the door. About ten minutes passed, then a Gardena police car drove up. Two cops approached and asked us to leave the premises because they received a complaint call. I told them that we are not breaking any law—the son called me and invited me to the house. If you don't believe me just ask the son. One officer told me that it must have been a prank call because this is the residence of a Gardena city elected official and his family does not have any problems. Richard and I left without meeting the young brother. I told a few of my Gardena contacts about the incident and asked them to tell the young brother to call up the YB house and I'd arrange a more convenient place to meet. Yesterday, two months later, is when his name appeared in the *Rafu* obituary section, but his cause of death was not mentioned.

What's really starting to eat at me is that when we first started the YB, I was sure that we had all the answers—now I'm not so sure. I don't know whether to blame misguided parents, faulty schools pushing bullshit curriculum, greedy drug corporations, unresponsive elected officials, institutional racism or community apathy. Yeah, at times it feels overwhelming, but what keeps me going is that even though philosophical differences within the YB leadership are starting to surface, the majority of YB youth still participate and remain committed to the program.

One unresolved rift in leadership is how we administer discipline. I side with the position that drug abuse is a symptom of a greater problem. Getting high and escapism is rooted in institutional racism, white supremacy, sexism, and vast economic disparity that promotes negative stereotypes, poor self-images, and self hatred, in people of color. No one is born with a negative self-image and self-hatred, it is a learned characteristic that needs to be understood and changed through political education. An opposite belief, held by the majority of YB leadership, views dopers as weak individuals, in need of "tough love"—putting it bluntly, an ass-kicking to get their heads straight. We never developed a consistent approach to deal with members "slipping" and getting caught being loaded. Consequently, organizational discipline is a matter of personal choice, and we're sending out inconsistent messages to the young. I can see them testing us, trying to find out our limits and boundaries. Man, I don't want to be an extension of their parents.

Despite our best efforts, we lost Donnie. Donnie's a nice, soft-spoken brother with a good heart. In stature he is bigger than everyone, but lacks confidence in himself. He gave the YB program a try, but succumbed to the lure of the streets. Now that his former Asian partners-in-crime no longer ran the streets, Donnie joined a Latino street gang, who gave him the "Chino" moniker. He ended up mainlining smack and in a drug-induced stupor, he held up a liquor store, shooting and killing a clerk who reached under the counter to pull out a pistol kept for protection. Donnie was sentenced to a thirteen-to-life sentence in San Quentin. I plan to make it a point to visit him.

Time to get back and concentrate on my school assignment—it's due tomorrow. "Yo, Tad, we need another warm body to run half court, you down? I promise, we'll take it easy on your old tired ass!" Looking down at my unfinished assignment, then up at smirking Richard, I instantly choose my priority. "I got your tired ass, chump! Let's ball!"

Summer, 1972

You'd think that I'd have learned by now—I bet I'm the only doofus in the YB organization attending summer school, to make up credits. If only I turned in my assignments! On the other hand, to see the expressions on their young faces as they walked the stage to receive high school diplomas was worth all my incomplete classes. Now, with no more excuses, no interruptions, I focus on a blank paper, preparing to write the essay that I should have otherwise finished last semester.

I still open up the YB house, but things have changed—the majority of the YB membership have recently graduated and are gradually moving on with their lives. Now they work, prep for college, are involved in relationships, are driving, and perhaps all of the above. Generally, during the day the house is empty, and perhaps out of habit, in the evening many of them gravitate back to the YB.

I could be elsewhere working on my assignment but for some reason, this is where I feel the most comfortable. Anyway, time to focus on the assignment. This shouldn't be too difficult because the topic is to describe an adverse situation and how you overcame it. Our teacher said, simply put, how you turned a negative into a positive.

In terms of negative, the first thing coming to my mind is Arthur. He was the first YB member to die of an overdose. I remember him having a tag-a-long type of personality. He was an underachieving kid from a good family. He hooked up with with some new partners that were basically like him: not rowdy cats, not into the school thing, and had no ambition nor direction. Arthur came by the house less and less; finally he stopped coming. Word was that he was spending most of his time with his new running partners. One night, Arthur and two others downed some reds. As time went on, someone came up with the idea of a suicide pact; in their clouded state they all agreed. They ingested the remainder of their stash, sat back, got into comfortable positions, listened to oldies on the radio for the last time, and closed their eyes. When one of the three felt he was starting to go under, he realized that he really didn't want to die, so he panicked and called emergency. The paramedics arrived in time to resuscitate two of them, for Arthur it was too late.

Man, this is adverse as hell, but no fuckin' way I can spin this into a positive light. Maybe if I describe Alex's tragedy, there might be a moral behind it that can shed light onto a positive interpretation. Let's see: Alex was a brother from the Pico Union area and he hung around the YB house at the beginning. He was a personable young brother and carried himself with swagger and confidence. I lost track when he stopped coming to the house, but a few months back he called. He told me that he was on probation for battery and recently got busted for carrying a concealed weapon in the trunk of his car. He also said that he was beefing with dudes in his neighborhood over some bullshit. He asked me for advice regarding his criminal case. I told him to enroll in school and find a job; take letters from his teachers and employers to court to give to his attorney. I said that a judge would be less likely to remove him from the community if he shows that he is doing something positive. I gave him a number to call for a mental health clinic in Little Tokyo. I told him to make an appointment with a therapist, even if he doesn't feel that he needs therapy. Since he is under a lot of stress, a letter from a therapist would carry a lot of weight in court. He thanked me and said that he will get back to me.

After we disconnected, I immediately called the mental health clinic and identified myself and why I was calling. I emphasized that Alex is a street brother and will put up a macho front, but he is undergoing a lot of stress and needs counseling. I explained that the mere fact that he will even show up at their clinic, speaks volumes. A few days later, Alex called to tell me that he went to the clinic and they had told him he didn't have to return because nothing is wrong with him.

When we finished our conversation, I called the clinic to find out exactly what happened. They said, "Alex wouldn't open up, so there is nothing that we can do for him." I said, "From jump street, I told you that Alex wouldn't fit into your textbook Freudian concepts, and that you needed to make him feel comfortable to gain his trust. I told you all this before he even entered your door: that he's street savvy, on probation for assault, got busted packing a piece, and has people in the neighborhood looking for him, so *pleeese* don't tell me there's nothing wrong with him!"

Two days later, Alex was on the late night news for allegedly committing a double homicide. The newscaster said that Alex was incoherent at the time of his arrest. I remember clipping out the newspaper article and personally delivering it to the shrink at the mental health center. After dropping it on her desk, I asked only one question, "Do you still think there's nothing wrong with brother-man?!!" Fuckin' educated idiot!! Man, thinking about this still makes me hot; it's hard just thinking about it, let alone writing it down on paper for my essay. Fuck it, I'll just wing it, make up some bullshit and turn it in—as long as I pass the class, it's cool.

Fall, 1972

"Hey Jeff, what's up?" He responded, "It's cool, everyone is out looking for a jobs, seeing their probation officers, or checking in with their ole ladies." I ask, "Is Cecil still here?" "Naw, he scored a full-time driving gig and secured an apartment in the jungle." Satisfied with Jeff's "progress report," I make my way to the backyard to shoot hoops. It feels strange not being the one who opens and closes the House on a daily basis.

I better get used to this feeling because everything's changed at the YB house. I anticipated a change but was unsure on how things would end up. At the close of summer, our members were no longer lost kids seeking direction. Most of them had graduated and the few still in school are on track to graduate. Some are attending junior colleges and most have full- or part-time gigs. Many are involved in personal relationships and some even have their own cars. I'd like to think that the YB served a useful purpose in their lives. They are now independent and while hanging out at the YB house is still a cool thing to do, it is no longer their priority.

I flick my wrist as the flight of the round ball finds its way to the center of the rim; the chain-link net jingles as the ball swishes through it. Nine for nine, one more make to meet my free throw quota. I take two dribbles, raise the ball slightly above my eyebrows, bend my knees, extend my shooting hand, flick my right wrist, and follow through with my fingers facing down as if I were reaching into a "cookie jar."

With the majority of the YB members venturing out on their own, we shut down the tutorial and after school programs, and the YB held fewer weekend activities. No one took it personally; both the older and younger members understood it was time to move on. We wanted to still keep the house open, but without a program, no one knew what direction to take. I didn't want to drop by everyday, just to see who was going to show up. We met and decided to pool our money together to hire Jeff, a responsible young member, to open the house everyday afternoon and close it around dinner time. Everyday an older member will swing by the house and check in with Jeff.

After our plan was initiated, it wasn't the after-school crowd that stopped by the house anymore. It became a drop-in center for the older street cats from the neighborhood. Age-wise, they fell in somewhere in between the OG Ministers and younger YB members. In fact a few, like Tony, used to be Ministers II. Their needs went beyond school, parents, and even drugs—their concerns are having a place to crash at night, meeting conditions of their probation, finding work, staying clean and out of jail. When Danny, an old Minister II, was released from the County, he had no place to stay and asked Jeff if he could stay at the YB house until he got himself together. Jeff brought us Danny's request. We decided that since no programs are running out of the house, at least it can be put to use as a safe haven for Danny, until he gets back on his feet. Subconsciously we were leery because we knew Danny may become the tip of the iceberg. Surer than shit, when other brothers were released from incarceration they, too, asked for the same opportunity we gave Danny.

In two months, the YB resembled a halfway house. Before letting anything get out of hand, we held a meeting at the YB house with our new "guests." Introductions weren't necessary because we all knew each other—all that remained was laying down the rules of the house. We made it clear to the street brothers that they are welcome to use the house only until they get their shit together. Absolutely no drugs or alcohol are allowed at the house, and do not come to the house loaded on anything. There will be no parties, outside overnight guests, or fighting inside the house. The house is to be kept clean on a daily basis. During the day, the house will be closed, and everyone is expected to be working, looking for work, or seeking other living arrangements because the stay is only temporary. They are to listen to Jeff because he speaks for us. If they can't police themselves and follow these rules, everyone will be "evicted." The street brothers are well aware of our history as OGs and know that we mean every word being said. Jeff memorialized the house rules on paper and posted it in the house.

Swish. Bingo! Ten for ten at the line. I can go home now. Yeah, the YB is now a halfway house.

TRAGEDY

Under Jeff's watch, the house rules were explicitly followed; everything ran smoothly. That is, until late one morning when I got a phone call from Jeff who frantically said, "Tony got shot! Get over here, quick! I gotta go!" Before I could ask him anything. I heard sirens from the other end of the phone, then a dial tone. I flew out of my pad, jumped in my VW and shot up Crenshaw heading to the YB house.

I PARKED ACROSS THE STREET because a LAPD squad car was parked in the driveway and another one was parked next to an ambulance in front of the house. Sprinting across the street, I saw Jeff, Russell, Danny and Glenn standing on the front porch being questioned by two cops. Fortunately, none of them were handcuffed; one of the cops was asking questions and the other was writing on a notepad. Upon my approach, the brothers stopped talking to the police; they looked at me, and Jeff said, "Tony got shot, he's dead." A cold numbing chill that I haven't felt since the Nam returned, I know better than to ask questions in front of the police. I asked, "Where is he?" Tony was inside the house lying on the middle level of the stairwell. As I headed toward the front door, the cop conducting the interview said, "No one is allowed inside, a crime scene investigation is taking place." I'm not in a mood for any bullshit, but I know a pig is a pig and I have to outmaneuver him. I step off the porch and head down the driveway to the back yard.

Damn, two more uniforms are manning the back door. Walking towards them, one asks, "Who are you, and what are you doing here?" I reply, "I got a call from a detective who asked me to come here immediately and identify the body of my cousin." They step aside and I walk in. I step through the service porch, the kitchen, and into the front room, making a quick right turn. I stop and stand woodenly at the bottom of the stairwell. On the platform, halfway up the stairs, the paramedics and cops are hovering over Tony's body. As I walk up the wooden staircase, the group turns and looks at me. Again I'm asked who I am; I reply, "That's my cousin, I need to be here!" They look at me, then at each other, shrug their shoulders, and redirect their focus back on Tony's body. I look down at Tony—he's laying in a pool of his own blood, his white tee shirt and khaki pants saturated in dark reddish-purple blood, and a grotesque, angry, wound in his chest, exposes where a bullet entered his body. Tony's eyes are open; it's eerie because his final facial expression captures a look, like he's trying to say, "What the fuck?" As the paramedics get into a position to lift Tony's body and place him on a gurney, I reach down to brace Tony's neck. We lift and place him on the gurney. Before they can put a white sheet over Tony, I ask, "Can I close his eyes?" Hearing no objections, I bend down, shut

Tony's eyelids for the last time, and whisper, "Rest in peace my brother, payback's a motherfucker." I follow the procession of paramedics and LAPD out of the house.

The brothers and the two cops are still standing on the front porch. When I exit from inside the house, the cop that wouldn't let me inside glares hard at me. Tony is placed into the ambulance and escorted by sirens and squads cars, heads south on Crenshaw, probably to the county morgue.

Now it's time to talk to the brothers. I can tell that they are still shaken. Russell tries to say something, but Danny quickly interjects, "Early this morning, before I came back to the house, I stopped at the ARCO station on Crenshaw. I was minding my own business, putting gas in my tank when this tall, narrow-ass, acne-face mothafucka jumps bad with me. I've seen his punk ass before and know he ain't shit. I said, 'What the fuck you looking at!' He didn't say shit but kept pinning on me; I said 'fuck it' and rushed him. To make a long story short, I fucked him up. I saw that my shirt was torn so I went to the garage, grabbed a tire iron and went back at him. He saw me coming, got up and took off; I chased his punk-ass but couldn't catch him. I threw the tire iron at him. He fell down grabbing his arm and started screaming like a bitch." I went back to my car and came back to the house. The biker dudes that work at ARCO were all standing around watching; no one did shit." Danny continued, "When I got to the house, I told the brothers what just went down—it was no big deal, just another ass-whippin' in the neighborhood."

Glenn picked it up. "A few hours later, I was in the front room and heard some motorcycles pull into the driveway. Before I could even get up, six biker dudes barged into the house. The punk Danny fired up was with them; his right arm was in a sling. One biker dude, a cat I've never seen before, was packing an automatic rifle. This cat is scary because he looked nervous. Just me and Russell were downstairs at the time. The chump in the sling asked where Danny's at. Tony, Danny and Jeff were upstairs. The biker dudes started heading towards the stairs, and the next thing I heard was Tony's voice coming from upstairs asking, "What's going on?" The bikers were at the bottom of the staircase and said that they're here to see Danny. Tony started walking down the stairs and when he saw the guy with the rifle, he stopped and said, "Man, you don't need to be doing all that, put the gun down and let's talk." The dude with the rifle didn't say shit and wouldn't drop his piece. Tony started walking down the stairs. He threw up his hands and showed his palms and said, "Man, just put the gun down, there ain't no need for this!" Tony was half way down the staircase when I heard a *blaaam!* Everyone, including the shooter, froze. The bikers pulled him out of the house and they took off. We ran over to Tony—he didn't have a pulse, he died on the spot."

Jeff finished off the story, "That's when we called the ambulance and I called you."

Continuing to talk on the front porch, the pieces started to fit. The dude that started the shit with Danny was Steve; the bikers that worked at ARCO were his partners. The shooter was an Asian dude from Long Beach, named Barry; supposedly he was a black belt in hapkido. Barry was shacking up with Sherry, a student at Long Beach. Jeff knew someone who had her address. We agreed to meet back at the house in the evening, enough time to get the address where the chump was hiding out, and enough time to come back locked and loaded—ready for payback.

Upon returning to the house, *beaucoup* brothers from the neighborhood are here. I'm informed that at his family's urging, Tony's shooter turned himself in and is in police custody. The other Asian bikers are making plans to split town—a couple of them have already left LA. At this point, we don't know what to do next; everyone's pissed off and frustrated.

Dave changes our mood by blurting out, "Tony's reputation finally caught up with him." No one understands where Dave's going with this, but since he is Tony's second cousin, we give him space to explain himself. Dave says, "I knew Tony all my life. He made his reputation by getting in the first punch; that's all he needed to knock motherfuckers out." So far, he ain't saying shit that we didn't already know. Dave continues, "One minute he's showing his teeth, smiling; the next second, he'd be flooring cats. When he was in junior high, he broke a store window, then sat on the curb waiting for the cops to arrest him. He wanted to be sent to camp so that he could pump iron all day and get buffed. He knew he'd be home before summer and would be bigger and stronger than before. Everyone knew Tony was a hardcore gangster. I know that Barry cat was scared shitless when he saw Tony coming towards him." What Dave says makes sense. At one time or another we all personally witnessed brother Tony drop someone with one punch. Reminiscing about Tony lightens the mood. Russell, one of Tony's tights says that when Tony was a little kid, his parents punished him by taking away his weights—fuck a time out! We're all cracking up—knowing Tony, it has to be true.

The brothers living at the YB house share how Tony was making an effort to change. They say that this time, maybe even for the first time, Tony was really acting as a peacemaker. They say that he respected the house rules and didn't want any trouble at the house. Dave sums it up, "First time, Tony does right and he gets wasted; ain't it a bitch!" We nod in agreement. Payback is put on hold. RIP, brother Tony.

Late that night after everyone left, the older YB leaders met—we decide it's time to close the YB house.

SERVE THE PEOPLE

In 1968 a cadre of older Sansei activists met weekly at the Alibi Club on Crenshaw Boulevard. At their gatherings, they'd discuss, debate, and argue about political issues and politics along with the beer, wine, shots of liquor and smoke. They were not student intellectuals; they were street savvy and blue-collar working class. What evolved from their gatherings was the development of a community grassroots organization, Japanese American Community Service, or JACS for short. By happenstance, the bartender who worked the late night shift, and grew fond of these spirited Sansei was Ben Yamato, Tony's dad.

AFTER THE YB CLOSED, I volunteered to coach my brother Renbo's JA basketball team. Coaching also gave me time to be with Renbo who is not a kid anymore. My team was eager to learn and I enjoyed teaching them basic fundamental skills. From this experience, I learned that the values of sacrifice, having each other's back, and unity, could be taught and coached through basketball.

When the basketball season ended, I went to Little Tokyo to check out the JACS office. I had met a few people who volunteer at JACS and they had nothing but positive things to say about their involvement there. They identify themselves as community workers and told me a little bit about the JACS "serve the people" programs.

The JACS office on Weller Street takes up the entire sixth floor at the old Sun Building. When I took the dimly-lit, rumbling elevator up to the sixth floor and the door squeaked open, I stepped out and found, to my surprise, I was in a beehive of activity. Sansei activists were on the phone, others were counseling people or walking from one part of the office to another. It was set up like an office with old sturdy wooden desks, folding chairs, phones, filing cabinets, bulletin boards, and a meeting room. People who didn't know me dropped what they were doing to greet me and make me feel welcome. I said I was stopping by to check out what is happening there.

I saw Carol, a sister from Long Beach State, who was a volunteer tutor at the YB. She was surprised and happy to see me; she gave me a tour of the JACS office. In the main reception area was a hotline phone, staffed around the clock by volunteer community workers. Carol explained that their community service programs are called "serve the people" programs, or STP for short. The programs serve the Issei population, hard-core street people, Asian American inmates, and at-risk youth. She said these groups are the most disenfranchised people in the JA community. So far, I am in agreement with the JACS analysis—in the back of my mind, I still need to know why are they doing this and what's in it for them.

Within the office, each room services a different STP program. I was given a brief synopsis on each program. JACS has an interesting mix of volunteer workers, from hard-core street people, students, ex-dope fiends, blue-collar workers, and even college grads. What impressed me the most is that everyone seemed to be working towards a common goal, and I sensed a basic level of respect and togetherness amongst the community workers.

Carol is involved in the Issei Welfare Rights program. During our conversation she asked if I'm available this weekend to pick up an Issei and take him food shopping at Grand Central Market. I told her that I'd help out. She said that the Issei man's name is Nishioka-san, and both of his legs are arthritic, which prevents him from using public transportation.

On Saturday, I parked my VW in front of Nishioka-san's address. He lived in an old, but well-kept apartment building in Boyle Heights. I went inside and knocked on the door to Nishioka-san's unit. No one answered, I knocked again; I was going to leave a note on the door, when I heard someone speak from the other side of the door, *"Chotto matte, kudasai"* (please wait a minute). I heard shuffling sounds and then the front door opened partially, but not entirely, because of the door's chain lock. I stood by the door and all I was able to see were parts of a small, frail Issei man with silver hair, wearing thin wire-rim glasses. Quickly, I introduced myself, "Carol had asked me to pick you up and take you grocery shopping." Even with the door partially cracked, I saw the old man's face brighten up with a smile. He said, *"Gomen nasai,* I will be ready in a minute," and closed the door. Five minutes later, Nishioka-san came out. I now had a full view of him; he was even smaller than how he had appeared to be from behind the door. He had on a yellow plaid flannel shirt, brown pants, and a light tan, button-down sweater. His clothes had the appearance of being well-worn, but like his apartment building, they were neat and clean. Nishioka-san stands slightly hunched over, and walks with a cane. I told him my car is parked in front of the apartment. Nishioka-san started to walk down the hallway to exit his apartment building. I observed that his average walking stride is eight to twelve inches in length. I don't want to stare at him as he struggles to walk, so I told him politely, "I'll wait for you outside by the car." He again apologized, *"Gomen nasai"* (I'm sorry), smiled and kept walking. When the old man finally made it outside the apartment complex, I noticed that the terrain leading from the apartment building to the street level has a downward slope. To get to my car, Nishioka-san would have to walk down a gradually descending slope of steps and then lift his legs up to get into the car. It hurt to watch him navigate painstakingly slowly and carefully down each step. I felt helpless, I don't know what I should or shouldn't do. A part of me wants to go help the old man, but another part tells me if I do, it could offend his dignity and pride. When I saw the oldtimer struggling near the top of the steps, I thought to myself, "Fuck it!" I walked over him, "Mister Nishioka-san, would it be okay with you if I carried you to the car?" Nishioka-san looked up at me, smiled and said, "Thank you." I lifted Nishioka-san up, and helped him into the car.

On the way to Grand Central Market, neither of us said very much. When we arrived at the market, I helped him out of the car and Nishioka-san began his eight-inch step walk. Again, I asked, "Would you like me to carry you? It's no problem for me." Nishioka-san answered, "Yes, thank you!" It wasn't a problem; Nishioka-san was light as a feather. Nishioka-san bought fresh vegetables, fruit, fish and a few other items. When he finished shopping, I placed him back in the car with his groceries. On the way back home, Nishioka-san became more talkative. He told me that he was nineteen years old when he came to America. He worked as a houseboy and attended school to learn English. When he became proficient enough in English, he enrolled in a high school, where he earned a diploma and he did well enough to gain admission to the University of California, Berkeley. At Berkeley, he continued to work and attend class and eventually graduated from Cal with a degree in biology. He said that after he returned to Los Angeles, the war broke out; he told me how hard it was after December 7th, and how the white neighborhood kids threw rocks at him and called him "Jap!" While he shared his personal history, I sensed no bitterness or anger in Nishioka-san's voice or demeanor. It kinda felt like he was apologizing to me for having to listen to his hardships. Nishioka-san's humanity touched me; in spite of all the racism that this man has endured along with his physical limitations; his spirit is strong.

He told me that after the war, despite having a college degree, the only types of jobs available to him involved manual labor. By the time I parked at his Boyle Heights residence, I had a new *tomodachi*. Before I could lift him out of the car, Nishioka-san reached over and tried handing me two one-dollar bills. I told him that it was okay because I just received my GI Bill and didn't need it. The way Nishioka-san insisted made me shut up and accept his generous gesture, I thanked him. I carried Nishioka-san and his grocery bags back to his apartment door. Nishioka-san asked me to place him and the grocery bags down and thanked me. I told him that I will help carry the groceries into the apartment, but Nishioka-san said that it wasn't necessary. Before leaving Nishioka-san in the hallway, I asked him if it would be okay if I take him the next time he needed to grocery shop. He smiled and replied, "That would be fine, Nagata-san." On my way home, I tripped on how ironic life is—in reality, taking Nishioka-san grocery shopping benefited me more than it did the old man.

The next time I met up with Carol, I told her that I would volunteer to take Nishioka-san whenever he needed to shop. Every other week over the next six months, I picked up Nishioka-san and the same pick-up and drop off routine repeated itself. Nishioka-san would always peek through the door when I came calling, and I would drop him off and leave him still standing in the hall in front of his door next to his grocery bags. During each grocery-shopping trip, Nishioka-san shared a different chapter of his extraordinary life with me.

I'm spending most of my time at the JACS office. By volunteering at JACS, my initial question, "why are they doing this, and what's in it for them," has been answered. The services JACS provides through the STP programs are good, but they are not "do-gooders." They don't intend to reform the existing "system." They are advocating "revolutionary change" through their practice, education, and community work. They are not idealists, but believe in the ideals of a socialistic society where human worth is valued over monetary gain.

The JACS office Central Committee asked me and two other Asian Viet Nam veterans if we would be interested in developing an Asian American veterans outreach group at the JACS office. We talked it over among ourselves, and decided to give it a try. We networked within the JA community and in other Asian ethnic communities to connect with other Viet Nam vets. Almost all of the vets are, or were, dealing with similar issues of confusion, anger and isolation. At our meetings we share our experiences both before the service, during their service, and what's going on now. Because most of us have similar backgrounds, we can relate to each other. Through this process, we've seen a commonality in our collective experiences—instances like being singled out in basic training for looking like the "enemy." As the political awareness of our vets group developed, we drew parallels of our experiences in the military to institutional racism and oppression in our community, in America, and ultimately, globally. As Viet Nam vets, we oppose the war. Unlike the white anti-war movement, we are not merely advocating to "bring the boys home," our message is deeper—we are opposed to the U.S. government's war of genocide waged on the Vietnamese people. To educate the Asian American communities, we speak at high schools, college campuses, churches, and temples. We share our military and combat experiences, and talk about the U.S. government's genocidal practices and policies. We also provided draft counseling to youth interested in resisting the draft.

VAN TROI YOUTH BRIGADE
AND
FAREWELL TO A TOMODACHI

Los Angeles, California

IN RECENT past summers, America has witnessed violence, looting, destruction of property and loss of lives as the slums, ghettos, and barrios of its inner cities went up in flames. Police brutality, inferior educational opportunities, disproportional unemployment, underemployment, racism and sweltering summer heat ignited insurrections in African American urban ghettos of Detroit, Newark, and Cincinnati. Not wanting to witness a repeat performance, Uncle Sam opened his pocketbook in the summer of 1973, to create summer jobs for inner city youth, hoping to keep them busy and in check. A program called Neighborhood Youth Corps (NYC) was created to meet this objective. In Los Angeles, Asian and Pacific Islander inner city youth participated in the NYC program.

The upshot of the NYC is that as long as bi-monthly paperwork is submitted to the NYC agency, the work experience for the participating youths is at the sole discretion of the community organization.

Grassroots movement Asian American community organizations took advantage of this opportunity to provide their youth with a summer of political education through community work and activities, all on Uncle Sam's dime. The JACS office, Gidra community newspaper, Jefferson Storefront, and Asian Woman's Center had NYC slots. Grassroots organizations in the Filipino, Samoan, Chinatown, and Korean communities, took advantage as well.

Renbo is now in high school and I encouraged him to sign up for the NYC program. Renbo and two of his partners signed on to work at the Gidra office, which publishes a monthly Asian American Movement newspaper.

Each organization selected a member to be a representative on a steering committee composed of each community group. The steering committee was responsible for setting up cultural exchanges and activities between the Asian ethnic communities.

For Renbo, this summer was his awakening; he became aware that he is part of a larger Asian American community that stretches well beyond the confines of Crenshaw. He made new friends, shared ideas, picnicked, ate different ethnic foods, partied, and exchanged phone numbers with other Asian young people. He participated in sports activities that were supposed to emphasize friendship over competition. I found it interesting that the Samoans from Carson's Omai Fa'atasi won all the competitions. I'm glad these brothers and sisters are on our side.

The NYC youth learned about Third World unity. Through rap sessions and drawing parallels from their own experiences they could analyze how institutional racism and stereotypes have divided and conquered people of color.

The more they were exposed to, the more they wanted to learn. The young took to their community work and "serve the people" programs like a duck takes to water. I was elated when these JA teens organized their own political education study group. They read, discussed, and conceptualized how corporate America, with the backing of the U.S. military, rips off Third World nations for their natural resources and labor in the name of profit. They learned about the Viet Nam War and the Vietnamese people's fight for self-determination.

By the time summer was finally nearing its end, this group of once-apathetic JA youths were now reading the teachings of revolutionaries like Chairman Mao, Che Guevara, Malcolm X, and the Black Panther Party. I kept my distance from Renbo and observed his growth from a distance; I chose to not invade his space. It felt good when he and the others in his study group invited a few of us "old heads" to one of their sessions.

When we met the study group, a member named Herman told us that they plan to address the apathy in the JA community by protesting against the war, in order to make a statement. The platform for delivering their message was going to be the Nisei Week Parade.

Renbo and the rest of them now joined the discussion. They said that locally, nationally, and internationally, people are speaking out and demonstrating to protest U.S. imperialism. Meanwhile, the conservative JA community remains silent with its head buried in the sand. While they are hep to the negative "mojo" the U.S. government put on our people through the concentration camp experience, they said it's time for a wake-up call.

Their protest would be twofold: to stop the war of genocide on the Vietnamese people and to oppose the re-building of Japanese militarism. They said President Nixon had escalated the war by ordering massive bombings in North Viet Nam. The tonnage of bombs dropped on this tiny nation surpassed the total amount dropped during WWII. The U.S. was also negotiating with the Japanese government to have Japan rebuild its military in direct violation of the peace agreement ending WWII. These discussions are taking place because the U.S. desperately needs an ally, a watchdog to perform its dirty work and protect its Asian assets.

They asked us if we would support them. I know, personally, our Asian vets group will follow their leadership. I felt proud knowing that Renbo is part of this progressive youth group and we are related by blood!

The Nisei Week Festival is the annual extravaganza for the JA community. Before WWII, it was organized by the Issei and was exclusively a Japanese community event to encourage business in Little Tokyo. Today, it showcases Japanese culture for all Angelenos to see. A parade held on the day after the festival's Nisei Week Queen coronation highlights Japanese and Japanese American culture, community figures and pageantry through traditional music and dance. The parade entrants assemble at a large lot behind Union Church; the parade route circles the perimeter of Little Tokyo and ends in the heart of Little Tokyo, at the intersection of Central Avenue and First Street. Every year, thousands of spectators line the sidewalks of Little Tokyo to get a glimpse of Japanese culture.

The parade participants are community dignitaries, organizations, churches, and temples. Organizational members may dress in uniforms like the Boy Scouts or 442 veterans, or in the case of traditional Japanese dance schools, wear matching colorful Japanese kimonos with obi sashes. The dancers carry fans and wear dress *zori* or the more casual wooden *geta* that make a clacking sound when the platform struts hit the pavement. Some schools wear wigs in a traditional hairstyle with white face makeup, or tie their hair up in buns; they all gracefully dance in unison to recorded music or the rhythms of the *shakuhachi* (bamboo flute) and *taiko* drums. The non-school street dancers often wear happi coats denoting their group identity or whatever they have available.

The young Sansei secured a parade participation permit and got busy organizing. They recruited neighborhood friends to attend their teach-ins, and they shared the true nature of the Viet Nam War with their peers. Renbo asked me if our Viet Nam vets group would speak at their teach-ins and provide security for the youth brigade at the parade. Of course, we obliged. They selected a name, calling themselves the Van Troi Youth Brigade, in memory of a young Vietnamese freedom fighter. Between their rounds of organizing work, they played and partied with equal zeal.

The conservative Nisei Week Committee never had a clue what the young Sansei were planning; if they had, they would have canceled their parade permit, yesterday. On the day of the Nisei Week Parade, over seventy teens of high school-age showed up at the Union Church parking lot to represent. After gathering, the Van Troi Brigade was surrounded by a sea of established community groups and colorful kimonos. The uniform chosen by the youth brigade consisted of white tee shirts, blue jeans, and blue and red head cloths (*hachimaki*) centered with a yellow star. The dance they were going to strut to was based on a Japanese folk song, called *Tanko Bushi* or Coal Mine Song. They improvised on the traditional steps, adding a taste of Westside flair to its rhythmic movements, and while sashaying to the beat of the *taiko* drums, they chanted in unison, "Go left, go right, now pick up the gun!" When they were on deck to join the procession, they unfurled their banner that read, "The Van Troi Anti-Imperialist Youth Brigade."

The Nisei Week officials were startled when they figured out what these renegade youth were up to and attempted to block their entrance to the parade procession. One step ahead, the Van Troi Brigade snaked around their flimsy roadblock attempt and became part of the Nisei Week Parade! They danced, marched, and shouted their mantra in unison while we older community activists spread ourselves out amongst the thousands of stunned and curious spectators and passed out leaflets that explained the principles of their protest.

The anti-war demonstration by itself shocked the JA community, but what really blew their collective mind was when the Van Troi Brigade stopped at the corner of First and San Pedro, unraveled a Japanese imperialist military flag, flipped open a Zippo and torched it. To the conservative JA community, opposing the Viet Nam War was one thing, but to burn the imperialist Japanese military flag was heresy.

The Van Troi Youth Brigade made the next day's front page news in both the *Rafu Shimpo* and the *LA Times*.

The youth brigade's anti-war demonstration served its intended objective—it stimulated anger, support, controversy, and debate—which opened up a long overdue dialogue between Nisei and Sansei in the once politically impotent JA community. In response, I received phone calls from parents who used to call only when their kid was in trouble, now wanting to talk to me about the flag-burning incident.

During the time when the Van Troi Youth Brigade was busily preparing for Nisei Week, the JACS medical committee organized young medical professionals who volunteered their services and hosted a Street Health Fair Day for the Issei population in Little Tokyo. On the day of the health fair, I picked up Nishioka-san and took him there. A trailer equipped with an X-ray machine was one of many services offered at the Street Health Fair. Later, when the medical clinicians review the charts and tests, Nishioka-san's X-ray reveals that he has tuberculosis.

Nishioka-san is admitted into a skilled nursing home in Lincoln Heights. Carol gave me the news and I go immediately to see him. I found Nishioka-san bedridden and not allowed to get up or to leave his room. Although Nishioka-san has had difficulty walking for some time, he was always was energetic and full of life; it bothers me to see my friend like this. I feel that the nursing staff isn't sensitive or comforting to Nishioka-san—they treat him as if he's already dead.

Lying on the hospital bed, Nishioka-san asked me if I could go to his apartment and bring back his radio and Japanese books. I told him to consider it done; he handed me the keys to his apartment. I left the nursing home and drove straight to Nishioka-san's Boyle Heights home. As I was about to enter the apartment, it dawned on me that as many times as I took him shopping, I have never been inside his unit. Actually, Nishioka-san never opened up the door wide enough to glimpse inside it.

I turned the key, unlocking the door; I felt a little hesitant before entering. I stepped inside and am relieved to see that his apartment room is no different from the single-unit tenements that the majority of the J-town Issei live in. The room is neat and organized. A hot plate, his magazines, books and radio are on a small table. I unplug the radio and stack up the reading materials while looking around the room to see if there is anything I missed. I see something strange on top of a fold-up wall bed in the corner of the room that draws me to it. I stare down and see underneath the covers of a neatly-made bed three dolls, all tucked in under the sheets with their heads resting on the edge of a pillow. The dolls are different sizes: the biggest one is the size of a 12-inch Barbie doll and the other two figurines, a boy and a girl doll, are smaller. I don't know what to make of it. It's too weird to think that Nishioka-san plays with dolls. I am confused because Nishioka-san is not weird, he is one of the most together people I know. It hit me—this is probably the reason Nishioka-san never invited me inside. I pack the radio and books and deliver them to Nishioka-san; nothing is said between us about the dolls.

What I saw in Nishioka-san's apartment bothered me to the point that I decided to confide in Carol. I told her about the dolls and immediately she looked sad; I saw wetness in her eyes. She gathered herself and explained that many of the first generation Issei men like Nishioka-san, never had an opportunity to marry, and legislation forbade them to marry outside our ethnicity. The dolls are Nishioka-san's make-believe family. Carol made perfect sense. I feel a lump in my throat—how lonely it must be for Nishioka-san and how his psychological survival depended upon creating his own sense of family through his dolls. Issei like Nishioka-san could have chosen a different path and become angry and bitter; he taught me that to maintain one's dignity and sanity in a racist society, we have to resist by any means necessary! In the early fall, Nishioka-san passed. Rest in peace my brother.

YELLOW BROTHERHOOD TWO

1974
"The revolution will not be televised"

Locally, nationally, and internationally, the struggle for civil rights, human rights and national liberation took center stage through protest, demonstrations, work strikes and armed resistance. Revolution was the word of the day. In Asia, Africa, and South America, national liberation movements were kicking Uncle Sam's butt. On the home front, people of color were organizing and mobilizing their own communities. Folks were no longer begging the "Man" for their civil rights; militant groups were demanding basic human rights. Past promises preaching for patience and "pie in the sky" deceptions, gave way to "seize the time" actions.

I QUIT SCHOOL. No longer do I pursue a college sheepskin to lead to a professional career, marriage, kids, mortgage payments, two-car garage, retirement and security. My priorities are community work; organizing, educating, and mobilizing people; and a commitment to a movement for revolutionary change. For me, it's more than destroying the existing order, it's being a cog in the gear of societal revolution. It is a tsunami that is committed to building a socialistic society where the basic needs for survival—food, clothing, housing, education, and medical treatment—are human rights rather than privileges. People I respect, and even my family, question my involvement. I'm told that revolutionary change will not happen in our lifetime. I understand that most of us will not make the same type of commitment I have chosen, I only try to show them revolutionary change is a process and not an event, and that this process is taking place as we speak.

I am not the lone ranger; many activists are equally if not more committed. I, three sisters and three brothers started an alternative living arrangement we call a collective. We combined our resources to rent a two-story house south of the Santa Monica Freeway, off the Arlington exit—we are known as the Westside Collective. We are attempting to change our lives by living together with a collective mentality. We are redefining the traditional roles of men and women and now share in household duties: washing, cleaning and cooking. We collectivize our earnings to pay for our living expenses. At our weekly house meetings we struggle over actual and perceived differences. It is difficult, but we try not to personalize problems arising between us; instead we utilize a constructive criticism approach to work out our differences. Our intention isn't to "put down" or to belittle; it is about struggle, resolution, and internal growth.

Our Asian sisters deal with an additional layer of oppression: sexism and male chauvinism. Unlike the white women's liberation movement, they don't view Asian men as the enemy. They understand that Asian men have been emasculated by institutional and overt racism and supporting their brothers and fighting together will only achieve our liberation. However, they are still quick to call a dog a dog, and will not tolerate macho bullshit.

On one such occasion, a street dude from the Westside named Dickey, kept a supply of drugs at his pad. He used his stash to entice women to drop by and perform sexual favors. What goes on between consenting adults is basically their business, but Dickey crossed the line when he hit a sister and gave her a black eye during an argument at his dope den. The Asian movement sisters found out about the incident and instead of letting the brothers deal with Dickey, they chose to deal with the chump themselves. The sisters, twelve strong, went over to Dickey's house on Hillcrest Boulevard. When Dickey answered the door, he knew something was up because the sisters didn't wait for Dickey to invite them inside; they stormed into the pad. Dickey had a trick up his sleeve—he picked up two kitchen knives that were on top of a table, put on his best mad-dog face, and performed his impersonation of a knife-wielding *teppan* chef. While Dickey was putting on his show, the room quieted; he got loud, profane and belligerent. Thinking that he had intimidated the sisters and was back in control, he made the mistake of placing the knives back on the table. One of the sisters, Candace, had measured Dickey and waited for him to slip up. When he put down the knives she closed the gap between herself and Dickey and with a powerful overhand left, tagged him upside his head. Like stink on shit, the rest of the sisters swarmed him. All of the sisters jumped in, fists and feet coming from every angle and direction. They unleashed years of pent-up anger and frustration on his sorry ass, calling him every name in the book as they beat his ass. They left Dickey curled on the floor in a fetal position. The stomping was righteous and sent out a message that if anyone fucks with one of them, you're going to have to deal with all of them. Dickey packed his bag and has yet to return to the Westside. Sisterhood is powerful!

Over the past two years, I've become a regular at the JACS office. Every day, I drive to downtown Little Tokyo for meetings and community work. While our efforts are serving the needs of the people and making an impact in organizing and educating the community, I feel a strong pull to build a revolutionary base closer to home.

One afternoon, a young Asian brother from the Westside called the JACS office hotline. He asked if someone could come to Mount Vernon Junior High immediately because the Asians and Blacks are going to fight after school. Since the school bell is about ring in less than an hour, I rush off. Arriving at Mount Vernon, I saw twenty or more young Asian brothers congregating around the school's side gate. I recognized one of them—Carl, the younger brother of Duane Ogawa who I had coached in the JA basketball league. I called Carl over and he told me that a group of niggers have been jumping on Asians and fucking them up. I am surprised to hear Carl calling African Americans "niggers" because Carl lives in the Avenues and when I used to drop his brother Duane off after basketball practice, Carl would always be outside playing with his black friends. I asked him, "Carl, are all your black partners niggers too?" He shot back, "Naw, they my partners and look out for me, but I'm talking about these other fools and fuck it, if they call us Japs then I'll call them niggers!" I knew that now was not the time nor the place for a political discussion with Carl so I asked him, "Who got jumped on?" Carl pointed out a young brother in the group with a noticeable welt under his right eye. He was pissed and animated as were the rest of the Asians in the group. Carl said that he was the latest one to get jumped on just because he is Asian; this caused the rest of the Asian brothers to unify and deal with the bullshit. I'm all for Third World unity but from personal experience, I know that to gain respect on the streets, both sides need to communicate in the same language. In this case, the only language their adversaries understood was, you dot one of our eyes and we'll close both of yours! I chose not to intervene because the young brothers already knew what needed to be done.

Minutes before the bell ending the school day rings, a black and white LAPD patrol car pulls up and stops in front of the Asians. The officers got out of the patrol car to start questioning them. I walked towards the group to tell them that legally, they don't have to answer the pigs. I got within earshot; the pigs were taking their names and writing them down. Before I could say anything, the brothers are blurting out fictitious names: "Zato Ichi," "Su Okaasan," and "Yojimbo Miyamoto," to name a few. As the police wrote the names, I wanted to crack up but held my mug. Eventually, the police left but the young people's targeted adversaries never came out the gate. When the group finally dispersed, going their separate ways, I called Carl over. I asked how his brother, Duane, mom, and family are doing. After catching up, I asked him if he remembered the old Yellow Brotherhood house. Carl did, and I asked him if he'd bring his Asian partners to the YB house to meet some of my partners. He said, "Why not?" We decided "Why wait," and plan to meet the next day after school.

I called for a meeting at the old YB house: Marlene, Larry, Brent, Greg, Willie, Steve, Victor and Chiemi arrived. Our commonality? We are all from Crenshaw, are active in movement organizations, and each of us has expressed an interest in restarting a youth program in the Westside. Most us have experience in working with dope fiends. At our meeting we talked about our frustration in dealing with drug addiction and the doper mentality. We acknowledged that drug abuse remains a problem but agreed our priority will be organizing the Asian youth in our community by starting a drug preventative program. Our youth group will be a part of the Third World movement; we want to educate, develop community workers, and build leaders in the struggle.

After school, Carl and the group of young brothers who were ready to throw down yesterday, arrived at the YB house. As an added bonus, a group of Asian sisters from Mount Vernon also attended.

We met as a large body and then broke into small rap groups. In a smaller setting it is easier to get people to open up and we wanted to hear what the young folks have to say. It turns out that the Mount Vernon youth were there for the exact same reason—they wanted to hear from us to find out where we're coming from. As they say, great minds think alike! Right on!

At first, the young brothers and sisters were a bit cautious but with an absence of positive things to do in the community, they kept returning to the YB house. Soon, they were at the house every day after school. We held a general meeting and the young teens were in favor of restarting a Yellow Brotherhood program. We defined the differences between YB One and YB Two. The original YB focused on getting the membership to stop abusing drugs and to end gang violence. Our organizational goals for YB Two are education, to build unity, start STP programs, and to develop new leadership.

We began by re-instituting a sponsorship program. The older members went to their homes and met with their parents to explain the purpose and goals of our program. The parents were receptive to our message, most likely because they knew that there were few, if any, programs for their kids in the Crenshaw community.

Academically, the majority of the young brothers were hanging on by a thread at school, so a study hall was instituted. The opposite was true for the sisters—they were excelling in school and to their credit, they attended the study halls and even helped tutor their academically lost brothers.

We took YB members to attend programs and events to expose them to other community groups involved in the revolutionary struggle. In addition, movement brothers and sisters from grassroots community organizations came to the house. We held study and rap groups: Asian American identity, Asian American history, Japanese American concentration camps, Third World unity, and the Viet Nam War, were some of the topics covered.

Our top priority is for the young to learn through exposure, interaction, personal experience and actions. To think it is fine, but to feel and believe it is divine!

The YB attended several annual Manzanar Pilgrimages where we were able to experience the harsh weather conditions that our parents and grandparents endured at this desolate Owens Valley location. The cold weather, strong gusting winds with dust kicking up in all directions—all are part of their education. We camped outside and each night, under the dark, starry sky, we encircled the campfire. After dividing into teams, each one performed a skit for the entire group. It is a unifying experience—our own version of amateur hour. Everyone put on a good show.

We caravanned to Delano, a small farming community in Central California, to support the Filipino United Farm Workers. Our contribution as a youth work brigade helped the Filipino farm workers build a retirement village for their elderly. The work was hard, the hours were long, but working side by side with a community of committed Filipino farmers and their families was an internal education in struggle and unity that cannot be replicated from a book.

We marched and demonstrated to protest against the Viet Nam War as part of a contingent with other Asian organizations.

The YB is asked to provide security for many movement demonstrations and events. Through repetition and practice, we've become proficient at coordinating our movements from location to location as a large organized body with minimum hassle—it is another lesson in unity where everyone cooperates and contributes to the process.

Meanwhile, the YB house is put to good use. Our YB film committee makes a connection with a progressive political film collective and at a nominal cost, we borrow political films like *Battle of Algiers, Young Lords Party,* and *Murder of Fred Hampton.* Included are cultural entertainment films featuring Zato Ichi, the Miyamoto Musashi trilogy, and martial arts flicks. On weekends, a Saturday night coffeehouse is organized and local musicians come to jam and perform to a neighborhood audience. The Physical Fitness Committee runs self-defense classes at the house with martial arts *sensei* volunteering their instruction. YB basketball teams enter the men's Nisei Athletic Union, and the sisters organize a YB Ninja team in the equivalent women's league. On weekends, progressive parents with young kids and toddlers use the house as a base for the Little People's Workshop program. I enjoy watching the YB youth take an interest and interact with the next generation. In between, we even have time to relax and kick back at a Big Bear Lake camping trip. For cash, we hold car washes, bake sales, and pancake breakfasts.

The young YB members have claimed the YB house as their own. The house is occupied with programs and activities every day after school and on weekends. Many of the original YB founders drop by the house to provide support and guidance, and to talk story with the young members. The young brothers and sisters now proudly identify themselves as members of the Yellow Brotherhood.

For Victor, Gary, Chiemi, Willie, Greg, and myself, organizing youth at the YB house is our full time commitment. Months earlier, my collective living experience had come to an end. We all parted on good terms and will always stay connected—we are better people because of this experience. Perhaps on this one, my folks were right on: I was a bit too idealistic.

To meet my financial needs I work part time gigs. Victor and I make extra cash by waxing and detailing cars. Our money is always funny and we survive hand to mouth. I always pay my monthly rent, buy groceries, and manage to have a little chump change left in my pocket.

During the ensuing weeks, months, then years, our unity was solidified and steeled. Unfortunately, only a few of the young made a commitment to revolutionary practice and ideology, getting ready to take their commitment to the next level. Our organizational dilemma? Although everyone is down with the "cause," the YB served more a social rather than a political need. Regardless, everyone involved identifies with the powerful feeling of unity that we all carry within.

CHANGES

July, 1978
Yellow Brotherhood House – Crenshaw

THE WORD IS OUT: an open community meeting is being held at the Yellow Brotherhood house where everyone is encouraged to come and discuss the future of the house. The older YB leaders ask me to chair the meeting. We are all aware that this may be the last meeting ever held at the YB house.

The meeting is scheduled for 10 a.m. but I arrive extra early to open up the house. For my own personal reasons, which I have difficulty articulating, I need time alone at there. I finish setting up the folding chairs for the meeting and sit down. Only two weeks ago the entire YB membership was together for a festive occasion: a high school graduation celebration at the Far East Cafe, in J-Town. I recall that everyone came and the Far East Cafe management gave us the entire upstairs floor to accommodate our large gathering. Over fifty of us who have been together for the past four years, ate, drank, and partied that night. We feasted on egg flower soup, house special chow mein, sweet and sour pork, broccoli beef, shrimp with lobster sauce, cha shu, and pork ham yuk. We brought in our own cake and snuck in a few bottles of liquor to honor the high school graduates. We honored, toasted and roasted all of the YB grads: Kenny I., Bobby, Carl, Nate, Mike, Jimmy, Tommy, Rick, Dean, Glen, Davey, Gary, Roger, Kenny U., Alfred, Patrick, Robert, Wesley, Scott, Kenny T., Kenny B., Wayne, Dennis, Iris, Gayle, Leslie, Diane, Vicky, Carol, Karen and Debbie. We partied late into the night.

Upon reflection, the dinner celebration symbolized the end of the second generation of the Yellow Brotherhood. The word that best describes what I feel this very moment is "bittersweet." To my comrades and me, our vision to build a revolutionary, militant youth organization fell short. Although the YB is on its last leg, we are one among just a few grassroots community organizations still standing. Most of the other community groups have disbanded or changed their organizational practice from STP programs to internal political study groups, struggling amongst themselves to develop a political ideology for revolutionary change. A few individuals were co-opted by the government. Uncle Sam did his homework and now pays people to do what revolutionaries and community workers did for free. The major difference is that a federally-funded agency answers to the government and not to the community. Social change was the goal of movement STP programs; reform and perpetuation of the existing rule is the underlying basis for federally-funded programs. The movement practice and mentality to "serve the people" was replaced by an agency mentality that views people as "clients" and "patients." Many other community workers, myself included, are opposed to federal funding; it advocates reform, not revolution.

Although the outcome of the Yellow Brotherhood was different from what I initially envisioned, I absolutely have no regrets on spending the last four years at the Yellow Brotherhood. Despite the majority of the members did not make a full-time commitment to social and revolutionary change, I know their hearts. If, and when, the shit hits the fan, I am confident that they will stand up for what is "just." It was sweet knowing that the Yellow Brotherhood organization had an active role in developing unity, a positive identity, and a strong sense of brotherhood and sisterhood in the community.

Slowly, YB members from the past and present trickle into the house. At half past ten, there are enough of us to start the meeting. No introductions are needed; we all know each other. I didn't waste time and got straight to the point of the meeting, "It's been months since we stopped running programs out of the house. The way I see it, unless there is another group that will committ to taking over the day-to-day responsibilities and run programs out of the YB house, then we probably should close it down." After a silent lull, Kenny Ito, a younger member who carries a lot of weight with his peers said, "It's not that the younger members don't appreciate the YB house and all the support you older folks gave us anymore, it's that most of us are into different things now and have gone our separate ways." We all nodded in agreement.

Greg, an older member, added, "I've been coming to the house almost every day for the last three years and for me, things are different now than it was three years ago. It started when Asian parents bussed their kids out of the neighborhood to go to schools in Westchester and in the Valley. Except for the YB members, there are no more Asians at Dorsey or LA High. There aren't enough Asians in Crenshaw to start a new program. I agree with Tad that we should close the house." Greg, a longtime community activist, voiced the feelings of many of the older members.

Willie reminded us, "Remember the last time we stopped running programs out of the house? That was when Tony got killed and unless someone else wants to take over, I say we should sell it and put the money into a youth fund." Willie majored in business and took care of the house's bills and property tax. Because of our lack of financial and business acumen, combined with a general feeling of burnout, Willie's proposal to sell the house was silently adopted in order to reach an immediate resolution. If we learned anything from our past, it is that running a half-ass program is asking for trouble.

By the time the meeting adjourned there was an unanimous agreement that the time had come to sell the YB house. There was no need for farewells, hugs, or kumbayas because all of us still live on the Westside and will be hanging out and seeing each other.

I am the last one to exit the house; I give Willie my keys to the house. On my drive home I thought about what Greg said at the meeting. It's true that the YB members that are just graduating, are the last group of Asians that attended a local neighborhood school. Over the years, Asian families have made an exodus from the *Seinan* community. When the JA families left Crenshaw, Asian businesses and the small mom-and-pop stores that made up the economic backbone of the JA community, closed down. Gone are New Moon Fish, Koby's Drug Store, Al's ARCO Station, Sam's Auto Shop, Grace's Pastry, Enbun Market, Kokusai Theater, Coy's Barber Shop, Kashu Realty, Saki's Liquor, the list goes on and on.

I know better than to dwell on the past right now. I need some time to sort things out in my head—I feel a bit lost and disillusioned but I know what I need to do first. I parked in front of Tag's Liquor and walked out with a six-pack of beer and a half pint of IW Harper. Greg's probably at his pad by now; I'll swing by and check him out.

FULL CIRCLE

Keough Hot Springs, Owens Valley, 1981

""There is a choice you have to make, in everything you do.
So keep in mind that in the end, the choice you make makes you."
Anonymous

I'M GETTING READY to soak my tired ass in the top pool at Keough Hot Springs, a natural oasis located off Highway 395, north of Bishop in the Owens Valley. It has six pools, with each pool able to comfortably accommodate a group of six to eight people. The pools are aligned on a gradually descending slope. Hot thermal underground water, flowing up from beneath the earth's surface, spews outward from a fissure into the uppermost pool at Keough. As the hot thermal water works its way downhill, it travels from one pool to the next and the water temperature cools off slightly. By the time it settles into the last resting pool, closest to the off the beaten track dirt road, the water is still hot, but comfortable enough to bathe in, nowhere near as hot as the water in the upper pools. I know about Keough because of its proximity to Manzanar. Whether the weather is warm, hot, windy, cold or freezing cold, the combination of the hot spring water surrounded by the rugged terrain and a scenic mountain backdrop, is a magnet that pulls me to this location whenever I pass through the Eastern Sierra.

I arrived at Keough a couple of hours before sunset; the site is free of locals and campers, so I have the entire *onsen* (hot springs) to myself. I stripped down and ever so slowly acclimated my body into the top pool. It's hot, just like I remember it. It takes me a while before I get my entire body stretched out in the *onsen*. With only my head sticking out and using a smooth rock on the side of the pool as my pillow, I let out a deep, "Ahhhhhhhhhhh," followed by, "That's what I'm talking about."

I have been on the road for the past two days. I stopped only for gas, a quick bite to eat, and once, to pull over on the side of the road to catch some Z's. It has been a long trip from the Crow reservation near Harding, Montana. What I was even doing there is a story in itself. Finally, I can relax in Keough's hot swirling waters, and reflect.

This journey began six months ago, when my younger brother, Renbo, moved in to share my back house on Fourth Avenue. Although my one bedroom pad was way too small for both of us, I gave Renbo the option to move in because it was obvious that he was going through a lot of changes. I felt that it would be a good change for Renbo to be on his own, to sort things through, and to find his center. In addition, it will give me an opportunity to spend time with Renbo and also relieve Mom and Pop of one less worry—after all, they *are* getting older.

I can relate to some of the changes Renbo was going through. Following the summer of political awareness and intense activism, he and many of the young activists in the Van Troi Youth Brigade felt the revolution was "NOW!" In reality, the end of the Viet Nam war saved the United State government. The majority of young, white liberals no longer felt a need to resist and protest—as far as they were concerned, everything was back to "normal." They were again free to climb the corporate ladder, make money, and to practice white skin supremacy and nationalism.

Leadership in Third World communities was silenced, neutralized, incarcerated, co-opted, or assassinated. Government edicts like COLINTEL, systemically locked up or assisted in the killings of community leaders like Malcolm X, Medgar Evers, Bunchy Carter, John Huggins, George Jackson, Fred Hampton, Jonathan Jackson, Marin Luther King, Geronimo Pratt, and others. Even on campus, student activism lost momentum and priorities had shifted from "serving the people" to "getting mine."

On a positive note, Renbo developed into an accomplished musician and is playing with different bands, seeking to find his groove through music. A side benefit of Renbo moving in is that I have access to one of the hippest jazz collections on the Westside, overnight. After Renbo moved in, we didn't hang out much because his gigs are always at night and he sleeps during the day when I am at work, driving a truck. I felt bad that I couldn't provide more support for him, but honestly, I am dealing with my own issues and trying to get my own damn self together. I am also involved in a relationship with a sister named Lynn.

About three months after Renbo moved in, I realized that I needed to take better care of my property because I am misplacing things, including money. Since I don't have a lot to start with, misplacing $20 is a huge setback. I quit throwing things around my room and kept track of where I put things. When another $20 disappeared, I knew something was haywire. That night, I stayed up until Renbo returned from his gig. I sat him down and asked him point blank if during the day, when I'm at work, he was inviting people over who could have ripped off my money. Renbo said that at times his partners did swing by, but none of them took my money. By the way he was talking, I sensed that something was not right, so I asked him straight up, "Did you take it?" When Renbo paused, my heart sank and my gut tightened. Renbo came clean that night; he told me that he took my money to buy heroin. I asked how long he'd been using and the extent of his habit. Renbo said that he had been using for the past four months and had graduated from snorting and skin popping, and was now mainlining—his jones cost him twenty dollars a day.

I felt numb—this ain't some neighborhood junkie, it's my kid brother. I didn't know what to say, I only wished that it wasn't true. Before I could regroup, Renbo said that he planned to check himself into a methadone maintenance program later that week. I tried telling him that those programs were ineffective and the best way to kick is cold turkey. I said I would help him but Renbo wanted to try it his way.

Renbo checked himself into a methadone program and voluntarily left the program a week later. It turned out that methadone made him feel worse than before he entered the damn place. He told me that he has it under control and will kick gradually by cutting back. He continued to use and I kept it from our parents because I knew that it would break their hearts.

On Thanksgiving Day, the entire family gathered at Mom and Pop's for supper. Ever since Renbo told me about his addiction, I've felt a permanent knot in my stomach. My family sat at the table enjoying the feast—I couldn't eat. I looked over at Renbo; the fool was tearing it up, scarfing up on dark meat, stuffing, mashed potatoes, rice, gravy, yams and cranberry. He was all smiles, stuffing his face without a care in the world. My mind snapped—I am the classic enabling chump, worrying about my kid brother to a point where I'm losing weight. I am more concerned about Renbo's addiction than he is. As long as I carry his burden, Renbo has no reason to quit. It's time to quit acting a fool!

After dinner I told Renbo to take a seat in the front room because we need to talk with the family. Renbo looked nervous but he knew he didn't have a choice. I asked the folks, older brother Shoji, and sister Akemi to join us in the front room. I told them about Renbo's heroin addiction. Mom looked scared but Pop kept his composure and asked how the family can help.

I told Renbo that he is quitting cold turkey and it's starting this very instant—no more bullshit! Now he looked afraid; he tried talking his way out the door, but to no avail. We confined him to his back room; a family member was assigned to his watch around the clock. Pop secured the back room window with hammer and nails. I estimate that it will take around three weeks to get the physical craving out of Renbo's system. The harder part will be dealing with his mental addiction.

The first three days were pure agony. Renbo's body temperature alternated from the chills to sweats; his body reactions from stomach cramps, squirming, and puking, to shitting his guts out. At the end of the first week, the worst of his physical addiction was over. After three weeks of staying clean and eating Mom's cooking, he got some of his color back and we saw glimpses of the old Renbo.

Now comes the hard part, staying clean. I know only a few people who were able to kick their dope habit and stay clean while returning to the same conditions and environment that contributed to their addictions from the jump. That's when our cousin Terry, from Chicago, came through. Cousin Terry is working at a medical facility at a Crow reservation in Montana. When she heard about our family crisis, she stepped up and said that Renbo can stay with her while she was fulfills her eighteen-month nursing contract at the rez.

It took me two days to drive to the rez. True to Terry's description, life on the reservation is a cultural shock. Here everything is the opposite from life in the big city. There are no sidewalks, streetlights, liquor stores, nightclubs, and even, no stoplight! Harding is the big city closest to the reservation, and it is over 100 miles away. One would have to look mighty hard to find trouble out here. Life on the rez reminds me of being on a permanent camping trip.

I stayed with Renbo and Terry for another day and by the end of the day, I knew it was time to leave. The next morning, I embraced Renbo and told him, "Be positive and stay strong." I thanked cousin Terry and hit the road. It had been a long two-day haul when I pulled into Keough Hot Springs.

Dusk was starting to settle in on the Eastern Sierra. It is my favorite time of the day when the surrounding shades and colors begin changing; the blue sky gradually fades until it's pitch black with hundreds of stars twinkling in the sky. If you are lucky, you can spot a comet streaking across the darkness.

I decided to camp out and stay overnight at Keough. The longer I soaked in the thermal pool, the more relaxed I felt. I was overcome with a sense of peace that I had not felt in a long time.

Later that night, I built a small campfire and while I stared into its hot red embers, I thought about my options. What if I get up tomorrow and just take off, seeing where I will end up, and experience something new! Through my movement connections, I know people in different cities throughout the country that I can stay with. Actually, this isn't the first time this thought has passed through my mind but now, being at Keough in the open air, I know that there may never be a better opportunity than now to follow this urge. Besides, I'm not even sure if my job will still be waiting for me.

Oddly, I don't feel the same excitement at the thought of breaking free as before. Seeing how my family pulled together these past months to support Renbo and being with him the past few days has helped me regain my perspective on the importance of family and community. I understand that everything in life is subject to change, but the love and support of my family has never wavered. The teachings and lessons I've internalized from working in the community have helped prepare me to handle our family crisis, and have now brought me to this moment in time.

I have no college degree, savings account, credit cards; nor have I ever written a personal check, but these perceived material necessities are not of significant importance. What I own is my sense of self: knowing who I am, where I am from, and my roots. There is nothing to fear, or to run from. Tomorrow when I wake up, I'll head home, and continue to fight the good fight!

Part IV

Yonsei

Yon = 4
Sei = generation.
Yonsei = fourth generation—great grandchildren of the Japanese
who immigrated to North America.

YONSEI

September 15, 2008
Los Angeles, California

LYNN PROBABLY got off work early because her car is parked in the driveway. *Damn, her paychecks are bigger than mine and she even gets off work earlier than me. Maybe I should have listened to her and gotten a teaching credential.*

No sooner than I step inside our modest three-bedroom house, Lynn calls out, "Tad, a letter just arrived from Masao. It's on the kitchen table, hurry and read it!" My mind races, *What now?* Not seeing Lynn, I shout, "Is everything okay?" From the bedroom, she says in a loud voice, "Just read the letter!" I am used to feeling immediate anxiety with anything having to do with our second son, Masao. I go to the kitchen table and see the letter. I begin to read:

September 8, 2012

Dear Mom, Pop, Taizo and Ayame,

I arrived at Fort Bragg two days ago and it is not as bad as I imagined it to be. It turned out that a lot of the military personal here are familiar with my court martial proceedings. Much of my apprehension has dissipated because everyone that I have talked to either supports my decision, and even if they don't, they respect my right to voice my dissent. Many soldiers returning from Iraq have told me that even though they do not agree with my decision to not deploy to Iraq, they respect my right to stand up for my beliefs, especially in light of the consequences of my decision. One guard even told me that he had just returned from serving a tour in Iraq and if his superiors ever ordered him back there, he would probably end up with me because he, too, would refuse to carry out their order. Overall, I have been treated well and am pleased to know that just about all of the military enlisted rank and file understand the position I am taking. This means everything to me because these men and women are my peers and other than the support of my family, their support in understanding the principles that I base my decision on, is very important to me.

Enough about me, how are all of you? I hope that my family is fine, because knowing this will ease my mind and make my time awaiting my court martial proceedings pass more quicker.

I realize how difficult my decision has been on all of you. I cannot help but remember the day when I first told you that I had made a decision to resist my orders

227

for deployment to Iraq. I can still visualize the pained expressions on your faces. What I failed to fully realize at the time was that the pain you felt was for me, and not for yourselves. As both of you told me from the beginning, you did not want to see me ruin my life.

I am forever thankful that instead of prejudging me, you listened to my reasons for why I chose this path, despite the probable consequence of being stripped of my rank and confined to a military stockade for up to seven years. I want to thank Pop because he had every right to throw it back in my face; he adamantly warned me not to enlist from the beginning. I didn't listen and signed up anyway, erroneously believing that it was my patriotic duty to fight the war on terrorism. Pop, thank you for your unconditional love and support, and never saying, "I told you so!" Having the support of my family is everything. That's about it for now. I miss you all.

Love,

Masao

After I finish reading, I stare at my son's letter. I can still picture in my mind the evening Masao told Lynn and me that he had enlisted in the Army and was going to report for active duty when he finished his semester at Santa Monica Junior College. At first, both of us thought our son was just being his usual self and kidding around. This was not the case. I was aware that watching the planes crash into the Twin Towers on 9/11 had deeply affected Masao, but never in my wildest imagination could I have envisioned Masao to be so emotionally affected by this tragedy that he would sign his name on the dotted line. In hindsight, from Masao's perspective, he must have felt that there was no way that he could approach and convince us that what he felt was his moral and patriotic duty to do. Probably, this was because from the time my kids were little, I always pointed out to them an alternative view from what the media, and even the schools, were trying get them to accept as the truth. Masao probably felt that it would have been unproductive to discuss his decision with us before he enlisted.

Whatever the case, after he made his decision, it was too late to undo what was done. All the family could do was support him and chant for his safety.

Actually, if any of our three kids was going to enlist post 9/11, it was going to be Masao. Taizo, the eldest son, is attending optometry school in Fullerton and he is too focused and practical to make such an emotional decision.

Our youngest daughter, Ayame, is a senior in high school. She is well-liked and involved in a lot of activities both at school and in the community. She enjoys playing basketball on her school team and in the JA leagues. She is enrolled in honors and advanced placement classes, hangs out with her friends, and even manages to find the time for an occasional date. No way is Ayame enlisting.

Now Masao is a different kid. It's not like he didn't do well in the classroom or isn't as smart as his brother and sister; he is more into having a good time and enjoying the moment. In private, both Lynn and I admit that of our three kids, Masao is probably the most fun to be around, but he is also the most sensitive.

After Masao reported and completed his boot camp training, his unit was sent to Korea for eight months. Lynn and I were concerned because it was the first time he was separated from the family for an extended period of time. When his unit returned from Korea, he came home on a two-week leave. I could tell that when Masao came back from overseas, he had matured and was more settled. During this time, all of his comments about his military experience were positive. He said that after his leave he had to report to Fort Hood, Texas, where his unit would be stationed for nine months before being sent out to Iraq. I sensed that Masao accepted and welcomed this upcoming assignment.

After spending time with Masao during his leave, the family had finally reached a point where we fully accepted that Masao is following his own path and doing what is best for him. Whenever he was able to come home, I kept my personal skepticism about the Bush administration and the 9/11 aftermaths to myself; the family just enjoyed Masao's presence and company.

Six months later, everything changed. Masao came home on leave and told Lynn and me that he had something important to tell us. My initial thought was, "Now what? He probably re-upped for another twenty years!" Before Lynn and I could settle in to get comfortable, Masao said, "I don't think there's a right way to say this, so I'm just going to say it. I am going to refuse my orders to be deployed to Iraq." We simultaneously responded, "Why?" As Masao explained, we sat quietly and listened to what our son had to say.

Masao said that during the past six months at Fort Hood, he had seen countless soldiers return from Iraq and most of them were disillusioned. Many were angry, depressed and confused. Masao started questioning what was going on over in Iraq. He said that many of the returning Iraq vets were willing to share their experiences with him. His resulting conclusion was that they did not return with any patriotic message or sense of duty; to the contrary, they, too, questioned our presence over there.

Masao said he started reading books and using the Internet to conduct his own independent research into how we ended up in Iraq, post 9/11. Everywhere he turned, the evidence overwhelmingly showed that Iraq did not possess any weapons of mass destruction, did not harbor Al Queda terrorists, nor did the Iraqi people pose a threat to America. He said that the Bush administration misled the American people and the preemptive order to invade Iraq was in direct violation of the U.S. Constitution. This meant that President Bush's order to the U.S. military to fight, kill and occupy Iraq was an illegal order, in violation of both the Constitution and the Geneva Convention. In contrast, Masao said that he understood his oath to serve in the military was to protect the American people and defend the Constitution.

By the time Masao finished laying out his train of thought, I felt different about my son's decision. If I hadn't listened intently to Masao, all I would have said was, "What the fuck's wrong with you, you're ruining your life!" Even after listening to our son educate us about the war in Iraq, both Lynn and I still felt that he should just go do his tour, get it over with, get his honorable discharge and move on with his life. I said in a quiet voice, "Are you sure you want to go through with this? You know that the government will make an example out of you. Mom and I don't want to see you ruin your life." Masao said that he thought about taking this path but if he did, he would know in his heart that he did not stand up for what is right when he had the opportunity to do so. He said that he hoped that others, especially other GIs would understand, but he needed to do this for himself. By the end of our conversation, Lynn and I have never felt so proud, but scared for him, than at this very moment.

When Masao returned to Fort Hood, he informed his commanding officer of his decision to refuse deployment to Iraq, based upon it being an illegal order in violation of the U.S. Constitution. In an instant, everyone's lives changed. Masao is confined to his barracks pending a court martial hearing. He has been asked by community organizations and anti-war groups to speak at their events about his decision and upcoming court martial. Many of our movement friends have provided us with political, monetary and spiritual support, along with re-kindling our bonds and friendship. Masao now has a top-notch attorney to represent him at the court martial proceedings.

I was so deep in my thoughts that I didn't realize that Lynn had joined me in the kitchen. "How was work today?" she asks. "I got tired of hearing all the crap, so I quit." After all these years, Lynn knows me all too well, "Yeah, right! So what did you make of Masao's letter?"

"It sounds like his spirits are up. I'm just worried that if the judge doesn't allow his lawyer to raise the illegality of the war issue as being the reason for his refusing to deploy, then it's a slam dunk for the Army at the court martial." Lynn could only say, "I know."

I see that she is starting to feel down so I quickly change the subject. "You know, Mike, Eddie, Sandy, Victor, Melvin, Janice, and Uncle Renbo, all plan to attend the court martial." Lynn responds, "Everyone has been so supportive, it feels like the old days."

"You know, I've been thinking. It's a trip how there are cycles in life, like how my *jiichan* was picked up by the FBI on December 8th and locked up at a federal prison; how Pop protested by saying, "No-No" and got locked down; and then here I come, enlisting instead of going to jail—now Masao follows his heart and faces confinement. Damn, I ought to write a book!"

Lynn smiles softly and says, "If I had known that I was marrying into a family with nothing but jailbirds, maybe I would have changed my mind when you knocked on my window sill and proposed!" I crumple a napkin on the table and playfully toss it at her.

We look at each other—our eyes express it all. No matter what the verdict is, Masao is going to make it. He has the unconditional love and support of his family, extended family, and community. The concept of family, extended family and community, started with the Issei pioneers, and has been passed on to Nisei, then Sansei. The torch is now passing to you—stay strong and follow your heart! *Gambare!*

Peace